RACHANEE LUMAYNO

HEIR OF
IMMORTALS
AND
EMPIRES

KINGDOM LEGACY BOOK SEVEN

Heir of Immortals and Empires

Kingdom Legacy, Book Seven

Copyright © 2025 Miss Lana Press

Editing and proofreading by Tom Loveman

Cover art by Fiona Jayde Media

Thank you for reading, I hope you enjoy Heir of Immortals and Empires. I'd love it if you'd leave an honest review on Goodreads or wherever you purchased this book. Thanks!

ALSO BY RACHANEE LUMAYNO

Kingdom Legacy

Heir of Amber and Fire

Heir of Memory and Shadow

Heir of Magic and Mischance

Heir of Crowns and Curses

Heir of Secrets and Spectres

Heir of Illusions and Others

Heir of Immortals and Empires

CONTENTS

JOIN THE NEWSLETTER

HELLO DEAR READER!

Here's a fun fact for you—the first book in the Kingdom Legacy series, Heir of Amber and Fire, was inspired by a character in a Dungeons and Dragons campaign that I never got to play. Even though the game never happened, the character's backstory stayed with me, and became the basis of Jennica's story.

Since the first book had such strong ties to tabletop gaming, a friend suggested I create a campaign set in the world of the Kingdom Legacy series. And so *The Mysterious Magical Emporium* was born, and I'd love to send you a FREE copy! Just sign up for my newsletter at www.rachanee.net/newsletter, and your new campaign will be sent to you right away.

So grab your friends, grab some dice, and grab a copy of *The Mysterious Magical Emporium*, and get ready to spend some time in the kingdom of Calia with your new friends, Jennica, Beyan, and Taryn!

1

CHAPTER ONE

"HAS ANYONE TOLD YOU, you're the prettiest girl here?"

I giggled as I turned my face to Tahn, a silent—and hopefully alluring—request for another kiss. "You have to say that, silly. Besides, I am the *only* girl here."

Tahn obliged my unspoken request. "I don't have to say it. And I wouldn't say it if it wasn't true."

I giggled again, snuggling into the crook of his arm. Together, we leaned back against the large oak that also conveniently hid us from prying eyes. In the distance, I could hear the faint voices of laughter and talk from near my house, but I didn't care. The party would keep. It wasn't like I was the guest of honor, anyway. No one would miss me.

Our lips had just met again when a pointed cough sounded somewhere above.

We broke apart to see my brother, Alistair, standing just a few feet away, a pained look on his face. "Forgive my interruption," he said, not sounding sorry at all. "But Mother and Father—among other people—have started noticing your absence, Idessa. I told them I'd go look for you."

I frowned. "Can't you cover for me, Lis?" I wheedled, falling back on my childhood nickname for him. Maybe that would soften him up.

But Alistair's frown matched my own. "I already did. Several times. Come on." He turned to go.

I sighed heavily as I stood up, brushing dirt and leaves from my dress. Tahn followed suit, and I grabbed his hand. We started after my brother, who paused, looking pointedly at our clasped hands. "Maybe you should return separately."

With that, he walked through the trees, not waiting to see if I'd follow.

I sighed again. "I guess I should go. Count to thirty, then follow me?"

Tahn shrugged. "Or maybe I should just go home. I don't think I can spend several hours being glared at by your brother."

"Oh, just ignore him," I said. "You haven't really met my parents yet. I know they'll think you're wonderful, just as I do." I looked up into his deep brown eyes, batting my eyes for good measure. "Please?"

He shrugged again, but nodded.

Smiling, I stood on my tiptoes for one last stolen kiss. Then I turned and hurried after my brother.

To my surprise, Alistair was waiting for me just on the other side of the trees. "You ready, already?"

"I thought you had already gone back to the house," I said.

He snorted. "Not likely. If I don't bring you back personally, Mother and Father will have both of our heads. Besides, I know you. If I don't keep an eye on you, you'd just stay out here with Tahn. Or worse, wander off with him."

"I don't know why you are always so down on him," I complained as we started walking.

"Because, Idessa. You can do so much better than him," Alistair said.

I rolled my eyes. Not this again. Ever since Alistair had returned from his Guardian year, he'd been insufferable. Gone was my fun-loving older brother, only to be replaced by some stuffy, boring person who was better suited to a straight-laced government job than his original dream of adventurer-for-hire in the Gifted Lands.

Which was why my family was hosting this party. As we got closer, I saw the painted homemade banner: "Congratulations, Alistair!"

A sizable crowd milled around our house, a modest one-story cottage. My parents didn't often host guests, as our family was rather private. But tonight was a special occasion.

Chatter and laughter floated on the air. I stopped my brother before we could reach the group—and while we were far enough away that they might not notice us. "Congratulations, Alistair," I said, echoing the banner's cheery sentiment.

He hugged me. "Thank you."

He tried to pull away, but I wouldn't let him go. "I'll miss you."

He laughed, and this time was successful in extracting himself from me. "Silly. I'll still be in Graenir."

"I know. But you'll be busy all the time, and who knows when we'll get to see you? And you just got back. We've hardly had any time together."

Alistair's smile faded somewhat. "And whose fault is that? I've been around for the last year, for the most part. You're the one who's rarely been home."

It was a familiar argument, and one I didn't want to get into. Not on today, of all days. Still, I couldn't stop the whine that crept into my voice. "Well, I'm not the one who changed. You used to be more fun."

Alistair snorted. "I'm still fun. Maybe not in a way you recognize, but ..."

"You know what I mean."

He stepped back, holding me at arm's length as he looked me straight in the eyes. "People change, Idessa. It's the one thing you can count on. And being a Guardian—it definitely changes you. You'll understand, when your time comes."

"If." It was a slim hope, but it was a hope I held onto nonetheless. I certainly didn't want to be a Guardian, even if it was a required duty.

Well. It's required only if you happen to be unlucky enough to be picked, I reminded myself.

Alistair shrugged. "True enough. *If*. And *if* it happens, then I hope it will change you as deeply as it did me."

He walked away, toward the house, leaving me no choice but to hurry after him.

As we approached, various guests greeted us, calling out their congratulations and well wishes to Alistair. With all that noise, there was no way I could slip in undetected. Sure enough, I soon found myself standing in front of Mother, who was chatting with some neighbors whose names I could never remember.

"Oh, and here's our youngest, Idessa," Mother said. "Idessa, meet Kal and Ellya Arnon. They live down by the pond."

I murmured a polite greeting, trying to avoid Mother's pointed stare. The one that said, *I know you skipped out, young lady. We'll discuss that later.*

"Idessa." Mistress Arnon beamed at me. "You must be so happy about your brother's new position."

"Oh, I am." I plastered a smile on my face. "Serving in the Archives is so exciting."

What a lie. Honestly, it sounded like the most boring job ever.

"It will definitely keep him busy," my mother said, sounding proud and sad at the same time. "He's only just returned to us, and now we have to give him away again in service to Graenir."

"Oh, that's right," Mistress Arnon said. "And now we're coming on the close of another year. They'll be sending out the summons soon." She turned to me. "Have you served as a Guardian yet, Idessa?"

"No," I replied. "But if I am called, then I will gladly serve."

Another lie. But it was the right thing to say—in fact, the expected response. Mistress Arnon beamed again. "Imagine if that were to happen! Two Guardians in the family."

Inwardly, I shuddered. But I just smiled again and nodded. "That would be exciting. If you'll excuse me, Mother, Mistress Arnon."

Mother waved me away, continuing her conversation with the Arnons. I made my way through the crowd, searching for Tahn's tall figure and blond hair. He should have been here by now. But I didn't see him.

I sighed.

"Why the sad face? It's supposed to be a celebration party, not a funeral," a voice teased.

I looked up. And bit back the groan that threatened to escape. Instead, I forced a pleasant smile on my face. "Hello, Oran." I looked behind him. "No Alistair?"

Oran grinned, waving at a group of people that surrounded my brother. "Not right now. He's lost in his throng of admirers."

I chuckled. "It's not often you two aren't joined at the hip. Except, of course, for when Alistair had to do his Guardian duty."

My brother's best friend—and practically a second sibling to me—Oran had been around for as long as I could remember. It always stumped me, how the two of them could be such good friends. Oran was steady and quiet, whereas Alistair was more spirited and carefree, sometimes bordering on reckless.

Or had been. Ever since Alistair had returned from his Guardian year, he had become more quiet and less fun-loving. In short, a lot like Oran.

Bo-ring.

In fact, it was Oran who had helped my brother get his new job in the Archives, where Oran had been working for a few years. From the way Alistair talked about it, you'd think that the Archives were the most exciting place in Graenir, let alone the Gifted Lands.

Yawn. No, thank you.

Oran nodded. "If it wasn't a solitary position, I would have gone with your brother. But, alas, I had to stay home."

"You sound like you want to be a Guardian." I pursed my lips, hoping I hadn't sounded too accusatory.

But Oran didn't take offense. "A whole year to just sit and be by myself, with only books and my thoughts for company? Sounds like heaven to me."

I smirked, shaking my head. "Sounds like a prison sentence to me."

He laughed. "Tell you what, if you get summoned, I'll take your place, and serve for you."

This time, a genuine smile bloomed across my face. "Deal."

2

CHAPTER TWO

THE FOLLOWING MORNING, I slept in. I figured, since it was the day after my brother's party, my parents wouldn't care. In fact, I'd be surprised if they were even up.

So I was surprised when I walked into the kitchen and found my entire family sitting around the table, lingering over the remains of breakfast.

"Good morning, Mother," I said, kissing the top of her head. She patted the hand I had rested on her shoulder. "Father."

My father stopped looking at the journals he had been studying long enough to nod at me.

"What's for breakfast?" I asked.

Mother waved at the sideboard. "Leftovers from the party. Help yourself."

I did as she said, grabbing an empty plate and filling it high with food before joining everyone at the table.

As I sank into my seat, Mother said, "What are your plans for today, Idessa?"

I paused. I didn't have any solid plans, other than seeking out Tahn, to hopefully pick up where we had left off yesterday. And to maybe ask him why he hadn't followed me back to the house. I had waited and waited, but he had never showed. It had put me in a bad mood, but other than Alistair—and maybe Oran—no one had noticed.

At least I hoped not.

Mother was still waiting for my answer. So I said, "I was going to go into the city today. To shop."

"Oh, that's perfect." Mother clapped her hands. "Alistair is also headed into the capital. You two can go together. And perhaps see what his new job will be like." This last part was said with a heavy dose of hopefulness. I half expected her to wink at me as well.

My jaw dropped open, then my brain kicked in and I closed my mouth on what I wanted to say. Which was, *No, definitely not. I don't think so.* Not only did I want to go find Tahn—alone—I also didn't want to spend a boring day with my boring brother at his boring job. No, thank you.

Across the table, Lis gave me a knowing look, one eyebrow raised. I narrowed my eyes at him. Whose idea was it for me to have a babysitter, anyway?

"It will be fun, Dess." He used my childhood nickname, as if that would somehow endear me to this idea.

"Oh, but I don't want to slow you down," I said to my brother, putting on the sweetest, most helpful little sister voice I could. "I'm sure you have a lot of things to do in the city to prepare for your big, important job." I debated fluttering my eyelashes for good measure, but then thought that might be a little too much.

"It's no bother. And I can help you with your … *shopping.*" That slight emphasis and that definite smirk cinched it. This outing had totally been Alistair's idea.

"There's really no need."

"Of course there is. What kind of big brother would I be, if I didn't help you out?" His voice matched mine in syrupy sweetness.

I gritted my teeth as my lips thinned. He had won the round, and he knew it.

"Perfect, it's all settled then," Mother said, oblivious to the conversation's undercurrents. "You two will have a wonderful time."

At least one of us thought so.

I took my time eating, hoping that if I drew it out long enough, my brother would get annoyed and leave without me. No such luck. Lis and Mother began talking, mostly about his upcoming job, what it would entail, and what he needed to do to prepare for it. Father kept paging through his books and papers, only occasionally contributing to their discussion. Nobody seemed inclined to hurry me, but my food only lasted so long.

The moment I was done eating, my brother stood up. "Shall we go?"

"I was about to get some more food," I hedged.

But Mother waved me away. "If you're hungry, get something in the market. There's some money in the drawer there. Not too much, since we spent so much on your brother's party. But there should be enough for you to do a little bit of shopping."

I sighed inwardly. Guess there was no help for it. I had to go to the capital with Lis. Lucky me.

Maybe I could ditch him once we got there. Or perhaps whatever he had to do with his job preparation would occupy him to the point where he wouldn't notice my absence for a little while.

I smiled as I picked up Mother's coin purse. And now I had a bit of extra spending money.

Lis already had his shoes and coat on by the time I joined him at the door. "Come on, we shouldn't waste any more time."

I rolled my eyes as he strode out the door. I followed along, hopping on one foot as I struggled to slip my shoe on. "Hey! Wait up!"

Lis didn't break stride, but his steps slowed somewhat. I caught up to him and swatted him on the arm.

That made him stop. "What was that for?"

I began to tick off the reasons on my fingers. "For not waiting for me. For forcing me to accompany you, instead of just letting me do what I want. And for so rudely interrupting me and Tahn yesterday."

My brother mimicked my finger counting. "You've already wasted most of the day. Mother thought it would be good for you to see what I'm going to be doing, and it's not like you had plans that ran counter to that. And as for you and Tahn ..."

I sighed. "What about him?"

Lis frowned. "It's just—I don't want to see my baby sister get hurt."

I crossed my arms and glared at my brother.

He sighed. "He's a bit too ... friendly with some of the other girls around Graenir. I know how much you like him, and—"

"And he's loyal to me. You have nothing to worry about." *I* had nothing to worry about. I huffed, angry at myself for letting my brother's words get under my skin. "Never mind. Don't even start."

We started walking again. An awkward silence stretched between us. Finally, as a sort of peace offering, I said, "What exactly are you going to be doing for your new job, anyway?"

Lis smiled. "You'll see, once we get to the capital. But the short version is, I'll be working with the Research and Excavation team."

Yawn. I frowned. "Really? Didn't you have enough of that during your year as a Guardian?"

My brother's eyes lit up. "Are you kidding? That's what got me interested in doing Research and Excavation in the first place. And then when Oran told me there was an opening ..."

Lis started to prattle on about the things he learned in his Guardian year. Great. Now I'd have to listen to this on the entire walk to the city. I could feel my eyes glaze over.

"When you serve your Guardianship, you'll understand," Lis said.

"*If*," I said, putting a heavy emphasis on the word.

He shrugged. "You might get out of it, but I doubt it. Graenir's population isn't as big as it used to be in previous years. There's a good chance you'll be summoned for duty."

"I hope not."

My brother eyed me sidelong. "You can't just hope the possibility away. What would you do if you do get summoned?"

What, indeed? Turning down the Guardianship was not an option. "I'd have to do it, I guess. Thank the gods the job is super easy. Just boring."

"Learning about Graenir's history—indeed, the history of the Gifted Lands—is not boring."

"Says you. Did you even commune with a god—any god—while you were a Guardian?"

Lis shook his head. "But it wasn't for lack of trying. The vault has been dormant for such a long time—several centuries, at least. Maybe even a few millennia. Perhaps the gods have moved on, or are sleeping. If they're even still alive."

I snorted. "Then why do we even bother still guarding the vault? The gods haven't tried to talk to any Guardian, ever. They might not even be there anymore. Why waste our time?"

"Because. Our god, Graenta, promised the people of Graenir, upon the kingdom's founding, that in exchange for unwavering, eternal Guardianship, he would impart to the chosen Guardian the wisdom of the ages. And, through that Guardian, all of Graenir, and perhaps even the Gifted Lands, would benefit."

I didn't even try to hide my smirk. "Spare me from the drivel that our teachers push on us every year. You really believe that crap?"

"I do."

"Why?"

For a long few moments, my brother didn't answer. The slap of our footsteps against the worn dirt road and the birds singing in the trees were the only sounds on our journey. And then, finally, Alistair spoke.

"I know that the old tales—of the gods founding the Gifted Lands, and of Graenir's god sealing all seven of them away in the vault—can't be proven. It's been so long, maybe they really are nothing more than stories by now.

"But there's something about them that resonates with me. Gives me purpose. I suppose that's why I'm so excited to join Research and Excavation—because maybe, in my lifetime, we'll finally discover something that answers all the questions that have been building up for forever. And because it gives me comfort and hope to believe in something bigger than myself."

The reverence in my brother's voice gave me pause. And it kind of made me uncomfortable. But I didn't know why, and I didn't really want to delve too deep into that reason right now. Maybe not ever.

"I don't know," I said. "I like things that I can see, and feel, and touch."

Like Tahn. I colored slightly, just thinking that.

Lis raised his eyebrows at me, as if he could read my mind. "You'll see. When it's your turn to be a Guardian, you'll understand."

3

CHAPTER THREE

BY THE TIME WE reached Graenir's capital, the city was already bustling. Even though half the day was gone, Market Day had still attracted a sizable crowd, with several merchants' stalls lined up right outside the gates, along the road, and many more inside the city as far as I could see.

Lis frowned. "I had hoped by now the crowds would have thinned out. It will take a while just to get through everybody to get to the Archives."

Seeing a chance to salvage my situation, I said, "And then you still have your business to take care of over there. And with so many shoppers, I don't want to lose out on the good merchandise. Maybe you should go on ahead, and I'll get my shopping done now, then meet up with you later?"

My brother's frown deepened—he knew exactly what I was trying to do. But he also couldn't deny that it made more sense for us to split up and do our separate errands than for him to force me to stay by his side. He sighed. "Fine. Don't take too long. I shouldn't be more than an hour. If you're not at the Archives by then, I'll come find you." His lips thinned. "And I won't be happy about it."

"Of course, big brother. I'll get my shopping done quickly, and then meet you at the Archives." I stood on my tiptoes and kissed him on the cheek. "Love you, Lis."

He smiled a bit at the childhood nickname, but reminded me, "Don't be late."

"Yes, yes. Get going. I'll see you soon."

Lis shook his head, but left, threading his way through the crowd. "Idessa!"

I turned at the sound of my name. My face broke into a grin when I saw who had been calling out to me.

My best friend Jele rushed up to me, a little out of breath. "I thought that was you! I'd recognize that hair anywhere."

My hand flew to my head, a self-conscious habit. Most people don't get white hair until they're at least middle-aged; I had been born with it, and had always been very aware of it. In a kingdom where most people had black or brown hair, I knew I stuck out—a fact that I wasn't too happy about.

Jele batted my hand down. "Oh, stop. You know you're gorgeous."

I embraced her. "I'm glad to see you. I wasn't sure I'd run into you today. By the way, where were you yesterday? I thought you were going to stop by Alistair's party."

Jele sighed and rolled her eyes. "Babysitting. Couldn't get away. Sorry about that."

"You could have brought Alara with you." Jele's five-year-old sister Alara was energetic, but well-behaved. My parents wouldn't have minded if Jele had come to the party with her younger sibling. Besides, Jele was practically family.

Jele shrugged. "It's okay. I was ... pretty busy."

I nodded in sympathy. "Likewise. And speaking of babysitting ..."

I told Jele about how my mother had shackled me with my brother today, and about yesterday's party. When I mentioned Tahn, Jele got a funny look on her face. I sighed inwardly even as I kept talking. First my brother, now my best friend ... was there no one in my life who liked Tahn?

"That's so annoying," Jele sympathized. She linked her arm through mine. "Come on, let's look around. It'll get your mind off things."

Together, we walked around, looking at the various items the merchants had on display. I picked up a leather belt, admiring the handiwork before putting it back down. Some lovely glass trinkets caught the sunlight—and my eye.

Jele was drawn to a merchant selling chocolates. I'd only had the exotic imported sweets once, but the delicious and unusual flavor had stayed with me. I watched, feeling jealous, as Jele picked out a few pieces and handed over the requested amount, not even bothering to haggle or fret over the cost.

But what really got my attention was a small wooden stall filled with gold and silver necklaces, rings, and bracelets. I'd always loved jewelry—I have a weakness for shiny, pretty things—but my plain, hardworking family didn't hold with frivolous adornments. Other than my parents' simple gold wedding bands, I don't think we had any other jewelry in the house. If we did, I had never seen it.

I was admiring a beautiful locket, perfect for holding a lock of your beloved's hair, when a low voice sounded by my ear, tickling my skin and sending a delicious shiver up my spine. "That would look great on you."

Startled, I jumped, then broke into a smile. "Tahn!"

He slung a casual arm over my shoulder. "You should get it. It's quite pretty, almost as pretty as the person holding it."

I blushed, but put it back down on the table. "I wish I could. Mother gave me some money for shopping, but she would be so annoyed if I came home with a new necklace instead of something more practical."

Tahn grinned and winked at me. "Don't lose hope. Maybe it'll be yours, someday."

Be still my fluttering heart. I leaned into him, enjoying his warmth and strength. Tahn looked over at Jele, and his easy smile faded a little. He nodded at my best friend. "Jele."

"Tahn." Her manner was just as reserved.

I sighed, loudly, so they would both hear just how exasperated I was. With both of them. "Sheesh, you two. Stop acting so sad. No one died, last I knew."

Jele forced a laugh, shaking off the odd melancholy that had settled over our little group. "You're right, Dess. Hey, did you two hear? Catrum just got back from completing his Guardianship. You know what that means."

I frowned. "Yeah, that they'll be picking the next Guardian soon."

Jele rolled her eyes. "Yes, and also—there will be a celebration tonight at the castle to celebrate his return."

That perked me up. "Oh, that's right. With all the fuss over getting Alistair's party together, I forgot about that. I'll be there. My whole family should be there, in fact."

I batted my eyes at Tahn. "How about you?"

He shrugged. "Of course. I'll meet you there?"

"Okay." I tried to keep my voice cheerful, but underneath I felt a little hurt that he didn't want to accompany me to the party.

He drew me a little closer. "And make sure you wear your prettiest dress. I have something I want to ask you about, tonight."

I shivered in excitement as my spirits instantly lifted. "Okay."

A flash of red, followed by a swish of blue, floated by. The red flash solidified into Fedra, one of our classmates, who looked stunning in a flirty crimson dress. Another classmate, Dienne, wore a more demure white blouse with a blue-and-white checkered skirt.

"Hello, Tahn." Fedra's voice oozed an open invitation while she pointedly ignored Jele and me. "So wonderful, running into you at the market."

Dienne had more manners than Fedra. Somewhat. She at least nodded to Jele and me, before turning all her attention on Tahn as well. But like I said, she somewhat had more manners. Even though he quite obviously had his arm draped around my shoulders, that didn't stop her from running her fingers up Tahn's wrist.

"Need some help shopping? We'd be happy to help you."

Across from me, Jele frowned at the pair. I grit my teeth. There were some choice words I wanted to say to both Dienne and Fedra, but I wasn't about to stoop to their level. Besides, Tahn would see right through their too bright smiles and fluttering eyelashes.

Wouldn't he?

"Ladies, as always, it's lovely to see you both," he said. "Thank you for the kind offer. Perhaps later, if we're all still around?"

"Of course, Tahn." Fedra leaned a little too close, giving Tahn—and the rest of us—a slight glimpse down her low-cut bodice. I couldn't help my soundless snarl of disgust. How obvious did she have to be? "We'll see you soon, hopefully. Goodbye, now."

"Goodbye," Dienne echoed, and the pair sauntered off.

"Well, that was ... something," I said.

Tahn laughed as his arm tightened around me. "Is someone a little bit jealous?"

"I'm not." But my petulant tone betrayed my feelings.

"Aww. How cute." He dropped his arm, and I suddenly felt a chill brush through me. Was I cold from the sudden loss of Tahn's body heat? Or was it nerves? I wasn't sure which—and more to the point, I was afraid of analyzing which one it truly was.

Tahn changed the subject. "Now, about tonight's homecoming. Who do you think will be the next Guardian?"

"I don't know, but it sounds horrid," I said, grateful to talk about something else besides my feelings. "Imagine, an entire year in solitude! Even the very slim chance of maybe talking to the gods isn't worth it. Who wants to talk to a bunch of dead gods anyway?"

Jele giggled. "If you're talking to them, then they probably aren't dead."

"You know what I mean. I'd hate to be away from you two—from everyone, really—for such a long time."

"There's talk that they're thinking of doing away with the whole Guardian thing," Tahn said. Jele and I both turned inquisitive looks on him. This was definitely news.

"Why?" asked Jele.

"There doesn't seem to be a need. In the entire history of the Guardians, the seal has never been broken. The gods have never tried to speak to anyone. And the interim time between Guardians has grown longer and longer, with nothing bad happening while the seal is unattended. So, Queen Yllulae feels like it might be an outdated tradition, and do away with it. Or perhaps shorten the serving term from a year to just a few months. At least, that's what my father has said." He sounded smug. Tahn's father was one of the queen's advisors, and Tahn often heard the news of the kingdom before anyone else.

"That's a good point. There was at least two or three weeks in between Catrum and the last Guardian. And everything was fine."

"Well, I just hope—"

But I didn't get to say what I hoped for. Oran approached our group, smiling as he nodded at all of us. The smile faded from his eyes as he noticed Tahn standing next to me, but he didn't comment. Instead, he greeted us, then asked, "Idessa. If you're here, is Alistair here as well?"

"He's at the Archives, making some preparations before he starts his new job." I paused, remembering. "Wait. Oh, dear—what time is it?"

"Well past the time we were supposed to meet," a pointed voice said behind me.

My heart sank at my brother's annoyed tone. I tried to put a little distance between Tahn and me—no easy feat, in the crowded market—and slowly turned to face my brother. "Hello, Lis."

"Hello yourself. I waited for you, but when you didn't bother to show I realized you had forgotten. Am I right?"

"Well ... ah ... you see ..." I flailed around for an excuse.

"Don't get mad at Idessa," Oran interjected. "I kept her here, talking her ear off."

Both my brother and I gave him funny looks, but even if Lis suspected his friend was lying, he wasn't going to call Oran out in front of the others. Instead, Lis just said, "Well, you can continue to do so while we walk home. If you want to join us. Ready, Idessa?"

I wasn't, not really, but I knew better than to make Lis even more mad. So I nodded, which prompted him to start walking. Oran gave me a sympathetic smile before following.

"I should go," I said.

Jele gave me a quick hug. "See you tonight."

"Definitely."

With a quick goodbye to Jele and Tahn, I hurried after Oran and Lis.

4

CHAPTER FOUR

I BRACED MYSELF FOR an awkward walk back, filled with glowering and stilted conversation. Or for Lis to lay into me the minute we passed through Graenir's city gates. I wasn't sure which would be worse.

But, to my surprise, neither happened.

"Did you get all of your shopping done?" Alistair's tone was pleasant, although his jaw twitched slightly.

"No," I admitted. "Once I saw ... Jele ... I just got caught up in talking with ... her."

"Even after Mother gave you all that money, you didn't spend a single cent?" He snorted. "I'm shocked."

"I saw a few things, but—" I shrugged. "I got distracted."

"I'll bet."

Before we could start arguing, Oran spoke up. "How were the Archvies, Lis?"

My brother's eyes lit up. "They were amazing. There's so much more history there than we were ever taught in school. And yet, all those supposed answers just bring up more questions."

"Are they going to have you doing cataloguing, for now?"

Cataloguing sounded incredibly dull to me, but Lis beamed. "Yes, they said that's how all new Archivists are trained."

Oran nodded. "Once you learn the cataloguing system, you can add in newer research. What kinds of questions do you have? Maybe I can help."

"Can you? I have so many questions. Such as, what was Graenir's power supposed to be? Did our kingdom's founder run out of time to infuse our people with it? Why seal away his fellow gods—wouldn't it have been easier and smarter to kill them for their crimes? And ..."

Oran and Lis got into a deep discussion about the history of Graenir and the rest of the Gifted Lands, positing questions and debating the answers. I tried to follow along, but found the conversation rather boring. Still, it kept Lis happy, occupied, and most importantly—not focused on me.

I yawned.

"Does the topic bore you that much, Dess?" Lis raised an eyebrow.

"Oh, no. It's just that I don't have anything insightful to say that could contribute." The lie sounded silly even to my ears.

"Well, let's talk about something that you can speak to," Oran said, ever the thoughtful one. "Will you two be going to Catrum's homecoming tonight?"

I gave him a sharp look. Like my now bookish brother, I thought all Oran did was hole up in his room and study. "How did you know about that?"

He grinned. "It's all anyone can talk about. You know it's always a big deal when a Guardian comes home."

I smirked. "I don't know why. It's not like the Guardians ever do anything important besides sit around in an empty tower all day."

"Still, every Guardian has said it's life-changing. Perhaps for some more than others, but still, it affects people deeply."

"Anyway." I drew the word out, letting Oran know that topic was done. "About Catrum's party. Yes, I'm sure I'll be there. Lis?"

He nodded. "Of course. For something like this, I would imagine pretty much the entire kingdom would attend. And it's such an honor. I know I enjoyed my homecoming."

Oran elbowed him. "As did several of your admirers." He chuckled. "Some still do, even though it's been over a year since you returned."

My brother blushed. "You have to admit, getting a stipend and a guaranteed placement in the capital is not a bad deal. You'd think people would volunteer to be a Guardian, instead of waiting to be picked."

"Not everyone can handle it. The isolation can drive some people crazy."

The three of us fell silent, remembering. The length of Guardianship used to be much longer, for five years instead of one. But a while back—about a decade ago, I think—the current Guardian had gone mad during his time of service, slowly starving himself. Nobody in Graenir knew what had happened until one day the messenger who delivered the Guardian's meals realized that the food had been piling up outside the tower door. By the time soldiers broke into the building, it was too late.

"I was just a child when it happened, but I remember hearing all the adults talking about it," I said. "And he was so close to finishing his term as Guardian."

"The poor man," Lis said. Oran murmured a blessing for the dead.

"And you wonder why I wouldn't want to do it."

"Well, ever since then, they've reduced the time of service," my brother pointed out. "And—for now at least—people who complete their time still get all the perks."

I shrugged. "Still doesn't mean I'd want to do it." I grinned at Oran. "Besides, Oran here said he would take my place if I did get summoned."

Oran grinned back, but Lis frowned. "Somehow I don't think it works that way."

We had reached our home. "Want to come inside for a bit?" Lis asked Oran.

"I would, but I have a few things to do before returning to the city for Catrum's celebration," Oran said. "I'll see you both tonight?"

"Probably our entire family," my brother said. "See you tonight, then."

We said our goodbyes and Oran continued down the road.

Lis sighed, his earlier good mood now gone. "Come on, Dess. I suppose we should get ready for tonight, too."

Mother was tending to the indoor plants when we entered. I waved, and was about to head to my bedroom when Lis fixed me with a pointed glare. Sighing, I turned on my heel and went to the kitchen instead to return my mother's purse.

Behind me, I could hear Alistair and Mother talking about the upcoming celebration at the castle.

"Right after you left, messengers came through to remind everyone," Mother said. "I'm just surprised Queen Yllulae left it so last minute."

"Maybe she hopes that, by doing so, less people will show? Less expense, less hassle?" Lis suggested.

"Maybe," Mother echoed, but she sounded doubtful. "My guess is that Queen Yllulae is just getting forgetful. Or more reclusive."

I put Mother's money in the drawer, then walked back into the room in time to see Mother swipe a dirt-stained hand across her forehead.

Both Lis and I started to chuckle.

"I don't think you meant to smear dirt on your face, did you, Mother?" I said.

Mother laughed too. "Oh, goodness. Apparently Queen Yllulae isn't the only forgetful one in Graenir. I'll take that as a sign that I should stop fussing with these plants and get ready for tonight." She looked towards the closed door to Father's study. "And I'll also need to pry your father away from his books, or we'll never make it to the castle on time."

"I'll get him," Lis said. "You go get ready."

Mother gave him a grateful smile, kissing him on the forehead before leaving the room. Seeing that I was still there, Lis waved me away. "You too, Dess."

I giggled. "There's dirt on your face, too."

Lis wiped at his forehead, groaning when he examined his fingertips. "Great. We'll make such a great impression tonight."

"I don't know, I think it suits you. Makes you look distinguished."

"Distinguished, huh? I'll give you distinguished." He waggled his dirty fingers at me, threatening to wipe them on my face. Squealing, I dodged him and then ran towards my bedroom, his laughter echoing down the hallway after me.

5

CHAPTER FIVE

"CLOSE YOUR MOUTH," MOTHER murmured to me. "One would think you've never been to the palace before."

I pressed my lips together, my eyes wide as I took in my surroundings. True, I had been the palace before. Once a year, in fact, when the outgoing Guardian was celebrated for completing his or her service, and the next Guardian was announced.

Despite my joking with Oran, once someone was chosen to be a Guardian, you couldn't get out of it. It was a Graenirian's solemn duty, and nothing short of death would be a good enough excuse to not do it.

Mother, Alistair, and I stood just inside the palace's great hall, to the side of the massive twin oak doors that were open wide to admit guests. Father had seen a professor friend of his, and had gone to engage him in what was sure to be an evening-long conversation about some boring scholarly topic.

My brother waved at someone across the room. "There's Oran. Excuse me." He threaded his way through the crowd to join his friend.

"Idessa! I love your dress!"

I turned to see Jele coming towards me. Her parents and little sister stood nearby. After Mother and I greeted everyone, I said, "Thank you. I ... I wanted to make sure I looked my best."

Jele smiled, but there was an uncharacteristic tightness around her eyes. "Well, you look beautiful. I'm sure Ta—a lot of others will think so."

I beamed at my best friend's compliment. The deep green velvet dress brought out the color in my own emerald eyes, and the dark shade made my white hair practically glow. Even Lis, upon seeing me earlier in the evening, had said that I looked like I had stepped straight out of his research on mythical creatures—*like a forest goddess*, were his exact words. I touched the cascade of ringlets piled upon my head, carefully curled for the occasion. I hoped Tahn thought the same thing.

"You two go mingle while we catch up," Mother said, shooing Jele and me away. She and Jele's parents started talking about current affairs in Graenir while Jele and I made our escape.

"I'm sure Catrum is around here somewhere." I craned my neck to see if I could spot the guest of honor in the crowd. "Maybe you can snag him for a bit before the queen makes the official announcement."

I spotted the recently returned Guardian, Catrum, near the front of the room, just to the side of the dais. A small crowd of admirers hovered nearby.

"There he is! Come on, let's go!" I grabbed Jele's hand and started in Catrum's direction.

But I didn't make it more than two steps forward when my hand met resistance. I looked back. Jele hadn't moved, although I had been trying to tug her with me.

"What's wrong?"

Jele had an odd look on her face, and the tightness was back. I couldn't tell what she was thinking, but whatever it was, it seemed serious. Which in itself was strange for my usually carefree, fun-loving friend. The fact that I couldn't read her emotions right away was also bizarre—we had grown up with each other, had been inseparable for most of our lives, and practically knew what each other was thinking without having to say it out loud.

"We don't need to talk to Catrum," Jele said. "I mean, he's got enough people hanging around, trying to get his attention."

I stared at her, surprised. "But you always want to talk to the returning Guardians."

Each year, at these homecoming celebrations, Jele had made it a point to try to capture the attention of the returning Guardian. Even my brother Alistair, whom she had known for forever and could talk to at any time. Befriending a Guardian was advantageous—and considering the last few Guardians had been eligible single men, with guaranteed good futures ahead of them, my boy-crazy best friend had been determined to catch their eye. She hadn't been successful—yet—but it was only a matter of time. With her distinctive red hair and beguiling blue eyes, she was often the life of the party.

Jele pulled at my hand, and I let go, confused.

"Jele, is everything all right?" I asked. "Has something happened?"

My best friend smoothed down her unwrinkled rose-colored skirt with nervous hands, then licked her lips. She took a deep breath. "Actually, yes. Idessa—"

Whatever Jele was going to tell me was drowned out by a sudden fanfare at the front of the room. The elderly Queen Yllulae had appeared.

Time and the stresses of royal life had caused her back to bow and her hair to grey, but she still moved with regal purpose. Since losing her husband the king a few years back, she had grown somewhat reclusive, favoring plain gowns with few adornments and showing a distaste for pomp and circumstance. Being a royal, she couldn't get away from formality completely, but many of the usual kingdom celebrations had been cancelled, the exception being the Guardian's homecoming and the naming of the new Guardian.

As the room began to quiet down, I whispered to Jele, "What were you going to say?"

She waved whatever it had been away. "It's not a big deal," she whispered back. "I'll tell you later."

I nodded, although I wanted to push Jele for information. But this was definitely not the right time or place to have a deep conversation.

Meanwhile, Catrum's admirers respectfully stepped back, blending into the crowd, as Catrum genuflected before the queen. She nodded once in acknowledgment, then raised her hand, palm up, indicating that he should rise as well. Once he got to his feet, he held out one arm and escorted her onto the dais. He left her alone in the center, bowing as he stepped back.

"My beloved people," Queen Yllulae started. "Another year has gone by, and with it, another successful period of guarding the Great Seal, as mandated by our kingdom's founder, Graenta."

I became aware of a tall presence by my side.

"Hello, Idessa." Tahn's whisper tickled my ear.

I looked up at him and smiled, grabbing his hand in a quick squeeze. He smiled back at me before exchanging a curt nod with Jele.

"... and accordingly, we have gathered to celebrate Catrum's safe return," the queen was saying. "And to pass on the mantle of Guardianship to the next person, as is our tradition. All eligible persons have been put forth by my advisors, and, as is also our tradition, the magic of Graenir will guide us to the name of our next Guardian."

What if it's Jele—or Tahn? I wondered. I'd miss either of them terribly, of course. If either one of them was chosen, I wouldn't be able to talk to them or visit them while they were in seclusion.

But maybe it would be good if it was *Tahn*, a small part of me whispered. Some time away from all the other girls in Graenir—and temptation—might do him some good. Might do *us* some good. And besides, didn't absence make the heart grow fonder? Time apart would just make him miss me more, right?

Queen Yllulae closed her eyes. "Oh, all-seeing, ever wise Graenta. We call upon you …"

Around the room, hundreds of mouths moved, soundlessly saying the words along with our queen. Even though we only heard these words once a year, the traditional prayer of supplication to our long-silent god was seared into every person's mind. Like everyone else, I mouthed the words, but my mind began to wander. It was hard to concentrate, with Tahn standing so close to me. After all this selection formality was out of the way, and the real festivities had started, would he claim me for a dance?

" … Reveal to us to your next champion, the one you have chosen to watch over the Great Seal, to commune with you and your brethren, to serve as our next Guardian."

The queen stretched out her hand, her fingers extended. Slowly, she swept her hand across the room, sometimes pausing for a moment, other times moving back over an area that she had already gone past.

And then her hand picked up speed, and her forefinger pointed.

Right at me.

"Graenta has made his choice. Please join me in congratulating our newest Guardian. In one week's time, they will take up their post on Zaela Island, to serve as Guardian for one year.

"Idessa Valdon, you are the next Guardian."

6

— · —

CHAPTER SIX

THE ROOM ERUPTED IN applause, but I couldn't hear it over the rushing in my ears.

Me? The next Guardian?

My life was truly, officially over.

I'd have to be sequestered for an entire year. One whole year!

The area around me erupted in happy sentiments from neighbors, classmates, friends, and strangers.

"Congratulations!"

"You're so lucky. What an honor!"

"Graenta hasn't chosen a woman in a long while. You truly are blessed."

I became aware of someone embracing me.

"Congratulations, Idessa," Jele said. She pulled back to smile at me, but her eyes were sad. And—somewhat relieved?

"Thank you." It was what you were supposed to say, after all, but I didn't feel thankful. I just felt numb.

My friend searched my face. "You look a little flushed. Are you all right?"

No, not really. "It is a bit stuffy in here."

"I'll go get you something to drink." Jele walked off.

A voice nearby echoed Jele's earlier words. "Congratulations, Idessa. Although we'll miss you, it will be such a good experience for you."

I turned to see Oran, with Lis next to him, beaming at me. "Thank you." Surprising, how quickly the false gratitude could spring to my lips.

I looked around. In all the noise, one voice had been absent. "Where's Tahn?"

Oran gestured behind him, in the direction Jele had disappeared. "Lis and I passed him walking that way while we were making our way over here. Why? Did you need him for something?"

"Oh—he was standing here earlier, and then after Queen Yllulae made her announcement, I didn't know where he had gone." I hoped Oran and Lis couldn't hear the hurt in my voice. "It's okay. You know how he is. He hates a ton of attention."

Lis raised an eyebrow at that, but didn't say anything.

More congratulations poured in all around me. Everywhere I looked, I saw a mass of faces, young and old, pressing in on me. Everyone seemed to think my new appointment as Guardian was the best thing ever.

The roaring in my ears came rushing back. The faces around me blurred, and the air really was stuffy and hot. I wanted to lie down, or hide, or throw up. Possibly all three.

Oran's concerned face came into sharp focus as he stepped forward to peer at me. "Idessa? Are you well?"

"I need to get out of here," I mumbled.

"Here, let me help you." Oran put an arm around me, guiding me away from the throng of people.

Lis followed behind. "I'll tell Mother and Father. And give your excuses to the queen."

He disappeared, even as my steps faltered. The queen! How could I have forgotten? As the new Guardian, I would need to present myself to her and receive her blessing. Traditionally, that happened at the homecoming event for the outgoing Guardian. But if I was about to be sick, surely she'd understand?

Oran steered me through still-congratulating crowd, towards the entrance of the great hall. To my left, I noticed Jele and Tahn standing near the generous buffet, in what looked to be an intense conversation. Jele was holding a drink—presumably the one she had promised to get for me—but her task seemed forgotten in the wake of whatever deep discussion was holding the two in thrall.

As Oran and I walked by, Jele and Tahn looked up, startled by the wave of well wishes they heard around them. When they saw me, Jele looked at the drink in her hand, as if she had just remembered she was holding it. She started towards me, but Tahn stopped her.

And then Oran and I were clear of the crowd and through the doors of the great hall, and into the blessedly cooler air of the castle hallways. Away from the stuffiness of the party, I felt much better, but still a bit nauseous.

Still—"Should I go back in there?" I asked Oran. But I wasn't thinking of presenting myself to Queen Yllulae. I wanted to talk to my friends, and find out why they hadn't come after me.

"It depends." Oran's arm was still around my shoulders, a warm presence of strength. "Do you feel well enough to return? You looked pretty green just a few moments ago."

I took a deep breath. "I—" All of a sudden, my stomach lurched, and the remains of my dinner ended up on the palace's otherwise pristine stone floor. My knees buckled, but Oran stopped me from falling. Gently, he lowered me to the ground.

Oran fished a clean handkerchief from his pocket and handed it to me.

I wiped my mouth, wishing I had something to wash away the lingering taste of vomit. "Thank you." I held the dirty cloth between the tips of two fingers. "I don't suppose you want this back. I'll burn it."

To my surprise, Oran took the handkerchief back, stuffing it into his pocket without a hint of disgust. "It's all right. That's what handkerchiefs are for. Besides, it was my grandfather's. I'd prefer if you didn't burn it to clean it."

I chuckled, then groaned, clutching my stomach.

"Come on, I'll take you home." Oran helped me stand, and, with his arm still supporting me, escorted me from the palace.

I spent the next two days in bed, recovering. The sudden "sickness" that had struck me at the homecoming celebration was largely anxiety over my new position, peppered with some embarrassment. My family was surprisingly solicitous, making sure I was allowed to rest and bringing meals to me in my bedroom.

But by the third day, even their concern had run its course.

"You can't stay in bed forever." Lis stood in the doorway, arms crossed. "You'll be leaving in just a few days—for a year."

I groaned. "Don't remind me."

"Like it or not, your term as Guardian will be upon you before you know it. You still need to present yourself to Queen Yllulae, at the very least. Even if you don't want to go to the goodbye party your friends are planning to throw for you."

I perked up. "A goodbye party?"

He nodded. "Jele came by the Archives yesterday to ask how you were, and to tell me about it. Assuming you're well, they'd like to hold it at the end of the week, right before you leave for Zaela Island."

I frowned. "I wonder why Jele didn't come here, to the house?"

Lis shrugged. "She probably thought you were very sick, and didn't want to disturb you. When you left Catrum's homecoming celebration, you also left behind a lot of worried people. Queen Yllulae even wondered if you would be well enough to take up the Guardianship in time."

"Why do I have to leave in a week?" I pouted. "Other people were able to wait much longer."

"I don't know. It's not for us to question the queen's decisions. And the timing is not determined by her, it's set by Graenta."

I rolled my eyes. "I doubt that Graenta's picking anything, let alone listening to our prayers. It's completely arbitrary, the whole thing."

"Maybe. But tradition holds that he is the one choosing the next Guardian. And traditions are important."

"Are they? Then you'd think, if he's able to pick the Guardians, he'd actually talk to one of them once they got to Zaela Island."

Lis shrugged again. "It's not for us to know the way of the gods. And speaking of tradition, are you ready to get the queen's blessing?"

I sighed. "I guess I'll have to be."

Lis chuckled. "Don't sound so excited."

I threw back the covers. "Well, I can't stop the Guardianship from happening. And if I don't go see the queen, then I don't get to have my goodbye party."

"And here I thought you were thrilled that two people in our family had been chosen to serve as Guardian. Most others would be delighted at the honor. Glad to see you have your priorities in order." Lis chuckled again. "I'll accompany you to the palace after you get ready."

7

CHAPTER SEVEN

THE REST OF THE week passed by in a blur. Besides meeting Queen Yllulae and getting her blessing—which went completely fine, with no fainting or vomiting incidents—I had to pack and prepare for my stay on Zaela Island, where the Great Seal resided in an underground vault, surrounded by a plain stone tower.

Fortunately, the island wasn't far. From the capital, it was about a half day's journey on horseback. But even though it was relatively close, I felt like it might as well have been across the continent.

While my meals and basic needs would be provided for, I could still bring some personal items from home.

"To make your year-long stay on the island more comfortable," the queen had said during our meeting.

Or more bearable, I had thought, but kept my mouth shut.

And now that word had gotten out that I was feeling better, the house was constantly filled with visitors. Neighbors, family friends, classmates. Even acquaintances I hadn't talked to in years, or only nodded to in passing when I saw them at the market. Cousins, aunts, and uncles. It seemed the entirety of Graenir had turned up on our doorstep to say hello, renew relationships, and wish me well.

Except for Jele and Tahn.

They're probably just busy preparing my goodbye party, I told myself. If the constant stream of people stopping by was any indication, it should be a big event, bigger even than my brother's "congratulations on your new Archives job" party.

Still, it hurt that neither of them stopped by, even for a short visit.

The day of the goodbye party dawned. I woke up with a mix of conflicting emotions. I was excited for my party—and to finally see Jele and Tahn—but I knew, once the festivities were over, my new life as a Guardian would begin.

A knock sounded at my bedroom door. "Dess? Are you up? Are you decent?"

"Yes. Come on in."

Lis opened the door, then laughed when he saw my room. Three large wooden trunks were pushed against the wall, with some smaller woven baskets and boxes stacked on top of them. "You're bringing all this? A year is really not that long, Dess."

"So says you. To me, it's forever." I waved a hand at my things. "Besides, I need all this stuff."

"Do you?" My brother lifted the lid to one of the boxes. He snorted, picking up the edge of one item, and I saw a swath of deep green velvet in his hands. "A formal dress? You really think you'll be going to any fancy parties while you're on Zaela Island?"

I swatted his hand away and shoved the dress back in the box. "I might. You never know."

Lis rolled his eyes. Shaking his head, he said, "I do know. I served as a Guardian, too, remember? And I certainly never went to any formal events while I was out there."

"Well, maybe I'll be the one to change that *tradition*." I emphasized the last word, smirking at my brother. "Leave it alone. Queen Yllulae said I could bring whatever would make me feel comfortable for the year."

"Yes, well, she's not the one who has to haul all your stuff to Zaela Island." He waved down the hallway. "Come on, everyone's waiting for you."

"Everyone?" I pushed past my brother and headed toward the kitchen. Lis followed, and I heard him mutter behind me, "We'll have to request that the palace send more help. Sheesh."

Gathered around the breakfast table were my mother and father—and Jele. My friend stood up when I entered. I squealed in excitement and gave her a huge hug. "Jele! I'm so glad to see you!"

"Same here." Her voice sounded a bit watery, and I could see tears shimmering in her eyes. "I'm going to miss you so much."

"Let's not think about that right now." I released Jele and we both sat down. "I'm just so happy you're here."

Lis brought over some full plates of food and set them down on the table—first in front of Jele, as our guest, and then in front of me, since I was the one they were all honoring. He served everyone else before sitting down with his own breakfast. We all kept the conversation light, knowing that soon enough we'd be saying our goodbyes.

When we were done eating, Mother took my dirty dish with only a token protest from me. "Go spend some time with your friend."

Wow. Twice in less than two weeks that Mother was letting me skip out on chores? Maybe there was something to this Guardianship after all. But I wasn't going to complain. Feeling impulsive, I kissed her cheek. "Thank you."

I quickly put on my shoes and joined Jele outside, where she was waiting for me. "Where are you headed?" I asked.

"Into the city. I have a few things to get for the party, and then I have to get home to prepare."

"I can help you," I volunteered.

"Oh, no, you won't," Jele said. "You can't go shopping for your own party."

"It's fine. Besides, how are you going to get everything home?"

Jele shrugged. "I have help. And I'm sure you want to spend time with your family the day before you leave."

I stopped myself from rolling my eyes. "Why does everyone seem so determined to get rid of me? Just wait a day, I'll be gone tomorrow for a long while."

My best friend blushed. "I'm not trying to get rid of you. I just—I thought—"

"How about this? I'll walk with you to the city, but I'll leave you alone to shop. That way I can at least spend *some* time with you before the party."

Jele nodded. "I'd like that."

We set off toward Graenir's capital. For a while, neither of us said anything, content just to enjoy each other's company. Actually, no. That was not quite true.

My unspoken question hung in the air. *Why have you not stopped by before today?*

I could have asked, but I didn't want to spend my last day before leaving getting into a potential argument with my friend.

And if I was being completely honest with myself, maybe I also didn't want to hear her answer.

As for Jele, she seemed a bit distracted. *Probably just preoccupied with preparations for tonight,* I thought.

I cleared my throat, which sounded overly loud in the silence between us. "Just in case I forget later ... thank you. For hosting my farewell party. And ... for being such a wonderful friend. I'm going to miss you."

Jele turned to me, tears springing to her eyes. She stopped and threw her arms around me. Her voice thick with emotion, she said, "I'm going to miss you, too, Idessa. You're the best friend a girl could ever have. How am I going to survive without you for a whole year?"

Sniffling through my own sudden tears, I joked, "Maybe we can sneak you in. I know! What if you were the one who brings me my meals?"

She chuckled, and we started walking again. "I like that idea, especially if I get to share the food with you. You'll get the finest food, whatever you want, since you're the Guardian."

"That's one good thing, I guess."

We fell silent again. Then Jele nudged my shoulder with hers. "What kind of food would you request, anyway?"

I laughed and started listing off all of the fine—and probably imaginary—meals I would be eating as the new Guardian. The silly conversation lasted us for the rest of our walk. And it was nice to joke and laugh with my best friend once more. Things had felt so cautious, so tense between us recently, that I had been afraid that we would never have our easy camaraderie anymore.

At the city gates, I embraced Jele once more. "I'm glad we got to spend some time together. And I can't wait for tonight's party."

"Me neither. It's not much, but I'm glad I can at least send you off in style and give you a night to remember."

Jele stepped back and gave me a little wave, then walked through the gates and into the city. I stood there for a few moments, watching her walk away.

A tall figure detached itself from behind one of the market stalls and stopped before Jele. Two little children raced by, nearly colliding with her. The tall person reached out, grabbing Jele's arm to steady her.

As Jele stepped to the side, I got a good look at her companion's face.

Tahn.

Huh. That was odd. I didn't even think they liked each other. But they had apparently decided to set aside their differences for the day so they could prepare for my farewell party.

A soft smile sprang to my lips. That they would do that, for me—I was truly touched.

With his hand still on Jele's arm, Tahn steered my friend further into the market. They were soon lost to my sight.

I turned and started the walk back home.

8

CHAPTER EIGHT

"THERE SHE IS! CONGRATULATIONS, Idessa!"

"Are you excited?"

"We'll miss you so much!"

I nodded at the group of well-wishers crowding around me, my head turning this way and that in a scattered attempt to follow all the comments people were firing at me.

"If you'll excuse us, we're going to get something to drink," Lis said, gently but purposefully pushing his way through. I followed him, grateful to get away.

And I still hadn't seen the two people I wanted to see the most.

The crowd thinned as we made our way to the refreshment table outside. Oran was already there and waved at my brother and me as we approached.

"Here you go, Idessa." Oran handed me a tall glass filled with a cold, red-tinted liquid that smelled strongly of strawberries and mint. "You look like you could use this."

"Thank you." I downed the glass in one swallow.

Oran laughed and took the now empty glass from me. "Apparently my hunch was correct. Let me refill that for you."

While he was doing that, I surveyed the area. Jele's family had generously opened their home to be used for my goodbye party, and the large crowd of guests had spilled over from the house's interior into their backyard. With the setting sun, the air had grown a bit chilly, so most people preferred to be inside. I didn't mind, though. The cold air was refreshing, and I actually relished the relative quiet outside.

"You'll have to go back in there and mingle, eventually," Lis warned me. "And it will take forever."

"I know. But I'd like to stay out here just a little bit longer."

Lis chuckled. "I never thought I'd see the day when you, of all people, didn't like having everyone's eyes on you."

I shrugged. "It's flattering—and you know how much I love being the center of attention. But not for this. I don't even want to talk about it, although it's all anyone wants to talk about."

My brother gave a mock gasp. "Could it be? Is Dess actually growing up?"

I punched him lightly on the arm. "Oh, stop."

Oran held out the newly refilled glass to me, but before I could take it, Tahn walked up to us. "Idessa."

I brightened upon seeing him. "Tahn!"

"Walk with me?" He didn't wait for my answer, but put his hand on the small of my back and steered me away from the refreshments table.

Behind me, I heard Oran say, "I guess I'll just hold on to this for you, then."

"I can't believe you're leaving tomorrow," Tahn said.

"I can't believe it either," I admitted. "I kind of hoped it wouldn't come, to be honest."

"Well, you can't stop some things. Like time." Tahn cleared his throat. "Idessa, I—"

I put a finger to his lips. "Before you start, I just wanted to say thank you."

Tahn's brow furrowed in confusion. "For what?"

I giggled at his expression. "For helping Jele get everything ready for tonight. I saw you at the market earlier today." Tahn opened his mouth to speak, but I kept talking. "I know you two can barely stand each other, so it meant a lot to me that you were willing to work together. For me.

"And for being such an amazing, wonderful person. I'll miss you so, so much." I stood on my tiptoes and brushed a quick kiss against his lips. "Now, what were you going to say?"

He shrugged, looking embarrassed. A surprising departure for the normally cool Tahn. "Ah—just that I think you're pretty great, too. And I'll, ah, miss you too."

I beamed and leaned forward to kiss him again.

But to my surprise, Tahn pulled away. A frown tugged at one corner of his mouth.

"Tahn? What is it?"

"I was just thinking ... you'll be gone for a whole year."

I pouted. "Don't remind me."

He shook his head, as if he was trying to clear his thoughts. "I wasn't trying to be rude. I know it's a sore subject for you. For both of us, really. I mean, a year is a long time."

I sighed. "It is. And yet, at the same time, it's really not, right? It will go by fast." I hoped. "At least, that's what people keep telling me."

Tahn clenched and unclenched his fists. I'd never seen him fidget before. He was always so suave, so in-control. His charm and easy manner was what drew people to him—I know it had worked on me. Seeing him nervous was a new experience.

I found it kind of sweet. My heart started racing. What was he trying to say?

"Tahn?" I prompted.

"Idessa ... like I said, you'll be gone for a whole year. And we won't get to see each other. I hate the idea of us being apart. So, I wanted to ask if—"

"Idessa? Idessa!"

Tahn and I both looked up to see who was calling my name. From the open door at the back of the house, Jele waved, although she frowned at the sight of Tahn and me together. "Idessa, get in here! We're all waiting for you!"

I looked around, realizing that while Tahn and I had been talking, the backyard had emptied of people. A few guests remained outside, but most had gone inside. Jele's house looked like a glowing beacon, with a generous amount of internal light spilling out to pierce the growing twilight.

Peering through the windows and the open door, I could see that most of the guests were sitting on chairs or the floor in a large semi-circle, with some leaning against the walls.

"I guess we should get inside," Tahn said.

"All right," I agreed. "And hey, you can meet my parents. Finally."

He raised an eyebrow at me before walking towards the house.

I followed him inside, staring at the strong lines of his back. *What had he been about to say?*

Tahn entered the house before me and stepped to the side to let me enter. When I did, the entire room burst into applause.

I gasped as tears sprung to my eyes.

The large main room of Jele's house was filled to capacity with friends, family, neighbors. Classmates, former teachers, even some of the merchants whose stalls I frequented on my shopping trips in the city. While my party wasn't nearly as big as Catrum's homecoming had been, there was still an impressive turnout of people who had come to wish me farewell.

The rest of the night passed in a blur of faces and hugs and sniffles and well wishes. Lis had been right—it really did seem like the mingling was endless. With so many people surrounding me at all times, I didn't have a chance to introduce Tahn to my parents. Or even get a moment alone with him again so he could finish what he had been about to ask me outside.

And when I finally had a moment to breathe and looked around for him, he was gone.

9

CHAPTER NINE

AFTER THE PARTY, I barely slept, just tossed and turned in my bed all night. When the weak morning sunlight pierced the horizon, I actually felt relieved, even though the lack of sleep made me sluggish and my head fuzzy. Time to start my new life. Might as well get it over with.

Three soldiers of the queen's guard arrived just after sunrise, with an extra horse for me and a wooden cart for my belongings. Their prompt arrival meant my family and I didn't have time to linger over breakfast or over saying our goodbyes.

I watched as two of the men loaded up the cart, their breath misting in the chilly spring air. In a few months, summer would come to Graenir, and it would be warm from morning to evening. But for now, the mornings were cold, sometimes grey with fog that would burn off by midday.

The donkeys tethered to the cart wheezed in protest when the soldiers piled yet another trunk in. I kind of felt bad for the poor animals. Maybe Lis was right, and I had overpacked?

Oh, well. Too late now to sort through everything.

The third soldier—who seemed to be the leader—was busy reassuring my parents, even though they had been through this with Lis about two years ago. "She'll be just fine. Even though she'll be unable to leave Zaela Island, she can still explore the grounds around the tower, and past Guardians have left their own items—books, journals, crafts—so she won't feel so lonely during her time there. Not to mention, someone will come by twice a week with meals to last her several days. So she won't be completely cut off from humanity."

"She's so ... high-spirited," Mother said. "More so than her brother. I just worry that this experience will either be quite good for her, or it will break her. I wish I knew which."

"Don't we all wish we could know our future," the soldier said. "Don't worry, madam, your daughter will be fine."

"I hope so," Mother replied, and left it at that.

One of the soldiers who had been loading my belongings came over to us. "We're all set, sir."

"Good," the leader said. "Shall we, then?"

Now that the moment was upon me, my earlier feeling of "let's just get it over with" disappeared. I wanted nothing more than to run to my room, bar the door, and hide under my bedcovers. Feeling numb, I gave first my father, then my mother, a hug.

"Be good, now," Father said absently, patting my head as if I were still a little child.

Mother clung to me, as if she could make me stay by holding on tight. "Be well, Idessa. We love you and we'll miss you, but we know you'll do us proud as a Guardian."

"I'll be fine, Mother," I said, parroting the soldier's earlier statement.

Lis was the last to embrace me. "Don't get into any trouble, Dess."

"I won't." I paused, then pulled Lis closer so I could murmur into his ear. "And—could you keep an eye on Tahn for me? He told me last night how much he would miss me. I don't want him to be lonely while I'm gone."

Lis snorted, but said, "Sure thing. I will."

One of the soldiers helped me mount my horse, and then the four of us set off. I turned in my seat for one last wave goodbye, tears pricking my eyes when my mother, brother, and even absent-minded father all waved back. Sniffling, I faced forward and focused on the journey ahead.

A few hours' easy ride brought us to the outskirts of Graenir, to the water's edge of the majestic Rehann River.

From the maps the teachers had shown us in school, I knew that the Rehann River flowed through a large part of the eastern Gifted Lands. It started somewhere beyond the northeastern kingdom of Shonn, feeding into the waterways by Graenir before going towards the southern kingdom of Annlyn. The dark blue-green water looked peaceful, but I had heard many stories of unsuspecting people who had been swept away by the Rehann River's swift currents.

From the riverbank, we could see Zaela Island. A lone tower loomed over the small forest scattered across the land.

"There should be some food already on the island in readiness for your first week," the soldier's leader said to me. "If you're so inclined, you can hunt or fish to supplement your food supply. If you have no weapons, we can send a spear, or bow and arrow, with one of the food shipments. But—" he looked at me sternly "—that is a privilege that must be earned. It may take a while for you to prove that you are worthy of it."

I nodded somberly, remembering how some had gone insane from their solitary service.

"Are you all going to stand around jawing all day, or can we get going?"

A thin, grizzled man stumped towards our group. He was hunched over slightly, and his weathered, slightly reddened skin spoke of someone who had spent a lifetime exposed to the elements.

The soldier who had been talking to me nodded at our new companion. "Ah, Harlan. It's good to see you again, my friend."

"Likewise," Harlan said, slapping the soldier on the back. The soldier just laughed, not offended in the slightest by the familiar gesture. "But we can catch up later. We should get going before the currents get rougher. It's always best to do the crossing in the morning before midday, or after the sun's gone down."

"You're the expert," the soldier said, chuckling. To me, he explained, "Harlan is the ferryman who will be taking us across the Rehann. And he's the best there is."

Harlan beamed, puffing his chest out. "That's true. Because I'm the only one there is. Come along, now. The ferry's down the way a bit. Follow me."

He turned and walked away. The soldier and I followed after him.

"He's quite fast, for—" I stopped myself, realizing how rude I sounded.

Harlan stopped and turned, smirking. "An old man? Or despite my injury?"

I grimaced at being caught out. "Your pardon, sir. I didn't mean to be disrespectful."

Harlan chuckled and started walking again. "I don't mind curiosity, which is what I sensed from you. I've been ferrying people across the Rehann since I was a boy. Learned the ways of the water from my father, and my grandfather. Others have tried to cross, and don't always succeed, but my family and I have never lost a single passenger."

I smiled. "That's definitely reassuring."

"Ah, but not losing a passenger is not the same as capsizing. I'd say I have a special connection to the Rehann—runs in my blood. But when I was younger, I was brash and reckless, and the river decided to teach me a lesson." He patted his injured leg. "I've kept that lesson close ever since."

We had reached Harlan's ferry, which, to my surprise, was no more than a simple raft. It was wide enough that it could hold three, possibly four, people comfortably.

Eyeing the pile of my belongings, Harlan said, "I don't think we can do this in one trip."

"That's all right," the leader said. He pointed at the trunks, boxes, and baskets, and asked me, "Which one holds your most necessary items? We'll take that across on this first trip."

Since I had just thrown whatever I wanted into whatever receptacle I had on hand, with no real eye to planning ahead or organization, I didn't know how to answer the soldier's question. I shrugged sheepishly.

The man sighed. Shaking his head, he waved me onto the raft. To Harlan, he said, "Take her across. I'll stay here and help my men load and secure her things to the ferry when you come back."

Harlan nodded and pushed off. As we floated down the river, he snorted. "I hope they're willing to haul all that up the tower stairs. I don't get paid extra for that."

"I guess I did bring a lot."

Harlan chuckled. "Now that's an understatement. But it's also rather amusing. It will keep those men on their toes."

I smiled. "So you've been a ferryman your whole life. Are you also the one who will bring me my meals?"

"That's right, miss. Sometimes one of the queen's guard will accompany me, but I'm always the one who brings them across. If you need anything, you just let me know."

"Do you—are you—" I paused, unsure of how to ask my question.

But the ferryman seemed to read my mind. "Allowed to visit with the Guardians? By necessity, we will see each other every so often. But I'm not supposed to seek you out, no. That would, in theory, steal away your focus and make it harder for you to commune with Graenta. But—if you need a friend, I'm happy to be that for you."

I sighed. "Thank you."

I never thought I would see the day I would beg an old man to be my friend. But, out here in the untamed wilderness, the loneliness was already beginning to set in.

Harlan smiled, revealing a mouth full of yellowed teeth, with dark gaps where some were missing. "My pleasure, miss."

10

–·–

CHAPTER TEN

Four months later

I sighed as I poked at the fire, trying to coax the wood to burn faster. Spring had lasted longer than normal, and the nights were still chilly. Or maybe it was just because this old stone tower was drafty.

My new home—the Guardian's tower—stood on the south shore of Zaela Island. Perhaps it had served as a former watchtower, although our southern neighbor Annlyn couldn't be seen from the tower's top. The rest of the island boasted a copse of trees, home to several species of small game.

There wasn't much in the spartan upper room of the Great Seal's tower. Just some plain wooden furniture—an old bed, a worn side table, a small dresser. Two full bookshelves. A fireplace. The room was tiny—after all, it wasn't made for more than one person, who was only staying for a year. Although I unpacked right away, I still didn't have enough space for all my things. Still, I was loath to send the excess back with the ferryman, even though it meant my little room was quite cluttered.

Going down the winding staircase brought me to the ground level, where a cozy study was tucked away to one side, near the tower's entrance. Another twisted staircase led to the underground level, where the Great Seal was housed.

When I had first laid eyes on the Great Seal and its environs, I had been disappointed. The room was plain, bare, and dark, except for the red light emanating from the magical lock. The gods' prison was a hole in the ground, covered over by the seal. It was solid enough to stand on, but nearly opaque. Still, that hadn't stopped me from peering curiously down, trying to spot the gods. I had thought I could see indistinct dark shapes moving about below me, in an area that was just a few feet smaller than the tower circumference.

Which, for seven gods, wasn't a lot of space.

I had knelt down, trying to get a closer look at the beings below.

And then one of the dark shapes had soared up and hit the bottom of the seal, the dull thud echoing throughout the chamber. I couldn't make out any features of what had hit, or hear any sounds from under the barrier, but for some reason, that lack scared me more than if I had been able to see the person—or thing—clearly.

I had screamed and scrambled back, even though whoever it was had not broken the barrier. Haunted, I had run frantically back up both staircases and into my bedroom, slamming the door behind me.

I didn't step onto the Great Seal again after that.

My days as a Guardian settled into a routine. A long, boring routine. Every day the first thing I would do after waking was check the Great Seal. (It was always intact.) Then I would eat, clean up, maybe study or knit or stare out the window. I could stare out the window in my boring room at the top of the tower, or in the equally boring study on the tower's ground level. Which was also filled with books, as well as a simple desk and chair. Apparently, the only thing you could really do on this stupid island was read. Or walk around Zaela Island.

Since there was nothing else to do, I would often do both.

Around midday I would check the Great Seal again. (It was still always intact.) In the afternoons I would commune with the gods—or at least try. If they were listening and able to talk back, they were being stubbornly silent. And frankly, after that first encounter with one of them, I didn't try that hard to commune.

I'd have my evening meal around sunset, then check the Great Seal before settling in for the evening. (And, of course, it was always, *always* intact.)

After just three days of this, I was already bouncing off the walls. A whole year of this? How would I even survive? But somehow the days passed and I kept at my Guardian duties. Because, really, what else could I do?

The highlight of my week was seeing Harlan. As he had said, he didn't seek me out, so our visits were restricted to when he came by with food for me. But he could give me news of the outside world, which I listened to eagerly.

Most of his news was about kingdom-wide happenings—new laws, citizen concerns, or how Queen Yllulae was faring. One time, he relayed greetings from my family, and even gave me a letter and small package from them, which was against the rules.

"But if I happen to drop them during my delivery and didn't notice, that's something else now, isn't it?" Harlan had commented, followed by a huge wink.

Of Tahn and Jele, he had no information. And even though I had read my family's letter top to bottom and twice over, it didn't contain any news of my friends, either.

Since there was little else to do, I had started reading through the surprisingly sizable library I found in the tower. Some were history books, and others were past Guardians' personal journals, recounting their time in service to help future Guardians. Despite myself, I found those fascinating. One previous Guardian, after months of meditation, had actually started to communicate with Graenta.

Or, the cynical part of me thought, they had gone crazy and these were the rants of a crazy person hallucinating their conversations with a god.

Regardless, their communications with Graenir's founder had been tenuous, at best, but they still had reached the god, somehow. And, according to this former Guardian, Graenta had an important task for them. But the connection had faded before the Guardian could learn what it was and act upon it.

Checking the dates in the journal, I had realized that the writer had been a Guardian quite some time ago. At least five Guardians back, and definitely before my brother's time.

But the mystery of how the past Guardian had reached our kingdom's founder would have to remain unsolved. The journals, history books, and other items left behind by my predecessors didn't give me any insights, and in the four months I had languished here, nothing exciting had happened.

Certainly not an unexpected communication from our god.

Now, with the fire built up to my satisfaction, I stepped back from the hearth. With the warmth of the fireplace at my back, I walked over to the tower's window and looked out over the landscape—something I did way too many times in a day.

Outside, the sun dipped low over the trees, casting long shadows on Zaela Island. The sky, streaked with purple, pink, and orange, reminded me of how the sunset had looked the night of my farewell party.

I sighed. I wondered how Jele was doing—what new trinkets she had found in the market, who else she was roping into her adventures.

And what about Tahn? Was he thinking of me right now, as I was thinking of him?

Perhaps I could ask Harlan to deliver some letters to them. Although I wasn't supposed to have any contact with the outside world, as it could potentially distract me from my meditations and duty. Indeed, since I was already imagining the things they would say in their return letters, I was already distracted.

I sighed again as I continued to stare out the window.

And then I straightened abruptly, craning my neck to peer out into the growing twilight. Had I really seen what I thought I had?

In the distance, the air shimmered and rippled. Below it, the Rehann River also glowed and swelled, as if it was reflecting the odd-looking air above it. The shimmer was getting brighter and bigger.

I gasped as my eyes widened. A huge wave, at least half as tall as my tower and steadily growing bigger, was headed straight towards Zaela Island.

And me.

Underneath my feet, the tower gave a slight jolt, as if a giant hand had pushed the island, and began to shake.

And that wall of water would be upon me soon.

Frantic, I reached out, trying to grab the window shutters so I could close them against the onslaught. But in my haste, my sweaty, nervous fingers failed to grasp the shutters properly.

And the water kept surging forward.

I gave up. One shutter was partially closed—it would have to be good enough. Not that two flimsy pieces of wood could keep out the increasingly angry river.

I dashed away from the window into the center of my room, grabbing onto the bed frame. I hoped that, if I held onto the heaviest item here, then I wouldn't get swept away.

The shaking under and around me grew more intense. I thought my very bones would shake out of my body.

Above my head, the rope—complete with clothes drying—that hung from the rafters swayed uncontrollably. Books and knickknacks tumbled off the shelves. The ceramic pitcher and bowl that sat upon my dresser fell onto the ground and broke with a resounding crash. Smaller crashes followed as more breakable items hit the ground.

And outside, the wave slammed into Zaela Island with a loud whoosh.

Water poured into the tower window. I screamed as the ground shook harder, with a huge jolt that felt like a giant's hand had pushed the island. The bed frame was ripped out of my hands as the bed and the dresser slid across the floor. A crash and the sound of wood splitting followed. The nightstand toppled over, as did one of my bookcases.

The partially closed shutter ripped off its hinges. It flew across the room, narrowly missing my head.

The water hit me, fast and forceful, sweeping me across the small room. It pushed me into the door to my tower room, where the small of my back hit the door handle.

My breath knocked out of me, and I doubled over, nearly blacking out. But despite the pain, I struggled to stay awake, knowing that if I gave into blissful unconsciousness, I could very well drown.

The meager fire in the hearth went out, leaving me in semi-darkness.

With one final heave, the ground stopped shaking.

Water still streamed through the open window, but not nearly as much or with the same force as before. I took in a few shallow breaths. My back throbbed, but at least now I was able to stand fully upright.

I surveyed the damage. Fortunately, the water in the room wasn't too deep, coming to just above my ankles. But even in the dim light, I could tell that the furniture was damaged. Indistinct shapes floated in the water.

With the fire out, the only light came from the moon outside my tower window. I had some candles and a tinderbox, but I usually kept them on a bookshelf—one that was now lying face down in the ankle-deep water.

I sighed as I ran a dirty, wet hand through my hair. I needed light, so I'd have to wade through the broken crockery and other debris to right the bookshelf and fish around for the items. I only hoped I didn't injure myself more in the process.

I looked down, ready to pluck up my soggy skirt from the water. And then I paused, confused.

A faint crimson glow had appeared around my feet. It faded the further it went into the room, so it wasn't coming from the window.

I turned to the door. It looked like the light was coming from it, or more accurately, from underneath it.

I stilled, straining my ears to listen. It didn't sound like there was anything out there. But that didn't explain the light.

Taking a deep breath, I opened the door.

11

CHAPTER ELEVEN

WATER STREAMED OUT AFTER me as I started down the tower stairs. I had to be careful as I descended—the wooden stairs were already slick with water from both my room and from a window across the way.

As my feet squelched with each step, I grimaced. Cleaning this place would be such a pain, although it would give me something to do. How bad was the damage, anyway? I wouldn't be able to assess it properly without light.

And speaking of light ...

The red glow I had seen under the door grew stronger the further down I went. I still didn't hear anything—other than my wet footsteps and a steady trickle of water. But despite the silence, I felt uneasy. I knew where I had seen this red light before, but it had never spread throughout my tower before.

I had reached the ground level of the tower, but the light wasn't coming from the study. A quick glance inside showed that one of the windows had broken, and there was some flooding. Fortunately, since the study faced away from the river surge, it hadn't received as much damage.

I still had one more floor to go. The Great Seal was housed in the tower's cellar, which also served as my food storage area. I had actually considered sleeping down there once summer came in earnest.

But now, I shivered as I descended the stairs. Whether it was from the cold night air and my wet clothes, or from the feeling of dread creeping over my heart, I wasn't sure.

The crimson light was so strong I had to shield my eyes as I approached. The air pulsed like a heartbeat. When I was higher in the tower, I couldn't hear anything moving down here—and in one sense, I still couldn't. But there was an odd vibration floating around me, one I could feel in my body just as surely as the earlier earthquake.

With my hand slightly covering my face and my head turned to the side, I couldn't quite see what was happening. The Great Seal lay somewhere before me, but I didn't have a clear view of it.

The pulsating grew heavier. With one final push, the light grew so bright, I had to shut my eyes against it. Then the vibration in the air suddenly stopped, and the intensity of the red glow faded.

Cautiously, I opened my eyes.

The last of the crimson light seeped away, leaving me in complete darkness. I swore and felt around by the entrance for the candle and flint that I usually left there. Thank the gods—it was there. I lit the candle and held it up to survey the room.

Before me, the Great Seal was open.

The Seal had been a perfect circle covering a deeper pit set in the tower's underground. From the things I had read, the barrier was impenetrable. It couldn't be hacked at or sliced open, or set on fire. Magic, of any kind or intensity, had no effect on it. The Guardians before me hadn't been sure if the barrier was the reason no one had been able to commune with the god Graenta, or if there was another reason for the god's overall, ongoing silence.

But now, the Great Seal was broken.

I approached it slowly, curiosity and fear warring inside me.

As if my meager light had called to something within the pit, a new glow emerged. Jagged spikes of red surrounded the circle, as if something had punched up through the seal to break through it. And a golden light shone from deep within the earth, steadily growing brighter.

Staring down at the open hole in the floor, it finally hit me.

The Great Seal was open. After centuries of the magical ward lying untouched and dormant, holding back whatever it was designed to enclose, it was now wide open.

And I was the Guardian who had failed to keep it intact.

Oh, gods.

I swayed as a wave of nausea hit me. I doubled over, heaving.

"Well, that's one way to get a god's attention."

I yelped at the unexpected voice and scrambled away. A hand reached out and steadied me, pulling me back from the circle's edge.

"Be careful, now. You don't want to fall in. It's an awfully long drop."

I stared at the hand on my arm, then the person attached to it.

Standing next to me was a little boy of about ten with dark hair and bright golden eyes. A pair of glasses in a hinged leather frame was perched on his nose. A streak of dirt was smeared across his left cheek. He sniffled and wiped his nose with his sleeve.

Ew.

Catching my grimace of disgust, he said, "What?"

"Nothing." I wasn't going to get into a discussion on manners with someone I didn't even know. Instead, I asked, "Who are you? And how did you get in here?"

The little boy gaped at me, then recovered and drew himself up proudly. Hands on hips, he said, "Don't you recognize me?"

I frowned and shook my head. "I can't say that I do."

The boy deflated, but shrugged. "Figures. I guess that's what happens when you're out of the collective minds of your people for centuries. Still, I figured, as a Guardian, you would know who it is you've been trying to commune with all this time."

My eyes widened and now it was my turn to gape. "Graenta? *You're* Graenta?"

The little boy nodded. "The one and only."

"For some reason, I thought you would be—"

"Older? Uglier?"

"Taller."

Graenta's expression turned sour. "I could be, but it's just easier this way."

He must have seen the confusion on my face, because he explained, "I'm a god. I can appear however I want, but it can be draining to be in certain forms all the time."

"And this is the form you chose?" The words slipped out before I thought, and I clapped my hands over my mouth. Graenta may not have looked like much, but if he *was* a god, he could totally smite me or something if he felt like it.

But Graenta just laughed. "It may not look like it, but it has its perks."

"Even the eyeglasses?" I figured a god would have perfect eyesight—or, if he didn't, the ability to give it to himself.

Graenta lowered his voice as if he were imparting a great secret. "Honestly? I don't need them. I just like how they look. I imagine they'll be super fashionable, in time."

I shrugged. "If you say so." I narrowed my eyes at him. "If you're really Graenta, prove it."

He raised an inquiring eyebrow. "All right. What would you like me to do?"

"I don't know. Something god-like. Um ..."

I perked up, thinking of something that was sure to stump him. "What was I thinking about before all this happened?" I waved a hand at the open seal and the damp tower.

Immediately, he responded, "Some guy named Tahn. Specifically, kissing him under the oak tree by your house, hoping none of your family or neighbors would stumble across you. Do you need more detail? You said, "Oh, Tahn, you're so—"

I blushed so hard my cheeks burned. "Oh, no, that's ... okay."

Graenta's eyes twinkled. "So am I right?"

I nodded, not trusting my voice. I cleared my throat. "Wow. It's like you were in my head or something."

"Well, you *are* my Guardian."

Even though I didn't understand, I nodded again. I looked at the gaping glowing hole in the ground. "So, then, how did you get up here? Aren't you supposed to be, you know, in there?"

Graenta nodded. "I was, along with the other gods. And then there was a rumbling, and a heavy feeling of magic in the air. There have been attempted breaches before, but this one—this had substantial power behind it."

The little boy grew somber. "I fear I have grown complacent over the years. I didn't realize how much power my fellow gods still held in reserve. When they felt the rumbling begin to chip away at the Great Seal, they added their own power to it and overcame the barrier. Before I could even react, they had all vanished."

Oh, wow. I couldn't believe it. According to Gifted Lands history, each of the seven kingdoms on the continent had been founded by a different god or goddess who molded their chosen kingdom into upholding their ideals. But after the kingdoms had been created, the immortals had found themselves at odds with each other. Various slights and skirmishes led to all the kingdoms meeting for what would be known as the Six Gods' War.

But the seventh god—Graenta—had lured his fellow gods and goddesses away from the battlefield and sealed them away on Zaela Island, preventing an even bloodier battle that would have surely killed the majority of the humans in the Gifted Lands. And to ensure that no gods could harm their new creation, Graenta also sealed himself away on the island.

Whenever we studied the founding of the Gifted Lands in class, I had never really believed it. It sounded like an impossible, silly story—kind of like believing that the Fae existed. If the gods had walked the continent, they had to have been long dead by now. Which, of course, would make being a Guardian a completely pointless endeavor.

And yet, I was standing next to the wide open, ruptured Great Seal, talking to a little boy with sparkling golden eyes who claimed to be the founder of my home kingdom.

Graenta studied me, head tilted in thought. "You're taking this quite well."

My breathing came in shallow gasps, and dark fuzziness was creeping into the edges of my vision. "Am I? That's good."

"Oh, dear. Here, sit down."

Graenta helped me to the ground, my back against a cool stone wall. The ground was damp and muddy, but I was beyond caring about the state of my outfit. I leaned my head back, trying to gulp in more air.

"You'll be all right," Graenta said. "That's it, that's it. One breath in, one breath out."

When the fainting sensation had passed, I took in another big gulp of air and then turned to Graenta. "Okay, so you're out, but you're not supposed to be. What now?"

Graenta tapped his chin in thought. Even though he was a powerful god who was older than time, the mature gesture looked funny and out-of-place on his ten-year-old face. "Hmm. For one thing, I can't go back in there unless all the other gods are with me. And then, of course, we have to make sure that whatever freed the immortals can't happen again."

"We?"

"Well, of course. You are the Guardian, are you not? My champion? So, the task falls to you."

12

—·—

CHAPTER TWELVE

I STARED AT GRAENTA, dumbfounded. "I may be the current Guardian, but it's not like I chose this! This was supposed to be an easy, boring job, for just one year!"

Graenta's serene smile somehow made him look like the ageless being he was, instead of a child. "You may not have chosen this, but I did. I chose you."

"Honestly? I had always thought the idea that you were guiding Queen Yllulae in picking the next Guardian was nonsense. Do you mean to tell me you really were leading her to choose me?"

"Sometimes, if she cannot sense my feelings on the matter, she will make her best choice. But other times, as in your case, I did my best to let her know my preferences, despite the Great Seal muting communication between us. As I said, I wanted you as my Guardian. And my instincts are never wrong."

I opened my mouth, ready to argue with him. I didn't care that he was an all-powerful god, I was no hero. But just as I was about to let loose, a pounding at the tower door sounded above.

Harlan's muffled voice floated down. "Idessa? Guardian, are you in there?"

In a rush, Graenta said, "You may tell him that the Great Seal was broken—the Gifted Lands will find out soon enough. But do not tell anyone that you've seen me." And with that, he disappeared.

"Graenta? Graenta!" I put my arms out, wondering if he had turned invisible somewhere nearby me. But my hands only met empty air.

Overhead, Harlan's pounding grew louder.

I groaned and stood up, then made my painful way back up the cellar stairs. "I'm here, Harlan! I'm here!"

Once I was back on the ground level, I unbarred the wooden door and opened it.

The ferryman practically tumbled inside. He put his hands on my shoulders and looked me over, making sure I wasn't bleeding or injured. "Guardian Idessa! I'm glad you're all right!"

"A bit bruised, and definitely frightened, but that's all. Do you know what happened?"

Harlan shook his head, his grey hair spraying drops of water. "No. I was at home when I heard a loud rumbling, and the ground started shaking. When I looked out my window, I saw a huge wave rolling along the Rehann, coming from the south. I thought for sure it would overpower my little riverside cottage. As it is, the rushing water broke some of my windows and my poor house is waterlogged."

"Oh, Harlan, that's awful. I'm so sorry."

He waved away my sympathy. "Nothing that hard work can't fix. That's what I get for living so close to the Rehann. She's beautiful, but she can be temperamental." He frowned. "Although, in all my years, I've never seen her behave like that."

I shifted uneasily, hoping he wouldn't ask me for my thoughts on the subject. But instead, he said, "How about you, Guardian? Any damage to the tower?"

"My room is flooded as well," I said. I told him about what had happened when the earthquake and wave struck. "I have yet to assess the damage completely, since I need light. And also ..."

Harlan frowned as my voice trailed off. "Also?"

I sighed. "The Great Seal is broken."

The ferryman's eyes grew so wide I thought they would pop out of his head. "My goodness! You don't say! You're sure?"

I nodded. "I checked, but you're welcome to look as well if you want."

Harlan shook his head. "No, I believe you, Idessa. Well, come on." He turned to go.

"Wait! Where are we going?"

He looked back at me. "Well, you can't stay here. Your room is in ruins, and there's nowhere safe on Zaela Island for you to stay now. Besides, you'll need to tell Queen Yllulae about the Great Seal."

I sighed again. He was right, of course, but I wasn't looking forward to giving the queen my report. "What about my things?"

"Leave them here. I can bring you back in a few days after the water has dried up, and you can salvage what you can."

"All right." I followed him out the door, making sure to close it behind me, then down the short beach to his waiting raft.

We pushed off from Zaela Island under the moonlight. Harlan skillfully steered through the currents, although now that the magical tremor had passed, the water was calm.

"I'm glad that you didn't get too hurt in that chaos," Harlan said. "I came as soon as I felt it was safe to cross the river."

"It's okay. I'm just touched that you came to check on me at all."

"Of course." The ferryman grinned. "But no more earthquakes, all right?"

I laughed. "Agreed."

I heard a high-pitched humming around my ear. I swatted at my hair, but the mosquito continued to buzz nearby. Pesky, annoying things. All the excess water, plus the oncoming summer's heat, would attract them to Graenir in droves. I waved my hand again, hoping I could shoo the bug away, but it kept coming back.

Great.

Harlan squinted into the distance. "My eyes aren't what they used to be, but it looks like you might have some visitors on the far shore."

Two hooded riders waited on the other side of the Rehann River. Two riders, but three horses. I frowned. Was it the queen's guard, already come to collect me and take me to the palace so I could make my report? I'd have to get it over, eventually, but a change of clothes and good night's rest would be nice.

I shivered in the night air, my damp dress clinging to my skin. Yes, I'd request at least a change of clothes—and an hour in front of a nice, large fire—before I went to see Queen Yllulae.

Harlan landed the raft on the Graenir shore and jumped off, pulling the ferry further onto the land. He held a hand out to me to help me disembark.

"Thank you," I said.

"Of course, happy to help," Harlan said. He looked up. The hooded riders had dismounted and were now approaching us. "I'll stay here for a bit, just in case you need some help."

I nodded, trying to suppress my nerves. "All right. Thank you."

The two people stopped in front of Harlan and me. Both tall, around the same height, they stood side by side as they regarded us. Then the one on the left put down his hood.

"Lis!" I breathed a sigh of relief at seeing my brother.

The other person removed their hood. "Oran! It's good to see you both."

I ran into my brother's open arms. I gave him a big hug, then stepped back slightly and swatted at his arm. "You two gave me such a fright!"

Lis laughed. "We didn't mean to. It's just cold out, that's all."

I swatted at him again, but there was no heat behind the hit. "Next time, announce yourselves!"

My brother chuckled, waving at Zaela Island. "I love how you assume there will be a next time."

I looked where he pointed. The moon shone down on Zaela Island, illuminating the destruction the earthquake and water had left behind. Trees were flattened or splintered, looking like skeletal broken bones. The tower still stood tall and proud, but I had a feeling that daylight would reveal cracks, rubble, and debris.

Harlan dropped the long oar he had been holding as a makeshift weapon. "Guardian, I assume I won't be needing this?"

I laughed. "No, Harlan. But thank you."

After a quick round of introductions, Lis said, "We felt the earthquake even in Graenir City and the surrounding areas. Once it was over, Oran and I came out here to make sure you were all right. And possibly bring you home, if needed."

"I'm glad you did," I said.

"Should we go straight to the queen to tell her what happened?" Lis looked at me expectantly, waiting for my answer.

That won't be necessary, I thought. *There's no immediate danger, nothing that won't keep in the morning. Go home, get some sleep, and a new, dry outfit.*

While I recognized the truth of my thoughts, I wondered why my inner voice sounded like Graenta's.

"No, we can go to the palace in the morning," I said. "But I'll have to go back home with you. My room on Zaela Island is wrecked. And so is Harlan's house."

"Is that so?" At Harlan's nod, my brother said, "Then you must come back with us. We can house you for the night, and for as long as you need after that."

"Oh, I couldn't possibly—" Harlan began, but Lis cut him off.

"I insist. It wouldn't be right, leaving you here in a ruined house."

I added my invitation to my brother's. "Besides, it's the least we could do to repay you for coming to get me."

Harlan paused, then nodded. "All right. I thank you."

Now there were four people, but only three horses. I ended up riding with Oran, with him sitting behind me on his mount. But honestly, I was fine with that. It was a well known fact—and somewhat of a family joke—that Lis didn't travel well. Even though the moon only lit our way so much, I could tell my brother felt a little queasy—either from the earlier earthquake, his ride over, or both.

As we rode off, a buzz sounded in my ear. That darn mosquito was back, or perhaps it was another one. I swatted my hand with such force that I startled the horse.

"Woah, easy there," Oran chuckled behind me.

"Are you talking to me, or the horse?"

"Both of you. You okay, Idessa?"

"Yes. No. It's just this stupid mosquito that won't leave me alone."

"Oh, yes. It will be bug season soon."

"Lovely."

To take my mind off my annoying little friend, I said, "I understand why Lis came here tonight, but how did you end up going with him?"

Oran said, "I wanted to make sure you were okay. Right after I made sure my family was all right, I went to check on Alistair. We both had the same idea—to go to the Rehann River, and see if we could get passage to Zaela Island."

"Oh." I was touched that Oran had thought of me. "That's very kind of you."

I paused. "Um. Did you see anyone else at my family's house? Or on the road, maybe?"

"No." Oran's voice sounded confused. "Should I have?"

"Ah, no. I guess not."

But it hurt, knowing that Tahn hadn't thought to check on me.

13

CHAPTER THIRTEEN

I FILLED ORAN AND my brother in on what had happened on Zaela Island, ending with my discovery of the Great Seal's rupture. They had stayed silent during my recounting, but when I mentioned that the Seal was now open, Lis sucked in a breath. "Did you see anyone? The imprisoned gods and goddesses? Were they there?"

That stupid mosquito kept buzzing in front of my face, back and forth. It landed on my nose briefly, then flitted away before I could squash it. Not that that would have been a good idea. I didn't really want to meet Queen Yllulae with a big red swollen spot on my nose.

Remembering Graenta's warning before he disappeared, I said, "Uh, no. I didn't see any of the immortals."

"Huh. Interesting." Lis paused, pondering. "It's been such a long time—I wonder if they're dead? But then, wouldn't you have seen their bodies in the ground, if they were?"

"But they're immortal," Oran pointed out. "That means they can't die, right?"

"Not necessarily," Lis said. "From the books and scrolls I've been studying in the Archives, they are long-lived, yes. Very, very long-lived. But extremely powerful magic could, in theory, kill them. An incredible, incurable illness. And—each other. If they turned on each other while in captivity, they could easily kill one another."

"That's fascinating. But—how would you define extremely powerful magic? As compared to any other magic found in the Gifted Lands?"

"That's a good question. I would say that powerful magic is defined by ..."

I tuned the two men out. A long-winded discussion on magic theory did not interest me. The horse's steady motion began to lull me, and I closed my eyes, soothed by the calm.

I woke up as we approached my family's home. I was leaning against something solid and warm. It was so cozy, and it smelled really good. I snuggled in, contented.

Now my mind was more alert. As I concentrated, I realized that whatever was bolstering me was moving slightly—like a heartbeat. And I could hear soft breaths above me.

I turned my head towards Oran. "Oh ... did I fall asleep?"

The solid, warm wall began to shake. With laughter. Oran's laughter. "Yes, you did. It's all right, you've had quite a night."

"Oh!" I sat upright, embarrassed. "Sorry about that."

Oran laughed again and, for some reason, I found myself missing the coziness of leaning against him. Ah, well. It was probably because I was still wearing this damp dress in the chilly night.

"It's fine," Oran said. "I didn't mind."

Lis and Harlan dismounted, then Lis hurried inside. A lone candle shone in one window, but just moments after Lis entered, the front windows bloomed with light. Lis poked his head back out. "Come on in, all of you."

Harlan disappeared into the house. Oran dismounted, then, despite my protests, helped me get down. I started after the others, then realized Oran wasn't behind me. "Aren't you coming in?"

He shook his head. "No. It's late, and I don't want my parents to worry. I'll come by tomorrow to see how everyone's doing, though."

"All right. Although I apologize in advance if you come by, and I'm already gone. I'll need to have an audience with Queen Yllulae tomorrow sometime."

Oran smiled. "No problem. I'll come early so I won't miss you. And if you need moral support, I'd be happy to go to the capital with you."

"Thank you." Once again I was touched by Oran's thoughtfulness. "I might be awhile, though. Not just meeting with the queen. But—there are some other people I was hoping to visit."

"Of course. I'm happy to accompany you on any or all of it." He nodded at the house. "Tell Lis I said goodbye."

He rode off, and I walked into the house where Lis was helping Harlan settle in. "You can take my room, it's the first door on the right. Tomorrow, I'd be happy to accompany you back and help you with cleanup."

Harlan chuckled, but it was tinged with sadness. "I think it will take more than a day to set things to rights. Still, I thank you for your hospitality. I'll see you both in the morning, then."

The ferryman disappeared down the hallway. I turned to my brother. "Where will you sleep?"

"Out here." He flopped down on the faded grey settee in our main room, swinging his long legs over the side. I giggled at the sight. The low couch was just a touch too small for Lis, and his feet hung over the edge.

"Looks comfy," I teased, and was rewarded by Lis throwing a small pillow at me.

When I made a sound of protest, my brother looked at me, all innocence. "What? I was just moving it so I have more room to sleep. I can't help it if it slipped out of my hands."

And then, "Oof!" as I tossed the pillow back at him.

He caught it, laughing. "I'll put this here, so we don't wake up the rest of the house." He put the pillow to the side. "What are your plans for tomorrow?"

I made a face. "Besides sleeping as late as possible? I need to present myself to Queen Ylllulae."

Lis smirked. "Forget sleeping late then. You should probably go see the queen at first light."

"But—"

"I know you're tired, Dess. But this is more important. And you *are* the current Guardian."

I huffed. Lis was right—which made me even grumpier. It didn't help that his words echoed Graenta's earlier statement, back in the tower.

And that stupid mosquito was back, buzzing around my head. My attempts to wave the pest away proved ineffectual.

Lis stared at me. "What are you doing?"

"Trying to get rid of this darn mosquito," I said. "Can't you hear it?"

But apparently he couldn't, since Lis continued to stare at me like I had gone mad. "Um. No."

"It. Won't. Leave. Me. Alone." I swatted the air so hard I nearly hit myself.

Lis grabbed my wrists and brought them down, holding them still. "Maybe you should go to bed, Dess."

Exhaustion washed over me as heavy and quick as the wave that had hit Zaela Island. "You're right."

"Would you like me to go with you when you see the queen?"

"I'll be fine by myself. You go help Harlan. Besides, Oran said he'd accompany me."

Lis raised an eyebrow. "Really? Well, you'll be in good company then."

"Yes." I started towards my bedroom, then paused. "By the way, have you seen Tahn or Jele at all in the last few months? I wanted to ask you about them but it didn't seem like a good idea while we were on the road with everyone else."

My brother stilled. For a moment I thought he was going to satisfy my curiosity. But then a huge yawn escaped his lips. "Sorry, Dess. It's been a long evening. Can we talk about this tomorrow?"

I nodded, disappointed. "Sure."

In my room, I leaned against the closed door and took in my surroundings. It had been a full season since I had been here last, and—except for the light layer of dust coating everything—my room had remained untouched. Gods, I had missed this place. I had missed being home, among my familiar things, and with my family. Even if they did sometimes annoy me.

I opened a dresser drawer and rummaged through my clothes for a nightgown. There wasn't much left, as I had brought the majority of my belongings to Zaela Island. I found an old, faded gown that had a frayed hem and a few small holes where moths had eaten the fabric.

I sighed. It wasn't pretty, but it would have to do.

Nightgown in hand, I turned around. Then gasped.

Graenta stood in the middle of my bedroom.

I clutched the gown to my chest, even though I was fully clothed.

"What are you doing here?" I hissed.

Graenta's brow furrowed. "Last I checked, we still had to get the other gods back to Graenir, close the Great Seal, and all that. And we haven't even started yet, so ..."

"But I thought you left. You disappeared when Harlan knocked on the door."

The little boy grinned. "I didn't disappear. I just changed forms, and went with you."

"Changed forms?" I blinked as realization dawned. "The mosquito? That was you?"

"Yes. And if I may say, you certainly didn't make it easy. Waving your hands around like that all the time."

I smirked. "I know you've been out of the Gifted Lands for a while, but I don't think anyone, in any time period, has ever liked mosquitos."

"Ah, but that's where you're wrong. Centuries ago, they were revered, worshipped even."

I gaped at Graenta. He clapped his hands and laughed. "Just kidding. Mosquitos *are* horrible."

"Glad we can agree on something. Look, I get that we'll be together for some time, at least until this whole mess is sorted out. So—could you pick a less annoying form to transform into?"

The god chuckled. "Sure. Any requests? Going smaller than my current form is always easier than going bigger, by the way. Takes less energy and concentration."

I smiled. "As long as it's not a mosquito—or any other bug—I don't think I'll be too picky."

"It's a deal."

A tentative knock sounded on my door. Graenta disappeared. I made a mental note to ask him, when he did that, if he actually disappeared or just turned invisible. And if he did disappear, where did he go?

The door opened a crack and Lis poked his head in. "Dess?" he said in a low voice, trying not to wake our parents or our guest. "I thought I heard voices. Who are you talking to?"

I laughed, a bit awkwardly. Great, now my brother thought I had returned from Zaela Island insane. "No one, just myself. Just ... listing all the things I have to get done tomorrow."

"Ah, okay." Lis eyed me skeptically. I didn't blame him. List making and being conscientious had never been my strong suits. "I'll leave you to it, then. Goodnight."

"Goodnight," I said back, and could have sworn I heard a slight echo behind my voice—as if someone else was repeating my sentiment, just a beat behind.

Lis blinked in confusion. Had he heard the second voice as well? He shook his head, as if to clear it, and shut the door.

A distinct giggle floated on the air.

I rolled my eyes. Blowing out my candle, I fell into bed, not caring that I hadn't changed into my nightclothes. Tomorrow, Graenta and I would have to have a discussion about how, exactly, this Guardian-god relationship would work.

14

·—·—·

CHAPTER FOURTEEN

TRUE TO HIS WORD, Oran came by in the morning. I was already awake, in part because some god-who-shall-remain-nameless made sure I was awake right at daybreak.

A bleary-eyed Lis answered the door. "Oran, good to see you again. Thanks for taking Dess into the city."

"It's my pleasure," Oran said with a nod to me. "If you like, I can head over to Harlan's afterwards and help you clean up."

"That would be great. I have a feeling it will take several days, if not longer, to get his place in order. And there's also Zaela Island to take care of."

"Oh, that's right. Are you going to help with that, too? What do you think you'll need?"

Since it looked like the two men were going to get into a detailed discussion about cleaning, I said, "I'll wait for you outside, Oran." Besides, I needed to talk to Graenta. And the last thing I needed was for anyone else to think I was crazy.

Oran nodded at me as I walked out the door.

Once I was outside and out of earshot, I hissed into the empty air, "Graenta!"

The god—in his little boy form—materialized in front of me. "Hello, Idessa."

"Geez, you scared me. Are you always just … there? How did you get here so fast?"

"As a god, I am everywhere and nowhere. But since you are my Guardian, you and I share a bond. If you call for me, I will be there immediately."

"That's actually what I wanted to talk to you about, before we get going. Being your Guardian."

Graenta merely raised his eyebrows at me in question.

"Okay, some rules," I said. I began ticking the points off on my fingers. "One, when you turn invisible—"

"Actually, I just head to the Other Plane. I find invisibility cumbersome, unless it's absolutely necessary. It's too easy for others to bump into me or trip over me when I'm invisible."

"All right, fine. When you disappear into this Other Plane, you stay there until I call for you. I don't want you lurking nearby, spying on me."

"I don't lurk." Graenta sounded offended. "And I have no need to spy on you."

"Fine. Whatever. Just give me my privacy, is all I'm asking."

"Of course." The god's voice implied he had been doing that all along. "What's your next point?"

I actually didn't have another point. The privacy thing had been my biggest concern. "Uh. Two. No more mosquitoes."

"We decided that yesterday."

"I guess that it's, then."

"Perfect. I have a rule of my own."

I eyed Graenta expectantly.

"No mention that you saw me, or that I'm accompanying you. Not until I tell you it's all right."

I frowned. "Not even to the queen?"

"No. I have my reasons."

"But why—"

With a small whoosh of air, Graenta disappeared. Again.

I looked up. Oran was walking out the front door, waving at me. "Idessa! Are you ready to go?"

I nodded, and we both started down the road towards Graenir's capital.

"Sorry for the delay." Oran grinned at me. "You'd think cleanup—even after such an event that befell you and Harlan—would be simple. Go to the place, sort through things, and that's it. But there was a lot more that your brother and I had to figure out."

I raised an eyebrow at Oran. "Really? Like what?"

"Like how we're going to get all your things off Zaela Island, for one thing. Along with all the other debris from the tower. How bad was the damage, anyway?"

I frowned. "I never got a chance to really look things over—it was kind of dark in there, and then when Harlan arrived I didn't go back upstairs. But I think it might be pretty bad. A lot of things broke, furniture fell over, and everything got soaked."

Oran nodded. "It sounds as bad as I'd expect. We'll have to ask Queen Yllulae to provide a boat, then, since I doubt Harlan's raft could handle all that."

"We?"

Oran grinned at me again, and I felt an answering smile bloom across my face. "Of course. I wouldn't leave you to face the queen by yourself. Not that she's scary or anything, but still."

Our walk to Graenir's capital city passed pleasantly. Just a few years older than me, Oran and Lis had been friends for as long as I could remember. Oran had always been around, and even though he was more bookish than my brother now was, we had an easy camaraderie that came from years of friendship and familiarity.

At the castle gates, we spoke to a guard, requesting an immediate audience with Queen Yllulae. The guard seemed disinclined to pass on the message, until Oran pointed at me and said, "Don't you recognize her? Idessa is the current Guardian."

Slow realization dawned on the guard's face. "Of course. I'll be right back." He scurried inside.

Oran and I stood waiting in the courtyard, trying not to appear awkward or uncomfortable. Luckily, we didn't have to wait long. The guard hurried back, waving us in. "The queen will see you now. Best not to keep her waiting."

Oran nodded at the guard in thanks. I bit my lip, trying to tamp down my nervousness.

The guard led us into the palace, back to the great hall where Catrum's homecoming had taken place just a few months before. A pair of thrones stood on the dais at the front of the room, one of which was occupied by the grey-haired queen. The other throne held a simple gold circlet—not the official ceremonial crown, but the "everyday" crown that Queen Yllulae's late husband used to wear. Although the queen had been widowed for many years, she had never shown any inclination to remarry after the king had passed away.

The queen herself was dressed simply, suggesting that this was an impromptu meeting and not part of her official open court for the public. Her silver gown lacked ornamentation, and the crown atop her head was as plain as the one on her late husband's throne.

We approached the queen, Oran bowing and me curtseying. The queen indicated we should rise. "Well met, Graenir's Guardian," she said. "Let's get right to it. Why are you here, and not at your post?"

"It's like this, Your Majesty," I said, and recounted the events of the previous night on Zaela Island. The queen's serene face grew more troubled as I recounted my tale. When I mentioned that the Great Seal had been opened, she grew pale.

"The Seal was open, but there were no other beings around, living or dead?" Queen Yllulae asked me.

I shook my head, not quite trusting my voice. I hoped my face wouldn't betray my lie. I was fairly sure lying to your sovereign was a punishable offense. Or, at the very least, frowned upon.

"I wonder what that could mean?" the queen murmured, looking pensive. "I suppose I'll have to send messengers out to the other rulers. But I would prefer not to, if I don't have to."

She looked off into the distance, her gaze unfocused. "I wonder—perhaps I should ask Joichan and Melandria what they think. They were rulers, once. They might have some good insights."

She continued to murmur to herself, forgetting that Oran and I were there. We stayed silent while the queen weighed her options, exchanging a questioning look with each other. I didn't know much about the other kingdoms in the Gifted Lands—I don't think anyone in Graenir did, to be honest. From what I knew of my home kingdom, we had always adopted a stand-offish, isolationist policy when it came to the other countries.

Which is why the entire kingdom had been shocked when Queen Yllulae had invited two ambassadors to her court several years ago—Melandria, the former queen of the northern kingdom of Calia, and Melandria's husband Joichan. They kept mostly to themselves, serving as observers of our culture and a still untapped liaison to Calia.

The queen nodded to herself, having come to a decision. "Yes, that's what I'll do. I'm sure they'll have some ideas."

She chuckled as she touched the small gold crown on the empty seat next to her. "My dear Rahnt always said I was too independent. Wouldn't he be surprised to hear that I actually want to ask for help."

I wasn't sure we were supposed to respond—or what exactly we were supposed to say—but Oran bowed again and said, "A noble plan, Your Majesty."

Queen Yllulae beamed, and for a moment her joyful, carefree younger self peeked out. "Thank you. And thank you for your report, Guardian Idessa. You both may go."

I spoke up hesitantly. "If I may, Your Majesty—a question before we leave?"

"Speak."

"What is to be done about Zaela Island, the tower, my things? And if the Great Seal is opened, am I still a Guardian?"

A small breeze blew past me. Startled, I turned my head to follow it—and saw a tiny blue butterfly flitting about the room. Graenta. I was sure of it.

Well, at least he's not a mosquito.

"I will send a group of guards and servants to Zaela Island," the queen said. "I'm sure you could use the extra hands for cleaning and moving heavy things. From your description, it doesn't sound like the tower is fit to stay in at this point, and won't be for a while.

"As for your Guardianship ..."

The blue butterfly landed on the top of my head. I debated swatting at it, but no one else seemed to notice that there was a butterfly on my head. So I fought the urge to brush it off, knowing I'd only look like an idiot if it really was Graenta, and he was invisible to the others.

"You can stay here on the mainland, as the island is uninhabitable. But even though there is nothing left to guard, we still need to get to the bottom of this. So, in the eyes of the Crown, you are still considered the current Guardian, until your time of service has been completed or Graenta himself releases you."

Oh, great. I doubted I would be able to convince Graenta privately to release me from my duty. The only other way I would be officially released by the god was during the transfer ceremony—such as what had occurred at Catrum's homecoming. So, the best I could hope for was for my remaining time as Guardian to go by quick.

Which would be at least another eight months.

Lucky me.

The blue butterfly fluttered around my face a few times before landing on my nose, forcing me to go cross-eyed to look at it. Could a butterfly giggle? Because I could have sworn I heard a little puff of laughter before it flew away, almost as if to say, *Gotcha*.

Great.

15

CHAPTER FIFTEEN

ORAN AND I LEFT soon after, our audience with the queen concluded. She mentioned that I might be called back to the palace after she consulted with the Calian ambassadors, so I should stay close. A nice, not-so-subtle hint to not leave Graenir for the time being. Not that I had anywhere to go, really.

Great. Lucky me.

"Is there anywhere else you'd like to go?" Oran swept his arm wide, indicating the city's daily market before us. We had arrived in the capital so early that the stalls hadn't been set up yet. But now the market was bustling with shoppers and merchants hawking their wares.

I shrugged. "Not particularly. But I don't really feel like going home yet, either."

"That's fair." Oran put his hand on my arm and gently steered me through the crowd.

We wandered from stall to stall, looking at the various goods for sale. Most of the items didn't interest me, but when we came across a familiar wooden stand, I perked up. It was the jeweler whose pieces I had been admiring the day I was appointed as Guardian.

He raised a hand in greeting as we approached. "Ah, it's the current Guardian. Well met, young lady. But shouldn't you be at your post?"

"It's a long story," I said. "But the short version is, I'll be back on the mainland for a while."

The jeweler nodded in understanding. "I don't suppose it has anything to do with the earthquake that rumbled through last night?"

"It does, in fact." I looked around the market. Overall, the stalls didn't show much sign of damage. "But it seems to have bypassed here?"

"We felt the ground shaking—a surprise indeed, since that rarely happens in Graenir—but fortunately it wasn't very long, or intense. A few things fell, but nothing more serious than a broken glass happened."

I raised an eyebrow. "Hmm. It seems to have been quite localized, then. Zaela Island sustained quite a bit of damage."

"My condolences, then." He dipped his head again. "And if you'd like a little something from my stall, I'd be happy to give you a discount."

"Oh, that's so sweet of you." I peered at his offerings more closely. While his wares were lovely, I didn't see the locket I had been admiring so many months ago. "There was a piece I was looking at the last time I was here—it was a while ago, so perhaps you don't have it anymore—"

"Ah, yes, the locket?" At my surprised look, the jeweler laughed. "I firmly believe that certain pieces of jewelry call to certain people. I remember who looks at what—and who buys what."

At his words, my face fell. "So the locket has been sold?"

The merchant nodded. "Yes, a few months ago. A gift for a young lady, from what I recall."

His eyes lit up as he spotted someone behind me. He pointed. "Oh, and there's the young lady now."

I turned around, curious to see who he was pointing at.

Two stalls away, I caught a flash of red hair. The person turned, and I saw a blessedly familiar face.

Jele.

I excused myself and hurried towards her, leaving Oran at the jeweler's stall. I pushed my way through the crowd, wedging myself between a small gap between two stands.

"Jele!" I called out.

My best friend looked up at the sound of her name. When she saw me, an array of emotions danced across her face. First confusion, then elation, which morphed into—guilt? But by the time I reached her, she was smiling.

"Idessa! I couldn't believe it was you!"

"It is! And I'm so glad to see you!"

I pulled her into a hug. She resisted me a little at first, then gingerly returned the hug. It was lovely to see her after all this time, but something about her seemed different.

I looked my friend over. Her face was fuller than I remembered, and—"Jele, not to be rude, but have you gained weight?"

She laughed, but she looked worried. "No, not quite. I mean, I guess, a little. Uh ... Idessa, I'm pregnant."

I blinked, not sure I had heard her right. "You're pregnant? Really?"

She nodded, her quick, nervous movements reminding me of a bird. "Yes."

"Wow! How far along are you? When will the baby be born? And ..." I lowered my voice. "Who's the father?" Before I left, Jele hadn't been involved with anyone.

She shrugged, her discomfort obvious. "Just a few months. We're expecting the baby to come sometime in late fall or early winter. As for who the father is ..."

"Hey, my love. There you are." A tall figure stepped out of the market crowd, bending slightly to kiss the top of Jele's head.

My heart sank. I knew that voice. I had dreamed of that voice—and its owner—for the last four months, while I had been isolated in the tower at Zaela Island. When I should have been meditating, or studying, or doing anything else—I had been thinking of Tahn.

And I thought he had been thinking of me.

I looked up. Our eyes met. Mine, wide and betrayed, tears threatening to spill at any moment. His, full of dawning horror.

"Oh my gods. Idessa ..."

"When?" I was surprised at how steady my voice sounded. "Just answer me that. When?"

Neither Jele nor Tahn answered me. Which was all the answer I needed.

"Were you two sneaking around together behind my back?" I whispered.

"It wasn't like that—" Tahn started.

"We didn't mean to—" Jele began.

My best friend—no, *former* best friend—reached out to me, putting her hand on my shoulder. I flinched away as if her touch had seared me.

Jele pulled her hand back, her eyes sad. Her fingers flew her to neck, in a subconscious gesture. And it was then that I saw it. I don't know why it took me so long to notice it.

Around her neck was the locket I had wanted all those months ago. The jeweler *had* been pointing Jele out to me. No doubt it held a lock of Tahn's hair, and would eventually hold a lock of their child's hair as well.

And on her left hand, a simple gold poesy ring. The rings, with their engraved hidden messages, were popular among sweethearts.

I gasped, and the tears I had been trying to keep at bay finally fell. "Are you two—married?"

Jele whispered, "We will be soon. Next month."

I had heard enough. Shaking, I pushed past the pair and ran. I could hear both Jele and Tahn calling after me, but I didn't respond, didn't stop. I just kept moving, threading my way through the market crowd, bumping into people but not caring about my rudeness.

At the city gates, I paused. Tears streamed down my face, and I was trembling so much I couldn't breathe properly. I fell to the ground, weeping.

A hand on my back caused me to startle. I flailed my arms in a pathetic attempt to get whoever was touching me to stop.

"Woah! Idessa, it's just me."

Oran's concerned face peered into my tear-stained one as he crouched down next to me. "Are you all right? When you left the jeweler's stand, I lost you for a bit, and then I saw you running through the crowd."

I sniffled and looked behind him. Aside from a few curious glances, no one else was approaching. I couldn't see Jele or Tahn anymore, but I could tell—they weren't coming after me.

"Do you want to talk about it? Or do you just want to go home?"

I wiped at my wet face. "I'd like to go home."

"Of course." Oran helped me to my feet.

We walked in silence for most of the way. When we were about halfway home, I blurted out, "Did you know?"

Oran looked confused. "Did I know what?"

"About Tahn. And Jele."

Oran sighed. I could tell this was probably not a conversation he wanted to be having, but I was past the point of caring. "I don't know if you were aware, but Tahn doesn't have the best reputation."

"I kind of knew, but I didn't care. He loves me. Well, he did."

"I personally wasn't aware of anything going on between him and Jele while you were here, but after you left for Zaela Island, I'd see them together often. I figured it was because they had you in common."

"But they can't stand each other." Or at least, that's what I had thought. Apparently a lot of what I thought had been wrong.

Oran nodded. "Yes, well ... and then rumors began floating around about Jele being pregnant. And now that she's showing a bit, they can hardly hide it anymore."

The tears came back in full force. "They lied to me. They both lied to me! I thought she was my friend! And I thought he ... I thought ..."

I stopped walking as I started shaking again. Oran put a comforting arm around me.

The blue butterfly from the palace appeared, flitting about my face before landing on my head. Was this Graenta's way of comforting me? It was a bit bizarre, and silly—but I was also touched by it.

"Listen," Oran said. "I could give you some speech about how you'll find a better man than Tahn, about how you'll find truer friends than Jele. Or that you're an amazing person who deserves so much more and now that you're free of them and their duplicity, you'll be able to find it."

I chuckled through my tears. "Wait, did you just give me an inspiring speech without giving me an inspiring speech?"

"Shh, I'm not finished." He put a finger to my lips. "But I'll just tell it to you straight: they're idiots for doing this to you. Both of them, but Tahn even more so."

On top of my head, the blue butterfly fluttered its wings once, in agreement.

I smiled. "Thanks."

Oran smiled back. "Anytime. Come on, let's get you home."

He glanced over at me as we started walking. "Huh. That butterfly is still on your head. I would have thought moving would have made it fly away."

I blinked. "Wait. You can see it?"

"Yeah. It's so distinct—I've never seen one like that before. It looks like the one that was in the palace earlier."

And with that, he turned back to face the road and changed the subject, telling me a funny story to take my mind from seeing Tahn and Jele. I laughed at the appropriate moments, but I was only half-listening.

If Oran could see the blue butterfly, did that mean he could see Graenta?

16

---·---

Chapter Sixteen

When Lis came home later that day from helping the ferryman Harlan, I confronted him about Jele and Tahn. "Did you know?" I demanded, after telling him about running into them at the market.

Lis nodded grimly. "I'm sorry, Dess. I knew you'd find out, eventually. I was hoping to soften the blow a little first, but last night was also not the right time to get into it."

I sighed. "I know. And I'm not mad—at you. I just—I feel so stupid. I should have known, right? But I really didn't see it coming."

Lis pulled me into a hug. "No one did. I mean, you know I never liked Tahn. But I didn't think Jele would betray you like this."

I sniffled, blinking back the sudden tears in my eyes. I had honestly thought I had cried myself out. Surprising that there were still any tears left. "Thanks, Lis."

He gave me a sympathetic smile. "Well, in good news, I brought back some of your things."

I brightened. "Really?"

"Yes. Help me unload it all?"

While most of my brother's day had been spent helping Harlan clear out his destroyed home, they had also taken a trip out to Zaela Island to assess the damage in the daylight. Lis had picked through the debris and taken a few salvageable items for me—mostly clothes, it looked like.

"They're dirty, but I don't think they're completely ruined," Lis said. "Nothing that a good scrub can't fix."

"I hope so." I eyed one dress, rumpled with streaks of dirt running down it, and shook my head. "But if they're all this bad—then cleaning them will take forever."

"Pack lighter next time," my brother quipped. I whipped the dress so it smacked him on the arm. "Hey!"

"That's what you get for making fun of me." I chuckled, then sobered. "But seriously, thank you for going out there and bringing this stuff back for me."

"Of course," Lis said. "But there's still so much more to sort through and clean up, both on Zaela Island and in Harlan's home. I've already let the Archives know I won't be in for a few days. Would you want to come with me tomorrow and help?"

I sighed. "Well, Queen Yllulae said I have to stay in the area. And I have nothing else to do—or people I'd like to visit. So I might as well."

"Please, try not to sound so eager," Lis said wryly.

I gave him a weak smile, then headed inside to try to get the dirt out of my newly returned clothes.

At sunrise, my brother, Oran, and I went to Harlan's to help him clean and repair his home. Shortly after our arrival, Queen Yllulae's promised group of soldiers and servants joined us. Harlan ferried the group across the Rehann River, taking three trips to bring everyone over.

I took a break from cleaning to see what was happening on Zaela Island. Shading my eyes, I frowned, not sure I was seeing things correctly.

"What's wrong?" Oran walked over to join me. "You look disturbed."

"I wouldn't say I'm disturbed," I corrected him. "I just don't understand what they're doing over there."

Oran followed my gaze. "They're setting up camp." His tone implied that "what they were doing" was rather obvious.

"I know that. I just don't know why."

He shrugged. "It makes sense. They'll be able to work longer hours, and they won't have to bother Harlan to bring them back and forth all the time. And now that things have settled, the wildlife should have returned, so they won't have to worry about food."

"Still. I would hate to do that. You're already going to get dirty and gross. Now you don't even get to sleep in a comfortable bed."

A thoughtful look crossed Oran's face. "You say that—and who doesn't like their creature comforts? But I think you're more resilient than you give yourself credit for."

He went back into Harlan's home, leaving me standing on the riverbank.

There were many things I would have used to describe myself—fun-loving, charming, effervescent. Lis, in true big brother fashion, would have probably added annoying, air-headed, or irresponsible.

But resilient? Definitely not something I would have thought.

Hoofbeats sounded on the path leading away from the river. I looked up.

A soldier bearing the queen's standard was riding straight towards me. He came right up to me, stopping his horse just an arm's length away.

"Guardian Idessa?"

I swallowed. "Yes, that's me."

"Her Supreme Majesty, Queen Yllulae of Graenir, requests that you come to court immediately."

My brother and Oran came out of Harlan's house to stand next to me.

"What's this about, sir?" Lis asked the soldier.

"I'm not privy to that information."

I looked down at my rumpled dress, dusty and dirty from the day's work. "I'll need to go home and change first. I can't go to court like this."

The soldier shook his head. "No, miss. The queen wants you to come right away."

"Can they come with me?" I waved a hand at my brother and Oran. "I'd prefer not to go by myself."

The soldier frowned. "I don't see why not. If Her Majesty doesn't want them there, they can wait outside in the courtyard."

That didn't sound very promising. Lis said, "Oran, why don't you go with Dess? You can take the cart horse. I'll stay here and continue to help Harlan."

"Are you sure?" Oran said. "I can stay here, if you want to go."

My brother shook his head. "That's all right. I'm in the middle of patching up the south wall. I'd rather finish it up—if I take a break now, I'll lose momentum."

I chuckled. That sounded just like Lis. When he got started on a task or a project, he was single-minded until he finished it.

"Okay, then." Oran unhitched the horse from the wooden cart. Then he held a hand out to me. "Let me help you up, Idessa."

Once we were both settled, the soldier took the lead, spurring his horse towards the capital. He kept up a fairly fast pace, so there was no time to ask questions. It took all I had to keep my seat atop the horse, who was enjoying the chance to run without being attached to an unwieldy, large cart.

Soon we were riding into the castle courtyard. Once Oran and I had dismounted, the soldier ushered us inside.

What's the hurry? I wondered. It's not like anything had changed in a day. At least, not to my knowledge. And I didn't have any new news to give the queen, so I wasn't sure why she wanted to see me so urgently.

The soldier strode to the doors of the great hall and announced, "Guardian Idessa, along with her companion Oran, are here, Your Majesty."

From the far end of the room, the queen called out, "Good, good. Send them in. And send a page with a few more chairs, please."

The soldier bowed and indicated I should walk in. I gave Oran a nervous smile, then stepped into the room.

The queen was sitting on her throne, the empty seat occupied by the gold circlet as it had been yesterday. Seated nearby were two people I didn't recognize.

Queen Yllulae stood up from her throne. "Come in, my dear, come in. I'm glad you got here so quickly. We have much to discuss."

17

CHAPTER SEVENTEEN

I APPROACHED THE QUEEN, dipping into a curtsey. Beside me, Oran bowed.

I was acutely aware of how messy and grimy and decidedly unpresentable I was, but there was no help for it. Would it be bad if I apologized for my appearance, thus drawing attention to it? Or would it be worse if I just ignored the state I was in, and pretended Queen Yllulae didn't notice? These were things that had never been covered in school.

The queen waved at the two seated figures near the throne. "Guardian Idessa, Oran, I would like you to meet Queen Melandria and Royal Consort Joichan, the Calian ambassadors to Graenir."

The pair rose from their seats as Oran and I both bowed and curtseyed again. Now I really wished that soldier had let me go home first to change. I brushed back a strand of hair that had fallen in my face. What must the ambassadors be thinking, looking at us?

The Calian queen smiled at us. "Just Melandria and Joichan, please. I don't rule in Calia anymore—that title is now rightfully our daughter Jennica's."

Queen Yllulae winked at Melandria. "Once a queen, always a queen, my dear."

Melandria chuckled. "In spirit, perhaps, but thankfully not anymore in duty."

Two pages hurried in with chairs for Oran and me. Queen Yllulae sat back down in her throne, and the rest of us settled into our seats.

"Now, then, to business," Queen Yllulae said. "The ambassadors arrived just a few moments before you did, Guardian Idessa. We talked about what happened on Zaela Island. Now that we are all together, I'd like to get their insights on the situation."

Joichan frowned. "Like everyone else in Graenir, Melandria and I also felt the earthquake from a few days ago. But since we are not from here, we didn't understand the possible implications it could have. If this Great Seal truly is broken—" He looked at me for confirmation. I nodded. "—Then the only conclusion we could have is that the gods have escaped. But to where, and for what purpose, is beyond us."

"If it's all right with you, Your Majesty," Melandria said, "I'd like to contact Jennica in Calia. At the very least, her scholars might have access to information we don't."

Queen Yllulae thought for a moment, then nodded. "Yes. I'll allow it. Let me send for the royal mage."

She rang a little bell by the side of the throne. A page appeared at the door of the great hall. "Yes, Your Majesty?"

"Please find Mage Fridan and bring him here, if you would."

"Yes, Your Majesty." The page left.

"Melandria and I thank you for your generosity, Your Majesty," Joichan said. "We understand what a sacrifice it is, to lift the binding of silence."

Queen Yllulae sighed. "I typically wouldn't, but if the gods have truly escaped their island prison, then this is something that affects not just my kingdom, but all of the Gifted Lands. I would be remiss as a ruler if I withheld that information from others. Perhaps it might be time to revisit my policy of standing apart from the other kingdoms."

Melandria and Joichan nodded in agreement. Oran and I exchanged curious glances—I didn't have any idea of what Joichan was referring to, and it didn't seem that Oran did, either.

Fridan shuffled in, leaning on the arm of the young page who had been sent to get him earlier. Although his steps were slow and unsteady, nothing missed his shrewd gaze. His dark eyes swept the room, sparking in recognition as he saw the Calian ambassadors. When he looked at Oran and me, he raised a single eyebrow, as white as his hair.

The page accompanied Fridan to the front of the room. The elderly mage bowed, with the page's assistance. "My queen. You asked for me?"

Queen Yllulae chuckled. "My dear friend. How many times do I have to tell you, you are exempt from bowing? I wouldn't want you to fall and hurt yourself."

Fridan laughed as well. "It never hurts to show respect. Besides, old habits die hard."

"I suppose they do." The queen addressed the page. "Bring a chair for Fridan, if you would."

Oran jumped up. "You can have my seat, sir."

Mage Fridan smiled at Oran as the page assisted him to Oran's now vacant chair. "I knew I liked you the minute I walked in the room, young man. You and your fair companion."

At his words, I blushed. "Thank you, sir," I murmured.

Once the mage was seated, he turned to Queen Yllulae. "Now then, my queen. How can I be of assistance?"

"The ambassadors would like to contact their daughter, the queen of Calia, about the recent earthquake. But they need to be able to speak freely with her in order to share and gather information. So ..."

The queen took a deep breath. "The ban of silence needs to be removed from them. Permanently."

Fridan gave his sovereign a sharp look. "Really? You do realize what this means?"

Queen Yllulae nodded. "I understand."

I still didn't know what they were talking about, but I knew better than to demand answers. Fridan must have seen my confusion, though, because he asked Oran and me, "Do you know what the queen is talking about? The ambassadors' ban of silence?"

We shook our heads.

Instead of answering, Fridan turned to Melandria and Joichan. "Why don't one of you tell them what it is."

Joichan opened his mouth to speak, but could only emit a few choked sounds. Strange, when he had been able to speak earlier. He tried again, and his face began to turn red. Beads of sweat formed on his forehead as he gasped for air.

Melandria, concerned, put one hand over his. "Husband, stop."

Joichan broke off from whatever he had been trying to say. His face returned to its normal color, and his breathing evened out. "I can't do it. I can't explain it. Can you?"

Melandria started to speak, but her words also cut off. She turned pale and started shaking. Her eyes rolled once, and I feared she was on the verge of passing out.

Joichan shook his wife, gently. "Stop, stop! It's not worth it."

Melandria leaned on Joichan, weak from her exertion. Panting slightly, she said, "I'm sorry. I can't explain it either."

Fridan nodded, as if he had been expecting this reaction from them both. "It's no matter. I will take care of it. Give me your hands."

Melandria put her hands out, one on top of the other. Joichan followed suit, placing his stacked hands on top of his wife's. Fridan placed his right hand on top of their hands, with his left hand, palm up, underneath. Closing his eyes, he began to murmur a spell under his breath.

I watched, fascinated, as their six hands began to glow.

Melandria and Joichan's were both a pale translucent silver—not quite as white as my hair, but nearly. Fridan's right hand—the one on the top of the stack—was a rich, deep golden color.

As Fridan continued his spell, the gold from his hand slid down into Joichan's hand, as if someone was pouring water or paint over them. The gold light continued to spread downward, covering both of Joichan's hands, then Melandria's.

As the color leached from Fridan's hand into the ambassadors', the pale translucent silver that had been in their hands began to cover Fridan's. Whether they were just switching magic, or if Fridan was truly pouring magic back into them, I couldn't tell.

The gold light stopped at Fridan's left hand at the bottom of their stacked hands. I wondered if it would continue to spill over into the mage's hand, but when it reached Fridan, the gold light refused to go any further.

"*Fiat*. So shall it be," Fridan intoned. The gold light pulsed once, engulfing all their hands except for Fridan's left one on the bottom, and then it winked out.

Fridan released the ambassadors' hands. Melandria and Joichan slowly pulled their hands back, flexing their fingers experimentally.

The mage leaned back, wobbling a little. Oran reached out to steady him, and Fridan reached up to pat Oran's hand. "Thank you, my boy." He turned to the Calian ambassadors. "See if you can tell our young friends about the binding of silence now."

"We're not allowed to talk about the things we've seen in or learned about Graenir." The words spilled out of Joichan in a rush. He stopped and blinked in surprise. "Wait. Did I just say what I think I said?"

Fridan nodded. Looking around, he said, "And now, if that page will help me back to my room, I'll leave you to make your call."

18

CHAPTER EIGHTEEN

JOICHAN HELD HIS HAND out and concentrated. "Jennica. Jennica."

The face of a lovely dark-haired woman appeared above the ambassador's outstretched hand. Her intelligent dark eyes surveyed the room. While she wasn't wearing a crown, she was wearing a dark red dress made of a fine rich velvet.

I leaned forward, curious about this new person, and about the spell. It was rather exciting to see magic performed twice in one day.

"Father, Mother. Hello," the woman I assumed to be Queen Jennica said. She nodded at the Graenarian queen. "And Queen Yllulae. It's a pleasure to see you again. I'll always be indebted to you for your help in rescuing my son."

Queen Yllulae nodded. "After today, you may consider that debt repaid. We have news for you that will affect not only your kingdom, but all of the Gifted Lands. But first, let me introduce Idessa, our current Guardian, and her companion, Oran."

"Well met, Idessa and Oran," the woman said. There was a question in her eyes—either at our presence, or because of the queen calling me a Guardian. But she refrained from asking. "I am Queen Jennica of Calia."

Oran and I both nodded and murmured polite greetings.

Queen Jennica turned to her parents and Queen Yllulae. "What news did you have to share with me?"

Joichan, Melandria, and Queen Yllulae shared a three-way glance. The queen nodded at the ambassadors, as if to say, *Go ahead.*

Melandria started, "Do you remember the histories your tutors would share, about the creation of the Gifted Lands? How each god created a country that reflected their strengths and values?"

Queen Jennica nodded. "And they nearly destroyed their newly made world in the process with the Six Gods' War. Until the seventh god lured them off the battlefield and sealed them away. Fascinating creation myth. What about it?"

Melandria took a deep breath. "Well, the story is true. The gods were imprisoned, here in Graenir. Until recently. An unexpected earthquake came through two days ago, up the Rehann River. It hit Zaela Island, where the gods were, and the Great Seal that magically guarded their prison has been broken."

Deafening silence met Melandria's words. I peeked a look at Queen Jennica, expecting her to be shocked. But while she looked grim, she didn't seem surprised.

"Lady Farrah had told me something about that when she returned from Faerie," Queen Jennica said. "Apparently the Fae historians are much more thorough than the human ones of the Gifted Lands."

"Could you ask this Lady Farrah about it?" Queen Yllulae asked. "I'd be most grateful for any insights she could provide."

Queen Jennica paused. "Queen Yllulae, how much can I truly trust you?"

Queen Yllulae didn't seem offended by the blunt question. Instead, she said, "I have lifted the ban of silence from your parents. Permanently. And I may never enact that ban on any future ambassadors, ever again."

Melandria and Joichan both nodded, silently confirming Queen Yllulae's words.

Queen Jennica sighed. "All right, then. Here's the situation: Lady Farrah is not able to assist us right now. And she might not be able to for a long while."

Tears shone in her eyes. She looked away for a moment to compose herself. "You see, we were recently in the kingdom of Annlyn, helping a new friend track down a mysterious magic that was affecting the country. We were able to stop it, but Lady Farrah was afflicted by the magic. She has been unconscious for several days now. Even though we brought her back to Calia recently, she has yet to wake."

The Calian ambassadors both looked shaken at this news.

Queen Yllulae said, "I am sorry to hear that about your friend. I hope she will recover soon."

"Thank you," Queen Jennica said, but she seemed distracted. "Wait. This earthquake you mentioned. When did it happen?"

"Two days ago," Joichan said. "At sunset, I believe." He looked at me for confirmation.

I nodded. "Yes, that's right."

Queen Jennica's brow furrowed in thought. "Father, you used to live in Annlyn. Are you familiar with Lake Vitrum?"

"In the hills north of Annlyn's capital? Of course. There was such an abundance of lovely, mundane goats in that area—delicious raw or cooked." Joichan sighed, reminiscing. Melandria smacked his arm. "What? It takes a lot to fill someone my size."

I eyed Joichan surreptitiously. His tall, lean figure didn't betray an overly eager appetite. But his comment about eating goats raw threw me. That didn't sound appetizing at all, but perhaps it was a cultural preference in the southern kingdom of Annlyn?

"A few days ago, I was imprisoned in Lake Vitrum," Queen Jennica said. Melandria gasped and started to say something, but her daughter held up a finger. "It's quite a story, and one I can tell you later. The most important part is this: the one who held me also trapped others from Annlyn, using Lake Vitrum as a large magical mirror. When our new friend—Endri of Annlyn—freed us, it also set off an explosion underwater. I would have thought the ripples from it would have faded out, but it was quite a lot of powerful magic."

Joichan looked thoughtful. "And the Rehann River, up here in Graenir, eventually feeds into Lake Vitrum." He turned to me. "From which direction did the wave hit Zaela Island?"

I frowned, thinking. The tower window I had been looking out of that night faced southwest. I had been able to see both the setting sun and the large wave as it barreled towards me. "The south."

Joichan nodded, as if expecting that answer. "The Rehann River flows from north to south. If anything, I would have expected that wave to come from the north, instead."

"Interesting that it went against the river's natural flow," Queen Yllulae said. "And if it was magical in nature, and that powerful, then I suppose it might have been strong enough to break open the Great Seal."

"Apparently so," Queen Jennica agreed. She frowned. "Perhaps I should go back to Lake Vitrum, to see what residual magic might be in the area. But ..." She paused, and swallowed hard. "I don't really know what to look for. Lady Farrah would—but she's unable to, right now."

Melandria touched Joichan's elbow. They exchanged a look, an unspoken conversation taking place between them. Joichan turned to his daughter. "Why don't your mother and I return to Calia for a little while? You and Melandria can visit while I see if I can do anything to help Lady Farrah's condition."

Queen Jennica brightened. "Oh, would you? Beyan and I have our hands full with taking care of Coran and overseeing the kingdom. Not to mention Beyan's been trying to keep Rhyss's spirits up during this whole thing. A bit of help would be most welcome."

Joichan nodded. "Of course." He turned to me. "Do you know how to do a calling spell?"

I shook my head. "I'm not really that magically inclined."

"Then you must come with Melandria and me back to Calia," he said. "That way, if Lady Farrah wakes up, you can tell her directly what you've seen."

"But ... am I ... ?" I looked at Queen Yllulae, unsure if I was allowed to leave Graenir.

The queen nodded, apparently liking Joichan's reasoning. "A wonderful idea, ambassador. And, should you get the answers we need—either in Calia or Annlyn—then you can contact me immediately."

I frowned as a sudden realization washed over me. Of course I was going to go. Did I really have a choice? But I'd be far away from home, and by myself among strangers. Except for my short-lived stay on Zaela Island, I had never traveled far from home. Most people from Graenir hadn't.

Oran gave me an assessing look before he spoke up. "Your Majesty, ambassadors. Would it be all right if I accompanied Guardian Idessa?"

Queen Yllulae paused. "I have no objections. Ambassadors?"

"That would be fine with us." Joichan spoke for both himself and Melandria. "I think I can handle three people."

Something about his statement struck me as odd, but I didn't have time to ponder it before Queen Yllulae turned to me, a twinkle in her eyes. "And you, Guardian Idessa?"

I blinked in surprise as I looked at Oran. He smiled at me, and I felt my apprehension melt away.

"I would welcome his company," I said honestly.

"It's settled, then," Queen Jennica said. "Mother, Father—when do you plan on leaving for Calia?"

"Soon. Just after midday, if we hurry," Melandria said. "If we leave by then, we should reach Calia by sunset."

"Perfect. I'll have the servants get rooms ready for all of you. See you then, and safe travels." With a wave, Queen Jennica ended the calling spell.

Now I was intrigued. What mode of travel did the ambassadors have, that they could reach Calia so quickly? Even the fastest rider, not stopping to rest and driving their mounts to exhaustion, would take a few days to reach Calia from Graenir.

"Is that enough time for you both to get ready to leave?" Joichan looked at Oran and me.

We looked at each other, our excitement beginning to grow. "Yes," I said. Oran nodded in agreement.

"Then I won't keep you any longer," Queen Yllulae declared. "Since you came here with one of my men, I assume you'll have to walk back?"

"We have one horse, Your Majesty. A rundown pack horse, but he should get us home."

"Nonsense." She waved my words away before ringing for a page, who immediately appeared at the door of the throne room. "Tell the stable master to get our two fastest horses ready for Guardian Idessa and her friend."

The page nodded and hurried away. The queen turned to me, satisfied. "That should help you save some time."

"Thank you, Your Majesty."

"Of course. All of you, return here just after midday so I can see you off. And ..." That twinkle was back in her eyes as she looked at Joichan. "I definitely don't want to miss that."

19

Chapter Nineteen

Oran and I rode out of Graenir's capital on two of the queen's finest horses, heading straight for my home. I wanted to ask Oran so many things. For starters, what did Ambassador Joichan mean, about handling three people? How were we going to get to Calia in less than a day, did Oran know?

And—why had he volunteered to journey with me? As a close family friend, my parents would have no objections if Oran was with me. And I supposed Lis couldn't just abandon his new job, although if the queen commanded it the Archives would, of course, go along with it.

But those questions would have to wait. For one thing, we were riding too fast for me to have a decent conversation with Oran.

And for another thing, as we approached my house, I saw two people conversing outside. My brother Lis—with my former best friend Jele.

I looked around, but I didn't see Tahn in the area. Which was fine with me. I didn't want to see him. I didn't want to see Jele, either, but since she was standing right there, I couldn't do much about that.

They both looked up as Oran and I approached. Lis looked both relieved and apprehensive as I stopped and dismounted. "Dess! Oran!

Glad to see you're back—but much sooner than I expected." There was a hint of a question in his voice.

"I didn't expect you to be home so soon." I pointedly ignored Jele, even though she turned a hopeful face to me.

"I forgot to pack a lunch for all of us, so I came back to get some food. Harlan is still at his place, working." Lis nodded at Jele. "I was just finishing up here when Jele stopped by."

Now that he had so obviously drawn attention to her, I couldn't continue to ignore her, even though I wanted to. Did I have to be courteous in this situation? I sighed. "Hello, Jele."

"Idessa. I'm so glad you're home. I really want to talk to you." The words tumbled out of her.

I held up a hand to stop her talking. "I don't have time. I need to pack and then head back to the capital."

"Speaking of which, I'm going to head home," Oran said from atop his mount. "I'll be back soon, Idessa, and then we can ride back together."

I nodded. Oran rode away.

"You have to go back?" Lis frowned. "Why?"

"I'm leaving. Soon."

"Where are you going?" Jele asked. "And how long will you be gone?"

Even though it was Jele who had spoken, I addressed Lis. "To Calia. With the Calian ambassadors. And I'm not sure for how long."

Lis raised an eyebrow. "Wow. It sounds like there's quite a story in there somewhere."

I smirked. "There is. Oh, and when you have a chance, the cart horse is at the palace stables."

My brother chuckled. "Noted. Perhaps I should go back with you and Oran, so I can go collect the horse. And also to hear about what's going on."

"But what about Harlan?"

Lis paused, but Jele said, "I can stop by the river and let him know you'll be along much later, if you like."

"That would be great. Thank you, Jele."

"Of course. I'm happy to help."

Like you helped by stealing Tahn away from me? But I refrained from saying what was on my mind. Instead, I started to head into the house.

A hand on my arm stopped me.

I glared down at the hand, and then at its owner. Jele blinked, letting go, but said, "Wait, Idessa."

I didn't respond, just continued to look at her.

"I'll go get some more food ready for your journey," Lis said, and hurried into the house.

Jele swallowed. "I know you're in a hurry, but I came by to talk to you."

"Make it quick, then. I don't have a lot of time." I knew I was being rude, but I was past the point of caring.

Jele's eyes shone with unshed tears. "I'm so sorry that you found out the way you did. That things turned out the way they have. For—everything."

"Everything? You'll have to be more specific than that, Jele."

"I mean—you know—"

"No, I *don't* know. Are you sorry you took Tahn from me? Are you sorry I couldn't stay on Zaela Island, so your deception could have been hidden that much longer? Are you sorry your betrayal got found out? What? What are you *sorry* for?"

Jele started crying. "For everything, Idessa. I'm sorry for hurting you. I'm sorry you were surprised. I'm sorry—I'm sorry we fell in love."

Hearing that, my throat tightened. *In love.* How could I be upset with Jele for that? Didn't she deserve love, as anyone did?

But why did it have to be with him? A little voice whispered in my mind. *And why didn't he ever love* me?

A faint meow made me look down. An orange cat—a stray, from the looks of it—padded over to me, wanting attention. It butted my leg with its head, then wound around my ankles.

"I don't have any scraps for you, little one," I said.

The cat meowed and rubbed its head against me again, then started purring. For some reason, the sound comforted me. I reached down to pet it, and it purred even louder.

Straightening up, I turned away from Jele. "I hear your apology. It doesn't mean I accept it."

"Please, Idessa. I ... I don't want you to leave Graenir still mad at me. You're my dearest friend. I want you to be in my life, in my baby's life. I—I can't do this without you."

I kept my back to Jele. I didn't want her to see my own tears that were now threatening to fall. In the steadiest voice I could manage, I said, "Perhaps you should have thought about that before you snuck around and stole Tahn away from me. Goodbye, Jele."

Behind me, I heard a subdued sob and some sniffling, then the slow crunch of her heavy footsteps on the dirt road. I swiped a hand over my face and entered the house.

Lis met me at the door, holding up a little sack. "I have some food for you and Oran."

When I met his eyes, the dam holding back my emotions burst. I let out a long wail, my heart breaking all over again. Lis gathered me into his arms.

"Oh, Dess. I'm so sorry."

"I—I wish it didn't hurt so much."

"I know, I know. It won't, in time."

I sniffled. "I guess it's good I'm getting out of Graenir for a bit."

My brother gave me a sympathetic smile. "Yes. Now come on, let's get you ready to go. You've got more important things to worry about than Jele and Tahn."

Lis led me to my bedroom and helped me pack. I let his innocuous chatter wash over me, grateful to just let him do the thinking for now.

I knew that I would have plenty of time to be alone with my thoughts on the upcoming journey. And I wasn't looking forward to it.

20

CHAPTER TWENTY

WITH MY BROTHER'S HELP, I was packed and ready to go in short order. I took the opportunity to change into traveling clothes—a more practical shirt and pants outfit than my earlier dress, which was dirty anyway from cleaning Harlan's house.

We informed Mother about what was happening—which she took surprisingly well.

"My darling Idessa, look at you," she said. "First becoming Guardian, and now going off to another kingdom to represent Graenir. I'm so proud of you."

"I haven't done anything, yet," I pointed out.

"It doesn't matter. You'll do great things, my darling, I know it. This is just the start." She sniffled. "But please contact us as often as you can. A mother worries, you know."

I smiled and hugged her. "I hope I can return soon. Please tell Father goodbye for me. I won't have time to stop by his work—not that he'd even notice. I know how focused he can get with his studies."

Kind of like my brother, even if it had taken Lis longer than expected to fall in love with research. Still, being around our bookish father had eventually rubbed off on him.

"I'm just glad Oran is going with you. I'll feel much better knowing he's there, looking out for you."

"I kind of wish I could go, too," Lis joked. When Mother and I both looked at him in surprise, he said, "I'm just kidding. I've got my new job at the Archives to keep me here. Besides, you know how I am about traveling."

We laughed. Lis could get sick sitting on the slowest horse. Riding across the Gifted Lands at top speed would not be good for him.

"But I will accompany you back to the capital," he said. "Mostly to satisfy my curiosity. Just ... take it easy, please."

I smiled. "Of course."

My brother smiled back. We heard a knock at the front door. "I'll get it. It's probably Oran. I'll take your things out while I'm at it."

He left with my now full pack, Mother on his heels. At the door to my bedroom, she paused. "Aren't you coming, Idessa?"

"In a second. I just want to ... say goodbye."

It sounded silly, even to my ears, to say goodbye to my childhood bedroom. After all, I hadn't even gotten this sentimental when leaving for Zaela Island. But something about this trip felt different. Like once I stepped outside, my life would irrevocably change.

Mother smiled in understanding. "Of course. I'll see you outside."

She left. Soon I could hear her voice join in conversation with Lis and Oran's. I took a deep breath, getting misty-eyed as I surveyed my bedroom.

A plaintive meow sounded at my feet.

Surprised, I looked down to see the same orange-colored stray cat from outside, when I had been talking to Jele. "How did you get in here?"

The air around the cat turned hazy and shimmered, and in another moment I was looking into the grinning face of Graenta.

I sighed. "I should have known that was you. So you heard all that earlier, huh?"

Graenta nodded. "Yes. Just like I was there when you discovered the truth about your friend and your former love."

"I thought you were that blue butterfly."

He bowed. "Did you prefer that form over my other one?"

"It was less annoying, to be sure."

"Well, I hoped to give you some comfort during a difficult time."

I smiled. "You know what? You did. Thank you."

The god beamed. "You're welcome. Well, what's next?"

Thinking back, I realized Graenta had been absent during my meeting with Queen Yllulae and the Calian ambassadors. "I'm leaving. For Calia. Now."

His eyes grew wide. "Really? The things I miss when I give you privacy."

I rolled my eyes. "Well, please don't stop. I need to get going, but if you change into another form and come along, you'll be able to hear the whole story as we ride back to the capital."

"Done." Graenta winked out, and a small blue butterfly appeared in the place where he had previously been standing.

Shaking my head, I headed to the front of the house.

Oran lit up when he saw me. "Idessa! There you are! Are you ready to go?"

I nodded. "Let's go."

"Would you want to ride with me, or Lis?"

I eyed Lis, who already looked a little apprehensive at the sight of the queen's horses. "I'll ride with you, Oran. I don't want to take my chances."

Lis stuck his tongue out at me. I responded in kind, and we both dissolved into laughter.

We set a good pace back to the city, but weren't so fast we couldn't converse. On the ride back, Oran and I told Lis about the morning's conversation with the queen and the ambassadors.

Graenta the butterfly flitted around my head, landing on my shoulder.

Behind me, I could feel Oran's curious stare. "I never knew you had such a way with animals, Idessa."

I shrugged lightly, trying not to throw Graenta off.

Lis looked at us curiously. "What are you talking about, Oran?"

Oran nodded towards my shoulder. "How could you miss it? A bright blue butterfly perched on your sister's shoulder like it's a flower or something."

Lis peered at me, frowning. "I don't see anything. But then again—" he groaned as he crossed his eyes "—I also don't feel that good."

I chuckled. "It's going to be a long ride back to Harlan's for you."

My brother groaned again. "Don't remind me."

We all fell silent, concentrating on the rest of the ride to Graenir's capital city. As we approached the gate, I was surprised to see the Calian ambassadors outside, along with Queen Yllulae and a small retinue which included a few servants and some of her royal guard. For some reason, when she had said she would meet us back at the capital, I had assumed she meant at the castle, not outside the city.

The elderly queen waved at us, excited. "Yoo-hoo! Over here!"

Lis said in a low, disbelieving voice, "Did the queen just say 'yoo-hoo'?"

I giggled. "It would certainly seem that way."

As we dismounted, a waiting servant stepped forward to grab our horses' reins. Oran and Lis both looked after the horses, with two very different expressions.

Oran's was full of admiration. "Magnificent creatures. I wonder what it would be like to own such a beast."

Lis shuddered. "They're beautiful, yes. But I'd rather walk any day, no matter how long it takes."

The three of us approached Queen Yllulae and the two Calian ambassadors. After quick introductions, Joichan turned to me. "Well, Guardian. Are you ready to go?"

I nodded. "I'm confused, though. I don't see any horses, and that servant just took ours away. How are we getting to Calia?"

Joichan smiled. "Like this."

His body began to glow, then pulse with a golden light. Perhaps the sun overhead made him shine brighter, because I had to avert my eyes from the brilliance.

"You might want to move back a little." Melandria's calm voice sounded in my ear. I felt her tug at my arm a little, pulling me away from Joichan.

The glow around him had dimmed somewhat, although he was still too bright to look at directly or for long. I shaded my eyes as I stared, dumbfounded, at what was unfolding before me. "Is he—what's happening to his body?"

Joichan's tall, slim frame was distorted, growing larger and—were those feathers? Scales?

"He's changing," Oran said in disbelief.

"He's transforming," Melandria corrected.

She was right. Joichan's tan skin turned the same shade of gold as the light surrounding him. His neck elongated, as did his torso. His arms and legs thickened, becoming covered with scales. My mouth dropped open as his hands changed, his fingernails extending into claws.

Strong, wickedly sharp-looking claws.

His face morphed, his nose growing bigger and longer until it resembled a snout. His eyes, which had been closed, now opened and eyed us with overly large eyes as golden as his skin.

The glow faded. Joichan's transformation was complete. He smiled at us.

I gulped. That was a lot of extremely large, extremely sharp teeth.

Queen Yllulae clapped, beaming as if she had been the one to transform, not Joichan. "Wonderful! Brilliant! I've always wanted to see you do that, Joichan. I missed it, the last time."

Joichan inclined his head—the dragon version of agreement, I guessed.

Melandria began walking towards her husband. After a few steps, she paused and turned to Oran and me, a big smile on her face. "Well? Aren't you coming?"

It was then that I realized that the Calian ambassador was also wearing a traveling outfit similar to mine. Which made sense, of course. It was just that I thought she'd be riding in a carriage, or sidesaddle, or something completely not like the idea that was beginning to form in my mind.

"Are we—" I gulped. "Are we ... riding ... a *dragon*?"

"Of course. How else would we get to Calia so fast?" Melandria laughed. "Come. I think you'll enjoy it, once you get used to it."

She turned and walked over to Joichan, nimbly climbing onto the dragon's back. Graenta, as the blue butterfly, crawled delicately up my neck, tickling me as he went, and burrowed into my hair. I scratched my neck, resisting the urge to do the same to my scalp. I hoped Oran and Lis didn't notice that a butterfly had just decided to become a stowaway. But both were staring in awe at the huge golden dragon before us.

"Mother and Father are never going to believe this. *I* don't believe this," Lis gaped.

Neither did I. But here I was, standing in front of a very solid-looking, very large dragon. The dragon—Ambassador Joichan—turned his big golden eyes on me, then snorted slightly, as if to say, *What are you waiting for? Get on up here.*

"Better you than me, Dess," my brother muttered. He gave me a hug goodbye. "Be well, be safe. I'll miss you, but I know you'll be just fine."

"Thanks, Lis." I released my brother. We exchanged a smile.

"Take care of her, Oran. And take care of yourself, while you're at it."

"Of course. We'll get in touch as soon as we can." Oran and Lis hugged briefly.

I blew out a breath, trying to tamp down my nervousness. Oran put a steadying hand on the small of my back, and I took comfort in that small gesture.

He guided me towards Joichan. The dragon was crouched low to the ground, waiting for us to join Melandria.

With Melandria's and Oran's help, I climbed on top of Joichan's back. Oran sprang up as if he'd always been riding dragons.

"Don't worry." Oran's breath tickled my ear. "I won't let you fall."

Any response I would have given was stilled by my sudden gasp as Joichan flapped his magnificent wings and began to rise into the air. It took all I had to hold on and not scream my head off—although I was tempted to.

Below us, Lis raised his hand in farewell. Even though it made me dizzy to look down, I kept my eyes on my brother until he was too small to make out.

Then I raised my head and took a deep breath.

Here we go.

I hope I'm ready.

21

CHAPTER TWENTY-ONE

AMBASSADOR MELANDRIA WAS RIGHT. Once I settled into the odd new sensation of riding through the air on the back of a large golden dragon, I did enjoy the journey to Calia.

For the most part.

I made the mistake of looking down, a few hours into the trip. Seeing the ground blur by as we flew caught me off guard, and I nearly lost the contents of my stomach. Oran touched my elbow, drawing my attention away from the sight. It grounded me—in the mental, if not physical sense. I took a few careful breaths and turned my head, just a little, to acknowledge him.

"Thanks."

"Just keep your eyes straight ahead, or up," Oran advised. "Don't worry about me back here."

My stomach lurched again, and I nodded as I slowly turned my head back to face forward. "Sounds good."

Stripes of purple and pink had started to streak across the sky when Melandria called back, "We're nearly there! I can see Castle Calia. We'll be landing soon, so brace yourselves!"

The words had barely left her mouth when I felt Joichan drop down a little. I bit back my scream, but Oran sensed my fear. "It's okay," he said. "He's just flying closer to the ground, gradually."

I nodded, not trusting my voice. *As long as we don't crash*, I thought. And then, feeling panicked: *Oh, gods. Can dragons crash?*

Joichan kept going down, down, down. As did my stomach. The only thing that stayed heightened was my fear and my growing certainty that I wasn't going to make it to Calia—in one piece, or at all.

"It's okay, Idessa. I've got you," Oran said. I felt one of his arms tighten around me. "I won't let you fall."

We glided over a small town, towards a wall that enclosed a much larger city. Calia's capital, from the looks of it. I figured we would land in the big, open area outside the capital's walls.

But no, Joichan headed straight for the stately pale stone palace at the far end of the city.

On either side of me, I gripped Joichan's scales for all I was worth. As we headed towards the ground and the castle—which were, even in the growing twilight, getting bigger as we approached it, way too fast, in my opinion—I leaned into Oran's strong arm, closing my eyes against the inevitability of impact.

Which ... didn't happen.

Joichan made a perfect, surprisingly gentle landing in the palace's courtyard. My heart jolted, as I swayed in my seat.

Two servants—who must have been waiting nearby—stepped forward to help Melandria down from the dragon's back.

"You can breathe again." Oran sounded amused.

I released the breath I didn't even realize I'd been holding. "We made it. We're here." *We survived.*

Once Melandria was safely on the ground, the servants turned to me. One extended a hand towards me, while the other cupped their hands to create a small foothold for me to step down on.

"Thank you." I idly wondered why they didn't just bring a step stool or a ladder, but perhaps Joichan's landing had caught them off guard.

They turned to Oran, but he had already jumped down behind me.

"Show off," I said, smiling. He grinned back at me.

Now that I was back on solid ground and could breathe normally again, I looked around in wonder. Even in the fading light, I marveled at the magnificence of Castle Calia. The castle glowed a soft pink, reflecting the vibrant hues of sunset. The path at our feet sparkled, first purple, then brown.

"It looks quite different in the daytime," Melandria said, coming to stand beside me. "The cobblestones are a lovely shade of blue and green—it rather gives you the feeling of being underwater. Which was the preference of the water mage who created this place." Her sweeping arm included the castle courtyard, the two impressive stone fountains that stood sentry on either side of the front entrance, and the castle itself.

"I look forward to seeing it in the morning, then," I said sincerely. Graenir's surroundings—much like its citizens—tended to be simple and discreet. We were a kingdom that was used to not calling attention to itself.

"Well, then. Shall we?" Melandria started towards the castle doors.

"But wait! What about—?"

Behind me, I heard a small whoosh and felt my hair ripple slightly in an unexpected breeze. I turned just in time to see the air around Joichan shimmer, and then his dragon form quickly collapsed in on itself, leaving behind the ambassador in his human form. I blinked in surprise.

"Me transforming? No problem, it's already done." On anyone else other than the dignified ambassador, I would have said that the smile Joichan gave me was cheeky. As it was, I wasn't sure if I should glare at him or smile back.

I settled on a smirk. "I guess we're all ready, then."

Joichan caught up to his wife, capturing her slim hand in his own. He addressed one of the servants who had aided Melandria and me. "Do you know where the king and queen would be at this hour?"

The servant eyed the sky, assessing. "I believe His Majesty is still with His Highness the Crown Prince in the dining hall. But Her Majesty should be in the great hall, in anticipation of your arrival." He bowed low, a sign of respect to his former sovereign.

"Perfect." Without waiting for the servants to scurry ahead and announce us, Melandria strode forward, Joichan at her side. Oran and I followed them into the castle.

With sure steps, the two ambassadors led the way to the great hall. I barely had time to take in my surroundings. Our quick walk left a vague impression of stone walls lined with ornate paintings—they all seemed to depict some interesting histories. I did, however, get a good look at the large picture hanging right by the doors to the great hall. How could I not? Not only did it hang in a place of prominence, a soft magical light set in a nearby stone illuminated it so it drew the eye.

The painting itself was magical—and as magnificent as the castle it was housed in. In vivid golds and reds, the painting depicted two large golden dragons and—was that Ambassador Melandria?—fighting against an evil-looking man, complete with wild red eyes, a sharp sword dripping with blood, and an ominous crimson haze that seeped from his outstretched fingers.

Below the breathtaking picture, a golden dragon figurine stood tall and proud on a pedestal, also illuminated by a magical stone light.

"My goodness," I said. "What an incredible battle scene—and an amazing painting. I almost feel like the artist was there, watching as the events happened."

"He was," Melandria said, giving the painting a cursory glance. "I was a bit distracted—being held captive and all—but I'm fairly sure I remember him in the courtyard. Hiding. I'm glad he painted the events a bit differently than how they really were."

Beside me, Oran raised an eyebrow and smirked. I couldn't think of the best way to respond, but fortunately I didn't have to—Melandria was already pushing the doors of the great hall open.

The two ambassadors strode forward, heading for the seated figure at the far end of the room. Oran and I trailed behind. I startled when I heard a soft click behind us. Turning to look, I realized a page must have discreetly closed the doors behind us.

"Darling, it's so good to see you again!" Melandria beamed, opening her arms wide for a hug. "You don't know how much I fretted, wondering if we'd get to see Coran before he got much bigger. Children grow so fast, don't they? Why, I remember when you ..."

Her voice trailed off as she got a good look at her daughter. Queen Jennica sat on one of two twin thrones on a dais. A low stool was placed to the side of the thrones—for an advisor, perhaps? I couldn't imagine a monarch allowing a supplicant to sit that close, no matter how informal the meeting.

Various weapons hung on the stone walls of the great hall, just out of reach for all but the tallest of persons. Above the twin thrones, one more sword hung. I would be the first to admit I didn't know anything about weapons, but even I could tell there was something beautiful and deadly about this one. Its edge looked a little too fine, and it sparkled with an otherworldly glow.

Queen Jennica stirred uncomfortably. I didn't know why—after all, this was her palace, and she was the current ruler. Nor could I understand the expression on her face. She almost looked angry—no, upset, I think would be more accurate—that we were there.

"Jennica?" Melandria said uncertainly. Her arms dropped to her sides. "Is everything okay? Aren't you happy to see us?"

The queen of Calia bit her bottom lip—not a gesture I would have expected from the woman who seemed so confident during our call earlier in the day. "You don't know how happy I am to see you and Father again, Mother. But it's just bad timing. I'm not happy about—"

A loud bang sounded behind us. Queen Jennica stood, alarmed. The rest of us turned to see what had caused such a commotion.

The doors to the great hall had burst open. An ethereal vision of a woman stood framed in the entryway. The air around her crackled with raw, untamed energy, and although there was no breeze in the great hall, her hair—streaked with shades of white, red, black, and gold—floated around her perfect, heart-shaped face.

"Me." The unearthly woman laughed. Even her voice was musical and exquisite. "The queen is upset about me."

22

CHAPTER TWENTY-TWO

THE MYSTERIOUS WOMAN STRODE into the great hall with supreme confidence, as if she, and not Queen Jennica, were the ruler of Calia.

We gaped at the newcomer—with the exception of Queen Jennica, who looked thunderous. I wondered why, if this person bothered the queen so much, she didn't call for the guards to take the woman away.

In my hair, my little stowaway stirred. I put a hand to my head. My fingers brushed against Graenta's butterfly form, halfway poking out of my hair. Was he having trouble untangling himself? But when I tried to part my hair a little to help him, I felt two little insect legs tapping at my fingers, as if to say, *Leave me be!*

So he wasn't trying to free himself, but rather he was … hiding?

The image of a little blue butterfly peeking over the strands of my white hair like a spy peering through the bushes nearly made me burst into laughter. I smothered my amusement, not wanting to miss what was happening.

Somehow, I knew that whoever this woman was, and whatever her purpose was here, was no laughing matter.

As she came closer, the woman paused. She sniffed the air.

"Who is that? The signature is different, away from the island prison …" she half-murmured. She looked around, suspicious. "Graenta?"

Oran stiffened and gave me a slight, questioning look. I shrugged, as if to say, *I have no idea what she's talking about.*

I felt the butterfly burrow a little deeper in my hair.

"Who are you?" Joichan's authoritative voice rang out, interrupting the strange woman's musings.

"Oh, forgive me." Her syrupy sweet voice didn't hide the undercurrent of gleeful malice. "I am the goddess Calianna, founder of this kingdom and therefore its rightful ruler, now and always."

I gasped. No wonder Queen Jennica was furious.

In a way, the goddess was right—as the kingdom's founder, she had the oldest claim to being its leader. But the seven kingdoms of the Gifted Lands had done well for centuries without the gods and goddesses who had founded them. And if the Great Seal hadn't been broken, then we humans would have continued to do just fine without their divine interference.

"Well met, Your Divine Grace." Ambassador Melandria sank into a deep curtsey, showing respect and also effectively hiding her own shock and rage. "What an honor to have you walk among us again."

"It is, isn't it?" The goddess preened. "And my first order of business will be to turn this kingdom into the bastion of magical might it was always meant to be. The current state of Calia is appalling."

"What do you mean?" Melandria asked. Her tone was polite, but I could see her jaw working.

Calianna sniffed. "No standing army! It's one thing to rely on your reputation, but Calia has just gotten lazy. Every mage should be well versed in all forms of battle magic."

Joichan frowned. "Calia relies on magic mostly for defense. Research and the healing arts are more prized here."

"Weak, as I said. There's no need for research, unless it's to find more efficient ways to take down your enemy. And there's no need for healing magic—anyone too weak to survive will be culled."

The nonchalant way Calianna spoke chilled my blood. How could she speak so carelessly of the Calian people? *Her* people?

The beautiful goddess yawned. "Well, it has been lovely chatting with all of you, but I think it's time to say goodnight, don't you? I'll see you in the morning—or whenever I have need of you next."

Queen Jennica started towards Calianna, hands raised in front of her. It looked like she was preparing to cast a spell, but no magic came forth. Realizing, the queen balled her hands into fists. "Now, wait just one moment—"

Calianna waved one lazy hand, almost as if she were swatting away a fly. The great hall turned hazy, and I had a sensation of being hurtled through something unseen. The feeling stopped almost as quickly as it had started. A bit disoriented, I looked around.

I now stood in a richly appointed bedchamber with a lit hearth on one side, a large bed on the other, and several comfortable-looking overstuffed chairs and a settee in between. Oran, Melandria, and Joichan were nearby, in the same positions we had been in when leaving the great hall. Queen Jennica was at one end of the room, in approximately the same place as the thrones had been, her hands still reaching out as if she was either going to cast a spell or strangle the goddess. Possibly both.

On the bed, a man sat, his head in his hands. He looked up when we poofed into the bedroom, running his hands through his disheveled brown hair before standing up to greet us.

"Jennica! Thank goodness, you're back. I was worried every moment you were away." The man embraced the queen, then turned to us. "Melandria, Joichan. It's wonderful to see you again, even under such circumstances. And who are these new people you've brought with you?"

"King Beyan of Calia, this is Oran of Graenir," Joichan said.

Oran bowed. "Your Majesty."

The ambassador turned to me. "This is Idessa of Graenir, and the current Guardian of the gods on Zaela Island."

I curtseyed. "Well met, Your Majesty. Unfortunately, there is nothing to guard anymore on Zaela Island, as the Great Seal is broken and the gods have all escaped."

"Which we knew from your news earlier today," King Beyan said, nodding at his wife.

"And we now are lucky enough to experience firsthand," Queen Jennica said ironically.

"What happened?" asked Joichan. "When we talked with you this morning—"

The queen put a finger to her lips and motioned for us all to come closer. "Talk lower. I wish I could muffle the sound in here, but—" She paused. "Maybe if Farrah was here, her magic could—" She stopped again, choking back a sob. Oh, yes. My heart broke for the Calian queen. Hadn't she mentioned her friend was currently in a magically-induced coma?

"We have much to discuss," Joichan said, his voice barely above a whisper. "But first, tell us about Calianna."

23

—·—

CHAPTER TWENTY-THREE

ORAN AND I PULLED over the matching plush chairs that were by the fireplace. Joichan brought over the settee for Melandria and himself. We all crowded close to the bed, where King Beyan and Queen Jennica sat.

"She arrived not long after we ended our call," Queen Jennica began. "There was a commotion in the courtyard—I could hear the guards yelling at someone to stop and stand down. Another guard ran into the great hall and told me they were going to shut me in, for my safety. But before they or I or anyone else could act, Calianna appeared, in a very similar fashion to how she showed herself to you tonight. She saw me sitting on the throne—Beyan was fortunately not in the room with me at the time—and demanded my immediate abdication and undying devotion to her. Of course, I refused."

"Which may not have been the best idea," King Beyan put in.

The queen shrugged. "I had no idea she would retaliate in the manner she did—or that she was even capable of it. It's not like anyone in our lifetime has ever encountered the actual gods of the Gifted Lands walking among us."

"If I may ask, what did the goddess do, Your Majesty?" Oran asked.

Queen Jennica closed her eyes, pain etched on her face. She whispered, "Calianna blocked my magic."

There was a collective gasp around the room, save for King Beyan, who presumably already knew the news.

The queen continued, "Then she locked me away in the royal suite. Because I wouldn't give her my authority. She suggested I 'consider my options carefully' and only let me out for that brief time in the great hall so I could meet all of you when you arrived. So you wouldn't get suspicious. Until it was too late."

"She got me, too," King Beyan said. "Jennica and I have been imprisoned for most of the day. We can't unlock the door or break it down."

"And I can't try it by magical means." Queen Jennica's voice broke.

"What about Coran?" Melandria asked, worried.

"Don't worry, your grandson is safe in the other room."

Melandria stood and hurried into the adjoining bedroom, where we could hear low murmurings, presumably to the sleeping boy.

Joichan frowned. "But when we arrived, the page outside said Beyan and Coran were in the dining room, eating. Do you mean to say they were lying? Are they now loyal to Calianna?"

The queen shook her head. "No. She placed a spell on the castle staff, so they think that Beyan and I are still moving freely around the castle, doing our normal routines. Although a servant did bring us meals earlier. We could hear him outside the door, talking to himself about it. He sounded very confused about why he was bringing food to supposedly empty rooms. I'll bet he has a nasty headache right now—the effect of trying to fight against magic through mundane means alone."

"Where's Taryn? Rhyss? Farrah?"

"Taryn was here when Calianna arrived, and unfortunately she got caught up in the memory altering spell like the rest of the staff. So she won't be much help right now. Farrah is still unconscious, but luckily, she's not at the castle. Rhyss insisted that she stay at his estate here in the capital, away from the busyness of court. So that's where he most likely is."

"But he's still in danger," King Beyan added. "He comes every morning to give us a report on Farrah's condition. With the servants compromised and Jennica's magic blocked, we have no way to send him a message warning him about Calianna."

"Not that my magic, when I had it, did any good anyway," the queen said bitterly. "I tried to attack Calianna, but my spells just ricocheted back on me." She touched her head and winced. "It will probably take a few days to completely recover. Maybe she did me a favor by stopping my magic."

On the top of my head, the little butterfly stirred. In a large mirror across the way, I could see Graenta climbing out from his hiding spot.

"Ouch!" I said as Graenta untangled his antennae from my hair.

Everyone looked at me, curious at my sudden outburst.

"Uh ... I just ... that is ..." I flailed about, trying to figure out a good excuse.

Graenta launched off the top of my head, fluttering around me once before landing on the floor in the middle of our group. Oran squinted at the insect. "Hey—that looks just like the butterfly in Graenir."

"Well, it's ... uh—"

The blue butterfly floated into the open area encircled by Oran and me, the two ambassadors, and the Calian royal couple. It landed on the plush rug.

Queen Jennica eyed it curiously. "There's a feeling of magic around that insect." She started to rise.

But before she could stand fully and inspect it, the air around the butterfly thickened. It turned opaque, shimmering in the firelight. The queen sank back down on the bed next to her husband, withdrawing her outstretched hand.

A slight breeze blew around the room, although none of the windows were open. It settled around the pulsing ball of light in the center, swirling along with the steadily growing circle.

Everyone looked on, wide-eyed in wonder. Except for me, of course. I knew exactly what was going on.

Oran, realizing that I was the only one not surprised by what was unfolding before our eyes, gave me a sharp look. But his attention was drawn away as the light grew even bigger, now becoming person-shaped.

The light pulsed once more with a final burst of brightness, and then faded. Spots danced before my eyes at the sudden dimness.

"You might have warned us that was going to happen," I said, my voice loud and cross in the still silence. I blinked rapidly, willing my eyes to adjust.

Graenta's voice was tinged with amusement. "Ah, but where would be the fun in that? A god has to make a grand entrance."

I heard a gasp—Melandria, I thought. And then Queen Jennica's voice: "A ... god?"

The spots faded, and I could see things in the royal bedchambers clearly again. Melandria and Joichan clutched each other, apprehensive. King Beyan looked torn, like he couldn't decide if it was better to attack the newcomer or fall on the floor to pay his respects. Queen Jennica's face reflected one part shock and one part curiosity.

And Oran was staring at—

Me.

With one eyebrow raised. I couldn't quite tell what he was thinking. But I had a feeling we'd be having a long conversation about all of this later on.

Graenta—in his favored form as a young boy—grinned from the center of the room. He somehow looked both authoritative and mischievous at the same time.

He bowed first to Melandria and Joichan, then to Oran and me. He saved his final bow for the Calian king and queen, adding an extra flourish for them. Then he pushed up his glasses, which had slid down his nose during his bowing. "Yes, Your Majesty. I am a god. One of the seven gods who founded the Gifted Lands, to be exact. I am Graenta, founder of the kingdom of Graenir, at your service."

24

CHAPTER TWENTY-FOUR

NEXT TO ME, MELANDRIA gasped. Her eyes rolled back slightly, and she slumped against her dismayed husband.

Queen Jennica reached for the bell pull that hung at the side of the bed, then withdrew her hand. "Oh, dear. I can try to send for a servant to bring smelling salts, but with Calianna's influence, I don't know if anyone will come."

"No need." Graenta snapped his fingers. Melandria suddenly sat up, eyes fluttering, gasping again, this time trying to breathe deeply.

She turned wide eyes to Joichan. "My goodness. I feel so ... strange. Lightheaded."

While Joichan fussed over his wife, the rest of us turned quizzical looks on Graenta. He shrugged. "Reviving a person is temporary. She should still take it easy, lest she have another fainting spell. But at least she'll stay awake, for now."

Queen Jennica gaped at Graenta. "Reviving someone is difficult, complicated magic—and even then, it doesn't always work. How were you able to do that so easily?"

Graenta smirked. "I'm a god, remember? Or do we need to go over that part again?"

I blinked. If I had any doubts as to Graenta's abilities, they were gone now. I didn't know much about magic, but if even the powerful queen of Calia couldn't awaken someone by magical means ...

Queen Jennica's dumbfounded expression changed to one of hope. "Not even the best mages here could do that ... how does it work? Can you revive someone who's been unconscious for several days? My friend Farrah ... if we can get you to her, out in the city ..."

Graenta looked thoughtful. "I can try—but like you said, it's a tricky bit of magic. It's easier to revive someone who's just lost consciousness, as opposed to someone who has been out for a while. The magic is more unstable, the longer you wait. I could revive your friend, only for her to fall back into unconsciousness, even deeper than before."

"Oh." The queen looked understandably disappointed. "We'd all love for her to wake up, but ... I'm not willing to gamble her health like that."

"What if someone's dead?" Oran wondered.

Graenta nodded, as if he had expected the question. "Same rules apply. Newly dead, not a problem. Dead for a while, forget it. And while I can revive someone who's just passed away, it's only for a short time—no more than an hour or so, usually enough to impart some last wisdom or to tell a loved one about something nearly forgotten. The person won't really have the strength or the energy to do anything more than that. And then they're gone again, and that's it. Once you're dead, you're dead."

It was such a matter-of-fact but disturbing way to describe his powers of revival that I couldn't do anything but gape at Graenta, wide-eyed. Looking around the room, I could see that I wasn't the only one feeling that way.

"Well, since you're here ... can you do something about Calianna?" Queen Jennica asked.

Graenta shook his head. "Not in the way you're probably hoping. She's much stronger than I am. They all are."

The queen blinked, taken aback. "Oh."

Oh, indeed. I had wondered why Graenta hadn't just overpowered them all, back during the Six Gods' War. But there was a simple reason—he couldn't.

And he was already so powerful, at least that's how it appeared to me. If the other gods were more powerful than he was ...

I spoke without thinking. "I'd hope that, being immortals, you'd all get along."

Graenta laughed. "The love among us comes and goes. With all that time on our hands, we're more often bored or annoyed with each other. It's no different than you humans. It's just made worse since we're so long-lived. And immortality doesn't mean that we're not impervious to dying. It's just extremely hard to kill a god."

Oran, ever the scholar, leaned forward, interested. "Really? How so?" Then he realized what he was asking, and colored. I hid a smile. He was kind of cute when he blushed. "Oh—forgive me. I wasn't asking—I mean—"

Graenta smirked. "Don't worry, I wasn't going to give you specifics. But killing a god may involve a complex ritual, or a very specific set of things to do to weaken them. It's not as easy as just swinging a sword or shooting an arrow at them, although those mundane weapons can be effective if the right kind of power is behind them."

"Power?" Oran blinked. "I'm assuming you mean magical power, not just strength."

"Of course, magic," Graenta smirked. "One to incapacitate, two to kill."

Before I could ask Graenta what he meant by that, Oran spoke up.

"Of course." Oran looked embarrassed. When I patted his hand in sympathy, he startled, then smiled at me.

"Graenta—" I heard gasps around me at how I addressed the god so informally "—I thought you didn't want anyone to know you were here. Why are you showing yourself now?" I paused, thinking. "If you can't do something outright, can you at least undo Calianna's magic on the castle? And on the queen?"

Graenta's face puckered, like he had tasted something sour. "No. To my everlasting sorrow."

Something about his statement seemed off, but before I could ponder it, the god continued. "But her spell on the castle won't affect me. So I can leave."

"You can?" Queen Jennica perked up. "Could you get a message to our friend Rhyss, then?"

At the same time, I muttered, "Lucky."

Graenta grinned. "Oh, don't worry, Guardian Idessa. You'll be coming with me."

"What?" I sat up straight, now worried. "Do I have to?"

He smirked. "You would rather be trapped here in the castle?"

He had a point. But still ... "Can we bring anyone else? Oran?"

Oran perked up, but his face fell when Graenta spoke. "No. Just you, Idessa. You're the only human I have a connection with."

"Oh. Okay, then. Oran, I'm sorry." I turned to the queen. "About this message—what do you want us to say? And how do we find him?"

Queen Jennica blew out a relieved breath. "As Rhyss would say, thank the gods—although now that we have one, live and here before us, that statement seems a lot more personal now."

Graenta bowed. "I haven't done anything yet, but I appreciate your thanks."

Together, King Beyan and Queen Jennica described their friend, Lord Rhyss, and how to find his estate in the city. "Tell him what happened here and warn him not to come to the palace," Queen Jennica finished.

"And tell him not to do anything rash or reckless in an attempt to free us," King Beyan put in.

The four Calians exchanged amused, knowing glances. Oran and I exchanged a glance of our own, but there was no amusement, just confusion. I supposed we'd find out what this Lord Rhyss person was like soon enough.

Graenta held out his hand to me. "Well, then. Shall we?"

25

———

CHAPTER TWENTY-FIVE

LEAVING THE CASTLE WITH Graenta was surprisingly easy.

Holding my hand, he walked straight towards one wall of the royal bedchamber, one that faced the outside.

"Graenta, wait," I said. "Shouldn't we, I don't know, use the door?" I gestured ineffectually at the closed and, I presumed, magically sealed door to the bedroom.

"This is much easier," the god said, and put his hand on the wall. His hand melted through the solid stone as if it was just an illusion of a castle wall, and not real rock.

"But ... but ..." I protested as he pulled me through. "We're several floors up! Aren't we going to—"

I froze as the cool night air washed over me. Above me—much closer than I would have anticipated—the inky black sky was dotted with bright white stars and a partial moon.

I looked down. Way, way down, somewhere in the darkness below, was the ground.

But the ground was definitely not directly underneath our feet.

"—fall?" I squeaked in a terrified whisper.

Graenta's hand still firmly covered my own. I was very aware of it, shaky and sweaty, and wished I could take it back so I could wipe it on my pants.

Then again, if Graenta let go of my hand, I would probably plummet to the ground.

Maybe it was better this way, sweaty hands and all.

There was a small tug on my hand, and I had a sudden fear that Graenta was, indeed, letting go of my hand. The slickness of my palm had proved too much, and now I was going to slip from his grasp and fall, fall, fall into the darkness....

The tug got more insistent. "Idessa. Idessa." I gasped and looked up at Graenta's impatient face, partially lit by the cold moonlight.

He looked at me sternly over the top of his glasses. "Come."

"But—how ... where ...?"

He didn't answer my unfinished questions. Instead, he continued moving forward, pulling me along with him.

No, wait. Not forward, at least after a few steps.

Downward.

Somehow, against all logic, we were walking down from where we had emerged several floors up from the darkened lawn and hard cobblestones below. Registering that I was now on an invisible staircase, I froze again, afraid of slipping.

Graenta, feeling the pull on his arm, turned around to look up at me. "Come on, Idessa."

"But ... what if I slip? Or fall off?"

The god huffed. "It's perfectly safe. You won't slip." He paused, looking thoughtful. "But you could fall off, if you wander too far to either side. Just stay close to me, and you'll be fine."

"Okay." I scurried down the invisible stairs, stopping just short of bumping into Graenta.

"Hey, be careful!"

"Sorry."

He continued to lead me down. Soon—but not soon enough for my panicked nerves—we reached the bottom. I put out an experimental foot, then another, and breathed a huge sigh of relief once I realized we were on level ground.

I rounded on Graenta. "Next time, warn me before you do something like that!"

"And give you a chance to worry?" He grinned, then put a finger to his lips. "And keep your voice down. We're still on the castle grounds."

I wondered why he didn't just throw a spell of silence over us to muffle any noise we might be making. But then the brief thought flew from my mind as I felt another tug on my arm. Without warning, I felt my body hurtle through the air. I had the fleeting sensation of traveling through gates and walls and across streets, the world blurring around me.

And then, just as sudden as the fast moving sensation had washed over me, it stopped.

Graenta released my hand. I stumbled forward, trying to catch my balance. And my breath.

Before us stood a two-story manor, its white stone making it look like a large phantom looming above us. We were in the well-manicured courtyard that belonged to said manor. The shrubbery, as indistinct forms in the darkness, made me feel like we were surrounded by monsters of all sizes, silently watching us.

Or maybe I was just jumpy.

"We're here," Graenta said.

I turned on him. "Again, some warning would be nice."

Graenta snickered. "And I told you, I'd rather not give you a chance to fret. Sometimes it's best to just plow through things instead of overthinking them."

He waved at the house before us. "For now, I'll let you do the talking. If you need me, just call for me."

And with that, he disappeared. In the darkened area, I couldn't tell if he had actually vanished or just changed forms or turned invisible. I waved an experimental hand in front of me, then turned around in a slow circle with my arm extended. Nothing but empty air.

As I completed my circuit, an amused voice said, "I've seen a variety of bizarre rituals in my travels, but I'm not sure what yours is trying to accomplish. Or why you're doing it on my lawn."

I looked up, startled. A tall, gangly man stood on the manor's front porch, silhouetted against the light from within.

I started to put my hand down, then stopped and awkwardly raised it again in a half-hearted wave to the stranger. "Uh, hello."

"Hello yourself." The man sounded like he was just barely holding back from laughing. "And please, if your ritual gives you comfort, don't let me stop you."

"Oh, it's not that. It's just—" I stopped, knowing I'd sound crazy if I said, *I was trying to find a god.* Instead, I said, "Um. I'm looking for Lord Rhyss?"

The man raised an eyebrow. "Who's looking?"

I curtsied, an even more awkward move than my odd wave. "My name is Idessa. I'm here on behalf of King Beyan and Queen Jennica, as well as the Calian ambassadors Melandria and Joichan."

The smirk the man had been wearing fell from his face. "You don't say? Come in, then."

He stepped aside and waved me in.

I didn't budge. "But you haven't said who you are yet, sir."

The man laughed. "Oh. I thought you knew. I am Lord Rhyss. Welcome to my home."

26

CHAPTER TWENTY-SIX

ONCE INSIDE, I GOT a good look at Lord Rhyss. He was definitely not what I had expected from a close friend of the Calian royals.

His easygoing, casual manner left me surprised. I would have expected a lord to be stuffy and proper. But instead, he flopped down on an overstuffed chair, his long legs hanging over the chair's arms. A smattering of freckles across his pale face and unkempt red hair completed the unorthodox picture.

Meanwhile, I sat ramrod straight in the chair across from Lord Rhyss, unsure of how to start.

"So, you just came from the castle?" Lord Rhyss prodded. "What's going on?"

I explained about Calianna's presence at Castle Calia, her threats to the queen, and how she was currently keeping the royals prisoner. "She's blocked Queen Jennica's magic, and they can't trust the servants right now. So the queen was unable to send you a message to tell you to stay away."

Lord Rhyss frowned. "That's quite a story, and one I find hard to believe. But I had wondered if there was trouble at the castle."

At my inquisitive look, he continued. "I received a call earlier today from King Addan and Queen Inari of Bomora—my home country.

They had tried to contact Jennica, but said they couldn't get through to her. So they contacted me instead, hoping I could pass a message along to her."

If I remembered my geography lessons correctly, Bomora was a small kingdom on the westernmost edge of the Gifted Lands. The Aentin Sea bordered it on one side, with a great forest and the military kingdom of Rothschan on the other.

Lord Rhyss ran a hand through his already mussed up hair. "I had debated going to the castle tonight to see what was happening, even though it's getting late."

"Well, I guess I came at a good time, then."

He smiled at me. "That you did."

"What was the message?" I wondered, then added hastily, "If you don't mind my asking."

Lord Rhyss shrugged. "I don't think it matters, the Bomorran royals didn't act like it was a secret or anything. And honestly, it sounded so far-fetched to me. They said there's a man there, claiming to be the god Bomor, the founder of Bomora."

I gasped. Lord Rhyss looked at me sharply. "Do you have reason to believe that what King Addan and Queen Inari told me was true? Besides your tale of Calianna returning to her country, which still sounds crazy to me."

"But it really *is* her," I insisted.

"There are a lot of powerful mages here in Calia," Lord Rhyss said. "It's quite possible someone is just impersonating her. After all, how would any of us know otherwise? It's not like the gods have walked among us recently."

"Well, actually ..." I began.

Lord Rhyss crossed his arms and leaned back—no easy feat, the way he was sprawled across that chair—and leveled a look at me that said, *Convince me.*

I took a deep breath. "Graenta? Could you—could you appear, please?"

A breeze began to blow through the room, similar to the one that had occurred in the Calian royals' bedchamber. It whipped up into a larger wind that ruffled our hair and clothes, blew the papers off a nearby table, and threatened the flickering fire in the hearth. A small circle of light shone to one side of the room, steadily growing larger and stronger. It grew so bright, Lord Rhyss had to shade his eyes. I squeezed mine shut and turned away.

With one final pulse, the light winked out, the wind stopped blowing, and the only sound in the room was the crinkle of the papers as they fluttered slowly to the ground.

I looked back cautiously. Graenta stood there, a wide grin on his face.

"That was ... flashy," I commented. Graenta's grin only grew bigger.

"Are you really a god? Graenta, the founder of Graenir?" Lord Rhyss breathed.

"What, my entrance wasn't enough to convince you? Fine," Graenta said. He snapped his fingers. The room around us started to shake. The table that had formerly held Lord Rhyss's papers shivered and toppled over. Books and knickknacks vibrated right off the shelf.

Outside, a thunderstorm seemed to have sprung up. Lightning crackled, followed by the loudest peals of thunder I had ever heard. Rain began pelting the manor, coming down hard and fast. An equally furious wind whistled around the house, looking for weaknesses in the walls.

"Graenta!" I yelled. "Stop that! It's not helping!"

The god sighed. "Oh, fine." With another snap, the shaking stopped.

I couldn't help but giggle when I got a good look at Graenta. "You made the room shake so much your glasses nearly fell off."

"Maybe I should rethink them," he said, pushing them back up his nose with as much dignity as he could muster. I giggled again.

A strangled cry brought my attention back to Lord Rhyss. I figured the man would also have found Graenta's comment funny. But instead, Lord Rhyss was facedown on the floor, arms outstretched in fearful worship.

"Even the most powerful mages of Calia can only command one element, if they can even command an element at all." Lord Rhyss sat up, trembling. "To be a master of earth, and wind, and the skies ... and all at the same time ... forgive me for doubting you, mighty one."

"That's better," Graenta said, a smug look on his face.

Lord Rhyss turned wide, amazed eyes on me. "And who are you, that you can just call a god up at will?"

I shrugged, uncomfortable. "I'm Idessa, of Graenir."

"She is my Guardian, and thus my champion," said Graenta. "We are linked together, and I will always come at her call."

Wow. The way he put it, it sounded impressive. *I* sounded impressive.

"Forgive me, my lady, for doubting you," Lord Rhyss said.

"It's all right," I said. "Um. Could you—could you please get off the floor now?"

Lord Rhyss scrambled up and into his chair so fast it nearly toppled over. Instead of sprawling over the seat like before, he now sat straight and proper. He made a fist with his right hand and placed it over his heart.

"Well, then. I never thought I would see the day when I would meet an actual god in person. God Graenta. Guardian Idessa. Whatever you need, I will be happy to do it for you. Just say the word. You have my sword and my service."

27

CHAPTER TWENTY-SEVEN

I BLINKED, STUNNED. GRAENTA'S childish giggle brought me back to myself. I cleared my throat, feeling silly. "Ah, that's great. Um. Now that we have the pledges of undying fealty out of the way, can we figure out how to get our friends out of Castle Calia?"

Lord Rhyss also cleared his throat. "Of course." He relaxed into his chair. Seeing that, I relaxed as well.

An awkward silence descended over the three of us. I realized that Lord Rhyss was waiting for me—or Graenta—to start the planning. But no ideas came to my mind.

Finally, I said, "I guess ... we need to break through Calianna's magic? Somehow."

"That's a start," Lord Rhyss said encouragingly. He gave me a quizzical look. "How did you two get out, anyway?"

I had been wondering that myself, but hadn't really had a chance to ask. We both looked at Graenta.

Graenta shrugged. "When you've lived your whole—immortal—life around others with more power than you, you learn that indirect methods are often the best way to accomplish your goals. Such as distracting them long enough for them to expend much of their strength—our power isn't infinite, after all. I cannot outright break

Calianna's spell, but I can manipulate certain elements of it, for a limited amount of time. That's what I did, in order to leave."

I frowned. "But then how were you able to bring me with you? Surely Calianna's spell would have affected me. After all, I'm not a god. I would have been subject to the same magic that affected everyone else in the castle. Right?"

"Yes, it normally would have—except you're my chosen Guardian, my champion. And thus, we are linked." Although his tone was proud, his eyes shifted, and he looked away.

My frown deepened. "What exactly does this mean, us being linked?"

Graenta didn't say anything for a long moment. Then, quieter: "It means my abilities affect you directly. If I use my powers to aide myself, it also aides you. But ..."

The god trailed off. When the silence grew longer, I prodded, "But what?"

Graenta sighed. "It also means that anything that hurts me directly also hurts you. And while it takes a lot to hurt a god, it takes much less to hurt a human. So you—*we*—must be careful."

I stared at him, open-mouthed. I was pretty sure my heart had stopped beating for a moment.

A crackling log in the hearth made me jump, startling me back to my senses. I shook my head, dismayed. "I've never heard of this before. Why didn't Queen Yllulae—or any of the past Guardians—mention this? I mean, it's kind of important."

Graenta shrugged, but his eyes were apologetic. "It's never been an issue before. After all, we gods were all locked away. When would any of the Guardians have had a chance to learn the extent of what Guardianship truly meant?"

I eyed him suspiciously. "That's a good point. So, if no previous Guardian had a chance to test this theory, how are you so sure it's true? Just because you were able to get me out of the castle as well, it doesn't mean we're that deeply linked. Maybe it just—"

"Because centuries ago, when all the gods walked the Gifted Lands, the human who served as my guardian died in the Six Gods' War." The words poured out of Graenta in a torrent. "I was hit with a particularly nasty set of spells—a one-two punch, courtesy of Bomor and Rothscha. It severely weakened me, which was just what those two wanted. But my poor champion took the brunt of the attack."

Graenta's voice shook and his small frame trembled as he relived the tragedy. "He died before I could even attempt to heal him." His voice dropped, coming out in a hoarse whisper. "Not that there was much left of him to try to heal."

Tears flowed freely down the god's face—an unexpected sign of vulnerability. "Humans had pledged themselves to me and the other gods before, of course. But in that moment before his life faded, I could feel his devotion and bravery, despite the agony that overwhelmed him. And I realized ... what an important gift he and the other humans, with their short and fragile lives, had given to us immortal and near indestructible gods."

"And that's when you decided to lure the others away and imprison everyone, including yourself, for all of eternity," Lord Rhyss breathed.

Graenta nodded. He removed his splotchy eyeglasses, wet from his tears, and wiped them on the hem of his tunic. It only served to smudge his eyeglasses further. He sighed as he swiped a hand over his open, young face to wipe the tears away.

A small snippet of memory floated back to me—a discussion of the Six Gods' War in a history class years ago. I had only been half paying attention, because who cared about events that had happened centuries before I was even born? I had been more interested in the party Jele and I were supposed to go to later that week.

"Why would Graenta bother to seal himself away with the others?" one of my classmates had asked. "Wouldn't it be better to subdue the other gods and goddesses, or only imprison them and stay free? Then they would know that he was the most powerful, forever."

The teacher had paused at the question. "Graenta could have done that, true. But it might not have worked, and it may have only caused more damage to the Gifted Lands and its people. Sometimes you show more power by showing restraint."

The enormity of Graenta's sacrifice centuries ago hit me. "Thank you," I whispered.

Graenta sighed again and snapped his fingers. The wet streaks disappeared from his eyeglasses, and he pushed them back onto his face. "It had to be done," he said simply.

"All right, then," Lord Rhyss said in the voice of one used to giving orders. "Let's figure out what we need to do. First, infiltrate the castle. Second, get rid of Calianna's spell on said castle. Third, rescue our friends."

"You make it sound so easy," I grumbled.

He grinned. "Eh, I'm used to impossible commissions. Besides, that's only the start of what we have to get done."

I raised an eyebrow at him. "It is?"

"Of course. We also have to stop a goddess from taking over Calia, and then after that, help stop another god from taking over Bomora. And if my guess is correct, we may have to do that for the other kingdoms in the Gifted Lands as well. It's going to be a long day. Would you like anything to eat before we start?"

It wasn't as simple as all that, of course. But hearing Lord Rhyss lay it all out so plainly made me feel better about the whole overwhelming mess.

Just a little bit.

Lord Rhyss rang for a servant. "I wasn't always a lord, you know," he confided as we waited. "And honestly, I'm still not used to it. But Jennica—the queen, I mean—insisted that I hire at least a handful of household staff. Just to take care of the place if I had to leave for a while, and whatnot."

The servant appeared. Lord Rhyss instructed him to prepare a quick, light meal.

"And in the meantime," Graenta said, "I will look over your betrothed. I understand she is unable to wake, and I might be able to help her."

"Really?" Lord Rhyss's eyes kindled with sudden hope. "Oh, if you could ..."

But when Graenta examined the unconscious Lady Farrah, he sadly shook his head. "My apologies, Lord Rhyss. I didn't mean to get your hopes up."

"You mean there's nothing that can be done?" Lord Rhyss deflated, his excitement dashed. He sank down on the pale blue and white quilt that covered his intended, reaching out to touch her cheek.

"Not nothing." Graenta withdrew his outstretched hands, which he had placed on Lady Farrah's forehead. The woman hadn't stirred at his initial touch, nor did she move when he took his hands away. In fact, she lay so still that I had thought at first that she was dead, not unconscious. Only a very slight rise and fall of her chest let us know that she was still alive.

Lord Rhyss looked at Graenta, confused.

"She's caught up in a very powerful, ancient magic," Graenta explained. "I can't revive her without triggering it—and it will put up a fight, dig in deeper to keep hold over its victim. Your intended would be caught in a magical tug-of-war. It would tear her apart, both mentally and physically. And without knowing who would ultimately be the victor, or how long it would go on ..."

Lord Rhyss hung his head. "I understand. Th-thank you."

"I wish I could do more. I'm sorry."

Graenta left the bedroom. Lord Rhyss continued to stare at his betrothed, as if the force of his gaze could somehow wake her up.

When I placed a tentative hand on his shoulder, he jumped.

"I'm sorry, too," I said. "We—we'll figure this out. Somehow."

Lord Rhyss smiled at me, though his eyes remained sad. "Thank you." He nodded towards the door. "Go join Graenta. I'll be right there. I—I just need a few more moments."

"Of course." I paused. "Would you like me to close the door?"

"If you wouldn't mind."

"Of course," I said again.

As I began to shut the bedroom door to give the two some privacy, I saw Lord Rhyss bend over to kiss his intended on the forehead. I closed the door on his quiet sobbing.

28

— ◆ —

Chapter Twenty-Eight

"Are you sure this is a good idea?" I whispered to Lord Rhyss for what was probably the twentieth time.

"Do you have any other ideas?" he asked.

"No."

"Well, then. There you go."

I gave an exasperated sigh. Ahead of us, the pale stones of Castle Calia gleamed in the moonlight. A few more steps and we'd be on the palace grounds.

In the courtyard. Or more precisely, right at the castle's front doors.

This was Lord Rhyss's brilliant plan. March straight up to Castle Calia, knock on the front door, and ... figure out something from there.

"No really, it's a great plan," Lord Rhyss had said when I had argued against it. "Calianna will be expecting us to try to sneak in, use brute force or some subtle magic to break through her defenses. She won't expect such a direct approach."

"You mean such a *foolish* approach," I had mumbled. "You do realize you're doing exactly what the king and queen asked you *not* to do?"

He had shrugged. His red hair had flopped down and he had shaken his head a little to get it out of his eyes, reminding me of a dog shaking off after a romp in the water. I had tried not to giggle. And then my desire to laugh had faded entirely when he had said quietly, "Farrah's the one who's good at coming up with a plan. Without her input, I don't really know what's best to do."

He had looked so forlorn, I had just nodded and agreed to go along with it.

But now, eyeing the castle in the moonlight, I wasn't so sure.

"Maybe we should wait until daylight?" I suggested now.

He shook his head. "That definitely wouldn't make sense, with what we agreed upon."

I sighed again. "You're right."

The butterfly in my hair fluttered its wings, somewhat erratically. I realized that Graenta, back in his former disguise, was probably laughing at our exchange. His rapid movements tickled my scalp, and I fought the urge to scratch my head.

"You ready?" Lord Rhyss asked me.

"I guess so."

At that less than enthusiastic response, Lord Rhyss looked to the top of my head and hissed, "Graenta! We're ready!"

The butterfly flapped its wings again, a more deliberate movement. A pleasant warmth, accompanied by a slight buzz, started at my crown, spreading downward over the rest of my head, my face, and my neck. Soon my entire body hummed with Graenta's magic.

And then my body morphed and changed, shrinking and collapsing in on itself. I waved an arm, realizing it was now a small, fragile wing. A butterfly's wing. And I could see so much more of myself and the world than I ever could as a human. My wings were an ethereal white, like my hair. I marveled at my new body, making a few loops in the air just for the joy of it.

Graenta, in his blue butterfly form, hovered nearby, peering into my face. "Hmm. Not bad, if I do say so myself."

I nearly fell out of the air. "We can talk to each other in these bodies?"

Graenta chuckled, his laughter sounding like a series of clicks. "Yes. And although Lord Rhyss won't be able to understand us—or even hear our butterfly language—it also means Calianna can't, either."

Oh, yes. Lord Rhyss. I had been so caught up in my transformation I had nearly forgotten our true purpose for it. I flew over to where Lord Rhyss was waiting for Graenta and me. Landing on his shirt collar, I carefully crawled down onto his shoulder, burrowing under his shirt. Graenta followed suit.

Lord Rhyss's large fingers reached under his shirt collar towards us, making me shrink back in fear. The fingers stopped just shy of where Graenta and I hid, scratching at the skin nearby.

"Gods, that tickles," he said. I cringed again. In this form, it sounded like he was practically shouting, even though he spoke barely above a whisper.

"Hold on tight," Graenta said to me, bracing himself.

"Wha—?" But I couldn't finish the thought, because Lord Rhyss started walking. I started to slide off, my legs flailing.

A black leg shot out and hooked itself around one of mine, pulling me back up onto Lord Rhyss's shoulder.

"Easy, now," Graenta said. Once he was sure I was secure and settled, he released my leg. "You okay?"

I took stock of myself. "Yes, I think so. Thank you."

"No problem." The clicking chuckles were back. "You can actually do a lot as a butterfly that you can't do as a human. Don't worry, you'll get used to it."

I shuddered, the sensation rippling along my wings. "Nothing doing, but I really hope not."

More clicking laughs ensued from Graenta.

Lord Rhyss stopped walking, causing us to jolt forward again. With a slight flap of his wing, Graenta motioned for me to be still. He crouched low and drew his wings in, making himself as small as possible. I copied his stance, trying my hardest not to quiver from nerves.

A succession of booms threatened to knock me from my perch again. What in the Gifted Lands was that?

When I heard the creaking of hinges, I realized that the loud thuds had come from Lord Rhyss, knocking on the castle doors. A voice spoke, carefully neutral. "Yes? How may I help you, sir?"

Lord Rhyss sounded surprised. "Don't you recognize me, Miven? I'm here often enough."

There was a pause. When Miven spoke again, I heard hints of how unnatural his tone was. Wooden, and somewhat thick, as if he was talking while falling asleep. "Oh, yes. That's right. Welcome back, sir."

"Thank you." But despite Miven's welcome, I could tell Lord Rhyss wasn't convinced that Miven recognized him. "Can you please tell King Beyan and Queen Jennica that I'm here, then?"

There was a slight pause. Then Miven said, "My apologies, sir, but Their Majesties are not receiving visitors. The hour—"

"If you truly know who I am, then you know that Their Majesties could care less about the hour, as far as my being here is concerned." An undercurrent of steel laced Lord Rhyss's statement. "If you don't want your sovereigns to be upset at you for not doing your job, then I suggest you let them know I'm here."

"But—I—" Miven stammered. He sounded confused, as if he didn't even really know what he was trying to say.

I felt a jolt as Lord Rhyss stepped forward. But just as abruptly, he stopped, as if he had changed his mind from continuing. Or perhaps something was in the way. "Listen, if you don't tell them—"

But I'd never know what Lord Rhyss would have threatened poor Miven with, because at that moment a new voice, low and musical, spoke. "Who is it that comes here, demanding an audience with the ruler of Calia?"

29

Chapter Twenty-Nine

I knew that voice. The goddess Calianna! I hissed in recognition. Well, if I had a human throat, I would have hissed. In my butterfly form, it came out as an agitated click.

Graenta twitched an antenna at me. I doubted Calianna could hear us, as small as we were and hidden under a layer of fabric, but she *was* a goddess. Perhaps she had extra sensitive hearing.

Lord Rhyss cleared his throat. "Good evening, my lady. I am Lord Rhyss, a close, personal friend of King Beyan and Queen Jennica's. I know it's a bit late to be visiting, but they are used to such unorthodox meetings."

"I see," Calianna drawled. "Well, Their Majesties—" did anyone else catch the sarcasm that laced her voice when she said Their Majesties? "—have retired for the evening. But if you are indeed such a dear friend of theirs, as you say—"

"I assure you, madam, I am."

"—Then I'm sure they'll want to see you, even if you are here at such at an odd hour. Come inside, and I will let them know you are here."

"Thank you."

Lord Rhyss moved forward again. The air around Graenta and me changed noticeably, from the cool night air to a more still, slightly warmer temperature.

As Lord Rhyss stepped over the castle's threshold, Calianna drew in a breath. "What was that?"

"What was what, my lady?"

There was a long pause. Graenta and I froze, too worried and scared to even breathe. Then finally Calianna sniffed. "Hmm. It must be nothing." Her light laugh reminded me of the water falling in the oversized fountains in the castle's courtyard. "I suppose my mind must be overactive. Come with me."

Graenta and I held on as Lord Rhyss followed Calianna. Eventually his steps slowed and we heard a heavy door open. A servant murmured, "Good evening, Your Divine Grace," as Calianna and Lord Rhyss moved past him.

"Just wait in here," the goddess told Lord Rhyss. "I'll be back in just a little bit."

Calianna's lighter steps faded out of the room. The door closed with a loud finality. After a few moments, Lord Rhyss said into the silence, "I think she's truly gone."

He pushed back his collar, holding the fabric away from his shoulder. "That tickles," he complained when Graenta and I crawled out from our hiding spot.

Graenta transformed back into his human form. He waved a hand at me, and I felt myself transform as well. I sat down hard on the floor, feeling disoriented.

"Oh, wow," I groaned, doubling over. My stomach threatened to give up its admittedly sparse contents. "I feel so funny."

Graenta pushed his eyeglasses higher up his nose and looked at me sternly. "I'm afraid you'll need to toughen up, Idessa. This is only the start of the magic I'll have to use on the both of us, until this whole mess is sorted out."

I groaned again. "Oh, gods."

Graenta shot me a dirty look.

"Sorry. I mean—ugh." I coughed as my stomach roiled again. "Just leave me here."

"Shh," Lord Rhyss admonished me. "Do you want her to hear?"

Graenta stood very still, eyes narrowed as he listened. "We're all right, for now. But we don't have much time."

"I'm assuming she'll lock me up with the others, if she doesn't try to kill me when she comes back," Lord Rhyss said. "Where will you two be?"

"We need to find the heart of Calia's power," Graenta said. "Not the king or queen, for rulers constantly change with the years and, sometimes, the will of the people."

"Isn't that it?" Lord Rhyss pointed at the far end of the room. I looked over to see the Calian thrones, sitting serene and stately on their raised platform.

"No," Graenta said slowly as he studied the thrones. "Those are symbols of power, but too common to any kingdom to be the true source. But—" he raised his eyes up to the bright, shiny sword that hung in a place of honor and prominence above the twin thrones "—that might be something."

"The Sword of the First King." Lord Rhyss patted his own sword reverently. "What a beautiful weapon. The king and queen use it for ceremonial purposes, now, but I understand that it used to be wielded in battle by King Aarna himself."

Graenta nodded in satisfaction. "I think that's it, then. Let's take a look at it."

But as he started to move towards the dais, Lord Rhyss said, "That's not the real sword. It's just a magical illusion. The real one was hidden away after the true sword was, ah, borrowed for a bit."

A telltale hitch in his voice made me look at him sharply. Lord Rhyss blushed a little, but didn't offer more explanation.

"Where's the real one, then?" I asked, but a sound at the great hall's doors made us all look over in fear.

"Quick, Idessa," Graenta hissed. He flew back to my side, grabbing my hand. My body shrank and changed, and when I blinked, I was staring at Lord Rhyss's black boots. The great hall looked even more cavernous than it had originally, and all the furnishings were now oversized.

My face twitched. Whiskers, newly sprouted on my cheeks, twitched with me. My nose quivered. I was now quite aware of how everything *smelled*. Lord Rhyss's boots. The somewhat dusty hardwood floor.

And danger. Coming from the slowly opening doors of the great hall.

A frantic squeaking from my left caught my attention. Graenta, also in mouse form, scurried towards a crack in the closest wall. I followed him, disappearing into it just as whoever was at the doors entered the room.

Graenta and I hid just inside the wall, trying to catch our breath. I looked around. The light from the great hall spilled into our hiding spot just enough for me to see Graenta, crouched across from me. Beyond us lay complete darkness.

On the other side of the wall, footsteps quickly approached the area where Graenta and I had just been. The steps stopped, then tapped an odd rhythm in place. Someone sniffed the air.

"Where is he?" Calianna's voice was hard and accusing.

"He, my lady?" Lord Rhyss inquired politely. I was impressed at how calm and composed he was. If I had been in his place, I would probably have fainted from nerves.

A slight squeaking drew my attention. I turned to look at Graenta, who was quivering all over. He continued to squeak, barely audible over the conversation on the other side of the wall.

I blinked in surprise as I realized that I understood Graenta's squeaking sounds.

"We need to go," he said.

"But ..." I stopped, marveling at my newfound ability to communicate as a mouse. I shook my head to clear it. *Focus, Idessa.* "What about Lord Rhyss?"

Graenta scurried away, then came back. Obviously, he wanted me to follow him. "We can't stay. We need to find this Sword of the First King."

He disappeared into the darkness.

I started to follow, then froze when I heard a scuffling sound coming from the great hall.

Lord Rhyss gasped. His calm demeanor slipped as he said, "Now, now ... Your Divine Grace, I'm not sure who it is you're looking for, but I assure you, I have nothing to do with it. Please, let's just discuss this calmly—"

My fur stood on end as I listened to Calianna's response. "Where is he?" she shouted. "Tell me."

"I don't know what—"

Her voice dropped to a menacing whisper. "Or I will make you talk."

Graenta's frantic squeaks came to me from the darkness. "Idessa! Come on! We need to go, *now!*"

I knew he was right, but I hated to leave Lord Rhyss behind with a crazed Calianna. With a last look towards the other room, I ran after Graenta, following the sounds of his scurrying and scratching as we headed deeper into the walls of Castle Calia.

Behind us, back in the great hall, Lord Rhyss let out an anguished scream.

30

–·–

CHAPTER THIRTY

I PAUSED, FEELING TORN. I wanted to turn back and help Lord Rhyss. Although as a mouse—gods, even as a human—I had no idea how I would be able to help.

But Graenta was expecting me to follow him. He had a plan—I hoped.

Lord Rhyss screamed again.

That did it. I turned around and darted back out through the crack in the wall, just as I heard Graenta squeak behind me. "Idessa, no!"

I felt a slight whoosh of air as he tried to grab my retreating tail with his paw. But it was too late. I had already left the safety of the internal wall and was now back in the great hall.

Staring up at the scene before me, I swallowed, instantly regretting my decision.

Lord Rhyss lay on the floor, curled up on one side. Thorny green vines had sprung up, impossibly, from the floor, causing cracks and ripples in the once smooth stone. Those vines now bound Lord Rhyss as Calianna stood over him. The air around her crackled with an otherworldly energy.

She pointed a finger, laden with magic, at him. "I ask you once more. Where. Is. He?"

I turned back to look at the hidey-hole where I knew Graenta was watching, hidden in the darkness and relative safety of the wall. I stared at the crack, willing him to come out and join me, but he didn't appear.

Which made sense, since Calianna apparently had quite a strong ability to know when Graenta was nearby. Perhaps all the gods could sense each other that way?

But did that mean she was aware of *my* presence?

Lord Rhyss let out a pain-filled moan. His breathing came in shallow pants, as if it hurt to talk. "I ... don't know ... who you're talking ... about."

Calianna's face contorted in rage. The feeling of magic in the air grew even heavier. Her eyes kindled, changing from gold to red to black to white, matching her multi-colored hair that swirled around her face in the sudden wind that had whipped up. I cowered, fearful that she would somehow sense me here and obliterate me with her magic.

And then, right before she unleashed a spell, she slowly curled her hand into a fist, stopping whatever magic she was about to send forth. "I could kill you right now, but I think not. You may have more use to me alive than dead. So instead, I will spare you. For now."

Calianna uncurled her hand, palm up. A magical web of silver and black shot out of her fingertips, encasing Lord Rhyss. His body convulsed once, then froze. I couldn't help myself—I gave a little gasp, which came out as a small squeak. The goddess had said she wasn't going to kill him, but from where I stood, it sure looked like she had.

Calianna paused, magic still crackling from her fingers. I shrank back into the shadows, hugging the wall. I didn't dare run back into the hidey-hole, even if that was the safer option. Any sudden movement might draw Calianna's attention to me.

The goddess sniffed the air and looked around. "So familiar, yet not," she whispered. "Is it you, or isn't it?"

She took two slow steps towards my wall. My whiskers quivered, and I closed my eyes against the inevitable squash or blast of magic that was sure to happen.

And then a low groan sounded from the center of the room.

Calianna whipped around. "You're supposed to be incapacitated," she said frostily, as if poor Lord Rhyss needed an explanation of his condition. She stared at her hands as if they had betrayed her. "Have my powers grown weak from being in captivity for so long? Graenta, when I catch up with you ..."

But her threat would remain unfinished. Instead, she waved her fingers at Lord Rhyss again, doubling the magical web around him. His next moan was abruptly cut off as silver and black threads wound around his head, silencing him.

I stared in wide-eyed horror, unable to tear my gaze away from watching Lord Rhyss's entrapment.

Calianna finished her spell, curling her fingers into a fist. "That should do it." The goddess yawned, brushing back strands of gold and red hair from her face. "Oh, my. That took more out of me than I expected. To bed, then."

She bent over Lord Rhyss, caressing his cheek as she admired her handiwork. He lay still, but I shuddered in fear, as I'm sure he would have if he could. "But I'm glad to know my magic hasn't faded completely." Another yawn overtook her. "I'll be back in a few hours, my friend. To figure out what to do with you—and the others."

With a light chuckle, she swept from the room.

When her footsteps had faded away, I scurried over to Lord Rhyss. The poor man was well and truly enmeshed in Calianna's magical web.

I could barely make out his features under the shimmery wrapping that had him trapped.

I ran around his prone form, trying to find a weakness in the spell. But while I could definitely tell that magic was holding Lord Rhyss, I didn't know enough about magic to know how to break it.

I ended up back at his head, sniffing at the spell. My little nose picked up something unusual. I slowly leaned forward, trying to figure out what, exactly, I was sensing, when—

"Don't touch him!" A pink paw swiped at my cheek, darting in between my nose and Lord Rhyss's face.

I jerked back, startled by the unexpected frantic high-pitched squeaking. "Don't *do* that!" I frowned—or at least, if I wasn't a mouse, I would have. All it did was cause my whiskers to twitch. "Why not?"

"Because." Graenta put his paw down, but continued to stand between Lord Rhyss and me. "You saw what happened to Lord Rhyss. If you get too close, Calianna's web could grab you."

"Then maybe you should move away, also," I pointed out. "Where *were* you, anyway? Why didn't you come out here and stop her?"

My voice came out sharper than I had intended, and Graenta hung his head as he stepped away from Lord Rhyss. "I'm sorry, Idessa. I was afraid that Calianna would be able to sense my presence—which she did, by the way—and I knew I wouldn't be able to stop her."

"But—that doesn't make any sense," I sputtered. "You may not be as powerful as her—which I find hard to believe, from what I've seen—but you obviously got the better of *six* other gods, once upon a time. *And* you kept them captive for centuries."

Graenta's whiskers worked furiously. Little squeaks—of rage? of embarrassment?—burst from him involuntarily. He flicked his long tail, annoyed.

He was obviously getting upset, but so what? *I* was pretty upset, myself. I had never wanted to be his Guardian in the first place, and now here I was, in a strange country, far away from my family, betrayed by my boyfriend and my best friend—okay, maybe that last one wasn't Graenta's fault. Not directly, anyway. But going away for four months hadn't helped that situation, either.

And now, here was Lord Rhyss, immobilized and who knew what else by sinister magic, and I was powerless to help him. And since I had dragged him into this whole mess, I felt responsible for what had happened to him. Which made me feel guilty.

And that made me mad.

My temper boiled over. "So what's stopping you from stopping Calianna? You've bested her before, why can't you do it again?"

Graenta exploded in a mess of flying fur and indignant squeaks. "Because! I didn't best her—or any of the others for that matter."

An appalled silence fell between us. When I finally spoke, my voice came out tiny and unsure. "But ... you lured them to their prison ..."

"I didn't use some impressive mind control spell, if that's what you're thinking," Graenta spat out. "No, I impersonated each god, planting untruths in their heads and poisoning their minds against each other. It was the best I could do, given there were six of them and one of me.

"After the imprisonment, the others had a chance to think about things, and realized the stink of my magic had been all over each of their 'appearances' to one another. My strategy, though successful, can never be replicated. They would see through it immediately." He sighed, his breath causing his whiskers to flutter. "As gods go ... I'm not a very good one. That's why I don't want to confront Calianna."

I stamped my paw against the hard stone floor—which, admittedly, would have been more satisfying if I was back in my human body. "So you're a coward, is that what you're saying?"

Graenta's eyes flashed. "Wait a minute. I'm not totally useless—"

"Yes! Yes, you are!" My whiskers quivered. "Just leave me alone! I'll help Lord Rhyss on my own!"

"Idessa—"

I turned my back to Graenta, ignoring him. *I'll show him*, I thought. *Stupid god, bringing me into this whole mess when I could have been back home, happy and safe ...*

Completely disregarding the god's earlier warning, I bit into the spell web, intending to chew through it to free Lord Rhyss. If my anger alone could have destroyed the net, the poor man would have been freed immediately.

Except my fury, no matter how strong, was no match for magic.

31

Chapter Thirty-One

The moment I latched on to the spell web, a jolt surged through me. Not good. I moved back, trying to disengage from the net—and the magic—but my teeth were still firmly attached.

I screamed, the sound coming out as a panicked, desperate squeak.

Behind me, I heard a series of answering, high-pitched squeals.

"Idessa!" Graenta sounded both frantic and frustrated. "I *told* you not to touch it!"

Too late now.

Calianna's magic continued to course through me. My muscles ached, my head throbbed, and a slow stiffness started to creep over my limbs. If I couldn't break this spell—and soon!—I'd be lost to Calianna's magic, just like Lord Rhyss.

And once she returned, we'd both be at her mercy.

Graenta squeaked again. I couldn't quite hear what he was saying over the rushing in my ears, but it vaguely sounded like, "Oh dear oh dear oh *dear*!"

"Can you stop fretting and free me from this?" is what I wanted to say. Except with my teeth still snagged in the web, and my face and jaw now frozen by Calianna's magic, I couldn't say much of anything.

"Idessa, hold on!" Graenta shouted.

There's not much else I can *do*, I thought at him sarcastically. My body was now completely locked, and although my mind screamed at my muscles to *Move! Twitch! Do anything!* my limbs refused to obey.

"No!"

Some detached part of me wondered what Graenta was screaming about, but then the magic and the pain intensified, and I couldn't concentrate on anything but my immediate sensations anymore.

My chest tightened as the edges of my vision grew uncomfortably bright. My eyes rolled back in my head just as everything went black.

I cracked open one eye, feeling disoriented. I sighed as I shut my eyes, not wanting to move.

A finger poked at my side, dangerously close to where my stomach was pitching a small rebellion.

"Hey!" I said, this time opening both eyes so I could glare at the offending finger—and its owner.

Said owner peered down at me, a worried frown on his face, completely unperturbed by my annoyed stare.

Idly, I noticed Graenta was back in his human form, appearing as a young boy again. I realized my own body felt different—my spine in a different spot, a fur-and-whisker free face, my senses of smell and sight not as keen as they had been before I blacked out.

"Are you dead?" Graenta asked me, pushing his glasses up his nose.

I groaned. "Clearly not. Now leave me alone." I turned on my side, hoping I could sink back into the blissfulness of oblivion.

Graenta poked me again.

"Stop that!"

"Not until you get up and get moving," Graenta said, unrepentant. "You might not have been out for very long, but we don't know how much time we have until Calianna gets back. We should all be well away from here by then."

If I had the energy, I would have stuck my tongue out at him and gone to sleep. But I couldn't refute the wisdom of his statement. With a sigh, I slowly pushed myself up on my elbows, then sat up.

A long sigh nearby echoed mine. Turning my head—wow, that hurt—I saw Lord Rhyss also sit up, one hand holding the right side of his head.

"What happened?" he asked, sounding as groggy as I felt.

"That's a good question," I said, giving Graenta a pointed look. "What *did* happen?"

"I'll tell you both later," Graenta promised. "For now, are you two able to stand?"

Despite the obvious pain that Lord Rhyss was in, he immediately got to his feet. Only the slight sway as he did so betrayed any lingering weakness. He held a hand out to me, as did Graenta. I grabbed both of their hands and let them help me to my feet.

"Woah." I stumbled a little.

Lord Rhyss put a hand on my arm, steadying me. He chuckled grimly. "It's all right. I know exactly how you feel."

Graenta wrung his hands as he bounced on the balls of his feet. "Are we okay? Are we ready? Come on, let's go!"

He headed towards the door, but stopped when I called out, "Wait! Where are we going?"

"To find the Sword of the First King." His tone implied that I was a dolt for forgetting.

"But we don't know where it is," I pointed out.

"We'll just have to hope we're lucky, then."

"Wait." Lord Rhyss drew his weapon and held it out to Graenta. "Before we go running through Castle Calia, at least take a good look at this. It will help you recognize the sword, should we come across it."

Graenta stared at the illusion of the sword that hung above the throne, then at the very real weapon that lay across Lord Rhyss's open hands. "Is that ... the actual sword? Do you mean to say you had it all along?"

"Gods, no." Lord Rhyss paused, a look of confusion passing over his face as he realized what he had just said. "I mean, uh, no. I once used the real thing—which upset the royals, I can't imagine why—and as a thank you, the former queen gifted me a sword modeled after the actual item."

I felt a bit confused myself—the Calian royals had been upset with Lord Rhyss, so they gave him a gift?—but before I could voice my thoughts, Graenta spoke.

"So that weapon you're holding, it's a copy of the real thing?"

Lord Rhyss nodded. "From what Queen Melandria—the former Calian queen—had once mentioned, it's an exact replica, down to any nicks, scratches, chips, or cracks."

Graenta's face lit up as he clapped his hands together. His glasses slipped, and he absently pushed them back up his nose. "Perfect! We can use that sword to find the true one!"

"Well, of course," I said, failing to keep the sarcasm from my voice. "Lord Rhyss just said that. We can compare any swords we find against his."

"No, no." Graenta hopped up and down, oblivious to my scorn. "Now that we have that, it will be easy! All we have to do is this."

He pointed at Lord Rhyss's sword. My eyes grew wide as the weapon, already shining in the torchlight of the great hall, grew blindingly bright. The blade glowed white, then faded into a shimmery pinkish-orange.

"There." Graenta's voice was smug. "That should lead us right to the Sword of the First King."

32

CHAPTER THIRTY-TWO

SPOTS DANCED IN FRONT of my eyes. I blinked several times, hoping I wasn't permanently blinded. Fortunately, the spots faded and soon I was looking around the torchlit great hall once more.

Next to me, Lord Rhyss rubbed at his eyes with one hand. His sword, still with that shimmery peach glow, dangled from his other hand.

"Next time, warn a person, will you?" Lord Rhyss said irritably.

"He does that," I said.

"Sorry," Graenta said, not sounding all that sorry. "I figured you would avert your eyes, or shut them, once you saw your sword glowing. That's what most people would do."

"Giving some sort of warning wouldn't take that much time—"

"Besides." Graenta continued on as if Lord Rhyss hadn't spoken. "I wanted to cast the spell while I was sure I still had some magic left."

I gave the boy a sharp look, but he just shook his head at me. I remembered what he had told me—he might be a god, but his power wasn't infinite. And he had used quite a bit of power in the last few hours, in our earlier escape from Castle Calia, to his display of power to convince Lord Rhyss. Not to mention the transformations into various animals.

"So how does this work?" I asked, indicating the glowing sword.

"We follow it."

"We follow it?"

"Um. Yeah. The light will grow brighter or dimmer, depending on how far away we are from the object we're seeking." Graenta shrugged. "Unfortunately, it's not more precise than that."

"Then we shouldn't waste any more time in here," Lord Rhyss said, striding over to where Graenta stood at the closed double doors. He pushed open one side, holding his shimmering sword aloft. "Shall we?"

"This is where they chose to hide one of their kingdom's greatest treasures? *Ah-choo*!" I punctuated my disbelieving comment with a sneeze and a sniffle. "Excuse me."

Holding a sleeve up to my nose so I wouldn't breathe in as much dust, I looked around.

I had figured we would end up in whatever room served as the castle's armory. Which would have made complete sense, and at least we would have Lord Rhyss's enchanted sword to help us locate the Sword of the First King as we sorted through the weapons.

But instead of a well-kept, well-stocked armory, we found ourselves in a nondescript storage area. Tiny and cramped, it overflowed with haphazardly stacked chests, shelves overflowing with random knick-knacks and linens and bottles. There was no organization to the dusty, forgotten room. It looked like a place where the castle servants stashed things that they weren't sure belonged elsewhere. Or, more likely, didn't care enough to put in its proper place.

Graenta looked as dismayed as I did, obviously expecting an item of such renown to be kept in a nicer area. Lord Rhyss, however, beamed as his replica sword glowed at its brightest, not heeding the inches of dust coating everything or the claustrophobic nature of the room.

"How clever of them," he murmured. "No one would ever think to look in here."

"I think your sword is broken," I said crossly, as I sneezed again. I wiped at my watery eyes and glared at Graenta. "Or, more accurately—maybe it's the spell that needs work."

Graenta crossed his eyes and stuck his tongue out at me. I responded in kind, eliciting a laugh from Lord Rhyss.

"Real mature, both of you," he said. "Kind of hard to take an all-powerful god and his Guardian seriously, when you do that."

Mostly powerful, I thought, sobering as I glanced at Graenta.

Lord Rhyss stood in the center of the room, slowly turning as he pointed his sword in various directions. He stopped with his weapon pointed right at me. I stepped back to avoid getting sliced, and bumped into a poorly stacked tower of wooden chests.

Lord Rhyss continued pointing his sword at me.

"Uh, you can put that thing down," I said. I would have kept backing away, but there was nowhere else I could go. "I'm on your side, remember?"

"No, no, I think the sword is behind you," Lord Rhyss said. He lowered his weapon a little. I would have preferred that he put it away completely, but at least that sharp tip—and its bright peach glow—was no longer staring me in the face. "My sword is actually quivering."

"Oh, good," Graenta said from the other side of the room. "That means the spell is working."

I rolled my eyes, then stepped to the side to give Lord Rhyss better access to the trunks.

"Ah! That's the one," he said.

Of course there were five heavy-looking, unwieldy trunks piled up against the wall. And of course the one we wanted was the fifth box, buried at the bottom.

I sighed and reached for the top trunk. It was surprisingly much lighter than I expected, just awkward to heft. I got it down and passed it to Lord Rhyss, who passed it to Graenta.

"I could just zap these out of existence," the god pointed out.

"Not without Jennica and Beyan's permission," Lord Rhyss said absently, piling another chest on top of the one Graenta held. "I'm sure they're keeping these around for a reason."

Graenta and I locked eyes over Lord Rhyss's shoulder. I smirked. The god grinned and turned to find a convenient place to put down the boxes.

Soon we were left with the final chest. Lord Rhyss knelt down in front of it, ready to flip the metal latch and throw back the lid. Curiously, there was no physical lock on the trunk.

"Wait!" I said. "What if there's a magic lock on that thing? You could get hurt."

"Since I'm not a mage, magic doesn't always affect me," Lord Rhyss said, but he looked at Graenta for assistance.

Graenta held out a hand towards the chest. He frowned. "I don't feel any magic. But you're right, Idessa. That's strange. Why wouldn't they put a lock, magical or mundane, on a chest that contains such a priceless treasure?"

Lord Rhyss grinned as he flung the chest open. Carefully, he lifted a blanket-wrapped bundle from the trunk's interior. "Actually, it makes perfect sense. You'd never expect the king and queen to hide something important in this room, and not even bother to secure it. Besides, knowing Jennica, there's other things to make sure a thief can't run away with with this thing."

The red-haired man sheathed his sword, then unwrapped the cloth. His eyes lit up as he got a good look at the item that the fabric had concealed.

I craned my neck to look at it. A shiny silver glint greeted my eyes. "Is it ...?" I breathed.

"Yes." Lord Rhyss's voice was filled with reverence. "It's the Sword of the First King."

"Well, that went easier than I expected," I said. I sneezed once more. "And I'll be glad to leave this dusty room." Even if I had no clue what we were supposed to do, now that we actually had the Calian treasure.

I opened the door and stepped into the cool stone hallway, which was quiet and—thankfully!—dust-free. Lord Rhyss and Graenta followed me out of the room.

And then a woman's scream pierced the silence.

33

CHAPTER THIRTY-THREE

"Jennica!" Lord Rhyss gasped.

The woman's cry was followed by a man's angry yells, which dissolved into an agonizing scream.

"Beyan!" Frantic, Lord Rhyss thrust the Sword of the Sleeping King, still half wrapped in fabric, into my hands, then sprinted down the hallway.

Graenta and I ran after him. "Where are you going?" I called.

"To help them!"

At the end of the corridor, Lord Rhyss dashed up a set of stone steps. Another scream tore through the air, along with another person wailing.

On the next floor, Graenta and I followed Lord Rhyss as he ran, sure-footed, down the hallway. I didn't recognize the area we were in—but I did recognize the voices that we could hear, growing louder, that were coming from a room with a half-open door.

"You're the only one who could have helped him." Calianna's drawl had turned into a vicious snarl. "I left him, completely incapacitated, in the great hall. And now he's gone. So, somehow you were able to escape this room and sidestep my magic. I want to know how you did it."

"Unhand my wife this instant!" King Beyan commanded.

There was a whoosh and a thump, followed by a scream and a groan.

"Your Majesty!" I heard Oran gasp. A woman wailed, quickly muffled. Her crying set off a baby's cry, but no one hushed the poor child.

Lord Rhyss, Graenta, and I paused just behind the door, out of sight of the enraged goddess. In a low voice, Graenta said, "Before we just go rushing in, we should figure out—"

Inside the royal bedchamber, Queen Jennica gave a strangled cry.

"Jennica!" Lord Rhyss cried, and ran into the room. Graenta reached out, trying to stop him, but the god's small hand only grasped empty air.

"Drat!" Panicked, Graenta turned to me. "What do we do now?"

"I don't know about you, but I'm going to go help them. However I can." I dashed into the room before Graenta could stop me.

Inside the room, I stared, wide-eyed, at the scene before me.

The plush chairs Oran and I had been sitting in earlier lay, overturned, on their sides. A small wooden side table was against a far wall, smashed and in pieces. The broken glass and spilled water gave me a hint as to what the table held before it was thrown across the room.

Ambassadors Melandria and Joichan were still seated on the settee, although now Joichan was comforting his crying wife. Although I could tell they were trying to avoid attracting Calianna's attention, they kept shooting worried glances towards the room's open internal door. Since that was the place where the baby's wails were coming from, I knew they were worried about their grandson, Coran.

On the floor, slumped against the bed frame, was King Beyan. Oran knelt next to him, checking for any injuries while he tried to revive the unconscious king.

And in the center of the room, Calianna stood over Queen Jennica.

The queen was on her knees before the goddess, her body stiff and twisted in an unnatural way. Although Queen Jennica didn't say anything, her face betrayed immense pain. Her normally olive skin had turned pale from lack of air.

Calianna towered over her, pointing a lone finger at the queen. Even though the goddess wasn't speaking a spell, anyone could sense the incredible power building up in the room.

As Lord Rhyss and I entered the room, Calianna turned. Her blood red lips curved up in a satisfied smile. "Ah, there you are."

Lord Rhyss drew his sword and pointed it at the goddess. "Let her go."

"Aren't we the bold one, now that we're all free again?" Calianna sneered at Lord Rhyss. "You should put that down, *before you hurt yourself.*"

Her words took on a strange resonance. Lord Rhyss yelped and dropped his sword, shaking his right hand. He glared at Calianna. His fallen weapon glowed a dull orange-red, from tip to handle. I winced in sympathy. I only hoped the magical heat wouldn't leave lasting burns.

"Nice to know you're open to my suggestions," Calianna smirked. "But you're being rather rude, don't you think? You're in the presence of a goddess, you know. *Show some respect.*"

Lord Rhyss stilled. Then his left arm stiffened, moving in a jerky manner. The rest of his body followed, and he lurched unsteadily towards the goddess. Then his right leg buckled underneath him, and he fell to one knee in a grotesque parody of a genuflection. His eyes were panicked, the only thing in his body that was still slightly under his control.

"Very good," the goddess purred.

I gasped. Calianna glanced at me, frowning as she looked me over. "I remember you. You were with this lot. How did you escape as well?"

"I-I don't believe I shall tell you," I squeaked. So much for a show of strength.

She sniffed. "It's no matter. I'll get my answers eventually. First, I'll finish with the queen, here, and then I'll see to you." She gave an evil giggle and waved the fingers of her free hand at me as her voice took on that commanding quality again. "*Bow before me, peasant.*"

I held my breath, anticipating that my body would respond the same to Calianna's magic as Lord Rhyss's had. But ... nothing happened. I shook one hand experimentally. No, my body was still under my control.

Calianna's face darkened. "I said, *bow before me.*"

I blinked, but I still didn't succumb to Calianna's magical command. I glanced at Oran, who had paused mid-ministration to King Beyan to stare at me, slack-jawed. I could tell what he was wondering as clearly as if he had said it aloud: *How are you resisting her?*

I had no idea. I didn't have any magic of my own to counter her, nor was I wearing or carrying any special talismans that would negate her magic. The only thing I had was ...

Furious, Calianna turned her full attention on me. Next to her, Queen Jennica gave a huge gasp and then doubled over on the floor, trying to catch her breath. Calianna ignored her, not seeming to care that she had released the queen from her choking spell. She thrust both of her hands out at me, sending some unknown spell my way.

But whatever the magic was supposed to do to me, its effects remained a mystery. I didn't feel a thing.

"What power do you have, that my magic does not affect you?"

I grasped the hilt of the Sword of the First King and let the fabric wrapping fall away. The weapon gleamed in the firelight, shining sharp and deadly in my hands. As I touched the weapon, a spark flared and a jolt of energy raced up my arms.

In front of me, a shimmery blue shield appeared, extending out-
ward from both sides of the sword. Somehow, the sword was either
absorbing Calianna's magic or deflecting it. I wasn't sure which, nor
did I care.

As long as it kept me safe.

Calianna renewed her magical attack. I stumbled back from the onslaught. The sword's defense held, but the shield wavered. A hairline
crack appeared on the right. I eyed it uneasily, wondering how long it
would take for the crack to grow and spread throughout the ward.

The goddess, however, didn't look winded at all, although she must
have used a fair amount of magic before I arrived. But I couldn't match
her in power, and I—or rather, the Sword of the First King—would
not be able to stand against her much longer.

I jumped, startled at a sudden touch. The weapon's ward wavered
even more, then steadied. Surprised, I saw that the shield had grown
stronger, and the crack I had spied earlier disappeared, now mended.

I turned a little to see whose comforting hand now supported my
elbow. Graenta smiled up at me. "I couldn't leave you to have all the
fun."

I smirked, grateful that he hadn't abandoned me. "Thanks."

Calianna's eyes grew wide once she saw who stood by my side.
"You!" she spat at Graenta. "I knew you were here! I knew it!"

Graenta gave the goddess a mocking little wave. "Lovely to see you
again, Calianna."

"I won't let you lock me away again," she snarled. The air around
her grew thick and heavy as it crackled with her power.

More power.

She pushed the full concentration of magic straight at us. "See if
you can withstand this!"

34

CHAPTER THIRTY-FOUR

CALIANNA'S MAGIC, FUELED BY her rage, hit our shield with so much force that I stumbled again. My feet slipped from underneath me and I fell square on my rear. The impact jarred the rest of my body and I quickly grabbed the sword handle with both hands, rather than risk dropping it.

The ward cracked again—this time in multiple places.

Get up! My mind screamed at me. But I hurt too much, and it took all my strength to just hold on to the sword, let alone do anything else.

Oran stood up, calling out to me as he started to move towards me. "Idessa!"

Calianna didn't even bother to look as she waved one hand his way. His eyes bulged as her magic slammed into him. He blew past the still unconscious King Beyan, his body hitting the far wall. I gasped as I watched him slide down, eyes rolling back in his head, stunned.

Please, please, Oran, don't be dead.

Above me, Calianna cackled and renewed her magical assault.

Graenta knelt down beside me. I thought he was going to try to help me stand, but instead he leaned close to my ear and said in a low voice, "You're not going to be able to withstand her. Throw the sword to the queen."

"Wh-what?" I panted, barely able to get the word out. Was Graenta crazy? Why would I get rid of the only thing keeping me—and him—from being annihilated by Calianna?

"You're doing a fine job, Idessa, but the sword is not for you," Graenta said. His voice was strangely calm, as if he were merely imparting some sort of lesson, instead of instructing me on how to save the both of us. "It belongs to Queen Jennica."

"B-but—"

Graenta ignored me as he stared up at Calianna. Lord Rhyss was still frozen in his forced genuflection before the crazed goddess.

But just behind her, Queen Jennica, now freed from Calianna's spell, had recovered somewhat. The color had returned to her face, and her breathing was more even. She was still on the floor, but at least she was now sitting up, instead of lying doubled over in pain.

"*Idessa.*" Graenta's voice took on the same commanding quality as Calianna's had with Lord Rhyss. Involuntarily, I turned to look at him, my head feeling a bit fuzzy. Then I blinked, shaking my head, and the feeling went away.

"Give Queen Jennica the sword." There was some residual magic in Graenta's words. I felt a strong urge to listen and obey, but something stopped me just shy of forced compliance.

Was it because I was his Guardian, and therefore connected to him? But I would think that would make his magic on me stronger. Maybe Graenta just wanted me to pay attention to what he was saying, but, unlike Calianna, wanted me to have the ability to choose what to do.

"Idessa, please!" This time there was no magic bolstering his words, just a pure, raw plea.

I called out, my voice ragged. "Your Majesty! Queen Jennica!"

She looked over at me, a question lighting her intelligent face.

I dropped the Sword of the First King, sliding it towards her with the last of my strength. I closed my eyes and cowered back, waiting for Calianna's magic to rip me apart.

So I was surprised when, moments later, I was still breathing, whole and alive.

Confused, I opened my eyes.

Graenta stood in front of me, arms spread wide as he shielded us from Calianna. Sweat poured down his shaking body—he wouldn't be able to hold out for long.

Across the way, Queen Jennica crawled forward. She reached out and grabbed the hilt of the Sword of the First King.

Calianna threw one final wave of magic at Graenta and me. "I won't let you stop me again, Graenta!" she yelled. "I won't!"

The queen anchored the sword, tip first, into the floor. Like an impromptu cane, she leaned on the weapon, using it to help her stand. Power swirled around her—not as dark and intense as Calianna's, but still impressive in its purity and might. Swirls of silver and blue floated in the air, and I could have sworn I heard the echoes of hundreds of voices cheering, "Hail, Queen Jennica!"

"You're right," the queen said, every low word dripping with venomous heat. "He won't stop you. I will."

Graenta's shield shattered. Most of Calianna's magic had been absorbed or deflected, but the god still caught a bit of backlash from her final blow. He flew backwards, tumbling to the floor right next to me.

"Graenta!" I gasped, patting his cheeks to wake him up. But the boy was out cold.

Meanwhile, Calianna turned to see who was speaking to her. Queen Jennica hefted her kingdom's symbolic longsword and thrust it straight into Calianna's heart.

The goddess screamed. I flinched at the agonizing sound, reflecting all of her anger and pain. Her scream cut off, becoming a grotesque sort of throat gargle. She crumpled to the ground between the queen and me, twisted and unmoving.

In the sudden silence, I found my voice enough to ask, "Now what?"

Queen Jennica approached the fallen goddess with caution. We waited for a few tense moments to see if Calianna would spring up, alive with fury, but the goddess stayed where she was. I held my breath as the queen reached out a tentative finger to poke Calianna's body. The goddess didn't stir.

"Is she dead?" I asked the queen.

Beside me, Graenta's hoarse voice said, "That depends on you, Your Majesty."

Both the queen and I turned curious eyes on him. Stronger now, he continued, "You've merely incapacitated her, for a time. Her power has been completely drained, but will eventually return. Unless you decide to end her now."

Graenta's words came back to me. *One to incapacitate, two to kill.* Now I understood what he meant.

We all looked down at the still form of the goddess. Queen Jennica's mouth turned down in distaste. "As much as I detest the woman, it feels wrong, killing the founder of my kingdom."

"Your compassion does you credit," Graenta said to the queen.

She smirked. "That doesn't mean I want her running around free to cause more trouble, though." She sighed. "What do we do with her?"

"With her in this state, I can easily send her back to Zaela Island," Graenta said.

"But the Great Seal is broken," I pointed out. "Won't she just escape once she wakes up?"

"Eventually," Graenta said. "But if we bind her, physically and mag-ically, that will slow her down a little. Not to mention it will be a few days before she even wakes up, and then it will take time for her to recover all of her magic."

35

CHAPTER THIRTY-FIVE

IT WASN'T THE MOST ideal solution, but it was all we had. Queen Jennica and Graenta got to work on binding Calianna. When she had fallen to the Sword of the First King, all her spells had fallen with her. The queen kept the castle servants busy, bringing ropes, chains, and spell components. She also called for smelling salts, water, bandages, and the Royal Healer.

Feeling a little unnecessary, I went to Oran to see if I could rouse him. Lord Rhyss, having recovered quickly once Calianna's magic had faded from his body, went to help King Beyan.

During all of this commotion, Melandria and Joichan peeked cautious heads into the main room of the royal suite. Sometime during the confrontation with Calianna, they had run into the antechamber, both to hide and also to protect their grandson, the Crown Prince Coran.

I brushed Oran's hair back from his forehead, peering into his face. He didn't react, but when I leaned in, I was relieved to hear he was still breathing.

Balancing the infant prince on her hip, Melandria asked me, "Do you need any help with your friend?"

Joichan stood nearby, ready to take the child from his grand-mother just in case.

"I'm not sure," I said honestly. "I'm not a healer, so I can't figure out what's wrong with him. I can only hope he—oh!"

Oran stirred and opened his eyes. I was still leaning close to him, my ear inclined towards him so I could listen for his breathing. When Oran moved, I startled, turning slightly to face him. We stared at each other for a few heartbeats, our faces so close we could kiss.

"You're awake," I said inanely.

Oran's hand crept up and locked around my wrist. I realized belatedly that my hand was still tangled in his hair.

Somewhere behind me, I heard Lord Rhyss say, "I think he's coming around!" followed by the rustle of Melandria's skirt as she moved towards her son-in-law. Was Joichan still around, paying attention to Oran and me? Probably not. But for some strange reason, I didn't care enough to check.

And we were still staring at each other.

"Here, Melandria, let me take Coran," I heard Ambassador Joichan say, a little too loudly. I looked up just in time to catch the twinkle in his eyes. He winked at me, then turned away and headed back into the nursery with his grandson.

I sat back, allowing Oran—and myself—some breathing room. I lowered my wrist, with Oran's hand still touching it. Somehow that evolved into him holding my hand. "How are you feeling? Do you need anything?"

"I'm fine," Oran said, then winced. "Okay, I lied. My head hurts."

"I'm not surprised. You hit the wall pretty hard."

"Yes ..." His voice trailed off as his eyes lit with remembrance. He sat up, looking around with fear. "Is *she* still here?"

"She is, but she's out cold. Graenta says she'll be unable to wake or do magic for at least several days."

"That's a mercy, at least. How's the king? And everyone else?"

"The king, I'm not sure about. Everyone else is fine, for the most part."

"Good." He sighed and leaned back. I noticed he didn't let go of my hand.

I shifted my body so I could lean against the wall with him and look around the room. The Royal Healer had arrived and was fussing over King Beyan, who had woken up at some point while I was attending to Oran. The king was waving away the healer's offers of medicines and bandages, while Lord Rhyss and Queen Jennica appeared to be in a deep discussion. Ambassador Melandria was absent, presumably back in the nursery with Joichan and Coran.

"I'll contact them now, then," Queen Jennica was saying.

"If you'll excuse me," King Beyan said to the Royal Healer, "I need to be a part of this. Really, I'm fine, thank you. If I need anything, I'll send for you."

The Royal Healer bowed and left the bedchamber. Lord Rhyss helped King Beyan get up from the floor, settling him in the bed before taking a seat nearby.

Queen Jennica held her hand out, palm up. "King Addan and Queen Inari of Bomora, if you can hear this, answer me."

Two images appeared above the queen's open hand. A handsome man with long brown hair, pulled back in a matching ribbon, smiled at the queen—an expression both welcoming and dangerous. Beside him stood a petite doll of a woman, equally striking with raven hair framing her heart-shaped face. Her bright blue eyes were sharp and assessing, and I got the sense that, despite her small size, she was not a person to be underestimated.

What surprised me, though, was that the Bomorran royal couple—at least, I assumed it was them—weren't dressed like any royalty I had ever seen. Instead of gold and jewels and fine fabrics, the pair wore loose-fitting, dark colored outfits, with no gems in sight. If I didn't know better, I would have thought they were vagabonds or thieves, not the rulers of a kingdom.

"Well met, Queen Jennica of Calia," the man said, his voice deep and velvety. "It's good to see you again."

"And we trust your family is well?" the woman inquired politely.

"They are, although it was a near miss," Queen Jennica said. "But as time is limited, let me get right to the point. Calia has had a most unexpected, unwelcome visitor—the founder of our kingdom, the goddess Calianna."

King Addan smirked. "I see Bomora is not alone. We, too, have had an unexpected, unwelcome visitor—our own founder, the god Bomor." He nodded at Lord Rhyss, who was standing a few feet behind Queen Jennica, supporting King Beyan. "As I am sure your friend has mentioned."

"He did, although the details were scant."

The Bomorran king sighed. "To be honest, there aren't many. Bomor arrived a few days ago, claiming to be our god and founder. He demanded that Inari and I turn over rulership of Bomora to him immediately."

"Which we of course refused," sniffed Queen Inari.

King Addan puffed up with pride. The smirk was back, teasing the corners of his lips. "Not even a god can mess with my queen."

Oran and I exchanged curious glances. I was dying to hear the story behind that statement, but the royals had moved on.

"We put word out to our network immediately," King Addan continued. "We anticipated that this person, whether truly a god or just a delusional human, would cause trouble and we wanted to be prepared."

Queen Inari took up the tale. "That's when we called you, Queen Jennica. We wanted to warn you, and to see if you had any insights. When we couldn't reach you, or Royal Advisor Taryn, we called Lord Rhyss."

Queen Jennica sighed. "Yes, thanks to Calianna's visit, Taryn was … not herself." She raised a quizzical eyebrow. "But you two seem awfully calm for having had Bomor show up on your doorstep."

"That's because he left our doorstep as fast as he appeared." Queen Inari shrugged. "Our spies kept a careful eye on him, but he disappeared sometime tonight, and hasn't returned. Yet. And we hope, not ever. In the short amount of time he was here, he broke into the palace treasury, injuring several of our men with unexpected traps."

"My goodness. Did he steal anything?"

"Surprisingly, no. We thought perhaps he did it just to prove he could. But—" the Bomorran queen's voice hardened "—he did set our ship, the Starchaser, on fire."

From Queen Inari's tone, and the set of King Addan's jaw, I did not want to be Bomor when they finally caught up to him.

My head spun. It hadn't been that long since the Great Seal had broken, releasing the gods and goddesses into the Gifted Lands and completely upending my life.

And, all of a sudden, I felt bone-weary tired. I yawned, fighting to stay awake. But despite myself, my eyes began to close. Distantly, I could hear Queen Jennica's voice. "I'll contact our allies in the other kingdoms, to see if they too have had these special 'visitors.' Then, I think it's best if we—"

But I never knew what it would be best to do. Exhaustion overtook me, and I fell asleep.

36

CHAPTER THIRTY-SIX

I WOKE UP SMELLING lavender and vanilla. Breathing it in, I realized it was coming from the linens that covered me. A heavy coverlet kept me nice and warm, and the plush bed I lay in was so soft and heavenly that I didn't want to get up. And, inexplicably, I was wearing a thin, light white gown, with lace at the collar, wrists, and hem.

Strange. I didn't remember putting this on. And I was fairly certain it wasn't mine. I didn't own anything so fine, and I definitely hadn't brought it with me.

I wanted to ponder everything a little while longer. But I became aware of a light, insistent tapping at my door that wouldn't stop.

"One moment, please," I called out. Sighing, I sat up and rubbed my eyes, looking around.

I was in a bedroom, much simpler than the royal suite, but still elegantly furnished. The lovely-smelling bed linens alone would have been one month's worth of my brother's salary at the Graenir Archives. This room boasted a simple four poster bed, a blue-and-silver rug as soft as the bed, and a small wooden nightstand. A matching armoire stood in one corner of the room. Sunlight streamed through the open curtains, some of it catching on a small mirror that hung on one wall.

The knocking grew louder.

"Hold on, I'm coming," I said loudly, finally getting out of bed. But instead of going right to the door, I went to the wardrobe and opened it. A few items of clothing hung inside, with some more pieces neatly folded on the bottom. I selected a cream-colored dressing gown and slipped it on. It was a little long, so I folded back the sleeves and hitched it up higher over the belt.

I flung open the bedroom door mid-knock.

Oran stood on the other side, his hand in mid-air. When he saw me, he hastily put his hand down. Then, once he got a good look at me, he blushed and looked away.

"G-good morning, Idessa," he said, looking somewhere near but not quite at me. "I hope you slept well?"

"I did, thank you," I said, somewhat amused that he wouldn't meet my eyes. I mean, I was fully covered, just not in what would be considered appropriate day wear. "But I don't even remember coming in here. I must have been really tired."

"You were." He smiled, remembering. "You fell asleep back in the king and queen's room, and you absolutely refused to wake up, even just long enough to walk down the hall."

"So how did I get here, then?"

He coughed, reddening again. "I carried you into this room, and then two of the queen's ladies-in-waiting helped you after that."

Oh. Now it was my turn to blush. I hoped I hadn't drooled or talked in my sleep or anything else embarrassing.

An awkward silence fell between us. Eventually, I said, "Um. What are you doing here?"

"Oh." He met my eyes, finally, being very careful to only look there and nowhere else. "Uh ... when you're dressed, the queen wants us—you, me, and Graenta—to join her in the dining hall for breakfast.

I guess there are some things we need to discuss, and she said it would go faster over food."

My stomach growled in agreement. It helped break through the unusual weirdness between us, and we both laughed.

"Sure," I agreed. "I'll need to change, first." I looked around the room. "I'm not sure where my clothes went, though."

A young woman appeared behind Oran, her arms full of clothing. Oran jumped when she spoke, causing me to giggle. "Good morning, miss. I have your clothes, freshly washed, and a few other options that might suit you better. If you'll excuse us, Sir Oran, I need to help Lady Idessa get ready for the day."

Oran smirked and raised an eyebrow at our new—and completely undeserved—titles, but stepped back to allow the woman to enter. "I'll wait out in the hallway for you, *Lady* Idessa."

I rolled my eyes at him, but he had already turned away, so my effort was wasted. Oh, well. The lady-in-waiting pretended not to notice and bustled into the bedchamber. She closed the door behind her and then dropped the bundle she was carrying on the bed.

"Forgive me for hurrying you, my lady," she said, "but we don't have much time. Their Majesties, along with the former queen, the former Royal Consort, and Lord Rhyss, are already gathered in the dining hall. So we need to get you dressed and out the door lickety-split."

I giggled at the lady-in-waiting's old fashioned language, then smoothed my expression at her stern look. I looked over the items on the bed. My traveling clothes lay on top, cleaned as the woman had promised, but a little dull from yesterday's adventures. And apparently I had also ripped it—a near-invisible seam ran down part of the shirt where it must have torn. A few faded splotches dotted the hem as well.

"The seamstress did a wonderful job, don't you think?" the lady-in-waiting gushed. "And those stains were pretty deep in the fabric. The launderer did his best, but it was hard with such a light-colored fabric. Still, you can barely tell."

I eyed the shirt with a skeptical eye. *I* could definitely tell, and I was sure it would be obvious to others also. Still, it wasn't like I had many other options.

... Or did I?

I looked through the assortment on the bed. There were some plain skirts and blouses, good for traveling. There were also a few pairs of trousers. Very practical. Perhaps that would be best ...

A bit of silver fabric caught my eye. I plucked it out of the pile.

"Oh, that used to belong to Royal Advisor Taryn," the lady-in-waiting informed me. "She needed something simple yet elegant for engagements outside of Calia. Light and easy to pack."

"It's beautiful," I said, holding it up so I could see it better in the sunlight. The shimmery fabric practically glowed. I admired it, entranced. "Can I ... can I wear this?"

"Of course, my lady!" The lady-in-waiting tittered. "That's why I brought it. Come, then. Let's get you dressed."

I felt a bit silly, letting some strange woman help me with a task that I had done by myself for years. Although I don't know how I would have gotten out of the nightgown otherwise—there was no way I would have been able to undo the row of ribbons down the back without assistance. Still, I felt slightly embarrassed, as if I was wasting the lady-in-waiting's time.

The Royal Advisor's former dress was fortunately easy to slip into. I could easily handle the buttons in the front, which was probably why its previous owner had chosen this style. My embarrassment came back when the lady-in-waiting insisted I sit down on the edge of the bed so she could fix my hair.

"It won't take long," she said. "And you'll be more comfortable with your hair out of your face."

I privately disagreed, but sat down and let her brush and braid and pin my hair to her satisfaction.

"There. You're done." Satisfied, the lady-in-waiting crossed the room and opened the door. "Hurry, now, my lady." She disappeared from the room.

Standing, I paused when I caught sight of myself in the mirror. I turned my head from side to side, admiring the woman's handiwork. She really had done an excellent job. Half of my long white hair had been braided and pinned back, but she had left the rest of it down to flow around my shoulders. I sighed. I wished the mirror was big enough so I could see how the dress looked on me.

Hearing footsteps behind me, I turned. I figured the lady-in-waiting had returned to admonish me to hurry, and I meant to thank her for the beautiful hairstyle.

But it wasn't the woman. It was Oran.

His eyes widened as he got a good look at me. Something in them sparked, and I felt an answering flutter. And, suddenly, it didn't matter anymore if I could see my reflection. The expression on his face told me more than any full-length mirror ever could.

"You look ..." Oran's voice faltered.

When he didn't continue, I prompted, "Yes? How do I look?" I aimed for a teasing tone, but a little insecurity may have crept in.

He smiled. "Radiant. Like a star shining in the night sky."

An answering smile blossomed across my face. "Thank you." I nodded towards the open bedroom door. "Shall we?"

He offered his arm to me. Beaming, I laid my hand on it and let him lead me to the dining hall.

37

CHAPTER THIRTY-SEVEN

As we entered the dining hall, we saw Queen Jennica and King Beyan seated at one end of the table. Lord Rhyss sat across from the king. Graenta was just sitting down, his plate piled high with food.

As Oran and I passed him, he gave us both a cheery, "Good morning!"

I eyed his plate. "How much food do gods need to eat, anyway?"

"None whatsoever," he replied with a big grin. "But the nourishment can help. Besides, I like how it tastes. Most of the time."

I chuckled and headed to the buffet, where Oran was already getting his breakfast. He handed me an empty plate. "For you."

"Thank you." I proceeded to follow Graenta's example and picked out a wide variety of fruit, cheeses, and meats.

As Oran and I both sat down, Queen Jennica said, "Perfect, I think that's all of us."

"Wait," Lord Rhyss said. "What about Taryn? And Melandria, and Joichan?"

"Taryn is briefing Mother and Father about the current state of things in Calia," the queen said. "They'll be ruling the kingdom in the interim while we're gone."

"Gone?" Lord Rhyss looked between Queen Jennica and King Beyan. "Both of you?"

The queen looked grim. "Maybe. That's part of what we need to discuss this morning."

Lord Rhyss nodded, falling silent so the queen could begin.

"All right, then." She took a sip of water from a crystal goblet before continuing. "Last night, after you left—" she nodded at Oran and me, and I blushed and looked down at my hands "—we still had more business to finish. Graenta was kind enough to send Calianna away and help Lord Rhyss get home."

"She's back in the vault on Zaela Island," Graenta put in. "We'll need to get back there soon to figure out how to imprison her more permanently, but she'll be asleep for a few more days, at least."

"Thank the gods—literally," Lord Rhyss said. He smiled at Graenta. "And thank you for sending me home with your magic. Saved me quite a bit of time."

"Of course. I'm just glad I had enough magic left to take care of both Calianna and you."

I frowned. "How are you feeling now, Graenta?"

"Much better. After I sent Lord Rhyss home I went right to bed." He beamed at the royal couple. "Best sleep I've had in centuries. I wish I had thought to outfit the vault with such comfortable furnishings."

The queen chuckled. "Coming from a god, that's quite an endorsement." Her smile faded as she turned to Lord Rhyss. "And how is Farrah doing?"

Lord Rhyss shook his head. "No change, unfortunately."

Although he masked his pain well, my heart still hurt for him. I wasn't a healer, and I definitely wasn't a mage, but I wished I could help his betrothed. But the only thing I could do was hope that she would wake up soon.

The queen reached out and touched his shoulder. Lord Rhyss grasped her hand and squeezed it in thanks.

"Well, as sorry as I am to hear that, I am glad you were able to get home quickly," King Beyan said. "Jennica and I stayed up late, contacting our allies in the other kingdoms."

"Their stories were very similar to what King Addan and Queen Inari told us," Queen Jennica said. "Princess Laersa of Annlyn reported that an unknown person arrived who was able to shift into multiple animal forms—something unheard of in all of the Gifted Lands. Their unique ability made it difficult for the guards to capture them, until they suddenly changed into an eagle and flew away. In Rothschan, their god murdered a contingent of knights in an attempt to seize the kingdom before Adalynn, who is able to mind-link with the entire army, realized what was happening. She had an uneasy feeling, a slight queasiness, that snowballed until it nearly debilitated her. Just when she thought she would pass out or even die from the pain, it abruptly stopped and left her."

Annlyn was a kingdom far to the south. I never knew they had shapeshifters there, although rumors had reached us in Graenir just recently about that possibility. The country had always seemed mysterious and exotic to me. Then again, I'm sure they felt the same way about Graenir.

The country of Rothschan was northwest of Annlyn, kind of in between Bomora and Orchwell. Everything I'd ever heard about that place sounded unpleasant—they had a deep hatred of all things magic, and were reputed to be cold and unfriendly towards outsiders. So it was a surprise to learn that Calia considered Rothschan an ally—or at least, had a friend among them.

"We're not quite sure what, if anything, happened in Orchwell or Shonn," King Beyan said, naming the kingdoms just south and east of

Calia. "Our contact in Orchwell, a Seeker named Kaernan, planned on visiting their palace later today to see if he could learn anything. Our relations with Shonn are neutral, at best, but we did send messengers to King Paxen and Queen Bettan, the rulers of Faerie's Seelie Court. The Fae don't usually mingle in human affairs—"

"—Unless it's for the occasional bit of mischief," Lord Rhyss put in, a reminiscent smirk on his face.

King Beyan chuckled. "But perhaps they will make an exception." He sobered. "The gods of the Gifted Lands breaking free from their prison is of concern to both realms."

Queen Jennica spoke up. "It might be some time before we hear anything from our messengers, though. It will take them several days to reach Shonn, even if they ride without stopping, and then they still need to locate the Veil to enter Faerie. And time runs differently between the two worlds, although I would hope the Seelie rulers would ensure that our messengers return in a timely fashion."

Lord Rhyss snorted. "If they returned one hundred years later, at least they would miss this whole mess. Maybe."

The queen of Calia chuckled. "There will always be some mess to clean up, whether it's now or in one hundred years. But let's get this one sorted out, so there will be a future mess for the people of the Gifted Lands to figure out in their time."

The king leaned over and kissed his wife on the top of her head. "Ever the practical one, my dear."

She gave him an affectionate smile, then sobered. "So, from what we could tell, it sounded like most—if not every—kingdom in the Gifted Lands was visited by their founding god or goddess since the Seal was broken. They demanded power or loyalty and caused some trouble, but then they all left just as suddenly as they arrived."

She turned to Graenta, who was busy cleaning his eyeglasses on the corner of his tunic. "Graenta, you're our best authority on how the gods think. Why would they go to their respective kingdoms, with the obvious intent of wanting to claim rulership for their own, just to leave before they even started towards their goal?"

The boy put his glasses back on, shrugging his shoulders as he did so. "I have as much insight as you do, my dear queen. I've never understood the power-mad minds of my fellow gods. But if I were in their place ... I would want to ensure I could never be imprisoned again. And I would also want to strike at the heart of the one who imprisoned me in the first place...."

His voice trailed off as he frowned, thinking. I started to ask him what was bothering him, but he held up a finger to silence me. *Wait.* Some important thought was hovering just out of his reach, if he could only remember it.

Fast footsteps approached the dining hall. We all looked up to see who the newcomer was, with the exception of Graenta, who was still trying to recall his elusive memory.

"Father?" Queen Jennica stood, concerned at the disturbed look on Ambassador Joichan's face. "What's wrong? Is everything okay with Taryn and Mother?"

Joichan nodded, but his worry didn't subside. "Yes, my dear, they're fine."

"Then what's—"

"We just received word from Queen Yllulae. The gods have returned to Graenir and declared war."

38

—:—

CHAPTER THIRTY-EIGHT

I GASPED. "WHAT? WHEN? Have they—how bad—?" The words stuck in my throat. I couldn't even form coherent thoughts, I was so shaken by the news.

Next to me, Oran reached out and put a soothing hand on my shoulder. He began to rub slow circles on my back in an attempt to calm me down.

Graenta looked up and whistled. "That's one way to get my attention, for sure. Smart."

"Smart?" I barely restrained myself from reaching across the table and shaking him.

The boy nodded. "Destroy the kingdom I founded, the seat of my power? It's an incredibly smart move. I don't know why they didn't do that in the first place."

"I wish they hadn't been smart enough to figure it out! Lis is there—my parents—"

"Shh, Idessa," Oran said softly beside me. "It'll be okay."

"No!" I shot up, toppling my chair over in the process. "I need to get back to Graenir. Now! Before it's too late!"

Queen Jennica frowned at me. "Your worry for your loved ones does you credit. And we will go. But we need to figure out a few things, first."

A gentle tug on my arm caused me to look down. Oran mouthed at me, *Sit down.* Feeling frustrated, I did as he suggested.

The queen turned to Ambassador Joichan. "Did Queen Yllulae give you any details?"

He nodded. "They gathered just outside the capital city this morning and went straight to the palace. Five of them, since Calianna is back at Zaela Island, and Graenta is here, with us. They killed or froze any guards who tried to stop them. A runner dispatched to the castle had just enough time to warn Queen Yllulae before they arrived." The ambassador swallowed hard. "She contacted me immediately to tell me, and was even giving commands to her guards as we spoke. But then I heard a crash, and our connection ended."

"Oh, dear." Queen Jennica looked grave. "I suppose they want to rule Graenir, just like they've been wanting control over the other kingdoms?"

"No." Graenta's sure voice cut through. "They want to draw on the power in Graenir, I'm sure of it. As the place where they were imprisoned for so long, it has the purest form of their power. They would be weaker in the other countries, which have been under human rule for too long. So they want that power. They want me. And they want Idessa."

I gasped in shock. "Me? Why me? Why not Queen Yllulae?"

"Although Queen Ylullae is the current ruler, in some respects, she is just a figurehead, and not the true symbol of the kingdom's heart. But you, Idessa, are the current Guardian. It ties you to me, and thus the country of Graenir, more than you can even imagine." Graenta didn't seem perturbed at all. He might as well have been talking about the weather, or what we would be eating later. "I would think they need both of us in hand to drain the kingdom of Graenir of its power completely."

"It makes sense," Oran put in. "As long as you—and Idessa—remain alive, you would be able to check their powers somewhat. But if they get rid of you—"

"Wait," I said. "I understand how Graenta, a god, would be able to counter a fellow god's powers. But I'm just a human. And I'm not a mage. So how could I do anything to stop them?"

"You're the link between the human worlds and the gods," Graenta said. "Notice how the Sword of the First King did not awaken until you held it in your hands."

"I thought *you* did that."

"I merely enhanced its power. But the sword is a human emblem. I could wield it as a weapon, but I would not be able to tap into its power."

I frowned, remembering the showdown with Calianna. "But you told me to give the sword to Queen Jennica."

"Once its magic was unlocked, its power would be more potent in the hands of one who has a direct connection to it. The sword belonged to the first king of Calia. Therefore, its current ruler, Queen Jennica, would be able to use its power more effectively than you would. But its magic needed to be awakened, first. And that was your purpose, Idessa."

The others had been following our exchange with interest.

"Graenta, are you saying that the only way to defeat the other gods is with weapons that symbolize the kingdoms of the Gifted Lands?" Queen Jennica said.

Graenta tilted his head, thinking. "They might not need to be weapons, but definitely items of importance to the history of each country. And it's not the only way, just an easier way."

Queen Jennica, King Beyan, and Lord Rhyss exchanged a three-way glance.

"We'll have to tell the other leaders," King Beyan said.

Lord Rhyss nodded. "But it will take time for the leaders to prepare. And then move their armies to Graenir. It could take a week, or longer. Can we afford to wait that long?"

"It can't be helped," King Beyan said. "We'll send the word out to the other kingdoms, and hope they can mobilize quickly."

"It's a good thing we don't have an army," Queen Jennica smirked. "Much less people to move."

"I could go to the farther kingdoms and ferry people to Graenir," Joichan said, but he sounded doubtful.

The queen shook her head. "It's a generous offer, but it would tire you out fast. And I don't know if it would be wise to split the other countries' armies like that. Besides, you and Mother are needed here in Calia. I think if we do that, it's a last resort. We'll talk to the other leaders first and figure out what can be done.

"All right. Beyan and I will contact the other leaders. Rhyss—"

"I'm going with you," he said. "There's no point in me staying here and worrying over Farrah, not when I can be useful."

Joichan said, "I'll check in on her while you're gone."

"Thank you."

Joichan nodded. "I'll head back to Melandria and Taryn, then. If Queen Yllulae contacts me again, I'll let you know right away."

He gave the queen a brief hug, then left the room. Lord Rhyss stood. "I'll head home right now to get my things. Is an hour enough time for you, Jennica?"

"Make it two," she advised. "We've got a lot of calls to make, and then we still need to make our own preparations."

"Perfect." He turned to Oran, Graenta, and me. "And what about you three?"

"Graenta, if you would be so kind as to be present when I call the other leaders, that would help immensely," Queen Jennica said. Graenta nodded. "Idessa, if you'd like to be there, you're welcome to, or if you and Oran have preparations of your own that you'd like to make, you can do so too."

"I think I'll go with Oran, Your Majesty," I said.

"Of course. The servants can help you with whatever you need. Let's all meet in the courtyard in about two hours."

As everyone else stood to go their separate ways, I couldn't help but think, *And let's hope we're not too late.*

39

CHAPTER THIRTY-NINE

I HELD UP A short sword, swinging it experimentally. "How does one use this, exactly?"

Oran's eyes grew wide as he stepped back, just out of reach. "Not like that. Put that thing down before you hurt yourself. Or someone else."

I dropped the weapon on the table like it had suddenly caught on fire. "Sorry."

Oran laughed. "Don't be. Just ... save that enthusiasm for the battlefield."

I grimaced as I looked around. We had our pick of any item in the castle armory, but I didn't know where to start. Nor was I all that excited. "I don't think I want to be that close to any fighting, thank you."

Oran's smile faded. "No one ever does. But we need to be prepared. We don't know what the situation will be like in Graenir when we get there."

"Oran, what if—" My voice caught as I burst into tears.

Oran put down the weapon he had been examining and gathered me into his arms. "Hey, Idessa. Come here."

I leaned into him, drawing strength from his steady presence. "When I think about my family, and whatever's happening back home, I—I ..."

"I know." He continued holding me, stroking my hair, even though his shirt was getting damp from my crying.

"How can you be so calm?" I sniffled. "Your family is back there, too."

"I didn't forget." A hint of resolve laced his voice. "But I try not to dwell on it, otherwise I'll worry about it too much, and descend into madness. Until we know for sure what's going on and how they are, I don't want to think about it. There are some things more pressing right now."

"Really? Like what? What could possibly be more—"

"You. You, Idessa."

Confused, I pulled back a little so I could look into Oran's eyes. "I don't understand."

He pushed a strand of hair back from my face. "Y-you're going through a lot right now," he stammered, surprising me with this unexpected bit of nervousness. "You need someone to be strong for you. I-I want to be that for you."

I stared at him, unsure of how to respond. The silence stretched out between us, heavy and awkward.

Oran swallowed and stepped back, releasing me. Cold air rushed in, and I realized I missed the feel of his arms around me. I blinked in surprise, trying to process this. This was Oran. My brother's best friend, and someone I had known for—well, forever.

He wasn't as dashing or intoxicating as Tahn had been, but his steadiness and sureness was compelling in its own way. And—maybe that's what I needed in my life right now, amidst all the craziness. Something solid and true, instead of exciting but fleeting.

Oran turned away, his hurt obvious. I know he wanted me to say something—*anything*—but I didn't know what to say. I was still trying to work through all these new thoughts and feelings I was having.

I didn't quite know what I wanted. But I did know I didn't want to see him hurt, and I didn't want him to walk away.

Not unless I was by his side.

I grabbed Oran's arm. He stopped mid-stride towards the armory door and turned to look at me, a question in his eyes.

I still didn't know what to say. So instead, I stepped forward, drawing him back. I lifted my face towards his and kissed him.

Oran's lips met mine, tentative at first. The kiss deepened as his arms tightened around me.

When we both finally pulled back, Oran had a dazed look on his face that I was sure mirrored my own. "Why now?" he asked in a low voice. "I've always been there. You've just never noticed—"

"I'm noticing now," I said, putting a finger to his lips.

He smiled. "Good."

Muffled laughter at the armory door made us spring apart, then both look over. Lord Rhyss and Graenta stood in the doorway, pretending to look over the array of weapons that surrounded us.

"Personally, I prefer a sword in one hand and a dagger in the other," Lord Rhyss said, his voice a touch too loud. "But I have a bad habit of losing daggers, save one. So I should probably grab a few before we leave."

"As a god, I don't necessarily need a weapon," Graenta said, trying and failing to keep the giggles from his boyish voice. "But they do come in handy, usually as a focus for my magic."

"We should probably pick out our weapons, then, and get going. We wouldn't want to keep the king and queen waiting. I wonder where—oh!" Lord Rhyss looked at Oran and me. "There you two are. Are you ready to go, or do you need more time to … look around?"

I giggled. Lord Rhyss, although a lovely and lively man, would never make a good actor. Next to me, Oran blushed bright red.

"We just need to pick up a few things," Oran mumbled. "We haven't quite made our selections."

"Really? I had thought it was quite the opposite," Graenta said sweetly. When I glared at him, he just grinned back.

"Oran, how comfortable are you with one of these?" Lord Rhyss held up a longsword, all business now.

"I'm fairly good with one," Oran said.

"He's being modest." I nudged Oran with my elbow. "He placed first in the sword competition in Graenir's annual tourney some two years past."

"And I haven't won since." Oran frowned. "*And* fighting in true combat is different than in a tournament for show."

"That may be true," Lord Rhyss said. "But you obviously know how to handle a sword, and that's better than most." He handed the longsword to Oran. "See if you like this one."

The two men started discussing the merits of various weapons in the armory. Graenta came over to where I stood, half-heartedly examining a wall of shields.

"I hope our teasing didn't offend you," he said in a low voice.

I shook my head. "No, it's fine. I'm not worried about that. It's just … everything is so overwhelming. I barely felt ready to be your champion, and now this." I waved a hand that encompassed Lord Rhyss, Oran, Graenta, and the armory. "I can't wield a sword. I can't shoot a bow. All I can do right now is worry." A little sob escaped me. "I'm not Guardian material, not one bit."

Graenta looked at me for a long moment. Then, finally, he spoke. "I'm not going to say it will all be okay, because, even as a god, I don't know. I can't see the future. But I can see you. And even though you may think you're not ready to be my Guardian, *I* know it. I wouldn't have chosen you otherwise. And I know, when the time comes, you'll be ready. And you'll be all right."

40

— ◆ —

CHAPTER FORTY

WITH THE SUN BLAZING overhead, I found myself on dragon back once more, flying towards Graenir.

Oran and I sat astride Queen Jennica, now a large golden dragon. Next to her, Ambassador Joichan carried King Beyan and Lord Rhyss. Graenta had transformed into an eagle and flew alongside the two majestic creatures.

Although I had known that the queen and the ambassador were related—and that Joichan could shapeshift—I had still been surprised and thrilled when the Calian queen had changed into a beautiful and fearsome dragon.

The king and queen had briefed us on the outcome of their calls to the other kingdoms. Bomora and Rothschan were both on the move, although it would take them a week or more to reach Graenir.

Annlyn, like Calia, did not have an army, although it was due to their former isolationist policies and not because they relied on the stronger, larger shapeshifters to fight. Their Princess Laersa had pledged to send her people as a backup, although everyone hoped it wouldn't come to that.

Orchwell, surprisingly, had wanted to stay out of any conflict, although the Calian royals' contact—Kaernan, I think his name was?—had promised to keep trying to convince the Orchwell leaders. Shonn was not in a position to spare help of any sort, as their numbers had been reduced due to the recent Fae unrest. Many of the kingdom's citizens had left and settled in other parts of the Gifted Lands when the Fae had threatened Shonn, and few had returned.

And right before we had left, another setback occurred.

One of the messengers the queen had sent to find the Veil and Faerie returned, exhausted and wild-eyed. He cradled his arm in a makeshift sling, and dried blood coated his blond hair and dirty face. With him was his companion's horse, riderless.

"We were set upon by bandits about a day and a half out of Calia," the man had said. "They killed Jonta, but spared me—barely—as a warning to not send anyone official-looking down 'their' road. I should have tried to fight through them, but—"

"No, you were right to return," Queen Jennica had told him. "Go straight to the palace and have the Royal Healer look at you, on my orders."

The man had bowed—nearly falling out of his saddle—and left. Queen Jennica had looked after him, worried. "How are we going to get word to the Fae? I don't want to send more people to their doom, but we need to get a messenger there."

"I can go," Joichan had offered. "I can more than hold my own against a group of bandits, if need be. After we go to Graenir, I can head north to Shonn and look for the Veil."

The queen's relief had been palpable. "And you can go faster than anyone on horseback. We need to do all we can to hasten things on our end."

Now, I settled into my seat, leaning against Oran and drawing from his strength. I might as well take what respite I could while I was able.

For better or worse—but hopefully not that much worse—we'd be in Graenir soon enough.

The sun kissed the horizon as we made our descent into Graenir.

Queen Jennica made a graceful landing on the banks of the Rehann River, with Joichan alighting next to her. Oran jumped down, then reached towards me to help me down. Lord Rhyss and King Beyan had already dismounted and were surveying the area.

Above us, Graenta flew in a slow circle, then landed somewhere out of sight. The two dragons shimmered briefly, and a moment later, Queen Jennica and Ambassador Joichan stood before us.

The crunch of leaves underfoot caught my attention. I squinted at the approaching figure in the dim light. Now that we were on the ground, it was much darker with the setting sun behind the trees.

"Graenta? Is that you?" I hissed, trying to keep my voice down.

"It is," a boy's voice answered me, equally low.

A familiar man's voice came from the shadows, in a near whisper. "Who's there?"

"Harlan?" I said. "I'm so glad you're here."

"Is that our Guardian?" The ferryman approached, his figure barely visible in the twilight. "It is! Well met, Guardian Idessa. Does your return mean you're here to save our kingdom?"

"Well, I—" I faltered. "I don't know. But maybe these people with me can."

Harlan grunted. "I didn't bring a lantern with me. It's not safe to draw attention, if you can help it."

"Quite understandable," Queen Jennica's voice cut through the twilight. "Is there somewhere safe we can go to talk?"

"My home's not far from here. Stick close together, now."

Harlan led us back to his little riverside cottage. It was hard to be sure in the growing darkness, but I thought his place looked mostly patched up.

"Come in, come in." He unlocked the door and ushered us in, closing the door and locking it against the night.

Inside, he lit a candle, its meager glow casting just enough light for us to see each other's faces, but nothing of the room beyond. The small cottage felt even more cramped with all of us in it.

"It should be safe to talk now, but don't get too loud," Harlan warned. "And even though I've got blankets covering the windows, I don't dare to light anything brighter than this."

"Harlan, what's going on?" I asked.

The flickering candlelight created deep shadows on his face, making him look gaunt and broken. "Some powerful people came through just after sunrise. I had just come back from my morning walk and saw them appear out of nowhere, on Zaela Island. So I stayed hidden in the trees until I was sure they'd gone. I'm so glad I did."

He shuddered. "They magicked themselves over to this side of the river, and when they saw my house, they went in to see if anyone lived there. Broke a bunch of my things, whatever had survived the flood. If I had been inside ..."

Oran put a comforting hand on the ferryman's shoulder. "I'm sorry they did that to your home, Harlan. We'll do what we can to make things right."

The ferryman squeezed Oran's hand in thanks.

"How many were there, do you know?" Graenta asked, worried.

Harlan frowned down at the boy, trying to place who the youth was. I could understand his curiosity. The god's clothes were of an older Graenir style, and his hairstyle was one that hadn't been popular in quite some time.

"There were five of them, a mix of men and women," Harlan said. "I couldn't get a good look at their faces, but their speech was a bit strange. In fact, they sounded a bit like you, young sir."

"They would," Graenta confirmed. "After all, it's been centuries since any of us walked this land."

Harlan nearly dropped the candle. "*Centuries?*" He looked at Oran and me. "What is the lad talking about?"

Clearing my throat, I said, "Uh. Yes. Harlan, let me introduce you to everyone here. You know Oran, already. And I'm sure you've seen Ambassador Joichan of Calia around Graenir." The two men nodded at one another.

"Also from Calia, this is Lord Rhyss, King Beyan, and Queen Jennica." I indicated each person in turn.

Harlan's jaw dropped. He tried to bow in all directions, but with the crowded cottage and the lit candle in his hand, it was hard for him to maneuver.

"Begging your pardon, Your Majesties, my lord," he said. "Had I known—"

"It's all right," I said soothingly. "You couldn't have known. *We* didn't even know ourselves, until a few hours ago."

"So, then, who's this?" Harlan's gaze settled on Graenta. "And what did he mean, centuries since he's been here? He doesn't look a day over ten."

"He's much, much older than ten." I raised my eyebrows at Graenta. "More like ten hundred, would you say?"

"Oh, at least," he smirked. "After a while you stop counting the years."

Poor Harlan. His rising confusion was palpable. Taking pity on him, I said gently, "Harlan, this is Graenta. The founder of our kingdom, Graenir. And—"

Harlan chuckled. "Oh, Guardian, you know better than to joke with an old man."

"It's true," Graenta said simply. "Look at me, Harlan."

Despite his disbelief, the ferryman stared into Graenta's eyes. Even I could hear the command in Graenta's voice, and found myself turning to look at the god, along with the others in the room.

There wasn't room for any flashy displays of power—not that that Graenta wanted to alert the other gods to his presence, anyway. Instead, his face and form shimmered and shifted. From his original form as a young boy with glasses, he changed into a taller, older man who bore a strong resemblance to Harlan.

The ferryman gasped. "Papa?" he whispered.

Graenta then cycled through more faces. A middle-aged woman, joy radiating from her. A younger version of Harlan, his features softened in a rounded, feminine face.

Harlan's eyes were so wide I feared they would fall out of his head. With each passing visage, his eyes grew mistier and I could feel his sadness and longing, they were so intense.

Graenta shifted into a final likeness, that of a beautiful young woman no more than twenty, her long brown hair braided in a crown circling her head. Her bright red lips curved back in a gentle smile, a pleasing contrast to her pale face.

Harlan let out a choked gasp and reached a hand towards the young woman. "Ranah? Have you returned to me after all these years?"

Graenta-as-Ranah didn't speak, just continued to smile at Harlan.

"My love," the ferryman whispered. "After all this time ..."

He reached out to Ranah, who grabbed his hand and held it to her cheek.

"I know it's not you, and yet it is," he said in wonder. Then, with a loud sob, he began to weep and buried his face in his hands.

"Are you able to bring the dead back to life?" he sobbed. "If you can't, then please—make it stop."

Ranah melted into the smaller form of Graenta, who studied the ferryman with pity. "Not even a god can bring back the dead. Once a soul enters the beyond, it is hard to call them back to the mortal world. But I was able to give you a brief visit from those that remember you."

Harlan wiped at his eyes and straightened. "You let me see my beloved Ranah once again, and I know she is well, wherever she is. And for that, I thank you. My sword and my service, however paltry they may be, are yours to command, my lord."

"Good." Graenta smiled with satisfaction, somehow looking regal and wise despite his youthful appearance. "Then let's go reclaim my country."

41

CHAPTER FORTY-ONE

BUT BEFORE WE COULD do that, we needed to hear Harlan's tale.

After the gods—for that was surely who the five people Harlan had seen were, minus Calianna, still unconscious on Zaela Island—had left the ferryman's house they had gone to Graenir's capital city. Harlan, curious, had followed at a discreet distance. Fortunately, they hadn't noticed his presence. Or perhaps they were too intent on their mission to focus on anything else.

The city gate had yet to open for the day. The group of gods had easily broken though and injured or killed the guards who had tried to stop them. They had descended upon the palace, confirming what Joichan had told us, but as to the exact events that had transpired inside, Harlan did not know. He had stayed hidden in one of the city's dark alleys.

"I think we can guess," Oran said grimly, and Harlan nodded.

"I fear for the safety of our dear queen," the ferryman said. "Once the people—the gods—entered the palace, the windows and doors magically sealed shut. The guards on the grounds were thrown forward, as if an unseen giant hand had swiped them aside. Screams and cries came from inside, but I didn't see anyone leave.

"And then, all of a sudden, the earth shook and huge vines burst from the ground. They covered the palace entirely, and any person unlucky enough to be standing near them was impaled on the sharp thorns that covered each vine. There were people in the streets who had come out to see what the commotion at the castle was, and they began to run away, screaming."

Harlan hung his head. "I'm ashamed to say, I did too. Seeing those men dangling helplessly in the air, all the noise and the yelling—I just turned and fled. As fast as these old legs could go. Through the city gate and down the road and all the way back to my little cottage, where I locked myself inside and hung up those window coverings and prayed to whatever gods who were still around and sympathetic."

"Don't be ashamed, Harlan." I gave the man a side hug, careful not to jostle the arm holding the candle. "Any sensible person would have done the same thing. There was nothing you could have done—and you might have been in worse trouble if you had stayed in the capital."

The grizzled ferryman patted my arm and smiled at me. "Thank you, Guardian Idessa. Now that you're back, I know Graenir will be all right."

I smiled back, but cringed inwardly. While I was touched by his confidence in me, it also frightened me. He and Graenta believed I was integral to Graenir's future, somehow, whereas I felt like I could barely make sense of the events of the last few days. And apparently the others believed in me, too, or they wouldn't have returned to Graenir with me.

I never would have thought Calianna was the merciful one. Graenta's thought sounded clearly in my head. *She just chose to enslave the Calians, instead of slaughtering them. Our poor people.*

"What now?" Lord Rhyss asked.

"I need to get going," Joichan said. "Now that everyone's here safely, I need to get to Shonn to see if I can find the Veil Between the Worlds."

"And then what?" Lord Rhyss pushed. "Do we break into the castle and try to save Queen Yllulae? Stay here in this cottage and hide?"

"That decision belongs to Graenta," Queen Jennica said.

"No," the god countered. "It has been a long time since I've walked this land. The one who really should be guiding us is Guardian Idessa."

Every head turned to look at me.

I swallowed. What should I say? I was no strategist.

"I think—" My voice squeaked. I cleared my throat and tried again, hoping I sounded more confident. "I mean, I *know* we should rescue Queen Ylullae. But not yet, not as we are."

I snuck a quick peek around the room at the expectant faces. No one looked bored or annoyed with me. Instead their faces were open and interested in whatever I might say. Encouraged, I took a deep breath and continued.

"Ambassador Joichan, when you visit the Fae, assuming they agree to help us, please see if they can send a troop of fairies right away. I know the Veil Between the Worlds is the easiest to travel through near Shonn, but the Fae have reach in all of the Gifted Lands. So, presumably, they could get to Graenir the fastest of all our allies."

Joichan nodded. "Where should I tell this group to go?"

"Graenir's capital, in the trees just outside the city. The rest of us will gather there as well, with whomever we can muster from the countryside. And the city." I paused. "If we can get to them, and if there's anyone left."

A grim silence descended over us.

"I will go, then," Joichan said, breaking the silence.

"Be safe, Father," Queen Jennica said, giving Joichan a brief hug. "And good luck."

Harlan cupped a hand around the candle flame, covering its light as best he could, as Joichan opened the cottage door and slipped out into the night.

A moment later, the candle's light flickered and the cottage rocked slightly as a large *whoosh* passed by. I resisted the temptation to lift the window tapestry to watch Joichan in his majestic golden dragon form fly away in the moonlight.

"All right, then," I said. "While the ambassador is in Faerie, Oran and I can go to our respective villages and see if we can rally support."

"What should we do, then?" King Beyan asked. Queen Jennica gave me a proud smile.

"If I may," said Oran. I nodded at him to continue. "I think if you come with us, it will give credence to our words as we tell everyone what happened."

"That's a good idea," Lord Rhyss said. "Jennica, why don't you go with Guardian Idessa, and Beyan and I can accompany Oran."

"What should I do, Guardian Idessa?" Graenta turned to me, eyes twinkling. I wondered if anyone else caught the faint emphasis he put on my title.

"Are you able to sneak into the palace and see what's going on?" I asked. "Or will the other gods be alerted to your presence?"

"It will be tricky, but I'll do what I can," Graenta vowed.

"Thank you. Even a little bit of information is better than none. Please be careful."

"Of course." The god grinned. "I can't abandon my favorite Guardian."

I rolled my eyes. "Last I checked, I was the only Guardian you have right now."

"Doesn't mean you're not my favorite. Just don't tell anyone."

I giggled, feeling strangely lighthearted despite the serious situation.

"I will accompany you, Your Grace, if that's all right," Harlan said to Graenta. "These old bones can't sneak into any palaces, but I can at least poke around in the city, see if anyone's still there."

"That's very brave of you," Graenta told him. "I will do my best to safeguard you."

With our plans in place, we headed out into the night.

42

—·—

CHAPTER FORTY-TWO

QUEEN JENNICA AND I watched Harlan ride off under the moonlight, headed towards Graenir's capital city on a horse that was actually a transformed Graenta.

"I hope he'll be all right," I commented. "Graenta mentioned that it's harder for him to become larger rather than smaller. That's why he often presents as a little boy."

"Fortunately, it shouldn't be too long before they reach the city," the queen said. "Hopefully the ride won't expend too much of Graenta's energy."

"Such a handy skill, that." I didn't bother to hide my envy. "I bet it would be amazing to be able to change into different creatures."

"It can be useful." I could hear the queen's amusement. "Trying to master it can be tricky, though. And I can only turn into one thing. Being able to transform into many animals would be something."

I chuckled. "I don't know, Your Majesty. Most people would consider turning into a dragon definitely *something*."

Queen Jennica laughed as we headed off in the opposite direction, towards my home village. King Beyan, Lord Rhyss, and Oran had already left for Oran's home, promising to spread the word in his hometown and further. That left Queen Jennica and me to visit my village and the other homes and farms between that and the capital. We had decided to meet in the woods just outside the city with whoever we could muster in a few days.

We'd still have to wait for help from Rothschan and Bomora to get here. There was no way reinforcements from either country could arrive sooner, even if they pushed themselves to their limit. But perhaps we'd have Fae assistance by then, and that, coupled with any information Graenta and Harlan could provide, would give us a better idea of what to do next.

Lord Rhyss had offered to stay with the queen and me, to serve as protection. But Queen Jennica—who, as a master mage and a dragon could more than hold her own in a fight—had insisted he go with Oran and the king.

"You've got more ground to cover, so it's good there's more of you," she had said. "Besides, it will be nice to have the chance to get to know our Guardian here a little better."

Now that I was alone with the intelligent and impressive monarch, I was a bit worried that she'd be not-so-secretly judging me.

"Do you think it will be easy to rally your people?" the queen asked me. She kept her voice low, even though we didn't need to worry about attracting any of the gods' attention. From the sound of things, they would be focused on whatever was happening inside the palace. And if Graenta wasn't careful while spying, then their attention would switch to him. Either way, they were too far away and too preoccupied to pay attention to two women walking around the countryside.

Even if one was a queen, the other the Guardian, and it was the middle of the night. Not suspicious at all.

Thinking of Harlan and Graenta's mission made me nervous. I took a deep breath, willing myself to not think about it.

"I hope so," I answered honestly. "We're a peaceful nation—we haven't been involved in a conflict for decades, maybe even centuries."

"You can thank Graenir's extreme isolationist policies for that," Queen Jennica said. "Calia didn't know anything about Graenir until Queen Yllulae kindly opened your kingdom to us a few years ago. Even then, there's still much to learn. And now, the other countries will be open to Graenir as well."

I sighed. "You mean, they'll be open because we'll be indebted to them after this."

"They're not just helping Graenir," Queen Jennica pointed out. "Stopping the gods will benefit all of the Gifted Lands. While we're grateful that they founded our respective kingdoms, there's a reason they faded into ancient history."

"I wish they had stayed there," I answered glumly.

"So do the rest of us." She fell silent, and I knew she was thinking of the chaos Calianna had created in Calia.

The silence stretched out between us. I coughed awkwardly. "Your Majesty, may I ask you a question?"

"You may."

"You mentioned, when Queen Yllulae contacted you, that you thought a disturbance near Annlyn was the cause of the wave that hit Zaela Island. I was wondering ... would you mind telling me more about it?"

"I'd be happy to, although there's not much more to say. I was trapped in Lake Vitrum, in my dragon form. The lake had been transformed into a large mirror, and I, along with the other shapeshifters of Annlyn, were caught inside it. When our friend Endri freed us, a huge blast of magic rippled through the mirror-lake and shattered it."

"Do you think this Endri's magic is what caused the Great Seal to break open?"

Queen Jennica was quick to correct me. "It wasn't Endri's magic, but a backlash from his breaking through the magic spell that imprisoned all of us. The one who cast the magic in the first place to hold us there was King Balor, the king of Faerie's Unseelie Court."

I frowned. The name and the titles didn't mean much to me, as I didn't know much about the Fae or the land of Faerie. Except that they were dangerous and charming, and both the place and its people should be avoided at all costs. Still ... "So it was this King who is ultimately responsible. Can we find him and make him reseal the gods' prison?"

"That might be a challenge." Even though her tone was grim, I could sense some satisfaction behind her words. "He was trapped in a mirror, the same as he tried to do to me and all of Annlyn. I believe he's still in there. And while I only know the basics of mirror magic, I do know that it's not easy to escape if you're inside. But if he does get out, and starts to cause trouble again ... well, let's just say, once I meet up with him, he'll know what *trouble* means."

I raised an eyebrow at her fierce words. Then realization dawned. During her conversation with Queen Ylullae, Queen Jennica had mentioned that she and her friend Farrah had traveled to Annlyn to investigate some disturbing magic.

This situation—the imprisonment in Lake Vitrum, and its transformation into a mirror—was probably what she had been referring to, with the end result that her friend Farrah had been struck unconscious by some magical ailment.

No wonder Queen Jennica sounded so angry when mentioning King Balor. The man was lucky he was stuck in a mirror. The queen of Calia would show him little mercy when—if—he ever got out.

Our conversation turned to lighter topics, with the queen asking questions about what general life and culture was like in Graenir. In turn, she was happy to answer my questions about Calia, and even the other kingdoms in the Gifted Lands. She was quite well-traveled, and offered great insights into what the other countries were like.

But the late hour was weighing on me. My steps felt heavy, and I could barely keep my eyes open. So I was relieved when I recognized my family's house in the distance.

"We're here, Your Majesty," I said, quickening my pace. "Even though it's late, I know my family will be happy to see us."

As we approached the front door, I dug into my pocket for my house key. Slipping it into the lock, I whispered to Queen Jennica, "You can have my room tonight, and I'll sleep in the front."

The key turned with a soft click. I pushed open the door and walked inside, still whispering, "We can explain everything to my family in the morning—"

A hand shot out and grabbed my arm, pinning it behind my back. I yelped, then stilled as a sharp blade touched my throat.

A menacing low voice spoke. "Don't move."

43

—— · ——

CHAPTER FORTY-THREE

WITH THAT KNIFE AT my throat, I'm certainly not going to, I thought.

The harsh whisper spoke again, this time to Queen Jennica, who stood in the doorway, framed by moonlight. "And you. Don't try anything funny, if you value the life of your friend, here."

My sluggish mind finally recognized the voice. "Mother?" I managed to squeak out.

"What?" The person holding me spoke in a more normal tone, releasing my arm and lowering the knife. I stepped away and turned around.

"*Illumine,*" Queen Jennica said, and a cold ball of light flared over our heads.

I squinted in the sudden light. The person who now held the knife uncertainly at her side was definitely my mother. "Mother, what in the Gifted Lands?"

"Sorry about that," Mother said sheepishly. "But it *is* late, and I didn't know you'd be coming home."

"Apparently," I laughed. I gently took the knife out of her unresisting hand and put it down on a nearby table. Now that she was safely unarmed, I gave her a big hug. "We were hoping to sneak in and explain ourselves in the morning, but I guess that plan failed. Does Father know you're awake and waiting at the door to greet strangers this way?"

Mother hugged me back, but when I mentioned Father, a small sob escaped her. "I was hoping he'd be back by now. I've been waiting all night for him to return. But when I saw two people at the door, I thought you were robbers, or worse."

I frowned. "Father's not here? Where is he? What about Lis?"

"That's just it. You've heard what's happened at the capital?" When I nodded, she sighed. "Alistair was in the city, at the Archives, when the trouble started. We waited for him to come home, but he never did. Finally, your father decided to go to the capital to see if he could find your brother. But it's been hours, and neither of them have come back."

Tears spilled down Mother's cheeks. I put an arm around her shoulders and guided her to a chair. "Sit."

My mother obeyed, sniffling. "We saw people pass by. So many people. All looking haunted and afraid. We stopped one of them to ask where they were all going. That's how we heard about what happened at the palace. If your brother doesn't come back—or your father—I don't know what I'll do—" She broke down, sobbing harder.

A small square of white linen appeared in front of my face. "Don't worry, it's clean," Queen Jennica said, waving the handkerchief at me.

"Thank you." I took it and handed it to Mother, who patted at her face.

"Thank you," she echoed, looking up at our visitor. "And forgive me for my rudeness. Welcome to our home. Please, make yourself comfortable." She waved at an empty chair.

"I understand completely," Queen Jennica said graciously as she sat down. "You've got a lot to worry about right now."

"Still, that's no excuse."

"Mother." I placed a careful hand on her shoulder. "I'd like you to meet Queen Jennica of Calia."

Mother gasped and tried to get up, but I firmly kept her in her seat. "Idessa! Why didn't you tell me right away? Forgive me, Your Majesty. Let me—"

"No, Mother, let *me*," I said. "I'll take care of any hospitality for our guest."

"But—"

The queen let out a big yawn. "Oh, my. Now I must ask you to forgive *me*. I'm afraid the only hospitality I would like right now is sleep."

"Oh, of course, Your Majesty," my mother said. "I'll—"

"*I'll* show the queen to my room," I said. "You should go to bed and get some rest."

"But what about your father? Alistair?"

"I plan on sleeping in here." I waved a hand, indicating the room we were currently in. "I'll stay up as long as I can and keep an eye out for them. All right?"

It wasn't, but she didn't argue with me. Instead, she said, "You could take your brother's room while the queen occupies yours."

I shook my head. "No, I would prefer to be by the door so I can know the moment Father and Lis get back." I turned to Queen Jennica. "If you'll follow me, Your Majesty."

Mother stayed in her seat, watching as I took care of our guest and then prepared the front room for myself. She allowed me to help her up and escort her to her bedroom.

At the door, she patted my hand. "My Idessa. You've changed."

I chuckled. "I haven't, although I'd like to. These clothes stink from travel."

Mother smiled. "I didn't mean that, silly. I mean you're different, somehow. More grown up."

I shrugged, feeling a little uncomfortable. "I'm just doing what I have to do."

She kissed me on the forehead. "That's a part of it, my darling. Maturity suits you." She opened her bedroom door and slipped inside.

As I walked back to my makeshift bed in the main room and settled in for the night, I thought about what my mother had said. Had I really grown that much, in such a short time?

That's silly, I thought as sleep came to claim me. *Like I told her, I'm just doing what I have to do.*

And as I pondered the true meaning of maturity, I fell asleep.

I awoke to the sound of the front door opening, followed by the sound of careful footsteps trying to be quiet.

The room was mostly dark, with only a faint sliver of moonlight to see by. I grabbed my pillow. Not the best weapon, but the only thing I could think to use on quick notice.

As the intruder came closer, I jumped up and brandished the pillow in front of me. The pillow made contact, and I heard a muffled, "Oof!"

Something small and metal clattered to the floor.

"Stop where you are!" I hissed. "Move one more step, and I'll scream and wake the house."

"Idessa?"

I dropped the pillow and peered at the stranger. "Father?"

"You pack a mean punch with that thing." My father rubbed at his cheek.

"Sorry about that." I dropped to my knees and felt around on the floor. My left hand brushed across the little metal object Father had dropped. I picked up the key and stood, handing it to him. "Here you go."

Father pulled me into a hug. "I didn't expect to see you home already, but I'm glad you're here. And that you're safe."

I looked over his shoulder. "Is Lis with you?"

"No. I couldn't find him. The city's deserted, except for the dead. I went to the Archives, but he wasn't there, and there was no one there who could help me." Father's voice shook. "Part of it was destroyed."

I gasped. Tears sprang to my eyes. "Do you—do you think he's ...?" I couldn't bring myself to finish the thought.

"Until I see it with my own eyes, I refuse to believe Alistair is dead," Father said firmly.

I sniffled, nodding. "You're right."

Father yawned, weariness etched plainly on his face. "Well, it's late. Perhaps we can think more clearly after some sleep."

He frowned as he saw my makeshift bed in the moonlight. "Speaking of which, why are you out here?"

"There's a queen in my bed. I'll explain later. Get some sleep."

He blinked as he thought better of questioning me. "Of course. Goodnight, Idessa."

"Goodnight, Father."

As my father shuffled down the hallway, I settled down for the second time that night.

Even though I was exhausted, sleep eluded me this time. Instead, I lay awake in the dark as I stared up at the ceiling, wondering where my brother was.

And if he was still alive.

44

CHAPTER FORTY-FOUR

"I'D LIKE TO SEE these Archives for myself. Perhaps I can use my magic to see if your son left any traces that can be followed."

"Oh, Your Majesty, do you think you could? If you could find him, we'd be ever so grateful."

Mother's eyes kindled as she regarded Queen Jennica. The Calian leader gave her a gentle smile.

"I can't promise anything," the queen warned.

"But it's better than nothing," Mother said, refusing to let go of this slim thread of hope.

My father squeezed Mother's hand. Turning to me, he said, "But first, you have a job to do. How about us? What can we do?"

"If you can talk to our nearby neighbors, that will save us some time," I said. "And then I want you and Mother to pack a few things and leave. Get out of Graenir. I don't think it will be safe here for a while."

Father paused, and I could tell he was considering my words. But to my surprise, it was my mother who spoke up.

"No. Graenir is our home, and it is our kingdom, our queen, and our loved ones who are in danger. We will stay and fight, or if we cannot fight, then we will help in any way we can."

Father raised an eyebrow at Mother's fierce tone. Then he smiled. "She's right. Besides, we couldn't leave unless we knew you and Alistair were safe."

Impulsively, I threw my arms around first my father, then my mother. "I love you both."

Mother gave me an extra squeeze before releasing me. "We love you too, honey. Now get going. You have a busy day ahead of you."

I chuckled. "So do you."

My parents waved as Queen Jennica and I set off down the road. The last thing I saw before I turned away was Father putting his arm around Mother, and her leaning into him. I smiled to myself, blinking back the sudden tears that filled my eyes. My bookish, aloof father tended to ignore his children, and only gave the barest of attention to his wife. While I was still worried about my brother, I was glad this crisis was bringing my parents closer together, something long overdue.

"Your parents are lovely people," Queen Jennica said. "And very steady. They're handling all of this surprisingly well."

"That's an understatement." I giggled. "I'm surprised we got out of the house at all."

This morning, my poor father had nearly fallen over when he realized we were hosting a queen. Meanwhile, my mother had gone into a hospitality frenzy, cooking up everything in the kitchen and apologizing to Queen Jennica repeatedly over the humble surroundings, food, and service.

Even though there were four of us, there was still way too much food left over. I had suggested taking the extras to the neighbors, as an excuse to visit.

Hopefully our neighbors are still there, I thought. It hadn't occurred to me until now, but there was a good chance most of the people in the area would have fled already.

My fears proved true. Several of the homesteads we stopped at were empty, abandoned by their owners in an obvious haste. Others refused to open their doors to us, even though I knew they recognized me as both their neighbor and the kingdom's Guardian.

The sun set on our first day of canvassing the area, and we returned home, discouraged. From the similar looks my parents wore, I knew they didn't have much luck either.

"Has everyone left, then?" I asked them over dinner.

"Some did," my mother confirmed. "Others were in the process of leaving when we stopped by."

"How about you?" Father asked. He nodded at Queen Jennica. "Surely with such a personage in their presence, those who stayed would at least listen."

The queen snorted. "They can't listen if they won't talk to us in the first place. I hardly think my status means anything here, let alone sways them."

"Perhaps tomorrow will go better," Mother said.

But the second day was even more dismal than the first. More empty homes, the remaining places shut tight against us.

"They're just scared." Queen Jennica tried to comfort me. "Especially for a country that has rarely seen conflict."

"But if no one will stay and fight, then there won't be a kingdom to come back to." I kicked a pebble down the road in frustration.

The pebble skittered away, getting lost in a cloud of dust that was rising from the road. The queen and I exchanged worried looks, unsure if we should stay on the road and greet whoever was coming, or look for a place to hide.

A group of travelers came around the bend, heading towards us. Worried parents herding their crying young children. Men and women of various ages, carrying bags or hauling small carts. An elderly couple who could barely carry their belongings as they tottered down the road.

I stopped one of the travelers, a middle-aged man with a small leather pack on his back.

"Has something happened?" I asked. "Where is everyone going?"

The man squinted at me, trying to place my face. His eyes grew wide as he recognized me. "You're the current Guardian, aren't you?" he said. "Guardian ... uh ..."

"Idessa," I supplied. "And yes. Although there's not much to guard these days." I waved a hand at the group. "But why is everyone leaving?"

The man looked at me like I was crazy. "Haven't you been by the capital?"

"I know the castle has been taken over, but—"

"The whole city has fallen. The castle is overrun, with that ghastly ring of vines around it. The queen is a prisoner. We're leaving while we still can."

I hope Graenta and Harlan are all right. We hadn't heard from them yet, but that didn't necessarily mean anything, since we had agreed to meet up in the forest three days after we had parted. Which would be tomorrow. But still ...

The man started to move away. My hand shot out and grabbed his wrist.

"Wait," I said. "Please don't go. We need to take back the city. Save Queen Yllulae. We have allies—Rothschan and Bomora are on their way. We've sent a messenger to Faerie. Please, stay. We need every person we can get."

The man gaped at me. A few of the other travelers had stopped and turned to watch our exchange. "Bomora? Rothschan? Where are they now, when we need them? It will take them a week, at least, to get here. And the Fae are fickle, if they even exist at all. By the time any of them arrive, perhaps those vines will have taken over the city. Or other horrors may be unleashed."

The man's companions murmured their agreement and started walking again.

"No! They're coming to help us, I swear. We need to defend our home." How could I convince him—or any of them—to stay, to hold on, until help arrived?

The man shook his head. "I'm not waiting around to die." He shook my hand off. "And if you're smart, you won't wait, either."

"If you change your mind, meet us tomorrow morning, in the glade off the main road about an hour's walk from the capital."

The man gave me a look. *Change my mind? Not likely.* Muttering to himself, he hurried down the road after the other travelers.

Queen Jennica placed a comforting hand on my shoulder. "Not everyone will run away, I promise."

I wiped away tears I hadn't even realized were falling until that moment. "I didn't realize the people of Graenir were such cowards."

"Not cowards," the queen said, showing much more grace towards my countrymen than I could have. "It's unknown, and it's scary."

Sniffling, I tried to lighten the mood. "I'm sorry. I completely forgot to introduce you. That might have swayed them."

"Maybe. But probably not." She shaded her eyes, peering down the road. "They'll be okay."

I wasn't surprised that the perceptive Calian queen had read my mind. "Do you really think so?"

"No," she said, startling me with her honesty. "But I have to believe it. Just as I have to have hope that we will, eventually, win the day. Otherwise, we'll have lost before we've even begun."

"You helped your little human get away, but you won't be so lucky."

Fear and worry weighed me down, but I fought against it. I had to keep my head clear, save my strength. Could I also escape?

I edged towards the window, but dark magic shot out and hit me square in the chest. Suddenly, I couldn't move.

"Come, little god. There's someone here who would *love* some company...."

More magic engulfed me, breaking through my mental walls to siphon away my power. Convulsing, I screamed.

I woke up with a gasp, my heart pounding and sweat pouring down my face. The scream had been so loud—at least, that's how it had seemed to me—I was sure it had woken the others up. But as I sat there, trying to get my erratic breathing under control, no one came to see what was happening.

The scream had only been in my head.

But it had been so real.

Graenta.

It was just an errant thought. I wasn't trying to commune with him or anything. Although he had spoken to me mind-to-mind before, I had never tried reaching out to him.

Could I?

I stilled and concentrated.

Graenta.

And then a faint voice responded.

... Dess ...

Graenta? Graenta!

But the small internal voice didn't speak again.

Unsettled, I tried to fall back asleep. But my mind kept racing.

Had I been dreaming about Graenta? And could I reach him?

But although I kept calling out to him, I did not hear Graenta's voice again.

45

CHAPTER FORTY-FIVE

IN THE GRAY LIGHT of approaching dawn, I embraced my parents, kissing them goodbye.

"Are you sure you won't leave?" I asked, hating myself for suggesting the coward's way for them, but wanting them to stay safe.

"Yes," Mother said firmly. "We will find ways to be useful."

"This is our home," Father added. "If those gods want Graenir, they will have to drive us out. We won't go willingly."

Or they could just kill you, I thought, swallowing the sudden lump in my throat. Looking at my smiling parents, I had a horrible, unwanted vision of them lying pale and still, eyes closed, in the unrelenting clutches of death. I shook my head, willing the vision away. I pasted a smile on my face.

"I love you both," I said, fighting back tears. "Please, please stay safe."

"We will," Mother promised. "And you both as well."

Queen Jennica and I started down the road towards Graenir's capital. Right before the house would have disappeared from view, we turned and raised our hands in farewell. My parents waved back, then went back into the house. Queen Jennica, her hand still raised, muttered something I couldn't quite hear and pointed at the house, waving her hand in the air. The hairs on the back of my neck prickled, the feeling similar to when a strong storm was in the area.

The queen of Calia turned away and started walking. I hurried to catch up with her. "What did you do?" I asked, curious.

"A small bit of protection, just something simple. If anyone comes by who is seeking to do the house or its inhabitants harm, they will get confused and forget their original purpose. It should last for an hour or so, enough for them to wander away and leave your family in peace. It won't work on a powerful mage, but for weaker magicians or those who don't use magic, it should do the trick."

"Really?" I looked over my shoulder, even though my family's home was now gone from view. "Thank you."

"Of course. It's not much, really. And it will only last for a few days." The queen sighed. "But I hope, even though it's a minor measure, it will be enough."

"I'm sure it will be," I said. "Again, thank you."

We continued the rest of the way in silence.

The sun had risen by the time we reached the meeting point, a small clearing inside the woods.

I sat down on a fallen log, looking around as I rested. "I hope the others get here soon." *And I hope they had better luck than we did.*

Twigs cracking and leaves crunching underfoot made me look up. Oran led King Beyan and Lord Rhyss towards the spot where Queen Jennica and I waited. The king, seeing his wife, quickened his pace. She smiled and went to him.

I glanced over Oran's shoulder. "It's just the three of you?" But even as I asked the question, I already knew the answer.

Oran nodded, looking discouraged. "We tried, we really did, but—"

"No one—at least, the people who were still around—wanted to fight," Lord Rhyss finished. "They would rather hide in their homes and hope the problem goes away."

"We had the same issue," Queen Jennica said, as she and her husband joined us, holding hands. She relayed what the traveler had told us about the capital, ending with, "It looks like we're on our own until Bomora and Rothschan can get here. And hopefully Faerie's Seelie Court comes through as well."

From the sour look on Lord Rhyss's face, he didn't think we could count on the Fae, but he refrained from saying so out loud.

I took a deep breath. "I guess it's just the five of us, then. Well, seven, once Graenta and Harlan get here. So, I suppose we—"

A twig snapped a few feet away, causing all our heads to swivel to see the source of the sound.

A young woman of maybe twenty stepped into the forest glade. "Pardon me," she said in a soft voice. "I'm looking for—oh!" She stopped when she recognized the men, dropping into a quick curtsey. "Your Majesty, Your Grace."

Lord Rhyss smirked, giving a little chuckle at her words. "I still can't get used to having a title."

King Beyan elbowed him, somehow making the gesture familiar and regal at the same time. "Hush, *Your Grace*." He turned to the young woman. "I remember you. Your father said he was sending you away, while he was going to stay behind and guard your house. What is your name?"

The woman nodded. "My name is Thea. And he did. Send me away, that is. But I decided to come here instead."

She looked around at all of us, her hands open in supplication. "I want to help. I'll fight, or cook, or whatever is needed. Graenir is my home. I can't turn my back on it."

Queen Jennica gave me a triumphant look, as if to say, *See? There are still brave people in your kingdom.*

I gave her a weak smile in return. I was glad her hope hadn't been misplaced, even if I still wasn't as sure as she was.

"Your courage commends you," the king said. "For now, just rest and wait here. We have yet to—"

We could hear more snapping twigs and leaves crunching. My eyes widened in surprise as five new people joined us.

"I think this is the place," the leader was saying. "I hope they're still—oh! Hello."

I gaped at the person who stood before me. "You're the man from the road!"

"I am. Hello again."

"What are you doing here?" I couldn't keep the suspicion from my voice.

The man had the grace to look sheepish. "I thought about what you said, as I was walking away. You're right, Graenir is our home. If we won't help it, who will?"

Our eyes locked and held for a long moment. Then, I stuck out my hand. "Well met, uh ...?"

"Dayviar." He grasped my hand, giving it a firm shake, then introduced me to the others. Eliyana and August, two people from the group of neighbors Dayviar had been traveling with. Kanyan and Halle, I didn't recognize. They must have randomly met up with Dayviar, Eliyana, and August on the road.

I introduced them to Oran—Kanyan and Halle already knew him—and the Calians. Dayviar's eyes widened when he realized that he had been in the presence of a queen earlier. "F-forgive my earlier rudeness," he stammered, bowing over Queen Jennica's hand. "Had I kn-known who you were—"

"It's all right," she said. gently extracting her hand. "You couldn't have known." She gave me a pointed look, but the amusement playing around her lips told me she wasn't upset with me.

"I would have gotten around to introducing you," I said. "Eventually."

The queen shook in silent laughter. "Come," she said to Dayviar. "We have much to discuss."

"I'll be right back," I told the queen. She nodded in acknowledgement.

I moved away from the clearing, towards the road. It was now well past the time when Graenta and Harlan should have joined us, and I was worried for their safety.

Standing in the middle of the road, I shaded my eyes and looked around. All I could hear was the occasional bird song and my breathing. Nothing moved, except for me, turning left and right. The sun beat down, promising a hot day ahead.

I sighed and started walking. I planned on walking a little further down the road, towards the capital, hoping I would see my friends. If not, perhaps I could see what was happening at the city.

I hadn't gone very far when I heard a faint groan coming from the side of the road. Curious but cautious, I crept over to spy on the source of the noise.

My hand flew to my mouth as my feet came to an abrupt stop.

Lying on the ground was Harlan.

46

CHAPTER FORTY-SIX

HIS FACE, COVERED IN scratches and dried blood, was red and peeling from sunburn. Dark red cuts scored his uncovered arms. Flies flitted around the poor man, and I had to fight off the urge to throw up as the strong smell of dried urine and baked sweat hit me.

I held my sleeve up to my nose, breathing shallowly through the fabric. Kneeling down next to the ferryman, I shook him gently. "Harlan? Harlan, it's Idessa. Can you hear me?"

Another groan escaped his lips, ending in a cough. His eyelids fluttered open, his eyes darting around until finally fixing on my face. "I-Idessa?"

"Thank—" I stopped myself before finishing, *the gods*. In light of our current situation, it seemed wrong to be thanking them. "I'm so glad you're alive, Harlan. Can you sit up?"

Feebly, Harlan tried to push himself up. I put an arm around him to help, turning my head to the side when the smell got unbearable. I tried to be subtle about my discomfort, but worried I was failing; I could tell Harlan was already embarrassed at his condition, and I didn't want to call more attention to it than was necessary.

Harlan sat upright, breathing heavily. Even just that little bit of exertion was hard on him. I examined him as best as I could. I was no healer, but it didn't look like he had any fresh wounds. Hopefully whatever cuts he had wouldn't become infected. From the sight—and smell—of him, he had been lying here for a while, and probably hadn't been able to tend to his wounds properly.

Once his breathing became more even, I asked, "Can you stand?"

Harlan grunted uncertainly.

"The others are in the clearing just down the road," I said. "They'll be able to help you more than I can. Take your time. I'll help you."

With my assistance, Harlan got to his feet. After a brief pause to allow him to gather strength, we made our slow way along the road, towards the glade.

We had taken only about fifty steps when Harlan's knees buckled underneath him. Quickly, I tightened my arms around him, barely able to support his weight. I had a fleeting fear that we would both fall. And if we did, I doubted I would be able to get Harlan on his feet again.

By some miracle, I steadied him and we continued walking.

Sweat rolled down my forehead, but I couldn't spare a hand to wipe it away. All of my energy was directed at helping Harlan walk.

And that energy was flagging fast.

As we approached the area where I had exited the trees earlier, I saw Oran standing on the side of the road.

"Oran!" I called out.

He turned, and when he saw us, he hurried over.

"Oh, my," he said. "Here, let me help."

He went to Harlan's free side and slipped an arm around the ferryman's waist, relieving me of some of Harlan's weight. Together, Oran and I half-helped, half-maneuvered Harlan into the clearing. The various conversations faded as the rest of the group got a good look at the three of us.

King Beyan and Lord Rhyss sprang into action, spreading their cloaks on the ground by the fallen log to create a soft place for Harlan to rest. Meanwhile, Queen Jennica sent Thea and Eliyana into the forest to gather some healing herbs.

"Yarrow would be best, if you can find it," the queen instructed. "You'll know it by its small white flowers. Also, it would be good if you could fill up some waterskins with clean, fresh water."

"I can get the water," Thea said. "I know this area well."

"I'll look for the plants, then," said Eliyana, and the two left the clearing.

Oran and I eased Harlan to the ground, settling him so the log supported his back.

Queen Jennica knelt next to Harlan, offering him her waterskin. "Drink," she commanded.

Harlan gratefully complied. Taking the water skin, he drank deeply, tipping his head back until there was nothing left.

"Sorry about that," he croaked, handing the empty waterskin back to the queen.

"I think there's some water left in mine," Oran volunteered. "I'll go get it." He stood up and walked over to a nearby tree, where a canvas pack lay propped against the trunk.

Queen Jennica started examining Harlan's half-healed wounds. Feeling useless, I asked, "Is there anything I can do to help?"

The queen paused. "If you want to gather yarrow or refill my waterskin, you can."

I shook my head. "I don't really know this area that well. I wouldn't want to get lost."

"Why don't you rest a bit, then? If I need anything, I'll let you know."

As the queen continued her ministrations, I stood and wandered away. King Beyan and Lord Rhyss were deep in a quiet conversation. Dayviar and August were in a discussion of their own, while Kanyan instructed Halle on basic fighting moves.

I frowned as I glanced back at Harlan. Although he looked a little better, he wasn't strong enough to leave the glade, much less fight if need be. And while I didn't want to distress him further, I was bursting with questions.

Most notably, where was Graenta?

Oran approached me. "If you could see your face right now ..."

I chuckled. "That bad, huh?"

He smiled. "Lovely, as always. But whatever you're thinking about, it must be heavy."

"It is. I didn't have a chance to ask Harlan how he came to be on the side of that road, or how long he'd been there. And why Graenta's not with him."

"It's worrying, to be sure."

A wheezy chuckle interrupted our conversation. Harlan, sounding much more like his usual hearty self, called out to us. "Hey, you two! Get over here."

Oran and I exchanged curious looks, then walked over to where Harlan sat.

The ferryman grinned at us, heedless of his sunburned skin cracking. "I know you two were talking about me."

"Oh! We weren't—I mean, we were, but nothing bad—" I tried to explain.

Harlan laughed and patted the log behind him. "Sit, you two, sit."

"You really should rest," I protested.

"There will be time for that later," the ferryman said, serious now. "We have a lot to talk about."

47

CHAPTER FORTY-SEVEN

IT WAS STILL DARK by the time Harlan and Graenta had reached the capital, although dawn was not far off. The pair made their careful and quiet way through the wide-open gates and into the city.

And stopped when they came across the first body.

Just inside the city wall, several fallen guards lay, their broken bodies a testament to their failed attempt to stop the invading group of gods. A quick search of the area did not turn up any survivors, just more fallen soldiers and an empty guard house.

The pair debated the wisdom of continuing further into the city, but the darkened streets, filled with mysterious shadows, made them nervous. And the late hour made them weary. So they decided to bed down in the empty guardhouse, taking turns keeping watch for the remainder of the night. Graenta refused to ward them, worried that using his powers would attract the other gods' attention.

When morning came, they were able to better assess the devastation in the city.

They had entered the capital unchallenged because there was no one left alive to challenge them. The streets were littered with the bodies of soldiers, as well as unfortunate citizens who had been caught outside during the initial invasion. Harlan's heart broke at seeing so many of his countrymen lying dead around the once fair city.

Shattered glass crunched under their feet as they walked, and they had to pick their way through splintered wood and broken brick. They tried to search a few of the buildings, but many of them were so damaged it would have been dangerous to go inside them.

As the day wore on, Graenta and Harlan realized that they weren't going to find anyone to join them against the gods. It looked like any survivors had fled, and with the city gates standing wide open, it didn't seem like the gods cared that they had no would-be subjects.

Ducking into an alley, the pair discussed the best course of action. The thorny mess of vines still covered the castle, the bodies of its victims warning others of a similar fate if they dared approach.

"Perhaps we should keep searching for survivors," Harlan said, his hopeful words sounding hollow even to his own ears.

"We could." Graenta sounded doubtful. "But I think our time would be better spent trying to get into the castle."

He's right, Harlan thought. *That's why we're here, after all. And who am I, to naysay a god?* He shuddered, recalling the magical hedge that had sprung up around the castle. *Still, those thorns look mighty sharp....*

The pair decided to spend the rest of the day resting where they were, hidden in the alley. When night fell, they emerged from their hiding spot and made their way to the castle.

Carefully, they circled the thorn-covered building in the moonlight, looking for a weakness or an opening in the vines. To their surprise, they got lucky. The moonlight revealed a small hole on the eastern wall of the castle, just large enough for Graenta and Harlan—if he hunched over—to pass through.

Harlan stared at the hedge, wondering why he could see the doorway so clearly. The light from the moon helped, but it was more than that. He rubbed his eyes. It looked like—

"Your Grace!" Harlan hissed. "The thorns—they're glowing!"

The god examined the thorns, being careful not to get too close. "Interesting. I wonder why. But it's quite helpful. Let's go." And the boy ducked through the entryway.

"Are we sure this is a good idea?" Harlan grumbled as he stooped down to follow Graenta.

"No," came Graneta's cheerful whisper. "But we have no other choice."

"Blasting our way in with magic would be easier." A dark lump of a shadow to his right caught Harlan's eye. Looking closer, he could make out the form of a soldier caught in the web of thorns, his sightless eyes forever in anguish. The ferryman shivered and quickly looked the other way.

"Then we may as well announce ourselves with a trumpet fanfare." The catch in Graenta's whisper let Harlan know he had also seen the dead man. "Like I said, we have no other choice."

Harlan fell silent, concentrating on following Graenta through the hedge maze. Although the castle itself was not far from the maze's entrance, the path to it wasn't straight. Harlan lost track of the turns they took, especially when they were forced to backtrack twice.

And he kept his eyes firmly on Graenta's back, not daring to look left or right. Seeing one poor soul impaled in the maze was enough for him. More of the same sight would make Harlan go insane.

After what felt like forever, the maze ended at a nondescript door set in the castle wall.

"A servants' entrance?" Harlan whispered.

Graenta frowned. "I think so?" He reached out a hand, but Harlan stepped in front of him, stopping Graenta before he could touch the door. The confusion on Graenta's face gave way to understanding, and then relief. He mouthed a silent "thank you" to Harlan, who nodded in return.

Taking a deep breath, Harlan touched the door's handle and gave it a slight twist. He expected it to resist. To his surprise, the door swung open soundlessly before him.

This is easy. Too easy.

He slipped through the doorway, Graenta behind him.

Inside, Harlan straightened, stretching his aching back. His old muscles screamed in protest. How had he gotten himself into this mess? He was too old for adventures. Best to leave this stuff to the young ones in their prime, the ones who had magic or swords. Or better yet, magic swords.

What I wouldn't give for a magic sword right now, Harlan thought as he followed Graenta again. *It was silly of me to come here without anything.* Not that he had any weapons stashed in his humble cottage.

And not that a magic sword would do much good against five powerful gods.

Harlan tamped down his less than cheerful thoughts. Gradually, he realized that, despite the fact that neither of them really knew their way around the palace, Graenta was walking sure and straight towards ... something.

Harlan whispered, "Where are we going?"

Graenta paused, turning wide, troubled eyes on his companion. "I don't really know. I just ... *know* ... where they are."

Like calls to like, Harlan thought. Graenta must have been drawn to his fellow gods because of their shared background.

Or was he enthralled for some other reason?

The pair moved through the hallways slowly, staying close to the shadows. It was easy—the faint moonlight that came through the various windows barely lit the darkened corridors. The unlit torches lining the walls stood as cold, small sentinels, silent witnesses to the tragedy that had so recently hit the palace.

At least they cleaned up after they ... well, after, Harlan thought. They passed a particularly dark spot with the strong metallic scent of dried blood.

Harlan fought the bile that suddenly rose up in his throat. *Oh, my. Okay, they* kind of *cleaned up.*

Up ahead, a door to some unknown room stood slightly open. Graenta paused just outside the room, trying to peer inside. Behind him, Harlan held his breath, straining to listen for any voices or other sounds.

But all was quiet.

Graenta put out a hand to open the door wider.

Harlan put a hand over Graenta's, a question in his eyes. *You want to go in? Are you sure this is wise?*

Graenta shook Harlan's hand off in annoyance. He nodded emphatically. *Yes. Come on.*

Graenta opened the door and slipped inside the room. Feeling apprehensive—although he had no idea why—Harlan followed.

They were in the castle's private chapel. Effigies of the gods of the Gifted Lands lined the walls, three on each side, each in its own individual recessed alcove. At the front of the room, in a place of honor, stood a statue of Graenta just behind a stone altar.

A skylight in the ceiling and two stained glass windows that framed the Graenta statue allowed moonlight to pour in, lighting the room more than the shadowed castle hallways.

The chapel looked to be one of the few places in Graenir that hadn't been affected by the gods' invasion. The city had been in shambles, and parts of the castle had shown signs of battle. But this place remained pristine, hushed and reverent.

And, except for Graenta and Harlan, empty of life.

Where are they? Harlan looked around, noting the stern faces of the stone statues that surrounded them. *Where are the other gods?*

Graenta's face mirrored Harlan's confusion. "I could have sworn ..." Harlan heard him mutter.

The young boy walked up to his statue, studying his likeness. He pushed his glasses up his nose, frowning. "Huh. Do I really look like that?"

A mocking laugh echoed around the room.

"No, my dear boy, you definitely do not, although at one point you did. Why you chose your current form is a mystery to us all. It was not something mere humans could have anticipated. They lack imagination, I'm afraid."

The speaker's laughter rang out again. Harlan and Graenta drew close together, trying to locate the source of the voice.

"Fortunately, we do not," the disembodied voice continued. "After all, we have had many, many years to dream up all sorts of things."

The statues lining the chapel's walls began to glow, eerily reminiscent of the thorns that had lined the hedge maze.

"Starting with, what we should do with those who have betrayed us."

48

CHAPTER FORTY-EIGHT

THE GLOWING STATUES GREW brighter, so bright Harlan thought a small sun had appeared in the middle of the chapel. He blinked, trying to clear the spots from his eyes.

When he could see clearly again, five people stood before him and Graenta.

Harlan stared at the newcomers. Each god, now in the flesh, bore a strong resemblance to their lifeless stone counterpart.

Against one wall, there stood Rothscha, founder of the military kingdom of Rothschan, resplendent in his famous red and gray, near-invincible armor. Gifted Lands legend held that the god's armor protected him from all physical attacks, unless the attack was bolstered by incredibly strong magic.

Next to Rothscha, the goddess Orchwen glanced this way and that. The founder of the Seeker kingdom of Orchwell was ever observant.

Not quite hidden behind them both was Bomor, trickster god and founder of the westernmost kingdom of Bomora. Despite the now well-lit room, Bomor favored the shadows, trying not to call attention to himself.

On the opposite wall, the goddess Shonnala regarded Harlan and Graenta with haughty disdain. The otherworldly beauty of the kingdom of Shonn's founder both unnerved and drew Harlan in. He tried to recall his Gifted Lands history as he stared at Shonnala. The continent's seven kingdoms had been founded centuries after the land of Faerie had been established, and it was quite possible that the beautiful goddess had Fae blood. He made a mental note to ask Graenta about her background later on.

Assuming, of course, that the pair survived.

Shonnala's hand was buried in the fur of a stocky black jaguar. The large feline regarded Harlan and Graenta with its round golden eyes. The ferryman shivered, eyeing the human-appearing statue of Annlynden, founder of the shapeshifter kingdom of Annlyn in the south. Whether in human or animal form, the shapeshifting god looked powerful and dangerous.

The jaguar yawned, revealing two rows of wickedly sharp teeth. Harlan shrank back against Graenta.

The only statue missing its living counterpart was that of the goddess Calianna. *Thank the gods for small favors*, Harlan thought, then smirked at the irony. He doubted he would be thanking these gods for anything.

Graenta stepped in front of Harlan. His small, slight form wasn't much of a shield for the grizzled ferryman.

Rothscha apparently thought so, too. His mocking laughter echoed around the chapel. "Do you really think you can best all of us, little man? How quaint."

Without warning, the god drew a dagger from his belt. He threw it at Graenta and Harlan.

Harlan tried to duck, dive to one side, anything—but found he was frozen in place. Meanwhile, Graenta yelled and threw up a hand. The dagger ricocheted off his hand, not leaving so much as a cut, and spun away. The knife flew past Rothscha, just missing him before embedding itself into the wall right next to the surprised god.

Rothscha turned and tried to pry the knife out, to no avail. With an annoyed frown, he turned to Shonnala. "My dear, if you wouldn't mind?"

The goddess smirked. "After all this time, you still can't admit that magic is more powerful than might?"

She snapped her fingers. The section of the wall around the stuck knife crumbled, allowing it to clatter to the floor. Rothscha bent down and retrieved the weapon, blowing the dust off before returning it to his belt.

"Let me show you how it's done," Shonnala said.

She began to weave a pattern with her hands. The air in the chapel grew heavy and thick. Harlan's chest tightened as he struggled to breathe.

"Stop it," Graenta said, angry. "Shonnala! This is between me and all of you. He's an innocent. Let him go!"

The goddess just laughed and continued her spell. Stars started to dance in front of the ferryman's eyes. The edges of his vision darkened.

"A smart strategy," Rothscha said. "I approve."

"I'm glad." Shonnala's voice dripped with sarcasm.

"Sometimes the indirect method is the optimal one," Bomor rasped behind Rothscha.

Graenta's small hand clamped around Harlan's arm. Warm healing energy flowed into the ferryman, partially blocking Shonnala's spell. Harlan's chest loosened somewhat. He swallowed in heaving gulps of air. The encroaching blackness receded.

Graenta released Harlan's arm and whispered, "Harlan, I'm sorry."

That was the only warning the ferryman had. A big gust of wind hit him in the chest, full blast. It pushed him backwards with such force that his body punched through one of the stained glass windows.

Harlan felt himself falling through the air. Time seemed to slow as he flailed about, trying to find something to grab to cushion his fall, but of course not finding anything. Despite knowing that death was imminent, all Harlan could think about was the beautiful window he had crashed through. Shame that his final act was to destroy a work of art.

And then he slammed into the ground, his right side taking the brunt of the fall. Pain shot through his shoulder. His stomach spasmed, and he threw up.

When the nausea had passed—somewhat—he gingerly sat up and looked around.

Broken glass glittered in the moonlight. Although he was hemmed in by the hedge maze, by some miracle, he hadn't landed on any of the thorns. Had Graenta's magic spared him somehow?

Harlan flexed his hands and took stock of his body. Aside from an overall soreness, he seemed to be all right. No cuts, although he was sure to find bruises later on.

Looking up, the ferryman understood why he had survived the fall from the chapel window. The now empty window frame was lit like a beacon in the night, clearly marking the chapel's location. But the window wasn't that high up. Well above the head of anyone standing below, but easily reachable by ladder.

Harlan eyed the broken window, wondering at the best way to reach Graenta quickly. Should he chance the hedge maze and try to find the servants' door back into the castle? Or was it possible to scale the wall, if he could find convenient handholds or a vine free of thorns?

A scream split the air.

Graenta.

Panicked, Harlan felt along the stone wall. Perfectly smooth. Another scream rang out, ending in a choked gurgle. Harlan looked around frantically, trying to get his bearings. Which way to go through the hedge maze?

The light above him went out. Silence descended, heavy and final.

Harlan picked a direction and started moving, half-running, half-limping. He was starting to feel the fall from the window—his body moved stiffly, screaming against every step he took. The thorns grabbed at him, brushing against his clothing and hair to slow him down.

The maze thinned out ahead. Harlan picked up speed, and reached—

The entrance.

Harlan cursed and plunged back into the hedge maze, picking a different path. But after a few moments, he found himself outside the maze of thorns again. And again, and again. No matter which direction he went, he always ended up back at the beginning.

Not only was it a fool's errand, his desperation to get back in the castle cost him dearly. The thorns, which had left him alone when he was with Graenta, now clawed at him, hindering his progress while they sliced through his clothes and skin.

The sky was starting to lighten overhead, and it had been several hours since Harlan had left Graenta in the chapel with the other gods. Exhaustion had set in long ago, and his broken and bruised body was on the verge of collapse after blood loss due to the thorn maze.

Harlan had to finally accept that there was nothing more he could do. And with daylight coming, it was best he get as far away from the castle and the capital as possible.

With one last look at the thorn-covered castle, Harlan left the city. He didn't even bother trying to hide, choosing instead the easiest paths to traverse. No one came after him.

Perhaps the gods were too busy with their new prize to bother with a mere mortal.

By noon, the city was well behind him, and he was close to the area where he and Graenta were supposed to meet everyone in a day or two.

The night's events, coupled with his hunger, thirst, and the sun beating down on him, finally caught up to him. His energy spent, he collapsed just off the side of the road.

As unconsciousness claimed him, he thought, *I'm so sorry, Graenta, Idessa. I've failed you both.*

49

Chapter Forty-Nine

After Harlan finished his tale, silence fell around our group.

Harlan coughed, the slight wheezes turning into deeper, rattling shudders. Queen Jennica began fussing over the ferryman again.

Thea and Eliyana reappeared, carrying bundles of yarrow and a few newly filled waterskins. As the queen waved them over, I moved away from the group, so they could tend to Harlan without us getting in the way.

Also, I wanted to think more on Harlan's story.sta

Thinking back, my vivid dream had occurred on the same night that Harlan and Graenta had encountered the gods in the castle's chapel. Graenta had told me that he and I were linked, although that Guardian bond had yet to manifest itself in any significant way beyond mind-speak.

I didn't truly understand how our connection worked, or what to do to make it grow deeper. And Graenta wasn't here to explain it to me. But if I could cultivate whatever small seed was there....

A hand touched my arm, causing me to jump.

"It's just me," Oran said. "Are you all right?"

"Yes." I didn't want to get into what I was really thinking, so I said, "Just thinking through our next steps."

"Really? Like what?"

"We need to save Graenta," I said. "And save Queen Yllulae, and stop the gods before they destroy everything. Which, since they're all in the same place, pretty much amounts to the same thing."

"How convenient," Oran said dryly.

"Convenient, yes. But not easy. And now that they have Graenta, I don't know if we can afford to wait for the other kingdoms to get here. Every moment we delay could be detrimental—to him, the queen, and to us." I refrained from saying that Graenta was our best way of stopping the other gods. His insights, and his power, were integral to our success. Without him, what did we have?

"A valid point, but we have a little bit of time," King Beyan pointed out, as he and Lord Rhyss joined us. "You are correct, Guardian Idessa, in that we can't wait *too* long. But we don't have to run in right away, either."

I eyed Harlan, who was leaning against the fallen log, eyes closed. I didn't see Thea or Eliyana. Perhaps they had gone back into the woods to get more herbs and water. The other Graenirians were setting up camp. Queen Jennica made a few final checks on Harlan, then stood up and brushed herself off. She started walking towards us.

I waited until she was within earshot, then said, "I don't know if it's wise for any of us to try to sneak into the castle. Even though the gods might not know how many allies Graenta has, exactly, they'll know he has at least one—Harlan. They'll be expecting someone to go back for him. But we're definitely lacking in strength and numbers."

"And power," Oran said. "Remember how we needed that fancy sword to take down Calianna?"

"That's true." I frowned. "Graenta had said we don't need each kingdom's emblem, but it would definitely help. And then, of course, we have to figure out how to use them."

"First things first." Oran put a comforting hand on my arm. "Do you want to go after Graenta, or wait for reinforcements?"

I bit my lip, torn. I didn't want to wait, but I didn't want to send anyone—or myself—into the castle to certain death. Neither option seemed ideal, but there really was only one choice.

"Let's take the rest of the day to rest, train, and gather supplies," I said. "And then, when night falls, I'll go to the capital. And the castle."

I tried to rest, I really did, but my nerves were on edge for the rest of the day. So I only managed a prolonged uneasy pseudo-sleep, where my eyes were closed but my mind was fully awake. It kept running over different scenarios, often leading to unhappy conclusions. What if I couldn't find my way through the hedge maze? What if I couldn't get through the servants' door? What if the gods set up some sort of guard at the city gates, or at the castle? *What if ... what if ...*

I also tried to mind-speak with Graenta again, but to no avail.

When the sky started to turn pink and reddish-orange, I got up, relieved. While I wasn't looking forward to infiltrating the castle, at least doing so would burn through the anxious adrenaline I had felt all afternoon.

I headed to the stream Thea had visited earlier. Kneeling down, I splashed some water on my face. Footsteps nearby made me look up.

Oran held out a hand. I took it, and he helped me to my feet. Once I was standing, he didn't let go of my hand, but instead pulled me towards him.

"I'm going with you," he said, holding me close.

"You should stay here," I said. "Two people will attract more attention than one."

"And if one by herself got into trouble, who would be there to help her? No, I'm going with you."

"But, Oran—"

"Idessa. If anything happened—"

Whatever Oran was going to say was interrupted by a shout from the direction of our camp. We both turned, and by unspoken agreement, headed back. Oran was in the lead, still holding my hand, walking as fast as he could through the darkening twilight.

When we arrived, only Eliyana was there. "Oh, good, you're back!" she said. "The others went to investigate, but I stayed behind for when you came back."

"What's going on?" I asked.

Eliyana motioned in the direction of the road. "Everyone's that way, if you want to investigate too."

Oran and I both nodded, and the three of us headed towards the road.

When we got there, we stopped, dumbfounded by what we saw.

The sun had fully set, leaving behind the purple shadows of deepening night.

But it wasn't completely dark. In the middle of the road was a shimmering doorway of bright white light, as if some giant had taken a knife and carved a starry seam down the middle of the air.

And streaming through that doorway were people. Hundreds of them.

50

CHAPTER FIFTY

FIRST CAME A CONTINGENT of proud soldiers wearing red-and-gray brassards—the color of the military kingdom of Rothschan. A striking young woman in a smart but simple red dress accompanied them. Gray ribbons were threaded through her auburn hair.

The people of Rothschan spilled onto the road, spreading out to allow the people behind them to come through.

Dressed in black and gray, or muted browns and greens, this new group was less attention-grabbing than the soldiers had been. But that didn't make them any less proud, or intimidating.

"Ah." Lord Rhyss grinned. "Bomora is here."

Curious, I studied the oncoming Bomorrans. They were led by a dashing dark-haired couple who, from their attire, looked like they would be more at ease on the deck of a ship than in the fields of Graenir.

Seeing the people of Rothschan and Bomora walk through a shimmering portal in the middle of Graenir was wondrous enough. But still more came.

The Fae.

Dryads, centaurs, pixies, gnomes. Elves, and even a few giants. Each otherworldly being possessed an unavoidable allure or deadly beauty.

Next to me, Oran chuckled and elbowed me. "Close your mouth, Dess. Gawking is not usually considered a polite way of greeting newcomers."

I blushed and tore my eyes away from the waves of Fae creatures pouring through the portal. My embarrassed gaze fell on Lord Rhyss, who smirked at me.

"I completely understand," he said. "My intended is part Fae, and there is definitely something compelling about her."

King Beyan chuckled. "I don't think her Fae side has anything to do with it, Rhyss. More like she's the only woman willing to put up with you."

The smile fell from Lord Rhyss's face. "Gods willing, she'll be able to do that for many years to come."

I winced, sensitive now to any invoking of the gods, but the words slipped out of Lord Rhyss's mouth without a second thought.

The final three figures that walked through the portal caught my attention.

Ambassador Joichan, back in his human form, walked alongside two Fae creatures. A male centaur sporting a spotless white jacket, his dark hair tied back, accompanied a petite woman with long, straight silver-grey hair. The woman also wore a dress so white it glowed. A grayish-white pelt hung at the woman's waist. A selkie, perhaps?

The silver-and-obsidian crowns atop the centaur's and selkie's heads marked them as Faerie's king and queen. My eyes widened, impressed. The rulers of Calia had a stronger pull with their allies than I had expected.

With the passage of the final trio, the portal closed. Lingering sparkles illuminated the area, making it feel almost festive.

The Faerie royals greeted Queen Jennica and King Beyan.

"Well met, our Calian friends," the centaur said warmly.

"King Paxen. Queen Bettan. It's lovely to see you again," Queen Jennica said, smiling.

The selkie turned to Lord Rhyss. "Lord Rhyss, it's wonderful to see you again. But where is the lovely Lady Farrah?"

Lord Rhyss bowed low, possibly to be polite. Or maybe to hide his discomfort. "I am delighted to see both of Your Majesties again. Alas, my intended is back in Calia, unwell. Her malady seems to be of a magical nature."

Queen Bettan's eyes grew wide. "Oh, my. That is indeed distressing to hear. When we have finished with our business here, we will send our best healers to her. Perhaps they will be able to help."

"I hope so," King Paxen said. "After all, we owe her—and you—a great deal."

I blinked in surprise. I didn't know what was more fascinating—the casual way that the Faerie queen discussed our impending battle against the gods, or the idea that the Fae royals were indebted to two humans from the Gifted Lands.

Lord Rhyss waved the king's words away. "It was nothing. We were happy to help. Although I must say, I'm surprised to see you here."

King Paxen said, "My wife, Lilliana, is back in Faerie, overseeing Seelie Court affairs."

Wait, what? The king and queen aren't married to each other? I made a mental note to ask Lord Rhyss how the Faerie court worked.

The Faerie royals moved away to oversee their people. The dashing pirate-looking couple I had noticed earlier approached. The dark-haired, petite woman embraced Queen Jennica, while the tall man bowed over the Calian queen's hand.

"A pleasure to meet our esteemed allies in person, at last," the man said. "Although it's a shame it had to be under these circumstances."

"That often seems to be the way of it," Queen Jennica agreed. "King Addan, Queen Inari, let me introduce you to my husband, King Beyan."

The Bomorran royals greeted the Calian king. "And I'm sure you remember Lord Rhyss," Queen Jennica continued.

King Addan clapped a hearty hand on Lord Rhyss's shoulder. Lord Rhyss stumbled forward from the impact. I snickered, covering my face with my hands so my expression couldn't be seen.

Oran's answering smirk told me, *Too late.*

"Of course, of course," the Bomorran king said. "We're looking forward to catching up. But for now, if you'll excuse me."

King Addan and Queen Inari turned to talk to one of their officials.

Finally, the striking red-haired woman who had come through with the Rothschan soldiers approached. "Your Majesties," she said to the Calian royals, curtseying low. "It is an honor to be called to fight by your side."

Queen Jennica held her hands out to the young woman, bidding her to rise. "Commander Adalynn Taethen. It is an honor to call you our friend and ally."

Adalynn Taethen smiled. "It's Grand Marshal, now."

Both Calian royals raised their eyebrows at this news.

"Really?" Queen Jennica said. "That's wonderful. Congratulations."

King Beyan added, "Impressive for one so young. You've risen in rank quite fast."

Grand Marshal Adalynn blushed. "My fellow knights insisted on it. I can't—and don't—want to rule the kingdom. I'd rather leave that to our current monarchs. But since I pretty much lead the Rothschan military anyway, they wanted me to be recognized officially."

Queen Jennica chuckled. "I see. Well, politically motivated or not, there's no one better to hold that position than you, Grand Marshal Adalynn."

"Please. Call me Adalynn, among friends, at least."

The queen nodded, smiling. The Grand Marshal beamed and curtseyed again. With her brief audience over, she too went to see to her troops.

That left Ambassador Joichan. He embraced his daughter, who said, "Father, how did—?"

"The Fae royals not only agreed to help, but they also offered to gather those traveling and give them safe passage through Faerie." He grinned. "It caused quite a commotion. Two giants were dispatched to find Rothschan, and several nymphs were sent to Bomora. The knights of Rothschan weren't sure if they should fight or immediately surrender, and the Bomorrans were too distracted by the nymphs' beauty to listen to their urgent message."

Queen Jennica laughed. "But I assume it all worked out?"

"Eventually. It's a good thing time flows differently in Faerie. We may have actually gained some lost time by moving through it to get here. But I understand the Rothschan army wants to train with the Fae giants now, and you wouldn't believe how many Bomorran marriage proposals I overheard on the way over."

Everyone laughed. But—to my ears, at least—our laughter sounded a little too bright and brittle.

What was better, I wondered. *Wallowing in reality, and knowing we might not make it through the next few days?*

Or pretending everything would be all right?

51

CHAPTER FIFTY-ONE

IN A MAKESHIFT TENT created by Faerie magic, the leaders of Bomora, Rothschan, Calia, and Faerie's Seelie Court met to discuss how best to free Graenir and thus, all of the Gifted Lands. Outside, all was calm and quiet. The now much larger combined camp had settled in for the night, but within the confines of the tent, the leaders couldn't agree on the best course of action.

"We should march on the castle tonight, while we have the advantage of surprise," Grand Marshal Adalynn Taethen said. "My knights—"

"Would be walking into certain death," said King Addan. "If you want to risk your people that way, so be it. But I will not risk my people like that."

"We have the numbers," Adalynn argued.

"And they have the power," King Addan said. "We could have double, triple our numbers, and it still wouldn't make a difference."

Adalynn took a deep breath.

"If I may," Queen Jennica said delicately. "You're right, Addan, that we do not have the same power that the gods possess. But I believe we may have discovered a way to perhaps turn things to our advantage."

King Addan crossed his arms and raised an eyebrow. "Go on."

The Calian queen nodded at me. "Guardian Idessa can provide you with that information."

Everyone's heads turned to me. I gulped, nervous at all these esteemed personages staring at me. Expecting me to have the right answers.

"Um." My voice wavered. I cleared my throat, willing my nerves to disappear. "Did each of you bring your kingdom's greatest treasure, as Queen Jennica asked?"

Adalynn and King Addan nodded. The Fae royals shook their heads, curiosity and confusion plain on their faces.

"Well. Um." *Get it together, Idessa.*

Oran, sitting next to me, surreptitiously put his hand over mine. That small gesture did much to steady me. I blew out a breath and straightened my spine. "A few days ago, in Calia, we—" I nodded at Oran and Lord Rhyss "—had to confront the goddess Calianna in order to free the royal family, and the kingdom, from her rule. Graenta helped me access the innate power in Calia's revered Sword of the First King to stop her. He said that the treasures from each kingdom would be the key to subduing their founders."

"Graenta," King Addan said, testing the name on his tongue. "Graenir's founder?"

I nodded. King Addan's face darkened.

"How do we know it's not a trick?" the Bomorran king demanded. "He's one of *them*, after all. Perhaps Calia's goddess allowed herself to be 'defeated' to lure you into a false sense of safety."

Sudden doubt sprang up on the Calians' faces. Queen Jennica, King Beyan, and Lord Rhyss exchanged a three-way glance. Oran looked at me, uncertain. I had to admit, King Addan had a valid point.

But although his logic was sound, something about it felt wrong to me. I thought over all my interactions with Graenta. He could have betrayed me or our newfound friends at any time, but he hadn't.

Idessa.

I looked around sharply, wondering where the whispered voice had come from. Everyone was looking at me curiously. No one had spoken.

Idessa. My Guardian, my champion.

The whisper sounded like Graenta. I closed my eyes, concentrating.

A slight sensation danced just out of my reach. It felt like ... I could somewhat sense him. Echoes of his fear, and underneath that, his anger.

And a thin thread of hope.

Answering hope flared in my chest. Graenta was still alive, and hadn't given up.

Yet.

Pushing that thought away, I shook my head. "No," I said with such conviction that it startled everyone, even me. "You're wrong." Belatedly, I added, "Your Majesty."

The Bormorran king looked ready to argue, but his wife put a soothing hand on his arm.

"Curious," Queen Inari said. "Explain, please, Guardian Idessa."

I took a deep breath. "I explained earlier my purpose as Guardian."

The others—minus the Calians and Oran—nodded. It had been one of the first points we had talked about, necessary so the other kingdom's representatives would understand why I needed to be involved in the night's discussion. It had also been a relief to stop their constant, curious glances. I had insisted Oran stay as well, as my "advisor". But it was mostly because his familiar presence gave me comfort.

"Part of being the current Guardian—indeed, his chosen champion—means that Graenta and I share a bond. A connection that, honestly, I still don't really understand. I have yet to explore what it really means. But I know—as certain as I know my own name—that he is true and honorable. I think, based on our bond, I would know if he was duplicitous. He is the one who imprisoned the gods in the first place, and he is still firmly devoted to his centuries-old duty of protecting the Gifted Lands from the others."

King Addan stared at me for a long moment. His fingers fidgeted, almost as if he were twirling an invisible dagger between them.

He slammed a fist down on the rickety camp table, causing the cups, plates, and papers scattered on its surface to jump. I winced as one cup overflowed and its contents spilled over someone's notes—a crude map of the castle's layout.

I hope that wasn't needed, I thought.

"All right, *Guardian.*" Did anyone else catch the slightly sarcastic emphasis he put on my title? "As you seem to know the most about this Graenta—and my allies in Calia trust you—I have no choice but to trust your judgment as well. But if your pet god betrays us, neither him nor you will live long enough to regret it."

Queen Jennica frowned, but before she could say anything, Queen Inari gently shooed her husband toward the tent's entrance. "Darling, why don't you go see how our people are faring?"

"If anything was amiss, someone would—"

"Just go check, my dear." The Bomorran queen's mild but firm tone brooked no argument.

King Addan stood and strode out of the tent without a backward glance.

"I must ask you to forgive him," Queen Inari said into the stunned silence that followed. "He's normally not so hot-tempered."

Lord Rhyss nodded thoughtfully. "From our encounter a few years ago, I would agree."

"Our pardon awaits upon your explanation," Queen Jennica said.

The Bomorran queen sighed. "My dear husband has been on edge lately, even before Bomor showed up in our kingdom and wreaked so much havoc." She laughed lightly. "This is probably not the best time to disclose this, but we are expecting our second child. After all this time. So, naturally, Addan is worried for our little one's safety. Among other things."

I frowned, trying to remember the history lessons I had had on the other kingdoms. I didn't think the Bomorran royals had any children, but perhaps my teacher had old information?

Although that lesson was just a few months ago, I realized.

Meanwhile, the Calian queen embraced her friend. "Inari, that's wonderful news! Congratulations to you both."

King Beyan and Lord Rhyss echoed Queen Jennica's sentiment.

"Thank you." Queen Inari beamed. "We're excited, but nervous. With what happened before, Addan wants to make sure nothing can harm our child. He didn't want me to come to Graenir, but I insisted. So this new conflict—with the gods of the Gifted Lands, no less—is more than he can handle right now. He just wants assurance that there is no way we will be in danger. Or lose."

"I wish I could guarantee that," I said. "But I do know, at least one of the gods is on our side. And I also know that tapping into each country's greatest treasure will give us an advantage."

Adalynn spoke up. "Considering not all of the kingdoms are here, I hope what we each offer will be enough."

I sighed. "It will have to be." I wished Graenta was here to advise us. I could only guess at what might work, based on my limited knowledge.

The Grand Marshal folded her hands together, ready for orders. "All right, then. What do we have to do?"

52

CHAPTER FIFTY-TWO

THEY FEEL LIKE MAGIC. Beautiful, but dangerous.

We stared at the items the Bomorran royals and the Grand Marshal of Rothschan had brought with them. The treasures—most prized in each of their respective kingdoms—were on display in the center of the tent.

Adalynn had presented a helmet, dulled from years of use and dented from countless battles. It didn't look like much. But despite its unassuming appearance, the Rothschan helmet radiated a feeling of power and strength.

"Our first queen wore this helmet into every battle and was victorious," Adalynn said reverently. "It heightens the wearer's senses, so they can anticipate their enemy's moves, as long as they don this helmet. It was a gift from the Fae, who created it and imbued it with its magic."

The Fae royals studied the helmet with interest.

"Paxen, I believe this is one of the pieces of Merla's Armor," Queen Bettan said.

King Paxen touched the helmet with an experimental finger. "I think you're right, Bettan. Smart of him to split up the set like that. No Fae would have ever suspected Merla would send part of it outside of Faerie. To think, the helmet was in Rothschan all along."

Adalynn raised an eyebrow at the Fae royals. "Do you mean to say there's more like this?"

The Fae king nodded. "There's a whole suit of armor. Merla, one of Faerie's most talented blacksmiths, created it. Each individual piece protected or enhanced the wearer in some way. Worn all together, the person was invincible. Naturally, wars were fought just to get a hold of it. Realizing what he had done, Merla tried to destroy the armor, but was unable to. So he gave away or buried or hid various parts of the set, placing a curse on it. If anyone gathers all the pieces and wears them, they will be invincible for one battle, but once that battle is done, they will be unable to remove the armor. It will shrink down until it suffocates them, and upon the wearer's death, the armor will turn to ash."

The Grand Marshal nodded. "Warning noted. Rothschan is more than happy with this singular gift."

Queen Jennica chuckled. "I'm surprised, given Rothschan's history and well-known aversion to magic, that they even acknowledge this helmet as their greatest treasure."

Adalynn grinned. "There was much in my kingdom's history that was concealed in the hopes it would be forgotten. The current royals had this locked away in a hidden vault. I had to search through my knights' collective memories to find this. With their permission, of course."

I gave her a quizzical look, but Queen Jennica nodded.

"One could argue that your ability to connect with the knights of Rothschan is the real treasure."

Adalynn ducked her head modestly. "It's invaluable, to be sure. But it's not an ability I want to have forever."

"Understandable. But in the meantime, how you're handling things is quite admirable." The Grand Marshal beamed as the Calian queen turned to the Bomorran royals. "Is your item also Faerie made?"

"No, but it has a similar intriguing history," King Addan, who had rejoined us, said. He touched his kingdom's treasure, a beautiful midnight blue velvet cloak, reverently. "This was woven by Bomor himself. Or so the stories say. He wanted something that would aid him in his exploits. But being somewhat of a trickster, he couldn't resist a bit of mischief."

Queen Inari took up the tale. "Bomor wove his will into it, so the item would be as whimsical and mercurial as he was. Perhaps it would help the wearer blend into the shadows. Or maybe deaden his footsteps, so none would hear the sound of his passage. On one occasion, it suffocated the thief who had stolen it so it could go back to its rightful master. It responds differently to each person, and there is no way to gauge what it will do until someone puts the cloak on."

Oran snorted, drawing raised eyebrows from the rest of the group. He coughed, embarrassed. "I don't know," he said. "It's a handy item, to be sure. But it sounds like it's a lot more trouble than it's worth."

King Addan shrugged, unperturbed. Perhaps his country's most prized treasure often got this reaction. "I suppose. But it really tests a Bomorran's mettle. And it ... senses a person's heart and character, somehow. Only a true Bomorran can use it and bend the cloth to their will, instead of the other way around."

Lord Rhyss chuckled. "One knave recognizes another, is that it?"

King Addan grinned. "A mutual respect between professionals, if you will."

"They're both very fine items," I said. "And their histories are indeed fascinating. So we have the what. Now we just need to figure out the how."

I frowned. "Last time, Graenta was here to help me. He ... used me as a conduit to awaken Calia's Sword of the First King. But now, without him ... I don't know how this should work."

"Even though he is not here, would you still be able to draw on his power?" Oran asked. "Your connection to him still holds, right?"

Recalling my recent awareness of Graenta's capture, I nodded. "Yes, I think so."

"Okay, then. Remember what happened in Calia, and replicate that. If it helps, pretend I'm Graenta." Oran put an encouraging hand over mine.

I touched the cloak, thinking back to the confrontation with Calianna. Graenta's presence had grounded me, helped me focus. It was through his steadiness, power, and belief in me that I had unlocked the Sword's potential.

I knew Oran wasn't Graenta. That flow of magic was missing. But through Oran, I could feel something deep and rich. His admiration and support of me, personally. But also the support and strength of the people of Graenir.

I had a vision then, of our countrymen returning back home. The ones who had fled in fear or in shame, coming back to claim the kingdom that was rightfully theirs. Their love for Graenir ran deep enough to call them back.

Tears streamed down my face, unchecked.

The dark blue cloak began to glow where my fingers touched it, as if lit from within by a small but intense flame. The glow spread and grew brighter, until it covered the entire item.

The brightness dazzled my eyes, making it impossible to see. A voice reverberated in my head. And in my heart.

"I obey the Guardian of Graenir. Command me as you will."

Was the cloak actually speaking to me? Could objects be sentient?

They possess a magic of their own, I thought. *Why* couldn't *they speak, then?* After so many years and so many wearers, it was entirely possible that each treasure had gained a life of some sort.

The blinding brightness stopped. The glow faded from the Bomorran cloak.

In the silence that followed, Lord Rhyss asked, "What was that? What just happened?"

Oran smiled proudly at me. He squeezed my hand. "That was our Guardian."

"It swore fealty to you." King Addan sounded impressed. And maybe a little bit jealous.

"You heard it speak?" I had thought only I could hear the cloak's "voice."

"We all heard it," Queen Jennica said. The others nodded.

"Oh, wow." I stared at the cloak, then my fingers, in wonder.

"But will it still work for me, or Inari?" King Addan asked. "Or does it belong to you, now?"

I shook my head. I didn't know how I knew, but I did. "It doesn't belong to me. It is still, and always will be, of and for Bomora. And it will work for you or whoever I ask it to."

The Bomorran king sat back, relieved.

I flexed my fingers, marveling at the lingering sensation of the unlocking magic. "Well. Now that we know that it works—I guess I should do the same with your helmet, Grand Marshal."

Adalynn nodded, then asked, "Does Faerie have a treasure?"

Queen Bettan smiled fiercely. It was unsettling for one who looked so demure and unassuming. "We Fae have our own unique claim. Our long history rivals that of the Gifted Lands' gods, which makes our power nearly a match to theirs."

The Fae king, Paxen, laughed. "Why do you think they discouraged us from settling in human lands? The kingdom of Shonn was our compromise, but even then we only visited the Gifted Lands twice a year, at Beltane and Samhain."

"I assumed the reason for your distance was because the Fae preferred their own lands," Lord Rhyss said.

"That's true. Still, just as mortals are curious about our realm, we Fae have always found you humans fascinating as well."

Adalynn looked at Oran and me. "What about Graenir's treasure? Were you able to recover it from your palace?"

I paused, frowning. "*Do* we have an item sacred to our kingdom? If so, how would we know what it is, or how to find it?"

But Oran was shaking his head.

"No?" I said. "No, we don't have a treasure? Or no, we don't know where or what it is?"

Oran smiled. "We do, but we don't have to hunt for it. It's already here."

"How do you know?"

"Every Archivist is required to study and memorize the histories before being assigned a specialization. The histories did mention that each kingdom had an object that held symbolic importance to it, but Graenir's ideals were never tied to an item. They were tied to a person. Not the reigning monarch, because our founder knew that monarchs could rise or fall, be good or corrupt. No, he wanted it tied to a person he had chosen himself."

At my confusion, he chuckled. "Idessa. It's the Guardian. It's you."

53

CHAPTER FIFTY-THREE

"MIND IF I JOIN you?"

I looked over to see Grand Marshal Adalynn strolling towards me. I nodded and indicated she join me, where I stood on the side of the road, a small distance away from the majority of our countries' combined camps. Most people had settled in for the night, and a feeling of quiet anticipation hung over everything.

Except me. Not-so-quiet dread hung heavy on my heart.

Adalynn looked up at the stars with me. "It's a bit overwhelming, isn't it?"

I snorted. "That's one way of putting it."

"Often our victories—or defeats—come about due to the way we 'put it'. In our heads, I mean."

I looked at her curiously.

"I wasn't born to command," she said quietly. "It was thrust upon me, in the form of an ability I didn't ask for and can't get rid of. I don't presume to understand why it came to me, and not someone else. But perhaps because of my own humble beginnings, I can be a voice for the common person when no else understands."

"Grand Marshal?" I wasn't quite sure what she was trying to say.

"I only say this because I see a bit of myself in you." She smiled. "I know we've only just met, and don't know each other that well. But kindred spirits can sense each other."

She placed an encouraging hand on my shoulder. "When the time comes, you will prevail, Guardian Idessa. We all believe it. You need to believe it, too."

With a final pat, she left. I stared up at the stars for a long time, thinking about her words.

I woke up the next morning to an unforgiving grey sky and a distinct chill in the air. I blew out a breath, dismayed that I could actually *see* my breath.

I sat up in my bedroll, instantly shivering. A steaming cup was thrust under my nose, just as I caught the smell of coffee rising from it. I looked over. Oran smiled at me. "Here you go. Thought you might need this."

I took the cup from him gratefully. Even though I hated the bitter taste, I needed to get warm, too. I took a careful sip. My nose wrinkled.

Oran laughed. "We'll take back the castle, save Queen Yllulae and Graenta, and then you can have whatever drink you want."

I sighed. "I suppose that's the order of things, isn't it?"

I continued drinking while Oran turned away and helped the others break camp. I grimaced, both at the drink and having to get out of my warm bedroll, but I knew I couldn't linger.

Soon enough, I was dressed and ready. I walked over to where Oran was standing with the other kingdoms' leaders, in a final discussion over the day's plan.

"It should be easy enough to get to the castle," Lord Rhyss was saying. "Harlan didn't see anyone. Alive, that is."

"I don't know," Queen Jennica said slowly, frowning. "Something feels wrong. I've been feeling unsettled since I woke up."

"Perhaps it's nerves?" Lord Rhyss suggested, not unkindly.

"Perhaps." But the Calian queen didn't sound convinced.

"We'll continue on with our original plan, then," Grand Marshal Adalynn said. "King Addan and I will accompany Guardian Idessa into the castle, with our kingdom's treasures. Once inside, we—"

A scout ran up to us, breathless. "Pardon me," he panted, sketching a hasty bow around the circle. "But I have news."

We all turned to him expectantly. My skin started to prickle. Something about the wild, urgent look on the man's face didn't bode well.

"The gate ... is no longer ... unguarded. The city ... is overrun," the scout said. He paused to catch his breath.

"Overrun?" Oran asked. "What do you mean?"

"There is an army outside the capital, guarding the gate," the scout said. "I couldn't get too close, but I saw some movement beyond the gate. I could only presume there are some guards just inside the city, as well. I'd estimate there were several thousand men, at least."

"But where did an army come from?" I wondered.

"I do not know, Guardian. But there was a foul stench in the air, and something about the soldiers seemed unnatural. I instantly felt uneasy, and was loath to get closer." The scout hung his head. "Forgive me. I was remiss in my duty."

"No. No, you weren't." I hastened to reassure him. "Trust your instinct. If it was telling you something was amiss, then you were wise to leave."

"Thank you, Guardian." The scout saluted me, then left.

Several thousand soldiers guarding the city gate? I turned to my companions in dismay. While we did have more people than originally, thanks to our Bomorran, Rothschan, and Fae allies, as well as some of our countrymen returning, we still were outnumbered. The Rothschan army, of course, were our strongest fighters. And we did have two dragons—Queen Jennica and Ambassador Joichan—on our side. But still ...

And where did the gods suddenly get an army?

"Unnatural ..." Queen Jennica murmured, deep in thought.

"We'll have to change our strategy," Oran said. "The most important thing is getting Guardian Idessa into the city, and the palace. But I don't think it's wise if King Addan and Grand Marshal Adalynn accompany her. Not anymore. All would be lost if all three were captured."

"What do you suggest, then?" King Beyan asked.

Oran looked at me.

"We should split up," I said, trying to sound confident. Inside, I was full of doubt. And worry. "That way, the enemy will have several groups to focus on instead of just one. And if we run the same standard with each group—all Graenir's, for example, instead of that of Bomora, and Rothschan, and Faerie—that might confuse them as well. They'll think we're all from the same kingdom and not know for sure which group to target their full force on. If some of the decoy groups can draw off the guards, so much the better."

Queen Bettan laughed. "We Fae are much better at subterfuge than direct confrontation. If confusion is what you desire, then that is what you will get."

"As are the people of Bomora," King Addan declared. He grinned savagely. "It might even be fun."

Grand Marshal Adalynn frowned. "Rothschan prefers action any day, but I see the wisdom in your plan. I will split my knights amongst each group, with the highest concentration in Guardian Idessa's group. They'll help you get through. King Addan and I will follow in our separate groups, and meet you inside the castle."

"Do you remember where the chapel is?" There was no guarantee that the gods would even be in that room, but it felt like the best place to start.

Adalynn tapped the side of her head. "I've got an excellent memory."

King Addan grimaced. "My apologies for that. I didn't mean to ruin your map. I'm glad you were able to memorize the castle layout so quickly. I, unfortunately, do not have so good a memory. I'll have to enter the castle with either you or Guardian Idessa, or I won't know my way around."

"We'll figure it out," I said reassuringly.

With our new plans settled, Grand Marshal Adalynn and King Addan went to oversee the formation of the various groups. The Fae royals left to give instructions to their own people.

Queen Jennica excused herself to talk to Ambassador Joichan. The two would go into battle in their dragon forms, although they hoped to intimidate, not attack. Unless it was absolutely necessary.

King Beyan and Lord Rhyss left to discuss things with the small group of people staying behind in the camp. This included Harlan, who was still recovering, and Queen Inari. The Bomorran royal was a bit put out at not being included in the action, but had graciously acquiesced when her husband insisted she stay behind.

"You're carrying the future of Bomora," King Addan had said. "If something should happen ..."

"I know," Queen Inari had replied. "It doesn't mean I'm happy about it, but I understand."

If anything bad happened—my mind danced around the thought, *If we all die*—then several scouts would be dispatched back to the camp to warn them to flee. They were to get Queen Inari back to Bomora safely, whatever it took.

That left Oran and me alone. I looked towards the capital, although I couldn't see it from this distance, and sighed.

"Hey," Oran said. "Are you okay?"

I shrugged. "As much as I can be, I guess. There's so many unknowns. We're taking such a risk, and there's no guarantee it will work."

"Anything we chose to do would be risky. It's just a matter of which choice has the least amount of risk in it." He put a comforting arm around my shoulder and pulled me close, looking deep into my eyes. "But that's not entirely what this is about, is it?"

I shook my head. "I'm just so worried. Worried that my parents won't be all right. Worried about Lis—where is he? Worried that this won't work and we'll all be killed and—"

"Hey. Shh." Oran kissed the top of my head. "There's no sense in worrying about the worst. We can only move forward and do our best, and take each moment as it comes."

I smirked. "When did you get so wise?"

He chuckled. "I always have been. You just didn't notice before."

Grand Marshal Adalynn rejoined us. "Guardian Idessa, Oran, are you ready?"

Oran looked at me. "Yes. I'll defend you with all I have. With my life, if need be."

I hoped it wouldn't come to that. And I wasn't ready, but I couldn't really say that. So I nodded.

"Good." Adalynn looked beyond us, to where several groups of combined Bomorran, Graenirian, Fae, and Rothschan forces milled about. "It's time."

54

CHAPTER FIFTY-FOUR

As we approached the capital, I understood the feeling the scout had spoken of. The air smelled rotten, and a sense of wrongness settled over me. I saw others in my group swallow hard or flinch, and knew I wasn't the only one affected.

Before us stood what seemed like an endless army standing between us and the city's entryway. The soldiers stood unnaturally still. Waiting, and watching.

A loud roar reverberated across the field, followed by the heavy vibrating thud of a large beast's footsteps. Make that two large beasts. Queen Jennica and Ambassador Joichan had both transformed, and two golden dragons now towered over the field. The two creatures bore a strong resemblance to each other, but I thought Queen Jennica's form was the slightly smaller one with delicate features.

Joichan snarled menacingly at the enemy army, who seemed surprisingly unaffected by this show of might.

What was wrong with these people? How could the sight of two huge dragons not have them quaking in fear?

My unease grew.

Queen Jennica lowered her head and let out a long stream of fire. Heat sizzled overhead as a wall of flame sprang up between the two armies.

Surely that would intimidate them. It wasn't like we wanted to fight. I didn't know where the gods had gotten their army from, but it was likely they were a mishmash of people from all over the Gifted Lands, just like our group was. Our hope was to scare some of them off, to convince them to surrender before the battle even started.

We waited for several long moments. The breeze whipped the flames higher. The only sound on the field was the crackle of the fire wall, or an errant cough from one of our people.

Something caught my eye. Some fuzzy shadows and movement beyond the wall of fire.

I drew closer to Oran, my sword at the ready. Although I had been outfitted with a weapon, I didn't really know how to use it. It was more a means for desperate self-defense than anything else.

Oran had volunteered to be my guardian—an ironic duty that both made me happy as well as fear for him—but even he wasn't to put himself in harm's way. The others with us, a mix of stalwart Rothschan soldiers, some of Bomora's finest archers, and the magical Fae, were tasked to protect us while creating a path to the city gate and beyond.

The indistinct figures grew bigger. And closer. Horrified, I watched as the first wave of enemy soldiers came through the fire. *Walked* through, completely unfazed, like the wall of dragon fire didn't even exist!

As I got a better look at the face of our enemy, I realized, with dawning horror, why that feeling of wrongness had been hanging over them.

I saw bloated faces with dried blood tracking down their cheeks. Here and there an eye was missing, or an arm. Clothes were torn and dirty, and I could see wounds through the ripped fabric.

Although their clothes and hair and bodies had caught on fire, they didn't react. No screams, no curses, no cries.

No spark of life in their flat, dull gazes.

Harlan had told us that when he and Graenta had come through earlier, the streets were littered with the bodies of Graenir's fallen soldiers.

My eyes widened. I now knew how the gods had raised their army. And I knew who these people were.

I turned slightly, retching.

Oran gasped. His face paled. "Idessa—the army—they're dead."

He was partly right. Most of them were dead. Or, undead. But sprinkled among them were a few people who looked whole and healthy—or had been until the gods' magic had compelled them to walk through dragon fire. My heart sank as I recognized that all the soldiers were wearing current Graenirian styles. I guessed they were the unlucky survivors who hadn't made it out of the capital city in time.

And all of them wore the same flat, lifeless expressions. Alive or dead, my countrymen had been turned into puppets to be used at the gods' whims.

Someone in our group swore. Next to me, a Rothschan soldier muttered a prayer.

Although the dragon fire had damaged some of the people, it hadn't slowed them down. Even with their bodies burning, they were relentless, human torches. I gagged at the stench of rot that filled the air, exacerbated by smoke and fire. The wall of fire had been a good idea.

If the soldiers before us weren't undead or possessed.

With low, unearthly groans, they raised their swords high.

"Fall back! Fall back!" Grand Marshal Adalynn called out.

We did so, hoping that the flames would do their work before it was absolutely necessary for us to engage with the enemy. Above us, Joichan snarled and raised a sharp talon. He swiped at some of the torched soldiers, sweeping them to the side. I shuddered. The men didn't make a sound as they flew through the air. No screams, no yelling, nothing.

Were their minds really and truly gone?

And then the enemy was upon us.

"For the Gifted Lands!" Oran yelled, raising his own sword. Around him, others took up the cry. The clash of steel on steel rang across the field as the two armies joined.

I stayed close to Oran, my own sword at the ready.

A blur of Rothschan grey-and-red slashed out at an undead soldier. The man moaned loudly as he fell to the ground, then twitched and lay still as fire licked at his body. I released the breath I hadn't even known I had been holding, relieved.

The Rothschan knight turned away, his sword meeting a new foe. More enemy soldiers had joined the first line, walking through the embers of the former wall of flame.

The fallen soldier's hand moved. And then another. And then the undead man was slowly getting to his feet, a chilling moan escaping his lips as he snarled and raised his sword again.

"To your left!" I cried out.

The Rothschan knight turned just in time to parry the undead soldier's attack, but it left him open to attack from his other opponent. The second soldier struck, slashing the knight's arm. He roared in pain and fury and renewed his own attack. He fought well, but I worried that he would soon tire from his injury.

All around us, our other allies fought just as passionately. But under the relentless onslaught of the dead, some were already beginning to slow down.

Smaller Fae darted amongst the enemy, casting minor magic to distract them or disorient them.

We were making slow progress towards the city, but there was still too much going on for me to feel confident about trying to run for the gate.

Nearby, a Bomorran's opponent caught my eye. I would recognize that form, that familiar flash of blond hair, anywhere. "Tahn?" I breathed. The two continued fighting. "Tahn!" I screamed, but he didn't turn.

A shuffle to my right was my only warning. I had just enough time to parry an incoming strike. My hands and arms shook from the force of deflecting the blow.

I got a good look at my adversary and gasped. "Lis?"

55

CHAPTER FIFTY-FIVE

THE MAN ACROSS FROM me was, indeed, my brother. He wore the official robes of the Archives, now tattered and stained. Although I was in shock at seeing him—and in such a state!—some distant part of me wondered where he had gotten the weapon.

Lis raised his sword again.

"Lis! Lis, it's me! It's your sister, Idessa!"

Lis paused mid-slash. Some faint hint of recognition sparked in his eyes. "I-dess-a?" He tripped over my name, as if he'd never said it before.

Relief flooded through me. "Yes! Yes, it's me, Dess!"

"Dess ..." Lis lowered his sword, thinking.

He'd be all right. He'd remember me, and that would break the spell, and we'd get him out of here, and ...

I stared up at my brother hopefully.

The light in his eyes went out. Snarling, he raised his sword again to strike. I weakly lifted mine, knowing that I wouldn't be able to withstand another jarring blow.

"Lis! Lis, please, wait—"

My brother slumped to the ground. I gasped. Oran stood behind him. A medium-sized rock fell from his hand to hit the ground with a thump.

"I couldn't kill him," Oran said, distraught.

I could only nod mutely.

"I hope he'll be okay. He'll be okay, don't you think? He'll be okay," Oran babbled on.

I opened my mouth to say something, anything that might comfort Oran—and myself—but didn't get the chance. Someone touched my shoulder to get my attention. I turned, seeing one of the Bomorran archers from our group.

"Go, go!" she yelled, pointing.

Somehow, the battle had brought us halfway across the field, closer to the capital. The way to the gate was, miraculously, clear.

Oran and I looked at each other. "Let's go!" he said.

"But, Lis—"

"We have to go, Idessa! *Now!*"

He was right. Heart heavy, I turned away from my unconscious brother. *Please don't let him get hurt. I mean, any more hurt than he already is*, I prayed. To Graenta? To any of the other Gifted Lands gods? I wasn't quite sure anymore.

Oran grabbed my hand and began running towards the gate.

"We'll shield you!" The Bomorran fell in behind us, bow at the ready. A Rothschan soldier joined us, hacking at someone who made the poor decision to try to attack me.

"Where's Pyana?" the Bomorran archer asked.

"He's gone," the Rothschan soldier said tersely. But there was no time for words of sympathy, for now that the enemy was aware of our goal, we were getting swarmed.

Ahead of us and to the left, a shimmery portal appeared. The Fae royals, King Paxen and Queen Bettan, were standing before it, their hands clasped. They each held their free hands up, presumably to call forth the portal. Some of the enemy soldiers streamed through the portal, either charmed or forced through by Fae creatures.

"They'll weaken and die faster in Faerie, due to the land's magic and the time issue," Oran called to me. I remembered something about time in the land of Faerie running differently than in the mortal world, which could prove instantly fatal for humans who lived in Faerie for a long time and then tried to return to the Gifted Lands.

"Why didn't we just create a Faerie portal and shove them all in it in the first place?" I wondered, breathless.

"It takes too much power," Oran huffed as we hurried by. "King Paxen and Queen Bettan won't be able to keep that portal up for long."

I glanced back over my shoulder. The portal was already starting to waver and shrink. I hoped that whoever found themselves in Faerie when the portal closed would come to a quick, merciful end.

Around us, groups of our allies swooped in, distracting and drawing the enemy away from us.

A giant of a man stepped into our path, his lips pulled back in a wordless snarl. Oran halted, torn. I nearly skidded into him. We were more than willing to fight our way through, but to do so would use up precious time, and our clear path to the gate was quickly growing smaller.

The Rothschan soldier stepped forward, taunting the man. "Hey! Over here!"

As the undead enemy turned towards the voice, our ally yelled, "I'll hold him here! Keep going!"

Oran tugged on my hand and we started running again.

Just a little bit more ... we were nearly at the city's entry ...

A cry ripped through the air behind me. I turned around to look.

Several feet away, the Bomorran archer sat on the ground, massaging her leg. A partially buried rock at her right foot must have caused her to trip and fall. She tried to get up, but then fell back to the ground, cursing through gritted teeth.

I started to move towards her, but she waved me away. "Don't worry about me. I'll catch up in a bit."

"But—" We both knew she was lying.

"Come on, Idessa." Oran tugged at me again, a gentle reminder not to abandon the larger goal. We kept going, but not before I snuck one last look behind me.

The Bomorran archer, having resigned herself to her injury, was shooting arrows into the enemy lines. Her face was a mask of grim determination—she knew she didn't have long before she succumbed to either the pain or the enemy. I turned back, tears streaming down my face, hating that her fate was inevitable.

We reached the gate and ran through it, into the city. Oran released my hand, and we stood back to back, ready to fight.

But no one approached us. The city stretched out before us, empty.

I turned back to the capital's entrance, which was wide open. There were a few undead milling around the gate. I presumed they had followed us, but why weren't they coming in the city after us? Surprised, I watched as they looked around and even into the city—right at us—then wandered away, their prey forgotten as they rejoined the battle beyond.

"I don't understand," I said. I walked back to the gate, even as Oran called out, "Idessa, don't!"

He needn't have worried. I bumped into something solid and invisible at the entrance. Confused, I put my hand out and felt around, from top to bottom. My hand—nor the rest of my body—couldn't pass through whatever unseen barrier was at the city gate.

"It seems you can only enter the city, but not leave," I said, turning back to Oran with a shaky laugh.

He frowned. "But why only us? It seems that we were expected."

I swallowed, not liking the sound of that. Oran's hand found mine again, comforting and warm.

Together, we turned towards the palace.

56

CHAPTER FIFTY-SIX

As WE HEADED DEEPER into the city, I found myself agreeing with Oran's hunch that *we were expected*. The capital was completely deserted of any guards, and it felt like even the castle itself was drawing us to it, impatient for our arrival.

All too soon we stood in front of the castle, surrounded by the thorny hedge maze that the ferryman had described. A stench of rotting flesh hung in the air, but the bodies Harlan had mentioned seeing in the vines were missing. I turned my head, feeling sick as the realization of where those poor souls had gone hit me.

"Didn't Harlan say that there was an entrance on the eastern side?" I said. "I hope it's still—"

Without warning, the impenetrable vines rustled and shifted, becoming an archway of thorns.

Eyes wide, I looked at Oran. "Do you think it's safe?" I whispered.

"No."

The vines rustled again, even though there was no breeze beckoning us in.

"What choice do we have?" I said.

"We have plenty of choices," Oran said. "But not a lot of time."

I nodded. "Okay, then. Let's go."

With trepidation, we walked through the thorn-covered entryway. I closed my eyes, waiting to be pierced through, but we
passed through unscathed. And even though I had been sure that
the hedge had been a thick, tangled, and impenetrable mess, the
path before us was wide and clear.

It's like the gods want us to find them, I thought uneasily. And
when we reached the castle doors—which swung open without us
having to touch them—my unease only intensified.

"Idessa ..." Oran's tone reflected my own fear.

"I know."

We headed into the castle.

I meant to go to the chapel. I was sure I remembered Harlan's
description of how to find it. But after walking for a little while,
I realized we weren't going there. I stopped and got my bearings.
Turning in the right direction, I started walking again.

But again, I still wasn't going towards the chapel. I deliberately
tried to walk in that direction. But my body resisted. Sweat broke
out on my forehead, and my breathing became labored.

"Idessa?" came Oran's uncertain voice.

"I ... don't know ... what's wrong," I panted. "I'm trying to ... go
... to the chapel. But something ... won't ... let me."

Oran blinked, brow furrowed, and shook himself all over. His
movements were fluid and easy. Whatever was happening, I was
apparently the only one afflicted.

I focused my will entirely on going to the chapel. My vision
began to blacken at the edges.

"Oran ..." My voice sounded faint even to my ears.

"Idessa! Stop," Oran said, grabbing me by the shoulders. "Don't
fight it, whatever it is."

I heeded his words, and my symptoms immediately stopped. Taking in a much-needed deep breath, I said, "But—the chapel—"

He shook his head. "I don't like it, but something doesn't want you to go there. So let's go where it *does* want you to go, and maybe we'll get a better idea of what to do from there?"

I didn't like it either, but what could I do? Either I wasted time trying—and failing—to fight this magical affliction, or I just went with it. And hoped for the best.

I nodded, and started walking again, carefully emptying my mind of any predetermined path.

After a few moments, I realized where we were going. I remembered walking this path well. I had done it the day I was named Guardian.

Soon, we stood in front of the closed doors of the great hall, in the heart of the castle.

Cautiously, I crept up to the door and put my ear against it. I couldn't make out exact words, but I could hear voices and movement inside the room.

I bit my lip, hesitant. Should we try to sneak in? Was there an alternate entrance? It would be foolish to enter through the main doors, but—

Oran touched my arm and jerked his head to the side. I gave him a quizzical look, but let him lead me around the corner and away from the great hall.

When we were a fair distance away, I stopped walking. My symptoms had returned, and I was afraid to test their limits. "Where are we going?" I whispered.

"Don't worry, it should be around here," Oran said in a low voice, looking around the hallway. Silently, he counted the doors, mouthing the numbers while he pointed at each one. We were standing between the third and fourth doors, and he opened the third one without hesitation.

A darkened corridor yawned open before us. A lone lit torch was attached to the wall, spilling a small amount of light just by the door but not too much beyond. The air was noticeably cooler than the main area we were standing in, and it smelled a bit musty. I sneezed, lifting my sleeve to my face just in time to muffle the sound.

Oran gave me a sympathetic smile as he ushered me into the passage. He closed the door behind us, and I tried not to panic. I wasn't scared of small spaces, but I didn't like how dark and unknown this area was.

"Where are we?" I whispered.

"Servants' passage," Oran replied, keeping his voice low. He grabbed the torch and started down the hallway.

"Really?" I said doubtfully, noting the thick layer of dust that coated the floor and walls.

"Well, that's what it was labeled as on the rendering I saw," he said. At my quizzical look, he explained, somewhat sheepishly, "A few months back, the queen wanted to build a new wing to the castle. I was tasked to review the castle plans, and I ended up memorizing them."

"It doesn't seem like the servants use it that much," I said, stifling another sneeze.

"I understand that past rulers preferred to have their servants hidden, but when Queen Yllulae took the throne, the fashion among Gifted Lands rulers was to have your servants visible to guests and outsiders. You know, as a show of wealth and power."

We fell silent, concentrating on navigating the twisty corridors. Oran counted doorways again, sometimes stopping to backtrack and recount. I wondered what the servants' hallways looked like on the castle map. The interconnecting corridors didn't seem that straightforward. No wonder royals preferred to have their servants come directly to the rooms they were needed in, instead of waiting for them to find their way through here.

After a time, we came to a heavy tapestry that covered the wall from floor to ceiling. Muffled movement and voices could be heard on the other side. Feeling that familiar tickle in my nose again, I put my sleeve up to my nose, trying to stay quiet.

Oran and I crept closer, and the voices became more distinct.

"Let her go," Graenta was saying. "You have me. You don't need the queen too. Send her outside to be with her people. She needs care."

Someone sighed loudly. A deep male voice said, "Is anyone else tired of his blabbering? I told you all we should have bound his mouth as we did his body."

"Now, now, Rothscha," a smooth female voice spoke. I could practically see her eyes rolling as she continued snidely, "If you want to waste your power on something so frivolous, my dear Rothscha, then be my guest. What with raising the army, creating the barrier around the castle, and then binding these two—it took quite a bit out of us. Not to mention—"

"Can we get on with it, already, Shonnala?" a bored female voice interrupted. "Must we have all these theatrics?"

"Theatrics, Orchwen? *Theatrics*?" Rothscha sputtered. "I'll have you know—"

"If you don't mind, I have a kingdom to subjugate. I've waited centuries for this, and I don't feel like waiting a moment longer," Orchwen said petulantly.

"She has a point," a raspy male voice said. "I'm as patient as the next god—"

"Which is to say, not very," Rothscha muttered.

"But what with that mishmash of an army on our doorstep, we should really get a move on."

"I agree, Bomor," Shonnala said.

My eyes widened at the sound of a sword being unsheathed. I shivered when Rothscha spoke, his voice laced with gleeful malice.

"Then let's get started."

57

CHAPTER FIFTY-SEVEN

MY HAND CREPT TOWARDS the tapestry, ready to twitch it aside and rush into the great hall.

Oran's hand shot out immediately, clamping around my wrist. Wordlessly, he shook his head at me.

He was right. But I didn't want to just stand here if there was something I could do. Except, what could I do, with a sword I could barely use, and no magic to speak of?

My hand dropped. I would wait, and listen to what was happening. For now.

On the other side of the tapestry, Shonnala said, "That's a bit much, don't you think?"

"No," Rothscha said fiercely.

"We need a slow bloodletting, otherwise it will be a waste of effort. If you don't have a dagger, borrow one from Bomor."

I gasped soundlessly. To Oran, I mouthed, *Now?*

He shook his head. *Not yet.*

Rothscha said grumpily, "My only dagger is dulled from the other night in the chapel."

Bomor said snidely, "Typical. Last time I lent him something, he lost it. And that was *after* damaging it beyond repair."

Rothscha sniped back, "If it was that badly damaged, why would you even want it back? Besides, I'm surprised you even remember that. That was centuries ago."

"It's not like I've had much else to think about over the ages," Bomor pointed out.

"Oh, please. Get over it—and yourself—already."

Bomor sputtered in indignation and started arguing with Rothscha. Oran and I exchanged a look. With the way these gods bickered, it was a wonder anything got done among them. As the argument got louder, Oran nodded at me and quietly pushed part of the tapestry aside.

We were to one side of the dais that held the twin thrones, hidden by the tapestry and a pillar. From where we stood, we could get a good look at most of the room.

In the center, stomping around in shiny silver armor decorated with red and grey shoulder plates, a big burly man whom I guessed was Rothscha waved his sword around for emphasis. A smaller, slender man stood a few feet away, circling Rothscha warily with a dagger in each hand, ready to throw. Bomor, most likely.

Nearby, a black jaguar growled at both men, obviously annoyed at their behavior. Annlynden, the god of shapeshifters. *That must be his favorite form,* I thought. *Or is he unable to transform into more than one animal?*

An elegant lady with an unearthly air about her stood to the side, looking irritated. Another woman stood next to her, yawning and idly examining her fingernails, as if the goings-on were beneath her notice. Shonnala and Orchwen, I was willing to bet.

My eyes swept around the rest of the great hall. I bit back a strangled cry as I got a good look at the figures sitting upon the twin Graenirian thrones.

Queen Yllulae was bound to the farther, left-hand throne. Her late husband's simple circlet, as well as her own crown, were piled on her head in a mockery of her status. But she was beyond noticing. Her head lolled to the side, and she seemed to be barely breathing.

Graenta sat on the right-hand throne, closer to where Oran and I hid. He was bound as well, but physical restraints alone wouldn't have been able to hold him. A strong sense of magical energy emanated from the area, suggesting his fellow gods had thrown a considerable amount of power into restraining him. His eyes flashed with anger as he watched the others.

Orchwen made a show of yawning, deliberate and slow. "Boys. This is so incredibly boring."

Rothscha and Bomor broke off their argument to round on Orchwen. Even Annlynden stopped his growling to glare at Orchwen, since he was presumably one of the "boys" to which she was referring.

Orchwen continued on, seemingly oblivious to the ire that was radiating off her fellow gods. "I've spent the last several hundred years listening to you two bicker." She gave an annoyed sigh. "You *both* need to get over yourselves."

Silently, I pointed to the pillars that were scattered around the great hall. If I was careful and quiet—and lucky—I should be able to sneak over to the dais. And hopefully free Queen Yllulae and Graenta.

Oran nodded. He waved me on, indicating I should get going. Taking a deep breath, I eased out from behind the tapestry and stood behind the pillar.

"Excuse me?" Bomor sputtered. "He breaks my best knife, and *I* need to get over it?"

At the same time, Rothscha said, "At least someone is finally speaking sense around here."

Shonnala said, "Please. It's not like you didn't have others, Bomor."

Bomor's voice turned deadly low. "I'm only cooperating with all of you until we ensure that we're never locked away again. After that, don't expect me to help any of you, ever again."

Rothscha swung his sword menacingly. "Noted, trickster. And likewise."

"Watch where you're swinging that thing!" Orchwen yelped.

The arguing renewed, this time louder and with more participants. Annlynden growled indiscriminately at the other gods and goddesses. I took advantage of the noise to creep over to the second pillar.

"Don't tell me what to do," Rothscha warned, an edge to his voice.

"I wouldn't have to if you had better self-control," Orchwen baited. "Both in temper and in handling weapons."

"I have perfect self-control, in all things!"

"She's right, actually," Shonnala said. "Or don't you remember what happened at Lake Vitrum, when Annlynden was trying to establish his kingdom?"

Annlynden growled in agreement.

I snuck over to the next pillar. Just one more pillar, and I'd be right next to the dais. From there, I should be close enough to easily hide behind the thrones.

Rotscha erupted. "Do none of you have anything better to do than hold centuries-old grudges?"

More shouting ensued. If there had been any small furniture or décor nearby, I might have been in danger of dodging thrown objects. As it was, I took advantage of their fighting to sneak to the final pillar. Honestly, I probably could have skipped or strolled over to it, and I doubt they would have noticed.

Nearby, Graenta's eyes grew wide when he saw me hiding so close by.

Idessa!

His voice in my head felt as loud as if he had yelled it across the room. I winced, rubbing my temples.

Sorry. Graenta's voice came softer this time.

I grimaced. *It's okay. I'm glad you're happy to see me.*

Am I ever. Listen, Idessa, we don't have much time. The other gods want to—

His internal voice broke off sharply as something over my shoulder caught his attention.

I looked back, down the length of the room. Oran had left the servants' hallway and was hidden behind the first pillar, following after me. With the gods arguing so intensely, I'm sure he could have just walked across the room to join me and been fine. I motioned to him. *Hurry! Get over here!*

Oran started towards the second pillar. I slipped around the edge of the dais. Just as I ducked behind Graenta's throne, I heard Orchwen say, "Wait. What was that?"

Footsteps started across the room.

I held my breath, sure I had been caught. But the footsteps weren't headed in my direction. Cautiously, I peered around the edge of the throne.

Orchwen was looking around the area where the pillars stood, a faint frown on her face.

"I could have sworn I saw something," she said.

Rothscha taunted, "Don't tell me your Seeking skills are slipping, Orchwen?"

She whirled, her investigation instantly forgotten. "My skills are as sharp as ever," she snapped. "Unlike some people I know."

I looked at the first pillar again, wondering what had happened to Oran. Then I saw a slight twitching at the tapestry, a gentle tug to make sure it hung straight. *Ah.* Oran must have ducked back into the servants' corridor to hide from Orchwen. I was glad he was safe, but now I couldn't communicate with him. Or have his comforting presence with me.

I ducked behind the throne again as Orchwen walked back across the room.

Are you safe, Idessa? Graenta's anxiety was palpable.

I'm fine. But Oran—

He'll be all right. But he probably shouldn't try that again any time soon.

"I tire of all this arguing," Shonnala said. "Rothscha, be a dear and start the bloodletting, if you would?"

"I thought you wanted me to have a different weapon for the task." Rothscha sounded like he enjoyed baiting Shonnala.

"I did say that, didn't I? Bomor, give him your dagger."

Bomor said, "But—"

"*Now*, Bomor."

The god grumbled under his breath, but he must have done as asked, because Shonnala said, "Good. Now you may begin, Rothscha."

Heavy footsteps started towards the dais and the two thrones where I was hidden.

58

CHAPTER FIFTY-EIGHT

Listen, Idessa. We don't have much time. The gods know they need specific Graenirian blood to overpower me, so they can drain me and the kingdom, but they don't know exactly whose. They're sure it's Queen Yllulae's blood that they need. We can't let them know you're here....

The footsteps came closer.

I froze, scared that the slightest breath or movement would give me away.

But fortunately—for me, at least—Rothscha's steps stopped in front of the thrones. To be exact, Queen Ylullae's throne.

Cautiously, I peeked out from my hiding spot.

Rothscha's back was to me, bent over the queen's still form. She commanded his complete concentration. I doubt he would have noticed anything else.

Rothscha murmured something. I winced at the sound of flesh being sliced open, closing my eyes as a wave of nausea hit me. A second wave came over me—Graenta's own horrified reaction.

What's happening?

Oh, Idessa. Graenta sounded sick. *He's cut her arm ... there's so much blood ...*

Graenta. We have to do something.

I can't. I could feel his frustration. *I can't break free from their collective spell.*

I *have to do something, then.*

No. *Idessa, you can't.* Graenta sounded panicked. *If they find you—get a hold of you—*

I understand. And I did. But I hated being unable to help my queen, having to weigh her life against Graenta's.

Queen Yllulae's arm hung limp over the arm of her throne, ribbons of blood threading down her skin.

"It's done, then," Rothscha said, straightening up. His back was still to me as he turned to face his fellow gods. His large form, the raised platform, and the oversized thrones all served to keep me hidden from the others.

"Good," Shonnala said. "As Graenir's ruler, she is the symbol and heart of this kingdom's power. We'll take some of Graenta's blood as well, eventually. But it's better to take from the creation instead of the creator. Graenta, after all, can make more of his little followers. But there's only one Graenta."

There was a long moment of silence. And then, eventually, from Bomor: "So ... now what?"

"I could be wrong," Orchwen said snidely, "but isn't something supposed to happen?"

Shonnala gave a disgruntled huff. "Stop looking at me like that, all of you! Yes, *something should have happened.*" She mocked Orchwen, who scoffed.

Without warning, Graenta screamed. Breathlessly, he called out something I couldn't understand.

From the center of the room, Shonnala shrieked. Bomor and Orchwen both yelped, then Orchwen started chuckling.

"For once I agree with you, Rothscha," she said. "We should have silenced Graenta."

Rothscha turned towards Graenta. The bloodied knife glinted in his hand. "It's not too late."

Speaking of too late—I ducked back behind the throne, but my movement caught Rothscha's attention. "Here, now. What's this?"

I froze, my heart hammering. I was too far from the servants' passage to try to run for it. Plus, I didn't want the others to discover Oran. Maybe I would get lucky and Rothscha would lose interest ...

A meaty hand clamped down on my shoulder. My breath whooshed out of me as I was hauled up unceremoniously.

Rothscha dragged me between the two thrones, to the center of the dais. He shoved me forward, causing me to fall to my knees. "Look what I found."

"So there was an intruder," Orchwen said smugly.

"Yes." Rothscha glanced down at me. "But what do we do with her?"

"That depends," Shonnala said. "Who are you, child?"

I paused. Shonnala waggled her fingers at me. Instantly, my body seized up.

"I asked you a question," the goddess said. "And I hate waiting."

I felt compelled to answer, to tell her the truth. But before I could speak, another wave of magic washed over me.

My body relaxed. I could feel Shonnala's spell hovering nearby, but this new spell kept it at bay.

Don't tell her anything of import, came Graenta's warning in my head. *Not even your true name.*

All right, I said. *And—thank you.*

I felt a slight warmth from Graenta in response.

"My name is Jele," I said, borrowing my former best friend's name.

"Jele," Shonnala repeated. I held my breath. Did she believe me?

"Well, Jele," she said. "What are you doing here?"

"I ... work in the palace," I improvised. "One of my duties is to clean the great hall daily ..."

Orchwen spoke up, her tone mild but with an undercurrent of accusation. "We took care of everyone here, or so I thought. As well as everyone in the city."

Bomor bristled. "I know how to do my job. I. Did not. Miss. Anyone."

"Well, apparently, you did."

Shonnala shushed them, then silently appraised me. "I'd hate to think Bomor overlooked someone, but you're under my compulsion spell. So you must tell me what I want, and not lie."

"Perhaps Bomor's not the only one getting rusty," Orchwen said.

Shonnala scowled. "I highly doubt that." Then, without warning, she threw more magic at me.

It was a renewal of her first compulsion spell, reinforcing it and bolstering it with additional power. I could feel Graenta's protection begin to weaken and crack as Shonnala's magic grew stronger. Soon it would consume his shield, and my mind.

Graenta ...

Immediately, he sent more magic to strengthen his original spell. The cloying feeling of Shonnala's magic began to recede. I breathed a mental sigh of relief.

I hope she doesn't try that again. Graenta sounded breathless. *I don't know if I can withstand her magic another time.*

I swallowed hard. *I'll do my best to make her believe I'm under her control.*

Please do. I know it's a lot, but ... please. Graenta's inner voice was faint, and I worried that, like Queen Yllulae, he would fall unconscious.

"All right, then, *Jele*," Shonnala said. "If that is, indeed, your name?"

"It is." I hoped my voice sounded steady.

"Good." She turned to Orchwen with a smug smile. "See? I haven't lost my touch."

Orchwen rolled her eyes.

"Jele, how did we overlook you?"

I cleared my throat nervously. Pitching my voice so it would carry, I said slowly, "I lost track of time waiting in the *servants' passage* for a ... for a rendezvous. He never showed, which is unlike him. I fell asleep, and then when I woke up I realized that more time had passed than I had originally thought. But *no one was in there*, except for me, so I came in here to clean."

"Servant's passage?" Shonnala said, startled.

"Yes. It's never used anymore, except by us. That's why we picked it, because *no one should be in there.*" I hoped Oran would understand my poorly veiled hint. I also hoped it wasn't suspicious that I was practically shouting.

"I knew it," Orchwen muttered. She stalked back to where she had been poking about earlier. It didn't take long before she announced, "Found it."

She swept the tapestry aside and disappeared.

I held my breath, waiting for her return.

She reappeared a few heartbeats later. And thankfully, she was alone.

At Shonnala's questioning look, Orchwen shook her head. "The girl is telling the truth. It's dusty and dirty, definitely not used anymore, although there were signs of recent passage."

I breathed easier. I had hoped that mixing in a little truth would make my overall lie seem more believable. But I had also worried that they would find Oran.

"I didn't sense anyone in there," Orchwen continued.

He was gone. He was safe. I hoped.

Shonnala nodded, satisfied. She eyed me thoughtfully as she turned back to me. "Just a servant girl, hmm?" she mused.

Rothscha grabbed my hair and pulled my head back a bit, placing his bloody knife at my throat. "If we don't need her ..."

"We don't," Shonnala agreed. I stiffened as the knife's edge touched my skin. "But don't do away with her just yet. She may be a nobody, but you never know when you a need a 'volunteer' for a spell."

Rothscha pouted. "Are you sure?"

"I am, Rothscha dear."

The god huffed in disappointment, but lowered his knife and released me. I scrambled away, my left side bumping against Graenta's throne.

Vines shot up from the dais, similar to the ones that guarded the castle outside. They snaked around my legs and crawled up my torso before I even registered what was happening. The vines kept climbing up my body, forming a grotesque necklace that stopped just under my chin.

I struggled weakly, but that only served to make the vines tighten. Small but deadly sharp thorns emerged down the length of the vines, and I stilled. The thorns rested right against my skin. If I continued to struggle, I would easily cut myself. Or worse.

Now that the matter of me was settled, Shonnala turned her back to me to address the others. With a light kick to my bound body, Rothscha stepped off the dais to join his fellow gods. I hissed as some of the vines dug into my skin.

Idessa. Graenta's weak voice popped up in my mind. *I am so sorry. I wish this hadn't happened. If only there was a way we could get you out of here.*

It's okay. Even as I thought it, I knew how inane it sounded. *We'll figure something out.*

I hoped.

In the center of the room, the gods' conversation had devolved into yet another argument.

How did you ever survive, listening to this day in and day out, for so many years? I wondered.

It was a long few centuries, came Graenta's dry response.

I started to chuckle, then instantly stopped when I felt the thorns grate against my neck.

If only I was free! The gods weren't even paying attention to Graenta or me. Their bickering had grown more heated.

"We'll just have to make do with the queen's blood," Bomor said. "Since we haven't had any success finding Graenta's Guardian."

All heads swiveled to Orchwen.

The goddess stamped her foot. "It's not my fault! I really thought it was that man we found in the Archives. I didn't realize it was just an echo of the past."

Man from the Archives?

I'm so sorry, Idessa. Graenta's response was tinged with regret. *I tried to protect your brother ... I failed. Since he was a former Guardian, Orchwen found him easily. They were enraged when they discovered he wasn't the current Guardian ... but even though they tried to break him, he resisted to the end.*

The end?

I blinked away tears, recalling how Oran and I fought that possessed shell of my brother outside. Was he truly beyond hope, then?

A commotion at the entrance of the great hall caught everyone's attention.

Rothscha smiled. "Ah. That must be one of our guards, here to give a report."

Shonnala waved a hand towards the entrance. The heavy oak doors flew open.

59

CHAPTER FIFTY-NINE

BUT INSTEAD OF THE single runner the gods expected, a wave of humans and Fae creatures poured in.

Near the head of the group, surrounded by her guards, I spied Grand Marshal Adalynn, Merla's Helmet shining on her head. And King Addan, his midnight blue velvet cloak swirling around his body as he strode into the room.

Shonnala cried, "What is this?"

Adalynn's command rang out loud and clear. "Surrender, all of you. Surrender peacefully, and we will be merciful."

"Surrender?" The goddess spat out the word like she had tasted something sour.

"Is that a no, then?" Adalynn's overly polite tone was laced with steel.

Rothscha gave a loud roar and charged forward, his sword at the ready. He tossed the dagger to Bomor, who caught it easily and fanned out to one side. Annlynden, still in jaguar form, padded alongside him.

Orchwen yawned and drew her own sword. But she seemed disinclined to get involved unless absolutely necessary. Meanwhile, Shonnala readied a spell. A mass of red and black swirled above her outstretched palm.

Shouts erupted as steel met steel. More of our people swarmed in from the doorway, filling the room. I didn't see Queen Jennica, Ambassador Joichan, or Lord Rhyss, although the Fae royals had joined the fray. I was heartened to see so many of our people safe and still standing, but it also made me wonder about the fate of the possessed souls they had battled outside.

Lis. I hope you're okay. Please be okay.

Sparks crackled in the air as magical shields went up. Shonnala's power was easily a match for several mages, and they struggled to hold their wards and fight her magic at the same time.

A scream ripped through the air as Annylnden sprang up, his sharp teeth sinking into one man's throat.

A blade at my back caused me to gasp.

"Idessa, be still! It's me," Oran's reassuring voice sounded low in my ear. "Give me a moment, and I'll cut you free."

Obediently, I held still, not even daring to breathe as Oran worked his knife carefully between the thorns. Finally, the vines gave way and fell off. I brushed them off, taking care not to cut myself.

Oran embraced me. "You're all right?"

I moved my head, relishing the freedom. As I started to stand, I sucked in a breath. There was no time to check the extent of the thorns' damage to my side. "For the most part. Now, let's get Graenta and the queen."

Two Fae were busy freeing Graenta. A dryad stood by Graenta's throne, her hand on the vines holding him in place. As she murmured a spell, her gnome companion furiously cut through his bindings. He gave a little cry of triumph as the cut vines fell to the side.

Graenta hopped down from the throne. The gnome and the dryad stayed nearby, weapons in hand.

"I thank you for your help," Graenta addressed the pair gravely.

The dryad blushed while the gnome bowed. "It's an honor, Your Grace."

Looking around, I realized—"You came in through the servants' passage?"

Oran nodded. "Just a few of us, really."

Oran's "few" was at least thirty people, spilling from the hidden hallway to surround the gods from behind.

Orchwen turned, her eyes growing wide as she spotted the newcomers. "Uh, Shonnala?"

Shonnala glanced over her shoulder. Her eyes grew wide. Cursing loudly, she threw a bolt of magic towards the dais.

Oran jumped in front of me, shielding my body with his. Others of our group scattered. Or tried to, but there was no way everyone would reach safety in time.

I grabbed Graenta's hand. I wasn't sure why. What did I think to do, drag him away? Pull him to hide behind Oran with me? Perhaps I just wanted to both offer and give comfort in our final moments.

I tensed and squeezed my eyes shut, bracing myself for inevitable annihilation.

Nothing happened.

Cautiously, I cracked open one eye. Then the other.

A powerful shield protected Graenta, me, and the others who stood on our side of the great hall. The shield emanated from Graenta's outstretched free hand. The youth looked stunned, as if even he hadn't expected it to work.

Shonnala's magic blasted against the ward, unable to break through. A dark purple and black mass coated the air directly in front of us, jagged edges spreading from its center.

But our protection would only last so long. Already Graenta was panting, winded. Beads of sweat appeared on his forehead from the effort of maintaining such a big ward. And he had already been so drained prior to this.

I squeezed Graenta's hand in encouragement. "Just hold on," I whispered. I looked down.

Our joined hands glowed silver, as if bolstered by the land of Graenir itself.

An errant thought tried to swim to the surface of my murky mind. I turned to Oran and grabbed his hand. The silver light around Graenta's and my hands glowed brighter.

My eyes widened. I nodded at the gnome and the dryad who had freed Graenta earlier. "Oran, take their hands."

"What?" Oran blinked, startled. But he did as I asked, and took one of the gnome's hands.

An earthy greenish-brown light joined the silver aura. Graenta breathed a little easier as new magical energy joined his.

Seeing this, the gnome grabbed the dryad's hand. She looked around, locking hands with a Rothschan soldier who stood nearby.

"Keep going!" I called down the line. On Graenta's other side, a Bomorran archer put her hand on the boy's shoulder. She linked hands with a centaur, who grabbed another Bomorran's hand. A few pixies flitted about, landing on people's heads or shoulders so they could also lend their strength to Graenta.

A gorgeous rainbow of colors flooded the silver glow. The red and gray of Rotshchan. Faerie's earthy tones. Dark green, symbolizing Bomora. More silver, from my home country.

And then, surprisingly, the blues of Calia.

I looked towards the servants' passage. Standing near the doorway were Queen Jennica and Ambassador Joichan, their hands joined to the others'.

Graenta didn't look so exhausted anymore. And his shield, now supported by the strength of our allies, easily held.

"I'm not going back!" Shonnala screamed as she redoubled her efforts. Nearby, the other gods wavered, unsure if they should lend aid to Shonnala or continue fighting against the original intruders.

Graenta didn't respond, but tears streamed down his face. To us, he yelled, "Get ready!"

"For what?" I asked.

And then I felt it. Graenta was calling to something within me, within all of us. It wasn't our magical power. Not all of us had magic, and those that did possessed it to varying degrees.

But we all had something else. Something in common. Something deeper, inherent within each of us.

Our ties to the Gifted Lands. And to each other.

Graenta's presence was polite but insistent, urgent. *May I?*

Yes.

A rush of energy surged through me. Graenta's power, searching for that core within me that bound me to him and all the others. Finding it, his power latched on and pulled it out of me.

But it didn't hurt, or leave me weak. Even as that essence left my body, to join the others' coalescing in Graenta, I felt power return to me, filling me with renewed vitality.

My eyes widened as realization dawned. Although I was willingly giving up my spirit to help Graenta, my shared bond with the others meant that that spirit would never really leave me. If anything, it was returned to me tenfold, bolstered by the others' power.

With our collective power, Graenta broke the ward.

60

CHAPTER SIXTY

WITH THE SHIELD GONE, Graenta immediately threw a concentrated bolt of magic at Shonnala.

The full force of his magic, strengthened with the collective will of the inhabitants of the Gifted Lands, hit her square on.

The room grew bright, so bright that I squeezed my eyes shut and ducked my head. Even with my eyes closed, I could still see bright spots beyond them.

She screamed as his magic enveloped her. As did Orchwen, who was standing close enough to be caught up in the blast as well.

Annlynden growled, but didn't attack. I wasn't sure why. Maybe he, too, was blinded?

The light faded to a more manageable level. I still saw some faint spots, and blinked them away rapidly. Wonderingly, I looked around.

Shonnala lay on the floor, deathly still. Orchwen knelt beside her, panting slightly as she checked Shonnala's pulse. Annylnden stood next to her, gently licking Shonnala's hand with a worried look on his black feline face.

King Addan stood over Bomor, his sword trained on the god. But Bomor, trussed up on the floor in the king's midnight blue cloak, didn't look like he'd be going anywhere any time soon.

Grand Marshal Adalynn was polishing her helmet. Satisfied, she held it firmly in the crook of her arm as she looked down at Rothscha. Three of her guards were holding the god at sword point, but, like Bomor, he seemed stunned. In fact, he was babbling incoherently in a language I didn't understand.

Graenta slowly lowered his hand as he surveyed the room. His face was a study in shock and grief, rather than triumph.

Orchwen looked around the great hall, taking everything in. She turned to us, tears streaming down her normally emotionless face.

"All right, Graenta. I'm not going to fight you. We're not going to fight you," she said, indicating Annlynden next to her. "You win. Again." She sniffled. "I suppose you're going to lock us away again, aren't you?"

Annlynden switched from licking Shonnala's hand to licking Orchwen's hand. She buried a hand, then her face, in the jaguar's dark fur. She gave a muffled sob.

"I was sealed away with all of you," Graenta reminded her.

"I know," Orchwen said, her voice somewhat indistinct as she mumbled into Annlynden's fur. "But I hated it. We all did."

I know. I did too.

Graenta's voice startled me, and I realized he had spoken internally, so only I could hear him.

Graenta? I reached out uncertainly.

A sob choked his voice. *I hated being locked away for forever as well. But what other choice did I have?*

I squeezed his hand. *Graenta.*

He looked at me, tears streaming unchecked down his face.

"Graenta, you don't have to go back," I said aloud. "Maybe ..." I took a deep breath, worried at the reaction my next words might cause. "Maybe none of you need to go back."

Sure enough, the great hall erupted in indignant shouts and questions. "What do you mean?" "Of course they need to be locked up!" "Are you insane, girl?"

Graenta held up a hand, and the room quieted. "What do you mean, Guardian Idessa?"

I cleared my throat, acutely conscious of the myriad of eyes upon me. I pitched my voice to be heard around the room. "The time of the gods is over. And they must be held accountable for the chaos they have wrought in each of your kingdoms, and here in Graenir. But they are our beloved kingdoms' founders. And they have also spent several lifetimes imprisoned.

"So, I propose that they be stripped of their power, and that that power goes to repairing our countries. They can choose to remain in the Gifted Lands or go into exile, but if they stay, they must abide by our laws and rules. Or they will face the consequences, up to and including death."

Orchwen lifted her head from Annlynden's fur and stared at me. "And if we do not agree to those terms?"

"Then you will be sealed away again, and each kingdom will take steps to ensure that it remains that way, forever," I said. "Any of you who do not agree will be imprisoned again."

The goddess bowed her head. After several moments, she looked up again. "I will do as you say. I give you my powers freely, and will be bound to the laws of Graenir, Orchwell, and the other kingdoms of the Gifted Lands."

The air around her swirled, as if a slight breeze had come into the room. Except the great hall, located in the center of the castle, had no windows, and no one was moving. As she finished speaking, the swirling air solidified into a light shimmer, settling on Orchwen. It pulsed once, and then disappeared. Orchwen slumped, then straightened. She seemed somewhat diminished, but held her head up proudly.

Next to her, Annlynden shifted his form slightly so that his human shape briefly overlaid his jaguar one. With a decidedly human voice, he said, "I, too, agree to give up my powers and be bound to the laws of Graenir, Annlyn, and the other kingdoms of the Gifted Lands."

The same pulsing shimmer descended upon him. When it disappeared, an average-sized, dark-haired man stood in Annlynden's place. He patted his body, taking stock.

"Can you still shapeshift?" Orchwen asked him, eyebrows raised.

The man closed his eyes, concentrating. When he opened them again, he shook his head sadly. Orchwen put a comforting hand on his shoulder.

Shonnala was still unconscious, and Rothscha, while now silent, didn't seem to understand what was happening around him. But Bomor, still bound by King Addan's cloak, swore the same vow Orchwen and Annlynden had given. After the god's power was taken, King Addan held out an expectant hand. The cloak whipped off Bomor and flew back to the king.

Queen Jennica and Joichan approached.

"Well done," the queen said. "But what should be done with Shonnala, Rothscha, and Calianna?"

"Calianna should still be on Zaela Island," I said. "It's probably best if we move Shonnala and Rothscha there as well, until we can get their answers."

"Do you need us to transport them?"

"No need," Graenta said. "I can easily send them there. I have more than enough power right now."

Queen Jennica nodded. "Perfect. Joichan and I will fly ahead to the island, then."

"I'll send them along shortly."

With that, the two Calians left. I stepped off the dais. Approaching Grand Marshal Adalynn, I asked, "What happened?" I waved my hand, indicating Rothscha, Bomor, and the first group.

She pointed to one corner of the room, where the wounded—fortunately, not many—were being treated. "It was hard to get the upper hand, let alone hold our own. Those gods just seemed to have infinite power. King Addan and I had our kingdom's treasures, but couldn't get close enough to use them. Not until Graenta overpowered them all."

I blinked, surprised. "All of them? I thought his magic only affected Shonnala and Orchwen."

"Not my magic alone," Graenta corrected as he joined us. Behind him, I saw Oran kneel down next to Queen Ylullae. "It was all of us—all of you. All that power, representing so many parts of the Gifted Lands. The five of them couldn't stand against that. Although I think Shonnala bore the brunt of it."

"Rothscha as well," Adalynn said. "He and I had locked swords at that point, and I took advantage of your surprise attack to push him into the magic's path. I think that, along with Merla's Helmet, broke his mind."

"How did that work, anyway?" I wondered, pointing at the helmet still tucked under her arm. "I saw how Bomora's cloak restrained Bomor, but—a helmet?"

Adalynn shrugged, but there was a mischievous gleam in her eyes. "I wasn't sure either. It's not like this came with instructions on how to take down a god. When Rothscha was distracted—and overpowered—by Graenta's magic, I threw the helmet at him."

I gaped at her. *You threw your helmet at a god? And you thought that would work?* was what I wanted to say. Instead, I settled for, "You must have excellent aim."

She ducked her head modestly. "He'll have quite a bump on the side of his head later, though. And a massive headache to go with it."

I grinned. "That's one way to use a helmet."

Graenta chuckled, but he seemed a bit distracted. One wave of his hand caused the rest of the gods to disappear.

I hope Queen Jennica and Ambassador Joichan made it to the island already.

I think we all breathed easier once the other gods were gone, although I noticed a few surreptitious, uneasy glances Graenta's way. He ignored them, instead pulling me aside.

"I'm going to head over to Zaela Island," he said.

"Are you sure?" I asked. "I mean, everyone else is either stripped of their power or ... incapacitated in some way. You can just relax now."

"I can't relax until I know Graenir—and the rest of the Gifted Lands—are truly safe."

I nodded in understanding. "We'll be here a while longer. We need to see what happened outside the city, first. And make sure everyone here is settled and all right. But we'll be along as soon as we can."

He sighed. "Perhaps you'll catch up to me sooner than you think. I plan on taking my time."

"You're not just going to magically transport yourself there, like you did the others?"

"Nah." He smiled, but it didn't reach his eyes. "I'd like to look around my beautiful kingdom one last time."

61

CHAPTER SIXTY-ONE

GRAENTA'S WORDS DISTURBED ME, but before I could ask him what he meant, King Addan called my name. Then he and Grand Marshal Adalynn joined me, and somewhere in all the commotion, Graenta slipped out of the great hall.

Oran joined us as we were finishing our discussion.

"I'll take my group back outside. Come join us when you can," Adalynn said, and left with most of the first wave of people.

I turned to Oran, my face lit with an unspoken question.

He shook his head sadly. "Queen Yllulae, may her name live on forever, is no longer with us."

Tears pricked my eyes. Bowing my head, I murmured, "May her name live on forever."

King Addan placed a comforting hand on my shoulder. "Bomora grieves with Graenir. Allow me to oversee her preparations."

I nodded numbly. Oran took my hand. "We need to get that wound of yours taken care of."

Fortunately, the vines hadn't pierced me too deeply, but they would still leave some ugly scars. After a dryad rubbed some salve on my skin and bandaged my side, she declared that I was ready to go. I thanked her before Oran and I left the great hall.

As we exited the palace, I noticed the vine maze that had surrounded the building now lay wilted on the ground. Even though we could easily step over the withered vines, we still had to be careful of the occasional thorn sticking up in our path.

The city streets looked much the same as they had on our earlier frantic run through them. Whatever magic the gods had used on their resurrected army, it hadn't allowed the possessed to come back into the city. As we approached the open gate, our steps slowed.

"I'm afraid of what we'll find out there," I admitted.

Oran squeezed my hand. "I am, too."

Taking a deep breath, we stepped through the gate.

The first thing I noticed was the stillness. No birds chirped in the trees, no insects buzzed around our heads. Even the air was eerily calm, as if no breeze would dare to blow and disturb the silence.

The deathly silence.

Strewn about the field just outside Graenir's capital were the bodies of those that the gods had taken and turned against us. With the battle over and their masters' powers gone, the undead were finally at rest, and lay unmoving on the ground. Sprinkled among them were some of Graenir who had been alive when possessed, and had also fallen during the fight. I saw a few of our number as well, but not as many as the gods' former army.

Who were all my countrymen.

Tears threatened my vision again. How much more sorrow would this day bring?

Adalynn and her team moved amongst the fallen, searching for anyone—from either side—who might still be alive. They conducted their work without words, as if they, too, did not want to break the unnatural quiet. To the side, Lord Rhyss stood with another group, silently observing.

Lord Rhyss saw Oran and me and waved. He carefully picked his way over to us, cradling one arm in a makeshift sling.

"What happened?" I asked, waving at his injury.

"A triple blow that I didn't see coming," he said ruefully. "Two sword hits back to back, fine. But I didn't see the last one—and those soldiers could really hit. The one time they have me lead a command ..."

I nodded, remembering the unnatural strength of the undead army. "Is it bad?"

"Nah. I should be fine in a few days," he said cheerfully, rolling his shoulder. He winced, then quickly pasted a smile on his face.

I giggled. Oran gave a cough that sounded suspiciously like an aborted laugh.

Lord Rhyss smirked, as if he knew our thoughts. Looking around the field, he sobered. "I'm so sorry you have to see this."

"There's so much devastation," I said, not wanting to believe my eyes.

"It will take some time to recover, for certain. But with your strong queen to guide you—"

"Our queen is dead," Oran said flatly.

"Oh." Lord Rhyss paused. "My condolences."

"Thank you."

We all fell silent, surveying the scene before us.

"Did Graenta come through here?" I asked, not wanting to think about Queen Yllulae's death and our kingdom's uncertain future.

"He did. He went that way." Lord Rhyss pointed down the road with his good arm.

I wondered what Graenta had thought when he had seen the people of his namesake country like this. And I wondered if he had any good ideas on what we should do next.

I may as well go and ask him, I thought. Plus, I didn't want to hang around this sad scene more than I had to. I knew the vision of it would haunt me for a good long while.

"Thank you," I said. "I guess I'll follow him, then."

"I'll stay here and help," Oran said unexpectedly. "I need to—I'll just be more useful here."

"Should I stay, too?" But I wasn't sure I was up to it.

"No. You go on and find Graenta."

I looked at Oran, wondering at his reasoning. He was holding back tears, but he sounded determined. I had a feeling I knew why he wanted to stay, and a rush of tenderness flooded me even as I wanted to break down sobbing.

He needs to make sure about Lis ... and he wants to spare me the shock. Dear, sweet Oran.

I nodded in thanks, and then headed down the road towards the riverbank as Oran and Lord Rhyss turned and waded into the field of the fallen.

I reached the Rehann River's shores quickly—and thankfully without incident. Once there, I was happy to be greeted by Harlan.

"It seemed safer to return home than stay close to the battle," he said. "A few people stayed at the camp, just in case you sent any runners. And if the worst happened, then we could escape down the river right away."

"We?"

Queen Inari poked her head out of Harlan's cottage. "Hello, Guardian Idessa! You're truly a welcome sight. The two Calian dragons passed by earlier today, and then Graenta not too long ago. If you're here, then I trust the battle is well and truly over?"

I nodded. "Not without some losses, unfortunately. Including our dear Queen Yllulae. Your husband has graciously offered to oversee her arrangements."

Queen Inari gave a small sigh of relief. "I am sorry to hear that, although I am glad to hear my dear Addan is alive and well. Could you tell us more? The others didn't stop by to give us any news."

I quickly filled them in on the events outside the city and inside the castle. I left out the part about seeing Tahn and my brother Lis on the battlefield. Some things were too personal to share.

"Did you need to go somewhere, Guardian?" Harlan asked. "Or did you just come by to tell us what happened?"

"I'd like to join Graenta and the others on Zaela Island," I said. "If it's not too much trouble."

The ferryman shook his head. "None at all. Just give me a moment to get things ready."

Soon we were on the water, headed towards the island. As I basked in the sun's warmth, I marveled at how different this trip felt. Before, Zaela Island was my prison, taking me away from all I held dear and trapping me in what I assumed would be a dull, uncertain future. Now, the future—both mine and my kingdom's—were still uncertain, but I didn't feel confined or resentful anymore.

I didn't know what the future would hold, but I knew that I wanted to be a part of rebuilding Graenir.

"I'm surprised Graenta didn't give you the news," I commented.

Harlan shrugged as he skillfully navigated around a rock. "Before I could go out to greet him, he just disappeared. When I looked again, he had reappeared on the island."

Hmm. Apparently Graenta really did want to be alone. I hoped he wouldn't be upset by my presence.

Well, too bad, I thought stubbornly. *He doesn't get to run away from his problems. Not as long as I'm his Guardian.*

We landed on Zaela Island. I waved away Harlan's offer to stay and wait for me. "I don't know how long I'll be," I told him. "Besides, between Graenta and the Calians, I'm sure I'll be able to find a way back."

Harlan smiled. "Still, to be safe, I'll look to the island every morning. If you need the ferry, just stand on the shore at sunrise, and I'll come for you."

"Thank you."

"Be well, Guardian." With that, Harlan pushed off, leaving me alone on Zaela Island.

I waved goodbye, then turned and headed into the remains of the tower. The area was noticeably cleaner, thanks to the queen's soldiers, but part of the building would be uninhabitable for a while.

My former bedchamber at the top of the tower was ruined, but the study on the first floor was intact. The broken window had been boarded up. A few abandoned bedrolls in the study told me that the queen's soldiers and servants had used the room as a makeshift camp. I continued past, heading downstairs into the underground area that once housed the Great Seal.

"Who's there?" a female voice challenged.

62

—·—

CHAPTER SIXTY-TWO

"IT'S GUARDIAN IDESSA, YOUR Majesty," I called out. As I drew closer, I saw Queen Jennica, Ambassador Joichan, and Graenta standing around a darker area in the center of the room. A cold ball of magical silver light danced on the ceiling, providing just enough illumination to see most of the room.

Queen Jennica smiled at me. "Idessa! It's good to see you again. And what perfect timing. We were just discussing the gods' fate."

"Has anything changed?" I wondered. I peered down into the hollow at my feet, the pit that had served as the gods' prison for so many centuries. Shonnala, Calianna, and Orchwen were all sitting on the hard ground, looking weary and defeated. Bomor paced the pit, impatient. Annlynden stood in one corner, staring at his hands as if he had never seen them before. Rothscha lay next to him. Sleeping, perhaps?

"Shonnala and Calianna have agreed to give up their powers," the queen said. "Which just leaves Rothscha."

"Did you ask him before he decided to take a nap?" I asked dubiously. If my fate was hanging in the balance, I didn't think I could just calmly go to sleep.

"We did," Graenta said. "But—he's not quite himself."

"Still?" I said, just as Calianna lashed out, "You ruined him!"

Shonnala and Orchwen were quick to hush her, turning wary eyes upward to see how their captors would respond to Calianna's outburst.

"Yes," Graenta said, responding to my question. "When we asked if he, too, would agree to exchange his powers for freedom, he didn't answer."

"He answered," Queen Jennica corrected, "but not in any way any of us could understand."

"I understood him. Quite well, actually." Graenta snorted. "Trust me, you weren't missing much by not having a translation."

The queen chuckled in response.

"So what should we do with him, then? And what about the others?" I asked.

"To their credit, the others refused to leave unless they could take Rothscha with them," Queen Jennica said. "But as he still has his powers ... even with his mind gone, he could still be a danger. Especially if, or when, he recovers."

"I don't know that he *will* recover," Graenta said, eyeing Rothscha's sleeping form thoughtfully. "And with Rothschan's treasure awakened, that should keep him in check."

"Still, it's a rather big risk to take."

"True." Graenta's eyes roamed around the room. "I wonder ... Your Majesty, are you able to do a basic binding?"

Queen Jennica paused thoughtfully. "Do you mean a binding to a place, an object, or a person?"

"Any of them, although to a place or a person would be best."

"Then, yes. Although, for me, to bind someone to a place would take more magical energy than I have. I would need to partner with a mage—preferably, several—to do that."

"I can help," Ambassador Joichan volunteered.

"As will I," Graenta said. "You'll need my magic mixed in with yours to make this work, anyway."

Queen Jennica raised an eyebrow. "What are you thinking?"

"We bind Rothscha to Zaela Island. If he ever regains his mind, then he can decide if he wants to give up his powers, or stay bound."

"No!" The collective protest arose from the other—awake—gods.

"No?" Graenta frowned down at them.

The gods exchanged a look. Shonnala gave Orchwen a little shove. Orchwen looked put out at being the group's unofficial speaker, but stood up and faced those aboveground squarely.

"Please don't bind Rothscha here," she began, in a surprising show of compassion. "Not to Zaela Island, not to this pit. None of us ever want to see this place, ever again. Losing our powers is a small price to pay to be able to walk the world again. If you must bind him, please—not here."

A heavy silence fell over the room. Part of me felt that, after all the havoc they had caused, they should have no say in their fates. The audacity! But if we didn't consider their feelings, then didn't that make us just as petty as they had acted?

"What do you think, Graenta? Guardian?" Queen Jennica and Joichan looked to us for guidance.

Graenta nodded at me. "This decision should be Idessa's, not mine."

"Me?" I gaped at him. "Why only me?"

"I can't say, just yet. But you'll understand soon enough. For now, let's just say I defer all decisions of this magnitude to you."

"But—but ... I'm no leader."

"You are. You have been, this whole time. And right now, you are the only leader your kingdom has."

I swallowed the argument I had been ready to give. He was right. Graenir had no leader. The late Queen Yllulae, a widow, had no children to inherit the throne, and no council to govern in her absence. The Guardian was the closest thing to a second-in-command Graenir had. Which meant Graenta and I were the most logical people to lead now. But since Graenta didn't want to lead ...

That left just me.

I took a deep breath. We'd sort out actual, permanent leadership later. For now—"Can we contact Grand Marshal Adalynn?"

Queen Jennica nodded. "Yes. Through a calling stone King Addan has, provided he and Adalynn are still near each other."

"They should both still be in or near the city."

The queen stepped aside to contact King Addan. Within moments, the Bomorran king's smooth voice pierced the air. "Queen Jennica! How goes it?"

"Overall, well," she responded. "Is Grand Marshal Adalynn with you?"

"She should be here soon. A runner just came by to tell me."

"Ah, perfect."

King Addan gave a nearby page instructions to send Adalynn to him the moment she arrived. The two royals made small talk while Queen Jennica waited. Part of that included reassurances that Queen Inari was safe and well. Graenta, Joichan, and I exchanged smiles. It was obvious the dashing pirate king adored his queen.

Adalynn's face appeared above the queen's palm. "Your Majesty! How may I help you?"

Queen Jennica's face broke into a smile. "Adalynn! Thank you for joining us. It's like this ..." She lowered her voice and quickly explained the situation to the Grand Marshal.

"If you did bind him to Rothschan, what would that mean? For him, for the kingdom?" Adalynn smirked. "If you tied them to our royals, I don't think any of my soldiers would object. I certainly wouldn't. But I don't think our king and queen could handle the responsibility."

Queen Jennica and Adalynn broke out in laughter.

Graenta stepped to the queen's side. "If I may, I believe I can answer your question, Grand Marshal. We'd bind him to the kingdom, to the land itself. His ties as your country's founder would hold him there more firmly than any prison ever could. His power will also be bound to the land, unusable to him, but able to help Rothschan flourish."

"And if he chooses not to relinquish his power?" Adalynn asked.

"He will be weakened, with his power locked away and our magic confining him to your kingdom. If he chooses to try to harm Rothschan, then you can deal with him as you see fit." From Graenta's tone, and the knowing gleam in Adalynn's eyes, I hoped—for his own sake—that Rothscha would willingly give up his powers as the other gods had.

"All right, then. Rothschan agrees to the binding. Do you need me to be present?"

"No. Your agreement will suffice."

"Is there anything else I need to know?"

Graenta paused, thinking. "After the binding is complete, we will bring him to you so you can bring him back to Rothschan. If we bring him there directly, that could weaken the spell."

"That is acceptable. I will take my leave now. We only came back long enough to rest and get some food. There's still much work to be done outside the city."

Graenta and Queen Jennica said their goodbyes, then ended the connection. They rejoined us, gazing down into the pit again.

The gods had heard practically every word of the conversation with Adalynn. The part that mattered to them, anyway. I was surprised to see tears in Shonnala's eyes, and Bomor had stopped his agitated pacing.

Orchwen gazed up at us, her own eyes shining. "Thank you."

63

CHAPTER SIXTY-THREE

WITH THE DETAILS SETTLED, Graenta and Queen Jennica turned their attention to binding Rothscha. It should just be a simple spell, confining Rothscha to the kingdom he founded. Bolstered by Ambassador Joichan's magic, it would be easy enough for Queen Jennica to do.

What would ensure his binding, and anchor Rothscha's power to the land, Graenta explained, was mixing in Graenta's magic with the queen's spell. The Calian's human magic would link Rothscha to Rothschan. But only Graenta's magic, the essence of a fellow god, would be able to hold Rothscha.

While they discussed spellcasting details, I headed back upstairs. I was no mage, and I didn't want to get in their way.

I wandered into the study. With nothing better to do, I began to tidy the room, moving the bedrolls to one side so there would be a clear path. Idly, I tipped a few books out, sneezing at the dust that brought up.

A shout from below pierced the silence.

I turned away from the shelf and hurried out of the room. Behind me, the books I had been looking at tumbled to the floor with a thud.

A second scream caused me to pick up my pace.

Taking the stairs two at a time, my feet nearly slid out from underneath me. I grabbed at the railing, barely catching myself in time.

I stopped, taking in the scene before me.

I had first thought that something had gone wrong, that the gods had regained their abilities and overpowered my friends. But a quick survey of the room told me that wasn't true: the gods, save Graenta, were all still in the room's center hollow. Queen Jennica and Joichan didn't look injured in any way.

But Graenta ...

I flew to where he lay on the ground, dropping to my knees by his side.

"Graenta! Graenta, what's happened?"

The boy god coughed and weakly tried to wave away my attempt to help him. I ignored it, tightening my arm around his shoulder as I helped him sit up. His face was pale, his hands clammy and cold even as I noticed the sweat on his forehead.

"Idessa, it's—" he started coughing harder.

I looked up at Queen Jennica and Joichan. They both shook their heads, as if to say, *We don't know what happened, either.*

"We completed the binding spell," Queen Jennica said, but she sounded uncertain.

"We did," Graenta croaked out. "Rothscha is well and truly bound."

"Then what happened?" I repeated. "You're so weak. It's like you lost your power, instead of just binding Rothscha's."

The minute I said it, my blood ran cold. I met Graenta's reluctant eyes, and I knew.

"You didn't," I whispered. Queen Jennica gasped, horrified.

"I had to," Graenta said. "It wouldn't have been right, making the others give up their powers, but allowing me to keep mine."

"Of course it would have been right! *You* didn't do anything! You helped the Gifted Lands. You've always helped us."

"I know, but ... it would be too tempting, if I still had my power. The others might try to sway me to share it with them, or use it against the people of the Gifted Lands. Or *I* might be tempted to do something—who would be able to stand against me? No, this is best, Idessa. My Guardian."

Tears streamed down my face, unchecked.

"But ... but ..." I didn't have any real arguments. Not that anything I could say would change things. I was too late.

Sniffling, I brushed some tears away. "Is your power truly gone?"

Graenta hesitated. "Not exactly."

Hope flared in my chest. "Really? So we can get it back—I'll be here, along with the others, to make sure you don't abuse it—"

He shook his head, and the small flicker died. "I can't get it back, nor do I want to. My power has gone where the others' has—into each of the kingdoms that is that god's namesake."

"I don't understand."

He sat up a little straighter. Some color had returned to his face, but he still looked drained. "It was never our intention to hoard our power. At least, that was what I had been led to believe when we created our countries. We were meant to share our knowledge and our abilities with our people, until we had given it all away."

"Given it all away?"

"Yes." He patted my hand. "Being an immortal is more of a curse than a blessing. When we created the Gifted Lands, even then, we had all begun to feel the weight of our immortality. So we agreed, over time, to siphon our power away." He sighed. "But after we created our kingdoms, some of the gods changed their minds. That's why I did what I did, and betrayed them to seal us all away."

"Does this mean ..." I stopped, swallowed hard, then tried again. I whispered, "Does this mean you'll die?"

He grinned cheekily. "Everything ends sometime." Then, more gently: "But, yes. I and the other gods—former gods—will die. Eventually. We've lived more lifetimes than we've ever wanted to. But dying—that will be a long way off yet."

I was crying. Still. Again. I wasn't sure anymore which one it was. But every time I thought my heart couldn't break one more time, it did.

A slim arm slid around my shoulders. I looked over to see Queen Jennica kneeling beside me.

"Here," she murmured. "Let's get you both off the floor."

I let her help me stand, then melted into her comforting embrace. Joichan assisted Graenta, then offered me a rumpled, but clean, handkerchief.

Gratefully, I took it and wiped at my face. When I felt a bit more composed, I looked around.

The other three were looking at me.

Oh, right.

I pushed down my grief and sadness. My broken country, Graenta's sacrifice—all of that I would have to ponder later, when I had the luxury of sitting with my thoughts. But first, there were more pressing things to take care of.

I cleared my throat. "So, all the gods are taken care of." All *of them. Oh, Graenta. No, don't think about that right now.*

I peered down into the pit. "With the exception of Rothscha, you are all free to leave. Wherever you go, whatever you do, always recall your promise."

The former gods nodded. Then, from Orchwen: "Uh ... how shall we leave?"

A fair point, since they were now powerless. Joichan spoke up. "I can bring them back to Graenir. Or another place in the Gifted Lands."

"I will go with you," Queen Jennica told her father, earning her a proud smile.

"We'll need to bring Rothscha back to Graenir and Grand Marshal Adalynn." I turned to Graenta. "Where would you like to go?"

He smiled. "With you, of course."

I grinned back. "Good."

Back outside, I was pleasantly surprised to see Harlan on the island, waiting with his ferry. "When I got to the mainland, I turned right back around. I was just so worried. I was going to wait until morning, to see if you needed me."

I threw my arms around him in an impulsive hug. "Thank you, Harlan. That's really ... I'm really touched." I sniffled. *Idessa, stop crying already!*

He patted my back awkwardly. "Ah, now. What do we have here?"

I turned to see Bomor and Joichan, with Graenta's occasional assistance, carrying Rothscha out of the ruined tower. I waved them over to the ferry. Harlan jumped to help, bracing the raft as the other men placed the unconscious Rothscha on it.

Queen Jennica, Shonnala, Annylnden, Orchwen, and Calianna emerged from the building. Once Rothscha was settled, the two Calians transformed into their dragon forms and flew away with the remaining gods, save Graenta.

Although each god wanted to return to their particular home kingdom, I didn't think they would be welcome for a while. So I had instructed Queen Jennica and Joichan to place each one in a random kingdom. They could make their way from there.

From the shore, Harlan, Graenta, and I watched them go, then set off across the river, back to Graenir.

As we drew closer, I saw a crowd of people waiting. Grand Marshal Adalynn, with a few Rothschan soldiers and a wooden cart. King Addan, with his arm around Queen Inari, who leaned her head against him. A few others who were a mix of Bomorran, Rothschan, and Graenirian people, and the Fae.

And Oran.

Once we reached the shore, I called out, "The rest of the gods have agreed to renounce their powers. Rothscha will be under confinement in Rothschan, until he either chooses to relinquish his powers or stay a prisoner of Rothschan for the rest of his immortal days. The age of the gods, if there ever was one, is over."

A ragged cheer went up from those gathered on the shore. Harlan and Graenta jumped out of the ferry, pulling it further up the shore. Two men wearing the Rothschan red-and-grey instantly appeared, ready to move Rothscha from the raft to the cart.

I joined Oran on the shore, where he enfolded me in a big hug. I buried my face in his chest while he kissed the top of my head.

I pulled back and looked up at him. In his eyes, I saw sadness, heartbreak ... and my future.

"What?" he asked. "What are you thinking?"

A lot of things. How we needed to rebuild Graenir. How I didn't want to lead forever, but I would do what I could to help my beloved kingdom get back on its feet. How, somewhere along the way, Graenir had become dear to me, instead of just a place to bide my time and waste my life.

Or how Graenta sacrificed so much to help us, and how I could ever honor that sacrifice.

There were too many things to think about, really. But I didn't need to think about them at this moment. For now—

I took Oran's hand. "Come on. Let's go home."

Epilogue

One Year Later

I kissed the tips of my fingers, then touched the gravestone, running my fingertips over part of Alistair's full name carved into the cool slate. The loss of my brother still felt fresh. I closed my eyes, preferring to remember his smiling face, his teasing, even his sternness when he was trying to steer me down a better path. The monster I had fought a year ago outside Graenir's city walls was not my brother.

Or so I tried to believe in my better moments. Far too often, I was plagued with doubt. Could I have tried harder to reach him? Had I killed him—or at least contributed to his demise? I'd never know the true answers to those questions.

When the gods had surrendered their power, their hold over the people of Graenir had broken. The possessed undead returned to their previously dead state. Those who had been alive when possessed either survived or succumbed to their wounds. Although for the survivors, death might have been more kind. The possession had broken the survivors' minds, to varying degrees, and none of them would ever be as they were before.

Tahn had been among those who had survived, but had been broken to such an extent that he spent his days staring at the wall, talking to unseen people. Jele had pledged to care for him, but when their baby arrived, the burden nearly broke her, too. We patched up our friendship, sort of—the kingdom had suffered so many losses that it didn't seem right to hold a grudge. I helped her out with her baby every so often.

Lis had not survived. I think I had known, when Oran and I left him unconscious on the battlefield, what my brother's fate would be. And I had seen the truth of it in Oran's eyes when I had returned from Zaela Island.

The news had devastated my parents. It had aged my father overnight; my mother had grown ill and frail, nearly giving up on life. But they were both strong people, and we had all worked through it together. But Alistair's absence would forever be felt in our minds and our hearts.

Thank the gods I had Oran. Although I don't think that phrase applied anymore in the Gifted Lands, but what else could we say? Steadfast Oran had gotten me through my darkest days, and I was glad I could be there for him as well. I know he keenly missed his best friend.

But we had other things to occupy our time. Mainly, running a country....

I finished tracing Alistair's name and placed the small bouquet of blue forget-me-nots I had brought on his grave. I stood, touching the gravestone a final time. "I love you, Lis."

Oran pulled me to him. I leaned against him, drawing from his presence, then sighed. Oran kissed the top of my head before we both turned and walked away.

"A messenger just delivered a letter for you," Oran said as he entered my private study in the castle.

Not that it was *my* room, any more than the castle was *my* castle. But as the kingdom's de facto leader for the past year, it had made sense to eventually move into the castle to oversee things, instead of traveling back and forth between my family's home and the capital.

I hadn't felt comfortable using the royal suites, though. Instead, I had taken up residence in one of the smallest, simplest guest rooms—"practically the servants' quarters," I had heard one of the servants comment—and preferred to hold public meetings in the dining hall instead of the great hall. I wasn't royalty; I wasn't going to sit on one of those thrones.

Besides, being in the great hall brought back memories of the battle. And other memories I would rather forget.

I looked up as Oran dropped a folded piece of paper on my desk. It landed awkwardly on top of the calling stone Queen Jennica had gifted me with shortly after returning to Calia. From what her accompanying note had said, I only needed to focus on her image while saying her name, and I would be able to reach her right away. But I hadn't used the calling stone yet, partly because I had been so busy overseeing Graenir's day-to-day affairs, and partly because there hadn't been an emergency that demanded I use it.

I picked up the letter, breaking open its golden-brown wax seal.

To Guardian Idessa, Graenta, and Oran, the letter began.

"Oh! You're included, too," I told him. "We can fill Graenta in later." I read aloud:

My apologies for not contacting you sooner. After I returned to Calia, I spent several months recovering. My arm injury was more severe than I had originally realized.

But, truth be told, I barely noticed it. For, upon my return, I found my beloved Farrah awake and healthy. And she wasn't the only one in Calia who had found themselves suddenly hale. I understand that when the gods' powers had gone to their respective kingdoms, it healed a myriad of maladies in each area.

"Huh," Oran said. "This is the first I've heard of that."

"I haven't exactly been good about communicating with the other leaders," I pointed out. "There's been too much to do here. And since Graenir didn't have any miraculous cures …"

"True. Still, we should ask Graenta about it."

I continued reading.

And that brings me to why I am writing. Finally—finally!—Farrah and I are getting married. We would be honored if the three of you could come to Calia to celebrate with us. I apologize for the late notice, but we want to be wed before anything else *happens.*

I smiled at that. I could practically see Lord Rhyss's smirk.

Our celebration will take place on the 16th.

"Idessa, that's …" Oran frowned, thinking. "In a week! We'd have to leave right now to get there in time."

"Hush, you," I teased. "I'm not finished reading."

I know it doesn't give you much time to get here, so Queen Jennica has graciously offered to go to Graenir to get all of you. By dragon, it will take hardly any time to reach Calia.

"That's true," I said, remembering our oh-so-long ago flight with Ambassador Joichan.

No need to send a response. Your always welcome presence will be the happiest of responses.

Lord Rhyss's blocky signature was scrawled at the bottom of the letter.

I picked up a little bell, ringing it twice. A smartly dressed page appeared almost immediately. "Please send a runner to find Graenta and request that he come to the palace."

The page nodded and left.

Oran and I looked at each other. "Well?" Oran said.

I put the bell down and picked up the calling stone. "I guess we're going to Calia."

Calia is much more pleasant when I'm not fearing for my life, I thought, watching the guests mingle at Lord Rhyss and Lady Farrah's wedding celebration.

There were easily two hundred people, maybe more, at this beautiful and lavish event. The couple's close friendship with the Calian royal couple ensured they had the use of a lovely venue—the courtyard of Castle Calia.

And it seemed like the newly wed couple knew most everyone in the Gifted Lands. My head spun from the myriad introductions to fascinating people from the other six kingdoms. Even the Fae royals, King Paxen and Queen Bettan, were in attendance, along with their advisor, Lord Chela.

Oran and I stood to the side, just people watching.

Lord Rhyss and Lady Farrah, who had been circling the courtyard talking to guests, approached us. "Guardian Idessa! Oran! I'm so glad you could make it. I was so happy when Jennica told me all of you could come. But where's Graenta?" He looked around.

"I believe he's getting a third helping. Or is it his fourth? I've lost count," I giggled.

Lord Rhyss smiled. "Good for him. Let me introduce you to my bride."

After we introduced ourselves and exchanged pleasantries, I said, "Lady Farrah, we were overjoyed to hear about your amazing recovery."

"Thank you." Her voice was low and musical. "As was I, when I was told about it. When Balor threw that spell at me, my last conscious thought was that he would be the only one who could lift it."

Oran and I exchanged a look. "We've heard this Balor person mentioned before," Oran said. "I even searched the Graenir Archives to find out more about him, but nothing turned up. I don't want to mar a beautiful day with a bad memory—"

"Of course. I'd be happy to tell you the whole story another time. But the short version is, Balor is—was?—the king of the Faerie Unseelie Court, and the one responsible for breaking the gods free from their centuries-long prison. When I and Endri of Annlyn tried to stop him, he drained me of my magic. I fell unconscious—"

"—And Balor ended up trapped in a mirror," Lord Rhyss finished. "As far as we know, he is still in there."

"Whatever his aim was in freeing the gods, we may never know." Lady Farrah's mouth set in a firm line. "And I, for one, will never break a mirror to ask him about it."

"I see." I definitely wanted to hear this story in its entirety, but Lady Farah was right—another day. "That's enough to make me eschew all mirrors from now on."

"Just be extremely careful not to break one." She paused, looking thoughtful. "I wonder if there's a way to enspell a mirror to make sure it never breaks?"

"I know that look," Lord Rhyss teased. "That sounds like a great new research experiment—*after* our honeymoon."

The two laughed and said goodbye, moving on to chat with other guests. Graenta approached, holding two plates piled high with food.

"Here you go," he said, handing Oran a plate.

"Thank you, but I can't finish all this," Oran protested.

"Oh, that's for the both of you." Graenta began to tuck into his food.

"It's odd, I figured you wouldn't have much of an appetite, now that you're mortal," I said. "Aren't you at least one thousand years old?"

"Oh, I'm well over that," the youth said cheerfully, his mouth full. He pushed his glasses up his nose. "But tell that to my adolescent body. I'm a growing boy, you know."

Oran chuckled while I rolled my eyes. "I didn't realize, when you gave up your powers, that you'd be a kid forever."

"Not forever. I'll grow up, eventually." Graenta shrugged. "I just don't know when, exactly."

I snorted. "I'm not ready to be a parent."

"You don't have to be." Graenta suddenly turned serious. "I'm staying in Calia."

"What?" I said, caught off guard. When I had moved into the Graenir palace, Graenta had moved in with me. There was plenty of room, and even though he deferred all major decisions to me, I still treasured his advice and insights. "You're leaving Graenir?"

"You don't need me," he said gently. "You're doing a great job running the kingdom—"

"I don't want to do it forever!"

"So set up Graenir's government however it suits you." He paused to put his mostly full plate down on a nearby table. "I won't be away from Graenir forever. I don't know how many years I have left as a former immortal, but I want to take the time I do have to get to know this beautiful world that we—my fellow former gods and I—created. I want to spend several years in each kingdom and adopt its quirks and its wisdom. And then, I'll return. Graenir is home, and always will be."

"I wish I could go with you."

"You can. Get Graenir completely on its feet, bow out of leadership, and come join me. Both of you." He smiled. "But something tells me you might have plans of your own that we can't foresee. We'll just have to face the future when it happens."

I smiled back. He was right. I had no idea what the future held. I could set up a new system of government and leave the country. Or I might stay, for longer than I had originally intended. Oran and I might travel the Gifted Lands and never return to Graenir. Or we could devote our whole lives to Graenir's reconstruction.

I didn't know. And I wouldn't fret about it. But what I did know was that whatever future I stepped into, it would be because I had chosen it.

Everything was possible.

Dear Reader: THANK YOU

WHAT A JOURNEY IT has been! I hope you've enjoyed journeying through the Gifted Lands as much as I've enjoyed writing about it and its people. Thank you so much for reading *Heir of Immortals and Empires.*

If this is your first foray into the Gifted Lands and the world of the Kingdom Legacy series, welcome! And if you're a returning reader, I'm so happy we were able to share all these adventures together.

But just because this is the end of *this* series, it doesn't mean the stories are done! I'm currently working on a new series of fairy tale retellings. I also have some more ideas of stories in the Gifted Lands world that I may revisit in the future.

I'd love it if you left an honest review on Goodreads or wherever you like to buy books and learn about new titles.

And stay in touch if you'd like to hear about new adventures first! Here's how:

Sign up for the Newsletter: http://www.rachanee.net/newsletter

Instagram: http://www.instagram.com/rachaneelumayno

TikTok: https://www.tiktok.com/@rachaneelumayno

YouTube: https://www.youtube.com/@rachaneelumayno

Twitter: http://www.twitter.com/rachaneelumayno

Join the community on Discord: Kingdom Legacy

READ ON FOR A PREVIEW OF
THE FIRST BOOK IN A NEW FAIRY

TALE RETELLING SERIES!

A NOTICE

To the citizens of Woodside:

There has been a recent rise in violence in the neighboring forest that gives our fair town its name. Several animals, both small and large, predator and prey, have been found dead, the cause unknown but a result of obvious unnatural attacks. We have also had an increase in reports of attacks on people traveling through the forest. The attacker or attackers move with such stealth and speed that the victims have been unable to identify who or what is attempting to harm them.

The majority of the attacks have occurred between sunset and dawn.

Caution is advised if you choose to traverse the woods.

Signed,

Joven Marley, Mayor of Woodside

CHAPTER 1

"CLARET? CLARET, HONEY, CAN you come here and mind the shop for a bit?"

I stopped mid-sneak and sighed. Turning on my heel, I called out, "Sure thing, Mama. I'll be right there."

I hurried down the hallway, towards the front of the house and our bakeshop. Grabbing a plain linen apron from a peg by the door, I pushed through it and entered the family bakery.

It may have been Daypito, the traditional day of rest, but the inside of the shop looked anything but restful. The counter was swarmed with impatient customers, with many more crowded behind them.

My poor mother rushed around, her stress palpable. "Claret, I'm so glad you're here. If you could fill some orders while I check on the ovens ..."

"Go, go." I shooed her away.

The next few hours passed by in a blur of taking orders, fetching items, getting payment. And then, repeat and repeat and repeat. Mama ran in and out of the bakeshop, refilling various food trays before going away to bake more.

Through the two large windows up front, I could see the store's wooden sign, "Rowena's Bakeshop," hanging outside. As time wore on, I eyed the light outside. The day was going by fast, but hopefully there would be a break in customers soon and I would be able to leave.

Finally, the crowd thinned. Mama came through the door, holding yet another tray of bread.

"This should be the last of it," she told me, placing the tray down on the counter. "Whatever we have out is it for the day."

"Oh, good," I said. "Do you still need my help? Otherwise, I'm going to head out."

Mama frowned. "Head out? Where?"

I sighed as I started to undo the strings of my apron. "It's Daypito. My day to visit Lola Cerise."

Mama's frown deepened. "It's been so busy, I forgot." She paused. "Honestly, Claret, I would prefer it if—"

The bell over the bakeshop door rang out, signaling the arrival of a new customer. I stepped back from the counter, hoping I could slip away. But I was trapped, with Mama on my right and the bakery wall to my left.

Frowning, I looked up into the most hypnotizing pair of green eyes I had ever seen.

The owner of said green eyes startled. "Uh, hello. I hope I have the right place." He glanced around, then turned to look out the window and peer at the sign. "This is Rowena's Bakeshop, correct?"

"Yes it is, young man," my mother said, nudging me slightly so she could address the newcomer squarely. "How can I help you?"

"Oh." He cleared his throat and eyed me sidelong. Belatedly, I smoothed my face into ... well, if not a welcoming expression, at least something more neutral. "Mayor Marley wanted me to give you this."

He plunked a piece of paper down on the counter. Mama picked it up and carefully looked it over. Her eyes widened. "Oh my goodness! He wants *how many* pastries in two weeks?"

The young man shrugged, brushing back a strand of dark hair that fell in his face. "I didn't read the message, madam. I'm just the messenger."

I narrowed my eyes at him. "I've never seen you before. Are you really the mayor's messenger? Or his secretary, perhaps?"

The man laughed, rich and melodious. "Neither. I'm the new sheriff." He extended a hand. "Hunter Tavish."

I gaped. "But you're so young!" Our last two sheriffs had been much older, the prior one around my Mama's age, and the one before him closer to Lola Cerise's age.

"Please accept my sincerest apologies, Miss ...?"

When I still didn't make a move, Mama swooped in. Taking Sheriff Tavish's hand, she gave it a firm shake. "Well met, sheriff. I'm Rowena Pangati, and this is my daughter, Claret."

"A pleasure, Madam Pangati." He looked at me, eyes twinkling. "And Miss Claret."

I nodded stiffly, just barely polite.

"Are you closing?" Sheriff Tavish indicated my trailing apron strings.

"Soon," Mama said. "There's not much left to sell." She looked at the mayor's note again. "My goodness. Between this weekend's festival and now this order, I'll be working overtime. If I'm going to get everything done on time, I should probably start right away." She began muttering to herself. "I'll need to check my stock. Do I have enough flour? And other supplies ..."

"Would you like me to stay and help you, Mama?" I asked.

She waved my question away. "No, no. You go on and see your lola. Don't forget to bring the basket with you."

"Where does your grandmother live?" Sheriff Tavish inquired politely.

"Past the forest, in the next town over. Cedarbrook."

Was it my imagination, or did the sheriff suddenly stiffen? "Oh. I'd be happy to escort you, if you like."

"Thank you, but I really don't need—"

"What a lovely idea!" Mama interrupted. "If it's not too much trouble, Sheriff Tavish—"

"It's not."

"—Then I would feel much better if you accompanied Claret. Really, that's just wonderful."

Glad Mama thought so. I had been looking forward to a quiet walk—by *myself*—to my grandmother's.

But it didn't look like I'd get my wish. Not wanting to waste any more of the day, I sighed and pasted what I hoped was a grateful smile on my face. "Again, I thank you, sheriff. Let me hang up my apron and get my things, and I'll meet you out front."

Sheriff Tavish nodded. "I'll be waiting. Good day, Madam Pangati."

He left the shop, the overhead bell ringing decisively in his wake.

"Go on," Mama said. "Don't keep the new sheriff waiting."

"First you didn't want me to go, now you do?" I grumbled as I removed my apron. "Make up your mind."

"I didn't want you to go *by yourself*," Mama clarified. "Now that you have that handsome young man to accompany you, I'm not so worried."

I'd be just fine on my own, I thought, but I knew better than to say that aloud. Ever since the mayor's notice about the attacks in the forest had been posted around town two months ago, Mama had, understandably, fretted about my weekly visit to Lola Cerise's. I had even stopped visiting my grandmother for a little bit, just to appease my mother.

But I missed my grandmother, so I pushed to start visiting her again. And when I had made several trips into the forest and returned home unscathed each time, Mama had relaxed. Somewhat.

Mama locked the shop door. "Go out the back, honey. Send my love to your lola. And don't forget the basket!"

"I will! And I won't!" I promised. I pushed through the door that separated the bakeshop from our private residence, grabbing the basket from the counter and hanging up my linen apron. I continued through the house. Before I exited out the back door, I made sure to grab my red cape, hurriedly throwing it around my body and tying the strings at my neck.

Rounding the house, I walked towards the front, where Sheriff Tavish waited at the bakery entrance. Seeing me approach, he stood straighter.

"Oh, Miss Claret! I didn't expect you to come from that direction." There was a slight question in his voice.

"Shall we?" At his nod, I began walking. Sheriff Tavish fell into step beside me. "Mama would prefer we use the front entrance only for the bakeshop. Anything personal, we use the back door. It's just a way to keep business stuff separate."

"That makes sense."

We turned down Main Street, passing the small complex of buildings that housed the mayor's office, the courthouse, and the sheriff's office. "There's your new office."

"Yes." Sheriff Tavish smiled. "It will be a while before I can settle in, though. There's quite a few repairs that need to be made, first. The building's a bit ... unusable, right now."

I chuckled. "That's a generous way of putting it."

He chuckled along with me. "I will admit, I was a bit dismayed when I saw how bad the building had been allowed to get. Holes in the ceiling, cracks in the walls. Not to mention the hay and manure on the floor?"

"Oh, yes. I think it was used as a temporary stable after the main one burned down."

"That explains it, then." He shook his head. "I'll do my best to get it repaired quickly, but that depends on how long the investigation takes."

"Investigation?"

We continued down the road, out of Woodside. The cobblestone of Main Street gave way to the dirt path that would lead through the forest to the next town, where my grandmother lived.

"Yes," Sheriff Tavish affirmed. "I was hired to investigate the recent attacks."

ACKNOWLEDGEMENTS

IT'S A BIT BITTERSWEET, closing the book on the Kingdom Legacy series. (For now, at least.) Writing the first book kept me sane during the pandemic, and the entire series has been such a big part of my life for the last five years.

But I'm glad that even though I have to say goodbye to such fun and familiar imaginary friends like Jennica and Farrah and Rhyss, I don't have to say goodbye to amazing readers who have been so encouraging (like you!) and terrific people who have helped me grow and get better as a writer.

My deepest thanks to:

Tom — you definitely top this list. Thank you for your patience, and your excitement over reading each new book. And sitting down for super-long calls to hash out notes. You are truly amazing, and I couldn't have written this series without you.

Jaime — for letting me bounce my writing ideas, woes, and questions off you all the time.

Lana — my sweetheart kitty, who has usurped Riley's spot on the chair! Your "encouragement" (in the form of loud meowing and equally loud purring) has been something to look forward to as I write.

About the Author

Rachanee Lumayno is an actress, voiceover artist, screenwriter, avid gamer, and amateur dodgeball player. She grew up in Michigan, where she spent way too much of her free time reading fantasy novels. She still spends too much of her free time reading fantasy, although now she writes them as novels, narrates them as audiobooks, and creates them as improv for various roleplaying campaigns as well. *Heir of Immortals and Empires* is her seventh novel. She is also a staff writer for an upcoming video game. You can find her online at her website, www.rachanee.net, or on Instagram, TikTok, or YouTube (@rachaneelumayno).